Bollywood **STORM**

An

Elanna Forsythe George

Mystery

Mystery lovers, rejoice!

...Publisher's Daily Reviews

N. K. Johel

Bollywood
STORM

A Novel in Two Books

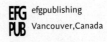 efgpublishing
Vancouver,Canada

ISBN   978-0-9917977-8-3

EFG PUB
efgpublishing
301, 1 0420 – 1 48 ST
Surrey, British Columbia.
Canada V3 R 3 X4
email: publish@efgpublishing.com

Or contact N. K. Johel on Bollywood Storm's website:

www.dhoomadakalakadhoomdhoom.com

Cover designs by Marvin Rayala & Gerald Rath for Signarama
Surrey. 'Mendhi' patterns used on the cover by Elena @ Art of Sun.
Editors: Alyssa Linn Palmer and Rab Feenie.
Proofreader: JC Chan.

For Simryn

Book II: MUMBAI

Scenes

"A dreamer of pictures
I run in the night
You see us together
Chasing the moonlight
My Cinnamon Girl."

"Names are language's most seductive sounds."
(Karmen MacKendrick)

The Big Deal

"Hey Mister American *sahib*.

"Hey, you!
"Over here, look over here!
"No, no, no. Over here.
"Because I know you are probably looking for me. . . .

"Now, listen, suno, I need to tell you something. Have you ever heard of the Bara Banta? 'The Big Deal'? No? Hmmm, I didn't think so. The Big Deal's a big secret; it's a secret underground place.

Yes, that's right. Haan!

Just imagine. A gigantic, opulent palace hidden under the streets of Mumbai for those looking for . . . forbidden delights? They even have a mahal for gambling there, in an ancient country where jua khelna has always been against the law.

So, you must know, not everyone is in on this?

Now usually, you have to know someone or *be* someone to go in there.

But *I* can get you in.

And boy, once you do go inside, then vah-he vah, you'll really see something. The place is huge. Cavernous. Big as any Las Vegas casino. It does business too. Millions, or maybe even billions of rupees flow across its tables every night, in and out of the hands of all those koob-soorati amir log you'll meet down there. You know, the beautiful people. Sexy stars and starlets, savvy producers and directors, protégées, personal assistants, the pretty lapdogs and all those scary Bollywood badmashes, and the polcia and their secret informants watching you on your every move.

Sounds exciting . . . no?

So, how do you get inside, you ask?

> Mein dhasta hai!
> That's easy.

> Neechae jana hai!
> You go down."

Down and down along the steep set of stairs that leads into Bara Banta. Across a wide and surprisingly well-lit hall that appears to have been cut out of white marble. Then down some more stairs, and around and around, until you come to the only entrance.

Knock the secret knock, and you're in. . . .

(Four loud knocks. A pause, just long enough for one big breath. Two gentle raps. Then four more loud knocks.)

The door opens. A mean-looking goonda in an expensive suit checks you out. You'll notice a large bulge under his suit jacket, and you find yourself hoping beyond hope that everything turns up neat and tidy, and that your name will show up on the guest list, just like they said it would.

Inside, it's a typical night. The place is hopping, abuzz with activity. It's early, only 8 P.M., but fortunes have already been won and lost. Some guests wail and cry. Others cheer with delight. The excitement of the Big Winners and dismay of the Big Losers punctuates the hum of other, milder conversations.

Across the hall, at the far side of the casino beyond the gambling tables, twin spotlights pierce the darkness on a stage to reveal a simple microphone. Standing alone, front and center. As if waiting for someone special to arrive. Behind it, a well-known skaa-banghra-hop fusion band from Chandigarh, Jagroop has begun to play. Their music is cooking. Jagroop's groove is founded on some deep percussion and a dense rhythm section.

Their Indo-African drums are patting out a complex groove:
Boom *dit-dit Boom Boom!* . . .*dit dit. Boom.* . . . *dit-dit* **Boom Boom** . . . *dit dit dit dit.*

A bassline booms out like thunder from below:
Bhoom*bara Boombara* **BHOOOM***bara* . . . *Boombara Boombara* **BHOOOM***bara.*

Above it all, the band's tinkly hand cymbals scatter the beat:
Tikka-tikka-tikka . . . *tah!* . . . *Tikka-tikka-tikka* . . . *tah!* . . . *Tikka tikka takka*

A subtle, sensual vibe emerges. Not too fast. Not too slow.
Just so.

Then, at an opportune moment, the dhol player cuts in:
Dhoom-a Dhoom-a Dhoom **DHOOM!** *Daka laka laka* **DHOOM!** *Daka laka laka laka* **DHOOM!**

In the pit before the stage, the dancing has begun. People are losing themselves in empathy to this beat. Some bump and grind, turn imaginary light bulbs. Others point to the sky, stirring the pot. One man spins-and-points a la Saturday Night Fever. Some younger ones twist, slam, and gyrate, pumping their vital hips and breasts.

It's a scene.

They sway.

They shake it on down.

It's an unchoreographed Bollywood freestyle.

The crowd begins to scream and shout as a thin, light-skinned South Asian woman in Elvis-blue hair and a silver sequined mini-dress steps up into the spotlights. She's Korina Mangel, Jagroop's lead-singer. She walks up to the mic and lifts it from its stand. She taps her fingers subtly on her thigh, testing the groove, then she lifts the microphone to her lips. Her eyes carry no expression. Her face is a cool mask; she'll give nothing away. She nods and moistens her lips, and as if on cue, a keyboard player behind her triggers some presequenced-recordings of her voice.

Her synthesized voices sing out from his keys in complex harmonies, as Korina stands silent.

> *Dhurhu Dhurhu, Dhurhu*
> *Dhurhu Dhurhu, Dhurhu*
> *Dhurhu Dhurhu, Dhurhu*
> *O-o-o-o-h Dhurhu Dhurhu*

Bhoombara bhoombara **BHOOOOOM** *bhoombara. . .*

The bassline booms even louder. Inciting a riot.

. . . The dancers feel it. Take it on. They break out. Dance even more wildly.

On the last of the Dhurhu Dhurhu's, the buxom lead singer joins the fray. Her face is set in a bland supermodel stare, as she blends her natural voice into the electronic versions of it behind her.

> *Dhurhu Dhurhu, Dhurhu*

Dhurhu Dhurhu, Dhurhu
Dhurhu Dhurhu, Dhurhu
Dhurhu Dhurhu, Dhurhu

Then, Korina launches off solo. (The sampled-backgrounds fall away.) Into the first verse.

Dhoor Dhoor dhiyan ha mere mitra
Mere ooncha mahaan seemaant he oh mere jan
Tera Mera Piyar ha saamaanya chaah
Chotae, neechae roop jeevan nirvaah chhaila
Mujhe pratishtha meinu Sapanae aate ha
O, Mujhe naseeb mein pralobhan ichchha ha

(Far far away are my thoughts, my lover
High and Grand are my dreams oh my heart
Your love and mine are common fare
for lesser forms and mere beautiful ones
Dreams of fame are chasing me
Desires for fortune are haunting me)

Meanwhile, in that very moment, on the stairwell leading into Bara Banta, a new Bollywood dream's about to appear.

She calls herself, 'Christine.'

Click. Click. Click. Her red, stiletto high-heels echo sharp against the granite of the stairs.

She's almost there.

She's on her way.

Her real name is Kristina Ivanovic Seredova, but she grew up in California, so she usually goes by the American version. The daughter of a high-profile Russian mobster, and a minor American actress, she's been hanging out in Mumbai the past couple of months, trying to carve out a career for herself as a dancer. Another dark-haired, light-skinned Slav girl who's trying to make it here. In Bollywood, where pale is beautiful.

It's tough, but tonight she's *close*, she thinks.

Inside Bara Banta, Christine turns to Deepak, the self-styledly suave Mumbai multimillionaire whose shady connections just got them through the door. She smiles a wry, sardonic smile.

"See ya," she says, as she walks flat away.

Deepak's mouth falls open.

What?

That bitch.

But Deepak only stands there. He doesn't even move. As if he knows already there's nothing he could do.

But why? he wonders.

Haran ha! He's had a million like her and none of them would have dared.

Across the room, the song's getting hotter.

On the chorus, the synthesized voices kick back in. With vengeance. Higher. Faster. Louder.

> *Dhurhu Dhurhu-Dhurhu*
> *Dhurhu Dhurhu- Dhurhu*
> *Dhurhu Dhurhu- Dhurhu*
> *Dhurhu Dhurhu-*
> *AAAAAAAAAAAA Aaaaaaaaaaa-hhhhhhhhhhhhhh*

The drumming intensifies.

WHAKKA *Tikka whap-pha thunnka* . . . **WHAKKA** *Tikka whap-pha thunnka*

Even funkier lines from the bass drive the vibe harder.

Boombara Boombara **BOOM***bara*. . . *Boombara Boombara* **BHOOOM***bara*

After she screams, Korina moves away from the mic into the half-shadows at the edges of the spotlights. Half-hidden in those shadows, her dance begins. Her silhouette spins wildly as she whirls, and she's more reckless than any dancer in the dance pit.

Sashaying and swirling with her shadows whirling and spinning she's winning your soul Elation Elevation Libational Vibration Sensational 'til you reach Satiation And the Creamy Steamy Spotlights Spurned Off they turn Lost gone What's goin' on? Tossed aloft Such a cost Turn it on Throw her down She Got a Sound Like Go Round In Dreams Schemes Screams Shouts She's About To Go: **Dhoom**-*a-daka-laka-laka* **Dhoom**-*a-daka-laka-laka* **Dhoom Dhoom** *Sha-boo-o-om!"*

She's got such daring moves, darling.
Oh, she's so . . . provocative!

On the other side of the hall, Christine's gone far past Deepak now. He's long forgotten. She's immersed herself completely in this vibe.

"Yeah," she says to herself, as she watches the half-obscured starlet twirling up on the stage, "this place will do."

She smiles.

"Better hold onto yourself, 'Lana, if you can, 'cause the fun's about to begin."

Suddenly she's hit by an overpowering urge . . . to yawn.

She smiles again.

Her extremely lithe limbs stretch out like a cat's.

Or a tigress.

Tonight she's feeling especially . . . powerful, inspiring, and drop-dead sexy!

Heads turn.

Mouths gasp.

Oh, she's so uninhibited . . . no, no, not at all appropriate.

People stare.

Men gyrate.

Women sputter.

Christine's hands drop to her hips. Her fingers achingly caress the taut curves beneath her red dress. The clingy fabric dances and shimmers, close to her.

She moans out loud.

"Uh Mmmmm-mmmh."

At a nearby craps table, a man loses control of his toss as Christine walks by. One die falls to the floor, while the other bounces off the table and hits a woman on the forehead.

Christine smirks.

"Hah. Watch this, 'Lana, if you time things just right."

An agile young waiter carrying a tray of drinks is about to pass by her. She lets out a deep sexual belly-laugh. Distracted, the young waiter trips. A woman close by screams as the alcohol douses the bodice of her dress. The man next to her shouts when the rest of the tray splashes down the front of his pants.

More heads turn to see what the fuss is about.

Some giggle.

Two Bollywood goondas in black suits move in quickly from the shadows. One apologizes and leads the angry, booze-splattered couple toward the rest rooms. The other pulls the waiter up off the floor and jostles him away. Christine's eyes widen, delighted with the results of her mischief-making. By the time the commotion dies down, she's stepped off into the crowd, looking for her next amusement.

She didn't have to wait long.

There he was, a young, lanky Indian man wearing Hugo Boss everything. He's talking to a diminutive woman with her hair up in a bob. Clearly he wasn't Christine's type. Too tame and geeky. Obviously newly money'd.

She sighs.

"Oh well, at least I can have some fun."

She puckers up her ruby-red lips and steps in between the couple. She grabs the man's tie and drags him away from his companion, who is left there in mid-sentence. She smirks at the woman screaming wildly behind her.

"What the. . . ? What the hell do you think you're doing, you whore!"

Christine keeps on walking.

Tell me something I don't know.

The woman's voice rises up higher. "Jeetain, Jeetain! Come back!".

Jeetain floats behind Christine like a lamb. She weaves him through the crowd by his tie. Her cold, blue eyes engage fiercely with anyone who looks at her. Men. Women. Tall. Handsome. Ugly. Short. Fat. All are fair game.

To her left, she hears a male voice. *"Mmmmm-hmmm, uh-huhh!"*

She spins round at the sound. A thick, rugged Indian male in an ill-fitting suit fills her vision. His tongue runs over his parched lips.

Her cold heart lurches.

Mmmmmm-mmmm, what a wannabe badmash. But cute. Strong-limbed too. No doubt he'd wet her whistle. She'd do the same for him. Too bad his wallet wasn't fat enough or she'd do him right now.

She glances back at Jeetain. And sighs.

So sad. Oh well.

She juts out her chin, tightens her grip on Jeetain's tie and drags him right past the lovely badmash. Suddenly, her nose wrinkles at the smell of his cheap cologne.

Ugh, what was I thinkin'?

Up on the stage, the band Jagroop is starting up again. This time with a slow, sad Hindi ballad. Korina's now-syrupy voice is blaring out like a banal, drippy siren. She's cooing the song, cuddling it. Smothering it; milking it for all its worth:

> *Koyi nahee janae mere dhuk chal*
> *Saub vekdhe apke kooshian*
> *Meri Dil*
> *Meri Dil*
>
> *Meri Dil*
> *Meri dil ka tara*
> *Utarna*
>
>
> *(Nobody wants to know my troubles*
> *Everyone sees only their happiness*
> *My Heart*

My Heart
My Heart
The star of my heart
Has descended.)

Out on the floor, Christine stops dead in her tracks. Her eyes narrow.

Omigawd, that sappy song!
What a crappy piece of *fluff*.

She looks up on the stage at the far end of the casino and sneers at the shapely buxom South Asian women in a sad version of Tina Turner's skank-dress, looking dead up there with a microphone in her limp, red nail polished hands. She was barely moving at all. Who did she think she was, Anne Murray?

It was so . . . lame.

People in the dance pit were moving their arms and hips around a little, managing to find some kind of beat. But there wasn't a bone in Christine's body that didn't want to retch.

"Aaaack."

She couldn't take it anymore. She drags Jeetain through the crowd by his tie toward the stage, bumping into people along the way. She protests loudly as she climbs the stairs up onto the stage. She turns and raises up a hand on Jeetain's chest.

"STAY!"

The lead singer's voice falters and stops as Christine steps out in front of her and wrenches her mic away.

"It's lame," she screams. "Lame, lame, lame!"

She glares at Korina.

"Puh-leeze. For God's sakes, stop. It's much too lame."

The amazed young pop-star just blinks. Baffled.

Christine sneers.

"It's lame. Don't you understand? It's far too lame!"

Tossing a scathing glance at Korina, Christine wanders to the back of the stage to speak to the rest of the band. The shocked and angry lead singer's left standing there, staring blankly in disbelief.

After a brief and animated conversation with the band, Christine moved back up into the spotlights. Something in her eyes must have woken the frozen-faced young singer up, because suddenly she made a dash for the stairs. She almost stumbles over Jeetain before she disappears into the dance-pit.

"Hmmmph. You call that world class talent? . . . We'll show 'em 'Lana."

The two spotlights dimmed to a warm glow. Christine stood quiet, commanding the room's attention. She turns back to Jeetain, still lingering in the shadows, and beckons him forward. He steps timidly into the spotlights, while trying to keep as far from her as he possibly can. She reaches out and tugs him in closer by his tie before turning her attention back to the audience. She places the mic back on its stand.

"Hah." Her husky voice imbues the casino. "Well, *I* thought that was lame, didn't you?"

Mutters of astonishment and outrage flutter through the audience.

Christine purses her lips. "Now I want to show you how we do it in America. But first, *suno*, I have something important to tell you."

She pauses. Her eyes flash.

"This one's for Simryn, Simryn Gill."

Her voice echoes.

What?

Simryn?

How'd she know about Simryn?

Christine frowns.

"Simryn's gone. But, take my word for it, she'd have been the biggest thing that Bollywood ever saw if a creepy goonda named Anil Negendra hadn't finished her off so . . . early."

That's right, Christine, she would'a been.

"But 'Lana dealt with him. The White Devil herself. Made sure he got his just desserts."

No, Christine. It was the Bollywood mob who 'dealt' with him. I only did what I could to bring him to justice.

Christine puckers up. "Ah yeah, anyway . . . 'Simryn'. Her name is 'Remembrance.' So tonight, I'm singing her this song."

Her sharp eyes look heavenward before she turns back to the band.

"Hit it, boys. Just like I told you. A real slow-tempo blues in B flat. And, don't worry, it'll be okay. Just follow me!"

"*One, Two. . . .*"

Her red stiletto-heel taps out a tempo.

"*Bamp-ba-ba-ba-***BAMP**." Twin horns shout.

A surly, sultry energy rises up.

The spotlights come back on full force.

Christine cries out:

"*Ba-by, Ba-by, Ba-bay.*"

She strokes her right hip.

Just *watch* me, 'Lana.

She grabs the microphone off the stand. Throws her head back. The band hits it.

> *Take it away*
> *Take it away*
> *I just think and taste and feel*
> *While I rub myself unreal*

She shines. Her powdered-white skin. Her breasts heave in contrast to her red dress. Red confessions of a Siren.

> *Not again today*
> *Not again today*
> *I'm about to overload*
> *On the seeds that I have sowed*
> *It's not the usual blue*
> *Not quite indigo*

Her impossibly-dark eyes glare. People move back. Ghostly debris. The bolder ones stand their ground. Christine shrugs. She tosses her hair back, lost in her own seduction. Yeah, she'd out-Marilyn Marilyn Monroe.

The spotlights blast even brighter as Christine throws her arm up in a forceful confession.

> *Got no alibis*
> *Got no alibis*
> *I just have to find a place*
> *Beyond your big bad soft-talkin' lies*
> *Sweet tender song*
> *Sweet sad and tender song*
> *You know I made it up so right*
> *But then I let it all go wrong*

Her eyes narrow. Brow-hooded, they say nothing. But tell, tell, tell, tell, tell it ALL.

> *And that's not the usual me*
> *So insensible*

A bluesy growl grows, rolls, then erupts, from the trumpet player. It flows. It's consumed. It seeps into every crack and crevice.
  Now, Christine's got it.

> *Ain't no story told*
> *Ain't no story told*
> *They'll just use you up and leave you*
> *All alone so bent and lost*
> *Over 7 million sold*
> *Over 7 million sold*

> *Yeah, they'll show you the whole thrill of love*
> *But ya cannot pay the cost*
> *And ain't that just the usual blue?*
> *So predictable*

Accusation. Irritation. Delight. She looks at the crowd. Yeah, she'll work it. Her hand moves down to her crotch and unleashes her wild, grind-bumping hips.

"That's right. Show 'em what it takes!"

> *Get your hands out of my pockets*
> *Quit thinkin' bout my sockets*
> *And if you wanna rock it*
> *Go behind that door and lock it*
> *And keep. . . .*
> *Keep your silly soul*
> *Don't bother me*

The fiery heat slowed to a simmer. Women gasped. Men perspired. Tipsy from the sultry, twisty, heady gyrations.

> *Take it away*
> *Take it away*
> *Don't wanna be alone*
> *But all you ever show me's made of stone*
> *Not again today*
> *Not again today*
> *The days are gettin' long*
> *But this daze just keeps goin' strong*
> *And ain't that the usual blue?*
> *Not so . . . . (trumpet solo)*
> *Not so. . . .(piano solo)*
> *Not so. . . . (drums solo)*
> *Not so. . . .*

(All the instruments go tacit, as Christine lifts the mic to her lips one last time.)

> *. . . un-us-u-al*

Christine slid the mic back onto the stand before turning to Jeetain. The crowd gasps and shouts as she pushes her body close up against his. He's hot. Trembling. She grabs his face and pulls it down to hers. She kisses him. Her tongue leapt inside his mouth. One horn squealed, as the other sang, "*Laa, Laa, Laaaaaaaaaaa!*"

At the drum roll, she releases him. He stumbles forward, legs wobbling, glasses askew. Christine's red lipstick is smeared all over his mouth. She grabs his tie and leads him back down the steps into the scandalized crowd.

On the other side of the dance pit, Jeetain whispers hoarsely in her ear. "I think you've made an impression. Certainly."

"Shush," she hisses back at him over her shoulder.

She'd sensed something.

A few seconds later, she follows the pull of intuition through the crowd. She drags Jeetain to the last roulette table at the back of the casino. It was hopping. 'Yeah', she thinks, 'this is it'. But there was no place to sit down, so she taps hard on the shoulder of a man sitting on one of the stools. He turns round with a start.

Christine frowns. "I want to sit down."

The man hesitated before getting up. But no, he decided he didn't want her kind of trouble. He inches away from his stool, keeping his gaze fixed on her eyes. Kristina Ivanovich was a beautiful and dangerous woman, '*An Icicle from a Hot Tin Roof.*'

She sits on the stool and turns to Jeetain.

"Bourbon. On the rocks."

Jeetain straightens his glasses before disappearing into the crowd. Christine settles in to study the table, the croupier, and the crowd, weighing their body language and their mannerisms. She takes in a deep breath and sighs.

"Smell that vibe, 'Lana? Somethin's cookin'."

Jeetain returns with a bourbon on ice and sets it in front of her. He stands close at her right shoulder as she lifts the glass to her lips. The first sharp, sweet, sensuous mouthful enlivens her waning energy. She's ready.

She places her first bet.

Square: *Black-11. Red-12. Red-14. Black-15.*

The croupier spins the wheel. —*Whirr whirrr whirr. Rattata, rattata.*

Rattata, rattata, rat tata rat tit at—The white ball leaps and bounces wildly, before it's finally captured.

People gasp. Then moan.

Red-12.

The croupier rakes the winnings towards Christine. It's not much, she thought, but it's a start. She was just contemplating her next move when the air around her began to crackle. Her eyebrows arch.

What was it?

She raises her eyes from the table.

Her heart stops.

She catches her breath.

A handsome and tall South Asian man is about to sit down at her table. He's wearing short black hair. He's got a strong jaw line. She takes in the quality of his well-tailored white shirt and his silk suit coat. His well-manicured hands. A large collection of casino chips. A few rings embellish his long fingers, but none of them is a wedding ring. (Not that it really mattered to her.) Christine realizes she's been holding her breath. She relaxes. Then she senses his pervading essence all around her.

What was it?

Was it his cologne?

His Big Brown Eyes flashed when he saw her eyes fixed on him.

Her Wild White Heart began to beat.

What was it? Was it Citrus-Honey. A hint of coriander? Sandalwood perhaps?

Mmm. Captivating. Was it Hugo? Chrome? Pi?

A knowing smile lifts a corner of the man's mouth.

It scratches Christine's soul.

She winces.

Then, I recognized him.

Johnny's handsome young 'Associate.' I'd seen him before in a restaurant keeping company with a marked and known, high-level Bollywood gangsta named 'Johnny.' I'd only just arrived in Mumbai then, and was sitting across the room with a couple of local Nomad operatives.

When was that?

It seemed so long ago.

Christine stares down at the table. She hesitates only for a microsecond before laying down her next bet. Three squares. Street. She leans back and looks up at The Associate, taking in his full lips above his strong, stubborn chin. I laughed out loud, thinking, "He's probably the worst kind of dog if he's falling for her cheap moves."

Christine's back goes up. A little.

Yeah, I thought. Sometimes she does hear me.

Johnny's Associate took command in that instant. The flow of his presence overwhelms Christine. She swallows hard, then opens up her mouth to get a little air. By the time she's stopped her head from reeling, he's sorted out his first bet and laid it on the table. A corner bet: Red, Black, Red, Black. His eyes narrow.

He nods at the croupier:

"*Spin it.*"

The ball whirrs inside the wheel, spinning counter to the now-blurry red'n'black numbers. It jumps. Stumbles. Jolts and rattles. Finally, it's snatched by a numbered pocket.

The croupier makes the announcement.

"*Black-Eleven.*"

The winnings rake toward Johnny's Associate.

Christine smirks.

Good for him.

She looks around at the spectators like she means business. Then she leans over the board and lays out two adjoining streets. She gazed back at him boldly. He wasn't going to get to her. She was still hunting prey. Losing to said prey is sometimes part of the game.

He glances up after laying out his bet.

The croupier reaches out and pulls the wheel. Christine narrows her eyes, willing the ball to fall in her favor.

"Black Four," is announced.

The Associate's eyebrows arch.

The chips sweep to Christine.

She tilts her chin up. Smiling.

Spin after spin, the night whirred by. After the first ten rounds, Jeetain, the man Christine confiscated earlier, had realized he was a third wheel, and slunk away unnoticed by anyone but me. He knew, now, he'd only been a means to a better means.

By 2 A.M., Christine was becoming ruthless and at times reckless in her betting choices. At 3 A.M., Johnny's Associate slid two-thirds of his winnings onto the table, covering half the board. Without flinching, Christine matches his bet. She leans back. The atmosphere is heady. She's enthralled by the game and the attention they're both receiving. A crowd surrounding the table watches the drama. Both players had won and lost throughout the night. She'd been down to her last RS5000 before winning again. The lowest he'd hovered was down around RS10,000. The bets were steep, and at one time, they'd lost a combined RS200,000 to the house. The most she'd won on any single spin was RS25,000.

Now, there she was, with RS75,000 on the table. All she had. Not two-thirds. All of it. Everything. She leans forward, thrilling. She feels the pressure of her expanded corpus clitorides.

Her heart beats faster.

Eyes narrow to slits.

Mouth and lips are getting dry.

Her breathing becomes shallow,

She anticipates the sensations that Fate's next kiss may deliver.

The croupier spun his wheel one last time. In my mind I saw everything, all the craziness of the moment. I watched as the ball whirr-r-r'd counter to the wheel's forward motion. I glanced over at Johnny's Associate. His gaze was locked on mine, telling me it's his victory.

Christine's eyes narrow.

She doesn't think so.

We all looked down at the wheel.

The ball, unable to resist the opposing forces any longer—jumps! It bounces and clatters, *rat-t—a-tat-ta-titty-tatters* all over the blurry, red'n'black numbered slots.

My stomach lurched. I felt dizzy.

Black-16 Red-1 Black-8 Red-15 Black-20 Black-22.

Finally Red-23 snatches up the white ball and holds it.

There's a pause.
Christine's heartbeat thumped loudly in my ears.
The onlookers explode into cheers and moans.
The croupier sweeps the pile of winnings to Christine.
Glances all around.
Shock and relief.
She's *won*.

After the crowd dispersed, Christine leaned forward to gather her chips in a bag provided her by the croupier.

The Associate's voice came to her from across the table, "Can I buy you a drink?"

Christine pursed her lips and glanced up briefly. Then she indicated her chips. "I'll take care of this first."

He nodded and leaned back.

She carried her winnings across the room to the customer service wicket, while glancing back at him several times over her shoulder. His gaze was staying fixed on her too, as he gathered up what was left of his winnings. Christine felt like a fish on a line. She'd fight, of course. She always did. Only a few could reel her in. She banked her entire RS500,435 with the house, and only then turned back to the table where he was waiting. She ran her fingers through her sassy, auburn-blond dyed hair, and said to herself that if he was her kind of man, she wouldn't need to spend a dime.

Back at their table, he was smoking a cigar, and absentmindedly watched a casino employee count up his winnings for him. The smoke rose lazily from his mouth and gently caressed his face. He snapped his fingers as soon as Christine sat back down. A striking young Indian waitress appeared, quickly placed a glass of bourbon in front of her, then backed away immediately. Christine's gaze follows the woman. She's not quite sure where she's seen her before.

"She's a would-be starlet working nights to earn extra money until she makes it," the Associate said.

Christine raised one eyebrow. Maybe they'd both been at the same audition or something?

The Associate wielded true power and command. And it seemed he wanted Christine. I wondered why. Who? Christine? A hyper-competitive little tramp on a Bollywood tryout circuit? Still, I thought, maybe she'd finally found us a link to the Bollywood underground.

I hoped so.

I didn't think I could take much more of her insanity.

The two lingered over a couple more drinks, exchanging glances and few words. His smooth, caramel smile played havoc with Christine's heart. She gazed into his deep brown eyes, and admired his strong look and lean body. I could feel Christine's awareness of him heighten. Her fantasies unfolded. She let her mind drift away imagining their encounter. The possibilities of such a liaison made her throat thick with desire. Mmm, it could be so delicious.

She started to get up. His knee brushed against hers as he got up, too, and put his cigar out in the ashtray. She settled back down into her chair. Her heavy-lidded eyes followed him as he began to make his way out of the casino. A moment later, Christine got up as well. She followed him at a distance. She watched him as he moved smoothly through the crowd ahead of her; she sauntered behind, not getting up too close, keeping just far enough back to have an eye on him. He stopped, for a moment, outside the main entrance to speak to a guard before exiting.

By the time she caught up with him, at the top of the long stair-well, a sleek, black Volvo coupe was already waiting at the curb. Without breaking his stride, a slim goonda in a black suit got out of the driver's seat, maneuvered his way around the vehicle and opened up the passenger-side door for Christine. He held it open attentively, as she slipped in, then the door shut tight behind her. She took in a breath. The car had a scent like sweet sandalwood, and, in spite of myself, my heart began to race too.

Christine pulled down the visor to check her lipstick in the mirror. Her fine, well-kempt eyebrows were lifted up high over her icy-cold eyes. Her mouth twisted up into a smirk. "He's something, isn't he, 'Lana? Yeah, I finally found someone who could be *it*. You better hold onto yourself, darlin', it's going to be one hell of a ride."

She said that every night.

Christine's exploits were more than I'd bargained for. Each night she worked hard to top the liaisons she'd had the night before. A shiver went up my spine as I swallowed back the bile from my weakened stomach. I didn't see how this one could be any different. I didn't see the purpose anymore, of all those one night stands. She was usually up and gone the next morning before anyone else woke, without a thought or a regret. Most often she met them after her steamy performances. Some nights, she ended up in opulent hotel suites, luxurious bungalows, or mansions. Other nights were high risk. One night she chose a man after a performance. He had all the main calling cards, well dressed, well moneyed, brutish with a thing for dangerous and expensive thrills. On the way, he called up a friend and asked him to join them at an exclusive venue, an opium den complete with private rooms, if clients desired some privacy. In their opium-induced daze, the two men had wanted to acquire a room, but Christine insisted on a public romp. Some passers-by joined in, and soon it turned into something that made the night in the Bollywood Planet seem like recess at an elementary school. Christine walked away satiated, like a lioness after an especially bloody kill. I still have nightmares about it.

By day, Christine auditioned for dance parts in Bollywood movies. She got almost every small part she auditioned for. She worked hard, making a special effort to satisfy the greedy, groping backstage managers, production managers, casting directors and choreographers, and danced, of course, like a well-oiled machine. She practiced every day. She could bump and grind in any style the Bollywood dance-fusionists could come up with, but, somehow, she could never land a lead part.

She didn't care.

By night, she sought out ever more powerful people to play with. She'd hit the jackpot somewhere; she'd find someone who would pay for all her thrills.

I had no control over her whatsoever. She never acknowledged me. She heard me all right, but always she gave me the cold shoulder. That is, unless I was . . . particularly disturbed. Then, she'd goad me.

"What's wrong, 'Lana? Can't take the ride? Want off at the next stop? Well, guess what? We're not stoppin'!"

After The Associate settled himself into the car, he turned the key in the ignition. The car purred alive. Christine took in his handsome profile and sighed. There was something 'extra-special' about this one. He was beyond handsome. Suffocatingly sexy. Christine was thankful I'd worn my best tonight. She leaned back in her seat as the car rushes forward along a Mumbai city-lit coastline. She allowed her hand to slip to the inside of his thigh and felt her way up his leg. He moaned appreciatively at the pressure of her fingers and kept driving. My head reeled as Christine unzipped his pants and lowered her head to his lap.

It wasn't long before the car was parked precariously on the side of the roadway. The reflected beams of headlights in the water revealed the shadows of two people, mouths drinking and pouring into each other. The man eased himself back into his seat. The vehicle rocked as Christine climbed out of her seat onto his lap, finding him unsheathed and waiting. We moved, grinding viciously, easing our needs. He buried his face in her still-clothed bodice. His hands wandered down her taut, slim body, slipped underneath her panties, and groped her bottom, hard. Then, he bit my nipple through her dress.

Christine gasped!

She let herself go and drove. My resistance gave way to her need and I don't know what happened after that. It was nothing like what had been happening the last few weeks, or even what happened that night in the Bollywood Planet. Christine panted rapidly for air as she accelerated her hungry devouring. I had nothing to hold onto. I was falling out of the sky. Then, a wind caught me, and I was flying . . . flying. . . .

The next thing I remember was hot, sticky bodies satiated. Smeared lipstick, tussled hair, sweat-stained clothes. I couldn't tell where any of us began, or ended.

"This is exactly how my life's supposed to be," she voiced. "None of this 'be happy with what you have' business. That's for people who weren't winners. Not like us, 'Lana."

I bit my lip.

And wondered at the cost of winning.

A few hours later, the black Volvo sports coupe pulls into the driveway of a bungalow style home just a few miles south of Mumbai. After their liaison by the roadside, they'd stumbled out onto the beach for air. Christine offered herself up in a playground among the monkey bars. I tried to remember whose humiliation it really would be, but it didn't help. I couldn't get away from it. I was in it whether I wanted to be or not. At one point the unnamed Associate turned Christine around and entered her. Christine thrilled at the forbidden sensations as cars drove by, exposing the act in the night.

In the driveway, the Associate cut the engine and turned to us. Christine stared back into his dark, brown eyes. He leaned in to her. She was intoxicated at his nearness; his breath was hot against her mouth. She launched her tongue inside his mouth and tasted him. It was delicious. Heady. Christine couldn't stop. She wanted more. I let go of all knowing and drifted off to a now-familiar place in the darkness, waiting for it to be over. I don't know how or when they managed to get inside the bungalow. I still have flashes of possible memories, but I don't trust them. I can't know how reliable they are. In fact, I don't like thinking about it at all, except it's relevant as to how far I would go, you know, for Simryn.

Eventually, I lost all connectivity to the world, and felt only a ravenous darkness with ocean-like swells of rising and falling. Night came and went. Morning became day. Day became evening, then night, as I rolled with the man and the woman. In a blue room. In a beige and green room. On a bed. On the floor. On a chair. In the shower. In all the rooms.

I saw their imaginings. They chased each other. Fell into a romance and withdrew. She became a goddess; he the worshiper. He, a lion; she, the prey. She rushed like a river. He was a swimmer whose chances were slim. She became a tree. He was the breeze passing through, moving her branches and caressing her leaves. I stood still near the tree and saw the breeze manifest. He raised his head, and I saw a nagh slithering in his forehead. He looked right at me. Quickly, Christine moved a branch to block the view. But was it too late? Had it seen me? I couldn't tell.

Then, everything went black.

It would be days before the sexual fury ceased. Just when I

thought they were both spent and satisfied, the torrents would rise again.

I'd never experienced such complete abandonment to one's own terms, and Christine's terms were shocking at times. I tasted, felt, saw and heard, and responded from places I had no knowledge of, nor any control over. Christine's strength was always to insist her needs be satisfied, and, in turn, she gave inexhaustibly. But it was more than that this time. More than just a calculated plan to participate in sex-gone-wild with her.

There was something about him.

His name.

'Sanjay.'

Sanjay.

Sanjay means 'Triumph.'

When he said it that night in the car, Christine had become utterly intoxicated, like someone who's had that one drink too many. She was lost in him and I was truly afraid. I was losing the ability to remember. I didn't know how much longer I could continue to exist, even only as 'Lana, just a forlorn and hidden voice heard only on the insides of another person. Soon, I feared, I'd dwindle away to nothing.

Then, it occurred to me.

"No, wait!

"I must be real.

"I *loved* someone once."

Stop Thief. . . .

2 P.M. CHATRAPATI SHIVAJI INTERNATIONAL AIRPORT IN MUMBAI, SOME MONTHS EARLIER.

"Damn," I thought, as I stared down the long, long lineup at the customs gate. "Why do I have to go through regular customs instead of the VIP gate when I came here on a private jet? The Nomads should have had this covered better. For God's sakes, what were they thinking?"

I looked back down the long line again.

"They *sure* know how to take their time here."

I was a mess. I'd freshened up and changed before I got off my private jet, but the sweat had soaked through my fresh white blouse as soon as I walked out into the hot, humid air. I stood there, fanning myself with a newspaper.

Why is it so damn hot? What's wrong with the air-conditioning? I should've worn something lighter. I should've remembered that, in Mumbai, May is the hottest month.

I sighed. This was fast becoming a test of my new, much-ballyhooed virtue of patience, wasn't it?

Just then, out the corner of my eye, I spotted a wandering official. He was sauntering slowly down the lineup, perusing all the new arrivals. He inspected each person thoughtfully, stroking his beard as he went. When he got to me, he stopped a few feet away and considered me. After glancing up and down the line a little bit more, he stepped in closer to me and cleared his throat, "Em, I can help you pass more quickly ma'am? Only two hundred, U.S."

I met his eyes.

Two hundred dollars? Was that all? I couldn't stand waiting any longer, so I slipped him the bills. He led me across the lobby to a much shorter line-up. Five minutes later, another official was rifling through my suitcases, frowning at my expensive pearl necklaces and inspecting my thong underwear. He shook his head as he sifted through my white suits, shoes and blouses. Finally he picked up the already-opened box of hedgehogs I'd purchased at JFK Airport. He wrinkled up his nose, as he grunted.

Then, he noticed the laptop I was carrying.

He waved his hand impatiently at me to lift the case up on the counter. He studied it carefully for a moment, squinting his eyes in mock-suspicion, then he looked back up at me.

"Do you have receipt for purchase of this piece of equipment, ma'am?"

I smiled.

Damn.

I dug a little deeper in my purse. "Okay, let's see what I've got in here. . . ."

$US700 and ten minutes later, I'd made it through Customs.

It wasn't all that much, I told myself.

In fact, I was quite sure I'd gotten off easy.

Out in the main lobby, I was jostled by the anxious throngs of people bouncing around, back and forth, to and fro, trying to get somewhere. I picked up on the soothing music they piped in to try to keep the crowds a little calmer. One track was from *Meri Dil Ka Tara*. The same tune had been floating around in the background during that nightclub scene when Simryn had appeared as a waitress, serving Karishma Chawla a highball. I frowned, wondering why Sharma had filmed it like that, why he'd allowed Simryn to obscure her sister Karishma, the lead actress, the star, even if it was for only a moment.

Why?

Why'd he use such an unorthodox angle?

Was it just a lame mistake? A dumb oversight? Well, that would be no big surprise; Sharma's movies were so lame.

But, what if, he were trying to tell us something?

I sighed, and brought myself back into present moment.

Here and now.

There I was.

Strolling down the Mumbai airport lobby.

Past the corrupt customs gate at last.

Sweating bullets.

I had a long look down at my soggy, sweat-stained blouse, and thought of home; I called up fond memories of my nice, cool, secure New York apartment.

"Simryn's the only reason I'm still in on this fiasco," I told myself.

I looked around the sweeping, silver-aluminum terminal, and noticed that, somehow, the mood of the travelers seemed lighter now. I watched as arrivals walked through the roped-off area, and made their way into the open spaces where relatives and friends would be waiting.

The dramas begin.

An older bearded man quickly makes his way through the crowd and stops in front of a young Indian woman. She drops her luggage and throws her arms around his neck. "Bapu ji!" A flood of tears erupt.

A few feet away, two small vilathi-born children cling to their parents' arms, unsure of the mamu, nana and nani they'd only ever seen in photographs. "Meenu, Raja, sung de kiyoon ha? Why are you acting so shy?"

Brothers and sisters laugh and cry as they reunite.

Old friends shout.

Businessmen with briefcases stride by.

A bride bends down, nervously, to touch her *suss*'s feet for the first time. She waits there. The older woman smiles and pats her head to bless her before bending down and helping her son's new bahoo up to her feet. The young woman smiles shyly, relieved at her good fortune: a good, loving mother-in-law.

I pass a short, fat, homely but newly green-carded man being greeted by his equally homely sister. She already has his itinerary in place, "We will find the highest-educated and best-looking bride, with the largest dowry for you, mere lal! People are willing to pay so much to have their daughters go to Am-reeka."

Sure, I thought, and I bet he won't ever have half the education she has. Nor the money. But she'll bring your family a good reputation and a goodly fortune, won't she?

I stepped back from those scenes to take a wider view. The airport was alive now with colorful clothing accentuated by the stark, white contrast of the sweeping, palatial backdrop in the lobby. People wore fashions from every era: pantsuits, suit pants, mini-dresses, dhoti's, sulvar kameez, kurta pajamas, turbans and fedoras and burkas. Oranges, greens, browns, ocres, reds, indigos, yellows, golds, grays, blacks and whites were scattered throughout the lobby, mindful and unmindful of current fashion trends; a world where everyone was allowed their own palette and fashion sense. Then I saw a man dressed in a long, flowing, white galabiyya mid-calf length tunic and a white Kufi skull cap. He seemed to float across the lobby. My gaze was fixed on him. There was something about him. Something ancient and venerable, and something familiar.

He was dressed like a Suni cleric, circa 1600.

I became mesmerized.

I took in a deep breath.

Future and past melded in my mind.

Fatehpur Sikri, India, June 8, 1488. Four men set down a Red-Royal wedding Doli. A ferenghi princess bride sits luminous behind the white Jali. Violins sing, clarinets swirl. The Jali is drawn back and the princess steps out, dressed in white, head to toe. She moves through the waiting crowd towards the throne. Her kohl-lined, green eyes keep their gaze fixed on her King, her patae.

Akhbar looks down at his new bride, and his heart swells with pride and love.

As the princess walks, the breeze blows her white translucent veil against her face, revealing her sensuous lips. Her white attire swirls like wings of an angel around her. Just as she arrives to stand in front of her king, a Cleric in white steps out and begins to protest, although he still holds onto his elbows, respectfully. Bitter words are minced with sweet.

The princess glances back at the cleric, then begins her ascent to stand next to her husband-to-be. The cleric's voice pierces the reverent moment and echoes in the hall. She glances over again. A glint of steel flashes in his hand. His other hand grabs her elbow and pushes violently. . . .

Back in the airport lobby, I found myself stumbling helplessly around, almost tumbling over and falling head-over-heels into the crowd.

What?

I steadied myself, gasped for breath and tried to get my bearings. Just off to my left, I spotted a dark-skinned, wiry little man in an orange shirt and khaki shorts, quickly scurrying away with my luggage trolley.

"I yam airport taxi driver ma'am!" he shouts back at me in broken English. "I yam take you safely where you go,"

Right.

And I was born yesterday.

I shot after him. "Stop thief!"

With amazing speed, the man jammed and wrangled his way through the crowd. He slammed the luggage cart into a woman. She screamed and fell down on the floor, clutching her shin. He kept on going, the crowds parting to let the crazy man through as the chase went on:

> "Deepa, Deepa, look out!"
> *"Aiiieeeeee, get out of my WAY!"*
> *"Watch where you're going, Oolu de patha!"*
> KA-THUMMMP!
> *"Stop, Thief. . . ! Somebody stop that man!"*
> "Whaaa. . . what's going on?"
> *"Oi! Chamariya! Vekh ke jao!*
> "No, wait. Come back here, YOU. . . ."
> *"Bachaou, oh bachaou!"*

The little man was very quick, and the wheels of my cart squawked loudly as it rattled further and further away from me.

I was about to draw my gun and shoot when a tall powerfully-built man stepped out in front of the cart and took hold of it. The sudden stop jolted the thief off his feet and almost over the cart. When he recovered from the jarring, the wiry little taxi-driver-man wiggled, pushed and pulled on the cart, but he couldn't budge it.

He cursed loudly.

"Bhan jot! You doing me what? I take memsahib in my taxi. Haram de alad."

I caught up with them, protesting. "I did not hire him. This thief shoved me aside and grabbed my cart."

"I am not chorrh, Memsahib. I am honest taxi man. You let me do my job!"

At that moment, I thought I heard something. A roar. A sound emitted from somewhere like an angry lion.

Did it come from the tall man?

His lips were still.

I took a step back, shocked at such raw, but untraceable aggression.

Then, the lion spoke.

"Array, Chuay ke poosh! You wiggly little mouse-tail, if you don't let go of this memsahib's luggage right now, I'll. . . ."

The mousy little man froze and caught his breath. His eyes turned big as saucers. He let go of the cart and backed away slowly, not taking his gaze off the tall man for a second, then he turned and high-tailed into the crowd.

I didn't blame him. That roar had been something else.

Immediately, I heard an outburst of laughter, sudden and robust. I turned back to the tall man. This time it's definitely him. He really is, visibly, laughing, I reassured myself.

He looked over at me and smiled.

"Works every time," he said. He was speaking aloud now in a normal way, but something else had changed about him. Was it my imagination? No. He seemed to be . . . morphing. It was subtle at first, but it was definitely happening. He seemed a different person now than when he first appeared. As if, his appearance could change along with his demeanor.

Or maybe *not*? That seemed ridiculous.

Perhaps it was some reflection off the stark, silver walls of the lobby that made him appear differently?

I wasn't quite sure.

That's when I recognized him.

"Wait a minute."

It was the same man as appeared in a photograph Beeji had emailed me during my flight. In the photo, he'd been standing next to a petite South Asian woman, who was wearing a blue sundress. The woman had been smiling shyly, and she had the most mysterious look in her eyes. The man was wearing a sports jacket and jeans, and he was sporting a goatee and a mustache. Maybe that's why I didn't recognize him? Now, he was clean-shaven and clothed in blue jeans and a black T-shirt recollecting U2's 'Unforgettable Fire' tour, just like Ricky's.

Ricky?

My heart jolted.

Ricky had worn that same black U2 t-shirt on our date, after the Festival, when we'd gone out to Giorgione's for pizza. He was look-ing exceptionally handsome that night, and. . . ."

Quickly, I recovered my composure and pushed those memories aside. I turned my attention back to the tall man, trying to assess his six-foot-plus frame. For a moment, I'd almost believed he was Ricky, but now, it seemed that wasn't at all how he appeared. In fact, he didn't look anything like Ricky at all.

The man flashed me yet another enigmatic smile. His brown eyes danced, cryptically, as he extended his hand.

"Ms. George," he exclaimed.

I tried to smile back, as I reached out my own hand.

"Hello, you must be Harshad."

At that moment, the small, slim Indian woman who'd been present in the same photograph emerged from the colorful crowd. She was dressed in stylishly faded denim jeans and a white short-sleeved peasant blouse. Her oval face was set in the same, serene Mona Lisa smile she'd been wearing in the photograph. With a curious gaze that seemed to match my own mood, her eyebrows arched up, then knitted, as she smiled at me in greeting.

Harshad reached over and pulled her in close to him. The woman looked up at him, and their eyes held each other brightly while he spoke. "Elanna Forsythe George, I want you to meet my heart of hearts, mere dil ki jahn, Laila."

The woman smiled. Her long hair framed small, delicate features. "I hope you don't mind my incorrigible husband. We've been married five years, and you'd think by now he'd have a little sharmai when he introduces me to people."

Harshad rolled his eyes and sighed. "Oh janae, mere jan, the day I stop introducing you in that way will be the day you'll complain to all your girlfriends that I'm not the romantic man you fell in love with."

Laila laughed. "Acha, acha, my desert poet, but it's time for us to go." She pushed him and my repossessed luggage cart along ahead of us.

I was still puzzling over Harshad's erratic changes in demeanor. He'd gone from ferocious adversary to lovestruck newlywed within seconds. Just then, Laila put her hand on my arm, brought me back into the present. She threaded her arm around mine as we followed behind Harshad. I didn't resist her intimacy, although I'd always found that level of familiarity a little uncomfortable. Even in the past, when Beeji'd walked with me like that in New York, for instance. It had taken me years to get used to it.

"How was your flight, Elanna?" Laila sang brightly.

"Fine."

That's all I had to offer. I was so tired from the trip and all the dramas at customs and in the lobby, and still reeling from the psychospiritual and temporal weirdness of the moment just before the little man grabbed my luggage. As we negotiated our way through the throngs in the crowded lobby, I just was happy to have someone there with me.

Truthfully? I hardly ever let anyone get close to me. Simryn, you may recall, was a rare exception. And so, as it turned out, were Laila Durga and Harshad Verma.

As we approached the terminal exit, Laila asked if I was hungry. "It's an hour's drive to our place, so we might want to get something to eat closer by."

Harshad looked back over his shoulder. "There's a great restaurant down the road, what do you say to Chinese?"

"Chinese?" I laughed. "Not authentic Indian?"

I saw an impish glint growing in Harshad's eyes.

"That would depend on which authentic Indian cuisine you were talking about. There's authentic North Indian cuisine. That includes Awadhi, Bihari, Bhojpuri, Kashmiri, Punjabi, Sindhi, Rajasthani, Uttar Pradeshi, Mughlai. Then there's the South Indian cuisine: Andhra, Karnataka, Kerla, Tamil, Hyderbadi, Udupi. . ."

"Harshad," Laila interrupted, her manner seeming ever-so-slightly exasperated.

He glanced over at her. "No wait, I haven't told her about the East Indian, North-East Indian and West Indian cuisines."

Laila smacked herself on the forehead with her right hand, then sighed. "Opho, baba bas karo." She turned to me, apologetically. "I'm sorry. He does go on and on. However, he is right. India is very diverse."

Once we got outside the majestic building, the hot, humid air swallowed us. The whole city was heavy under the unrelenting heat and still anticipating the moment the monsoons would arrive. Across the street, taxi drivers stood outside their cabs shouting at travelers, aggressively offering their services, bullying and coercing passengers into their cabs. Others stood back, minding their own business, tacitly waiting for patrons who would brave the gauntlet of angrier, more resolute drivers.

In the moving crowd, I spotted a stout middle-aged woman in a parrot-green-yellow-red sulvar kameez, struggling with a 'grabby-cabbie'. When he wouldn't let go of her bag, she raised her left leg, and stomped her heeled shoe on his sandaled foot. The man finally released her bag, howling and hopping, his eyes darting around in search of relief from pain. Without an apology, the woman wheeled her suitcase to a more placid driver, who promptly bowed before he opened the back door for her, stashed her safely inside, and only then did he place her suitcase in the trunk of his vehicle.

"Ah, the human drama," Harshad mused, as the scene developed before us. "Welcome to Mumbai, Ms. George, you'll notice here that people are sometimes very direct."

"Don't forget, Harshad, Elanna is from New York City," Laila retorted.

Harshad raised one eyebrow, as if to say, 'And your point is?'

Still, when it came down to it, Harshad was correct. I could sense the unfamiliarity of the vibes all around me. New York is big, beautiful, rough and tough, the great American city, but Mumbai was different. There was so much more color in the landscape and people, the linguistic and cultural mixes. Psycho-mystically, I'd already discerned many layers of entitlement and lack all around me, including, but not limited to, complex class and traditional caste divisions. There were other differences, too, ones I'd often noticed in non-Western countries; the depths of the long history; the traces of many peoples; the marks of many civilizations who had come and gone, and especially those that had taken the country by force.

Culture of cultures.

Riches of riches.

Beyond your wildest dreams.

A way of living had evolved over centuries to accommodate every ferenghi who wanted to become a desi. A democracy was developed later in an attempt to allow all the religions, languages, and the subcultures of subcultures to try to co-exist, even though people had lived here for centuries and didn't bother to pretend that there were no differences. With so many groups adhering to their own faiths and practices, it was no wonder there were supposedly over three hundred million Gods, Goddess or Deities in India. New York seemed stark and uniform in comparison. Sameness and equality on all levels was the goal there. Nice ideas. Even if, sometimes, they seemed only another mask for intolerance and division.

Harshad was still loading the luggage in the back of his cyan-blue Jeep as Laila and I climbed into its suffocatingly hot interior. She got the air conditioning going right away. I noticed the Jeep's steering wheel situated on the vehicle's right hand side. I let out a breath. Okay, it would take me a few days to get used to driving in Mumbai. I wondered what the traffic would be like. I hoped it was better than Delhi. I was there as a teenager with my mother and had taken a tour of some of the great temples and shrines around Rajistan and Punjab. Since my mother is a nervous type, I'd done all the driving. Beeji made a joke once about how, in India, lines on the road were 'only a suggestion' and I'd already known what she meant. In Delhi, I'd learned that roadkill was a not-infrequent event, sometimes a sport, and not always limited to wayward animals.

Except, of course, for cows.

Harshad drove out of the airport onto Sahar Road and turned right on DN Path. From there we took Vaikunthlal Metha Road en route to the Tulip Star Hotel on Juhu Beach, and within fifteen minutes, we were strolling into the lobby of the five star hotel, and following the signs that lead into the Shansui Restaurant. It was great to be out of the stifling heat of the parking lot, into the air-conditioned comfort of the hotel hallways, and, even though I was feeling quite exhausted, the aromas that met us as we entered the restaurant perked my appetite immediately.

As the young host led us to a table, Harshad gushed. "You'll be totally, one hundred percent, utterly amazed by the food here."

He was right. I was amazed. It was authentic. Authentically Chinese-Indian; 'Chindian,' as they called it. Manchurian chicken, chili paneer, gobi manchuria, flat hakka noodles, fried rice, and three servings of naan.

It tasted great. The real treat, however, was the "Sizzling Brownie" for dessert. A chocolate-covered, impromptu delight sprinkled with walnuts, served on a hot plate splattered with extra chocolate sauce, and an extra dollop of ice-cream on top. The entire meal had been pleasant enough, but with little conversation, for which I was thankful.

Then, halfway through the dessert course, Harshad suddenly began chattering in a loud and inane manner. I looked at him, narrowed my eyes and wondered. He was going on and on, talking about 'different similarities' between America and India; those were his exact words, 'different similarities'. I'd barely known him for an hour, but it seemed as if he'd already manifested, not only numerous physical appearances, but four complete personality changes too. He'd been fierce at first, then charming and chatty at the airport, rather quiet in the car and for most of the meal, and now, suddenly, he was acting just plain silly. It seemed as if he was cycling through some odd kind of bi-polarish mania.

I began to wonder if I'd done the right thing, promising Beeji that I'd meet up with these two. Beeji hadn't wanted me to be alone in Mumbai, and despite my protestations that I'd be okay, she'd insisted. She told me it would make her feel better. Now I started wondering if it'd been wise to give in so easily. As always, I supposed Beeji had her reasons for recommending them. That woman had a way of always turning out to be right in the end, and even if it seemed like she was wrong in the moment, somehow she'd always come out smelling like a rose. She had a serendipitous gift for knowing just where she needed to be, and just what she needed to do or say when she got there. And she never panicked.

But clearly, at that moment, Harshad was oblivious to both my contemplations and my discomfort; he just kept prattling on and on. His attention was now settled on the supposed 'different similarities' between the Hollywood and Bollywood film industries. He told me he was a self-proclaimedly 'huge' fan of the movie industries from both our countries. I confessed to him that I didn't know much about Bollywood, having only ever seen 'Meri Dil ka Tara.'

"Then you ain't seen *nuthin'*," he avowed. "Myself, I have just about the greatest collection of Hindi films ever, and soon I'll show you my perspective on the best of the best that Bollywood has had to offer: Andaz, Mother India, Sholay, Bobby. . . . " He continued to unfurl his mental list of favorite movies. "Haan, I do know the 'Who's Who of Bollywood' in all its entirety, and all its what's and wherefore's."

He snuck a peek at Laila. "Go ahead, mere jaan, ask me anything."

Laila opened her mouth to speak and. . . .

"Smita Patil!" Harshad exclaimed.

Laila glared at him. "Chi, chi! Why are you telling me to ask questions if you aren't going to give me a chance to speak?"

"Because, oh my beloved Laila, I know you so well. I know how you fancy socially-conscious movies about oppressed women who overcome an unjust society." Harshad leaned away just in time to avoid a backhanded laphar. "Just remember, it's all typecasting my darling. There's more than one woman in India who is oppressed, isn't there? And they don't all look like Smita Patil. Kamala ha! That one, she should have been more forward thinking and tried to break the mold. She might have tried for more romantic roles sometimes and expanded her range somewhat. Or perhaps she should have done a dance extravaganza!"

"Hiy oi rabbah! The man is so profound in his idiocy," muttered Laila as she darted a look at him. "I was doomed from the first day I ever laid eyes on him."

Harshad put his hands behind his head and leaned backward in his chair. "True, true. You see, Ms. George, it was Fate. Destiny. Kismet. Karma. Picture this:

"It's a Tuesday. Bhuddavar Savera Sham. Lunchtime at the Tata Institute of Social Science, Mumbai. Laila Durga, the heroine of our story, sits under a mangosteen tree reading and sipping a pink Fanta. Me, Harshad, the hero, is walking, reading and sipping an orange Fanta. I accidentally walk into her and fall over. Next thing you know, I am wearing pink Fanta and she is wearing orange Fanta. It was like Holi come early."

He sighed, as he gazed heavenward.

Laila covered her face with her hands and moaned. "Enough of this, Harshad. Bas Karo!"

Harshad stopped suddenly dead at the reprimand, with his feelings hurt, like a lost child.

Laila stared at him sternly. Then, she couldn't help herself, and her lips broke out into a wide, Mona Lisa smile. "Baba, you are so right, our lives are exactly like a Bollywood romantic-comedy."

Harshad's frown lifted, and he too smiled widely. "Arr-r-ray, I knew you couldn't stay mad at me for long."

Watching the pair of them for a moment, I suddenly didn't mind being there so much; the warmth between them was infectious. I took a deep breath and began to look around the restaurant. Then I noticed a man sitting across the room at a dark, obscure table. He was wearing a dark suit too, along with opaque sunglasses, and it seemed as if he was studying me. Suddenly, the man jerked his head away, and pretended to be interested in something else, outside the window.

I looked back over at Laila and Harshad, and tried to act as if I hadn't even noticed the man, but I was sure I could feel some kind of presence, as if something were trying to dig inside my psyche. *Rage. . . . Sorrow. . . . Aggression. . . . Regretful. . . . Sibilations. . . . A sudden sliding alongside my head as if trying to dig a hole. Something like a tunnel.*

Somewhere inside, a cold hunger was forming.

Soon, I'd be starved to death.

Just then, Harshad fell into an even more ridiculous comedy routine. He knelt down next to Laila and began to grovel and paw at her hand, as if trying to 'kiss it' with a clownish, pseudo-romantic flourish. Laila, forever the straight-person, brushed him off with a look of disgust. It suddenly occurred to me what I had to do. I threw my head back and laughed, very loudly. It was a bit forced at first, but as Laila indignantly smacked Harshad away with a rather sharp back of her hand, an honest and strong belly laugh came out of me. I could feel the psycho-energetic pressures on me become less intense. I caught a look at Harshad out the corner of my eye. He was wearing a smirk. After a while, the man across the room got up, paid his bill and left. A bit later and with much ceremony, Harshad tipped the waiter and paid our bill. Afterward, the three of us walked out of the restaurant, giggling and joking our way, loudly and boisterously across the hot, humid parking lot.

Inside the Jeep, the mood was different. Laila and Harshad had suddenly become very quiet. Harshad surveyed the parking lot. "That man. The one wearing sunglasses. I recognized him at the airport. I knew he would follow us, so I thought we'd lead him to a place where we could give him, as you might say, 'the runaround'."

"He was following us?" I hadn't sensed anything at the airport. Perhaps I'd been overwhelmed by the whole experience, the sweeping silver interior, the colors, the people and the drama. I sighed. Who was I kidding? Ever since my experience at the Bollywood Planet, my powers and intuitions were off. I was still raw, and I needed to be patient, because healing from trauma and tragedy takes time.

Harshad looked back over at me. "Yes, Ms. George. And in fact, I know who and what he is. His name is Rashbir Dulku. He is a highly-paid, very skilled assassin. A special sort of assassin; one with paranormal abilities. He is, what we call in India, an 'atma katan vala,' a 'soul reaper.' These types of assassins, so they say, kill by drawing out powerful and traumatic past life experiences from their victim's soul in such a way that the energies and confusion overwhelm the psyche. Then, a brain hemorrhage, a sudden and massive stroke ensues. The victims, however, don't all die immediately. Sometimes, they linger in a comatose state for months. But Dulku is an especially powerful 'soul-cutter' and no one yet has recovered from one of his attacks."

Harshad paused. "I have no doubt he was following you all the way from the airport, Ms. George."

I gaped at him. I had no idea of the magnitude of that man's powers. No extra-parasensory activity had shown up at all on my radar. This was frightening. Clearly, I was having a much harder time coming back after the Bollywood Planet incident than I'd hoped. I had to admit, then, that connecting with Harshad and Laila at Beeji's insistence was, perhaps, not such a bad idea, and I began to regret my overly-rushed opinion in the restaurant that they were both nothing but clownish, obtuse, and embarrassingly loud buffoons, and, in fact, obnoxious.

Then, something else occurred to me.

"So, Harshad, what you're saying is, the way you've been acting, um, ever since I met you, has all been. . . ?"

"That's correct, it's an act. That's – ah – one of my superpowers." Harshad continued.

"Honestly, I hardly ever say a sensible word in public. Most of the time, everyone within earshot thinks I'm a fool. It can be quite advantageous."

I turned to look at Laila.

She nodded at me, solemnly.

"Huh?"

Her eyes had penetrated me.

Inside myself, I felt the world becoming very still. As if time itself had suddenly slowed down.

Then Laila spoke. But her lips seemed to be moving out of sync with her words.

"Not . . . even . . . our . . . parents . . . know . . . about . . . our . . . . powers."

I shut my eyes tight. and shook my head.

"Laila, what's happening?"

Harshad responded. "You can feel that stillness, can't you? Relax, you're safe. It is one of Laila's abilities. The effects will calm you."

When my eyes opened again, Laila's eyes were no longer on me. She'd turned back around to face the front. Time was returning to normal and all the warbling in my mind had ceased. In fact, it seemed now my perceptions were becoming sharper and sharper. Soon, all of my senses seemed as clear as notes played on a well-tuned guitar.

Hmm, that was better.

"Tell me more, Harshad," I finally said. "How were you able to fool that man back there – 'Dulku' was his name? – even if, as you say, he's not an ordinary person?"

In the rear-view mirror, Harshad smiled back at me. A slightly wry smile. "Yes, that's correct. My ability to mask myself and others transcends the physical and mundane levels and can operate effectively on psychic planes as well. That's why Dulku couldn't quite recognize us, that is until you began to pay attention to him and try to figure it out with your mind. I initiated the joking around strategy to distract you, and, in the end, I think you realized, intuitively, that you were in trouble enough to help us pull you out of there. Dulku lost interest in us simply because we seemed like, well, just every day, ordinary people. And a bunch of mindless fools to boot. So I am able to fool the gifted much of the time, and not just the normals. Yet, to be frank, even I couldn't begin to tell you how it all works, how all those less tangible spheres of our personal realities come together in such ways that some of us have access to them."

I bit my lip. Okay, I thought, after all who could explain that? I am first and foremost a scientist, and I'd much rather deal with physical evidence: blood and hair samples, DNA, and so forth. I don't really understand any of this psychic quantum-jumping, para-phenomenological stuff either. Oh, it's true, I've studied spirituality and meditation with many great teachers and learned a few things, but I doubt anyone could give satisfactory explanations to the 'heebee jeebee stuff,' as Sergeant Martin once put it. The entire psychospiritual realm is utterly uncontrollable, completely unquantifiable. Even so, I was suitably impressed and surprised by my hosts. It was clear that both of them were extremely powerful, paramystical agents.

Harshad spoke. "I'm sorry about your delay at the airport, Elanna, but it seems to have been brought on by something quite serious."

I looked up from my ponderings and studied his profile in the driver's seat.

Now what?

"You see, one of our best agents, a normal named Arti Jain, functioned as an administrator in a downtown government office, while working for us, in an undercover capacity, of course. Then, when she didn't turn up for work this morning, we were alarmed because she was one the most relied-on people in the whole Mumbai Nomad organization. If things had gone on as usual, she'd have been the one who made sure your arrival was better coordinated today, and we'd have had you whisked through the airport, not let you be exposed to so much danger."

Damn.

More people had gone missing.

"We looked everywhere. They finally found her in an alcove on one of the upper floors of the office building she worked in. She was unconscious, an apparent victim of a stroke. So then, when I sensed Dulku's presence at the airport, it all made sense. Dulku'd taken Arti down in an effort to get to you."

Laila spoke up, her voice seeming to catch a little. "It was a great loss for us. Arti was very valuable. Very resourceful and kind."

The silence that followed seemed fitting. A moment for Arti. I immediately thought of Simryn. How can anyone come to mean so much to someone so quickly? I reflected on all the people in the Nomad system in New York who'd given me support over the years. Aside from Beeji, Ricky and Captain Stewart, I'd never given any of them much thought.

Then, a disturbing idea hit me:

Maybe I'm a cold fish?

I thought about my parents and tried to remember the last time they'd been involved with my life. To this day, they still didn't know me or have a clue about what I did, and, if they did know, they'd surely think I was ill and try to make sure I had the best 'help' that money could buy.

I shuddered.

It had always seemed a better move never to bring my true life up with them. The time I'd spent with Beeji, however, had led me to believe that an Indian family's attitudes might be different when it came to psycho-mystical oddities. Then I smiled, as I remembered Beeji, her boisterous demeanor, her wisdom, her cooking, her kindness; suddenly, I felt a bit forlorn, and a long, long ways from home.

"Elanna, how many years have you known Beeji?" Harshad asked me.

I was startled.

What?

How long had he known what I was thinking?

I stared at him.

"Oh, sorry. Yes, I often do know what people are thinking, and sometimes, I annoy them by speaking up prematurely."

I was a bit taken aback.

"Harshad, what you're saying is. . ." I finally responded, "you and Laila are not only powerful paranormal agents, but each of you possesses a multiplicity of gifts."

"Mmm. That's right," Laila replied. "and we're assigned to be your primary contacts here in Mumbai."

"A few minutes ago you told me that your parents don't know anything about your abilities. Do you hide your 'giftedness' from them, Laila?"

Laila turned again to look at me from the front seat. I was surprised this time when the world didn't wobble or slow down to a halt. "When I was a small child Beeji lived on the same street as us, and I've known her daughter, Davina, since we were both two years old. Beeji recognized my abilities early after I came over to play with my friend. She introduced our family to some parent-agents when I was only three, who made a point to become closely acquainted with us. So, even after Beeji moved to America, I was well guided, and even today, my parents don't suspect a thing."

I pondered her story. "Beeji is a genius. To look at her, you'd never suspect she had an ounce of guile."

"Precisely."

Harshad turned the key in the ignition and the Jeep roared to life. "And that's how we all need to be. Crafty and sly. You're too straightforward, Ms. George, too overconfident. That's why we almost lost you a few moments ago. You should lose your excessive cool here. I'm glad you caught on to our charade in time, but you would do well to have less akkarh, be a little less arrogant and uptight while you're here in India. Fortunately, at least for now, Rashbir Dulku thinks we're just a bunch of imbeciles."

As Harshad began to maneuver the Jeep out of the parking lot, Laila broached another topic. "Beeji told us quite a bit about you. She said you're an extremely private person and will resist help. That's why we're charged to keep a special eye on you."

I stiffened up.

Harshad stopped the vehicle at the hotel exit, waiting for a break in the steady traffic. His eyes in the rearview caught mine once again. They were clear and sharp.

"Being what we are is difficult, and we need to rely on the resources of our organization. Taking matters into your own hands puts questions in the minds of other operatives. Yet, throughout your career you've done exactly that, and on a number of occasions, you could have been. . . ."

"Lost forever, I know"

Harshad's gaze returned to the road. "We should *learn* from our mistakes, Ms. George."

I rose up in my seat, a bit.

Rush-hour traffic along the route had cleared enough now for Harshad to start for home. We drove along in silence for a time. Outside, it was muggy and hot, so I was doubly-glad for both the quietude and air conditioning, as I gazed out at the Mumbai city-sights passing by. Trucks, rickshaws, cars meep-beeping, jeeps rushing to and fro; men and women in western suits and boots rushing to their businesses; vendors, young and old, selling their wares; beggars crying out for a few annas. The colors and contrasts, outrageous as they were, formed a seamless reality.

A bit later, we turned onto the Western Express Highway. The Jeep was moving much faster now, and our newly-found speed seemed to lift our communal spirits.

After a time, as I watched the scenery race by, Laila spoke up again. "Beeji tells us that your abilities are not only powerful, but also random and unpredictable. Our orders are to stay close by you, because in India, you might have more trouble understanding the ways things manifest."

"She mentioned something like that to me, too. But I wasn't quite sure what she meant."

Laila paused. "The energies flow differently here. Experiences on the ethereal plane can form and alter more quickly, and be more haphazard and dangerous than one might expect."

I could hear all her subtexts and innuendos. I tried not to sound sullen when I responded, but I hate it when people know things about me. "I suppose . . . it would be better if I could learn how to control my abilities," I said.

I caught another sharp look from Harshad as he glanced back in the rear-view mirror. "It's a matter of trust. An unshakable trust that the universe will send you just what you need, just when you need it, that's what's needed. There's no use looking for it. You might not like what you find."

That's true, I thought. But all too often, I wasn't quite sure when to wait or when to act.

Laila replied. "Elanna, that's something only you can decide for yourself. We can't tell you when and how to respond. Ultimately, deciding to confront the spirit of Rajesh Sharma all alone, without support either inside or outside our organization, was a decision you made. You'll have to live with the results. So, who are even we to tell you it was the wrong choice?"

I pursed my lips and silently thanked Laila for that. It was time to let it go. Of course, it was still the wrong thing to do from the Nomads' organizational point of view. I'd put myself, and perhaps others close to me into dangerous circumstances. But I wasn't thinking about losing my affiliation with the top-top-secret organization. I'd only been thinking about Simryn's death, Suraj, Saramma, and their surviving half-sisters and brothers. After two weeks of uncovering nothing but chaos and confusion, a face-to-face confrontation with Sharma's ghost was the only plan I was able to come up with. And, even though Sharma was dead, and therefore, not going anywhere, I'd felt an urgency.

And somehow, it had to be me.

That night in the Bollywood Planet, I'd entered into a wild vision after encountering Sharma's ghost. He put on a spectacular show for me illustrating how he died during a sexual tryst with four voluptuous and sex-crazed starlets. Sure, right. Believe me, I knew the vision was badly overacted and over directed, with choreography done by some hack amateur. Sharma had definitely blown the budget on visual effects. But, after witnessing the nauseating performance, I wasn't any closer to knowing who poisoned him or any of his illegitimate children. All I'd got, in the end, from Sharma was a weird 'clue' that he whispered in my ear, just before he unmanifiested.

Rajesh was right, I told myself, as I watched the Mumbai cityscape flying by outside my backseat window. Murder mysteries were definitely *not* his genre.

I'd woken up in a crazed psycho-sexual rage. It took me weeks to get it under control. I winced as I recalled the young valet at the Bollywood Planet Hotel, the first person I'd encountered after I emerged from the ghostly experience. That young man was still under observation by the Nomads. After my recovery, I returned to Captain Stewart and argued to stay on the case. He told me that it'd gotten too personal for me now and that the Nomads would prefer I handed it over to someone else. But I wouldn't budge.

He'd called me a cowboy. A 'lone gunman'.

Well, okay . . . but could I help that? Perhaps it was my root American-superhero complex, but it always seemed to me that I was the one who had to get it done. So, I waited it out in his office and stared him down, until he'd finally conceded, gave me what I wanted.

BEEEE-EEE-EEE-EEE-EEEEMP!

A loud blast from a horn roused me from my musings.

I turned to see a bright orange truck coming up from behind us. A blue Lord Krishna, painted above the cab, gazed down his nose at me. The words 'Goods Carrier' were painted underneath it. The impatient driver rode our tail.

Harshad maintained his speed.

BEEEE-EEE-EEE-EEE-EEEEMP!

The driver moved up even closer and beep-beeeeep-beeped loudly on his horn once more.

Harshad slowed down.

BEEEEEEEEEEEEEEEEEMP ... BEEEEEEEEEEEEEEEEEEEEEEMP!

Harshad maintained his cool. He wouldn't budge. The irate driver behind him was having his patience stretched to the utmost.

BEEEEEEEEEEEEEEEEEMP! . . . BEEEEEEEEEEEEEEEEEMP! . . . BEEP-BEEEEEP! ... BEEP-BEEEEEP-BEEMP!

"Acha baba," Harshad muttered, as he finally turned right onto Jogeshwari Vikhroli Link Road, and the impatient driver behind him sped away. We rode past building after building. Many banks. Their architecture ranged from ancient times and eras to modern designs. Images of devas and devis in many incarnations stood painted on signs out front of some of the buildings. Lakshmis, Shivas, Ganeshes, Varahas, Krishnas. I wondered what Americans would think if they had paintings of Jesus, Superman, Batman and Wonder Woman outside our banks. Or Nomads. I laughed to myself, imagining paintings of Captain Stewart outside a bank, or various other Nomads painted on freight trucks and taxicabs.

I smirked, widely.

Harshad suddenly blinked, as he caught a glimpse of me in his rearview mirror.

". . . Ms. George?"

"What? Oh, it's nothing."

I let out a breath and quickly changed the subject. "Harshad, may I ask you two a question?"

He nodded.

"What can you tell me about yourselves as . . . ah, 'members of our organization'."

Harshad faced his gaze back to the road. "We have abilities opposite to one another, and in many ways, Laila and I shouldn't be able to get along at all."

Laila turned to me and smiled. "Still, I suppose the heart has the final say."

"You see, Laila, as she demonstrated earlier, has very deep focus. She has an ability to become so still that she can tune into things everyone else will miss, and people are often completely oblivious to her presence. And me, I'm able to pick up on seemingly random signs and messages. I can see things formulating in advance and act according to my instincts. For instance, I always know at a distance when-ever people have a high level of interest in me."

Laila jumped in. "If his mother decides to call him, he will know in advance and call her, just so she doesn't have to pay the long distance charges. She'll always say, 'Harshad baeta, may you have a long life, I was just thinking of you!'"

"I also have an ability to sense individuals in a crowd," Harshad went on, "which is how I knew the assassin, Rashbir Dulku was at the airport and tracking you. Our abilities don't manifest at will, as yours don't, but they usually come out when we need them. As to how we accept our situations, well, we've both been dealing with this for a long time, ever since we were children. We had excellent teachers with their own special abilities, who, from an early age, taught us to 'go with the flow,' as they say."

"We also have abilities in common." Laila said. "Each in their own way, Harshad and I are both masters of disguise. It can border on shape-shifting. However, all of that's pretty minor compared to what Beeji told us about you and your abilities."

I swallowed. I'd trust Beeji with my life and she was usually very discreet, but why had she thought it necessary to reveal so much about me to these strangers? I took in a very deep breath, let it out, and stared out the window at the scenery racing by.

"I felt a little disturbed when I first met Laila, too." Harshad said, reading my mood. "It felt strange being around someone who . . . just knew me. Apart from her extraordinary powers of stillness, I didn't realize I was dealing with another, equally powerful and unpredictable force."

He glanced over at her.

"I didn't know it, at the time, but it was love at first sight."

Laila laughed at the recollection. "We couldn't be near each other for very long at first before our powers would short out. Things became very heavy, and at times, dark. I thought it was crazy but we couldn't stay away from each other. Harshad found a way we could spend time together, by keeping things light, making jokes. What keeps us mobile out in the public sphere is laughter, music, and seeming to be engaged with only the superficialities of the world."

"The only place we can afford to be serious is at home," Harshad added.

"By the way," Laila said, as she glanced back at me over her shoulder. "You'll be staying with us for the duration of your visit. No ifs, ands or buts."

"Thank you for your hospitality." I smiled. "And I've not an 'if', an 'and', nor a 'but' to offer."

"This is good." She laughed again. "I think we're going to get along quite well."

I smiled. I was feeling like that might even be true, so I relaxed as best I could back into my seat and allowed myself to feel a bit more comfort. About an hour later, we were pulling into the cool, underground parking lot of their apartment building in Navi Mumbai. Harshad helped me with my luggage, while Laila went over to hail the elevator.

"It will be great to have you here. It's been months since we had a house guest," Harshad said.

I was puzzled. "You and Laila entertain guests? How do you find the time?"

"Most of our relatives have adjusted slowly to modern living. When a relative comes to visit, we'll take a day or two off and spend time with them. But gone are the times when guests could come and stay for weeks. When we were children, some relatives came and stayed for months. My mother took us to live with our nani and nana ji when she was pregnant with my sister so my grandmother could take care of her when she had her baby."

His face lit up like the sun.

"My mother is from Punjab and my grandfather had some zamine. I had fun as a child running and playing wherever I wished. We'd walk into nana ji's fields, and pick whatever sabzi we wanted, cauliflower, potatoes, eggplant, and then nani ji would make dinner for us. And, anytime I wanted a big, juicy watermelon. . . ." He stopped and shook his head. "But, look at me, I've already started my trip down memory lane, and we haven't even settled you in yet."

At least, they're *good* memories, I said to myself.

Harshad and Laila's apartment was spacious, clean and comfortable. If

I hadn't felt the exotic heat and humidity and seen the sights on the way, I might have sworn I was back in New York. Their home had every convenience. I walked to the window and looked out on the cityscape. Even though I was very tired, I felt a strong urge to get out and explore the sundry temples and shrines I'd seen along the way, but I knew they would have to wait.

"Would you like a cup of chai, Elanna, or would you prefer English-style tea?" Laila asked.

I smiled. "I love chai, but a cup of nice, plain tea sounds very good at the moment."

"Darjeeling? Jasmine?"

"No, just plain black tea. Thanks."

"Done," Laila said as she disappeared around the corner of the kitchen. I sat down on the sofa next to a red silk covered pillow, with an embroidered woman in a sequined dress carrying a clay pot on her head. I sighed and looked around the room. Along with the television, stereo and DVD player, there were pictures and sculptures of various gods and deities. To the far left of the room stood a short book case. My gaze fell on a statue of the Goddess Maha *Kaali* sitting on top. She stood on one leg, many arms held up in balance. Black as black can be. Skirt adorned with severed arms. A necklace of heads. She looked wild and chaotic. As if she were ready to propose the world a frightening new question, one that would open the door to some paradoxical new universes.

"*Quite* the enigma, isn't she?"

What?

Laila's voice came from beside me.

I shook my head and came out of the vision.

My eyes darted around the room and fell upon a fine china tea-set waiting on a coffee table in front of me. Steam was pouring out from the spout of the tea pot.

"How long was I, um, gone?"

"Long enough for the tea to brew nicely," Laila said, as she poured the tea into the waiting cups.

"Would you like milk and sugar?"

"No, thank you," I replied. I shook my head a little. "I must be more tired than I realized. I was thinking just a single thought, and then you materialized right in front of me."

She bit her lip. "Yes, I have a way of doing that. And it's not only you who has trouble with it, don't worry. It is kind of spooky. I have a gift for moving through time so quietly that, to most people, it seems as though I'm not affected by its passing."

"Fascinating. How do you and Harshad manage to live here in the same residence? I mean, with being investigators and all?"

"We cope. As other people do."

I took a sip of the hot, steaming tea and felt my body soothe a little. "Being a super-sensitive para-mystical agent is never easy, and, in fact, most of the time I feel like I can barely deal with living."

Laila paused.

"Harshad and I are both aware that we can use our talents only when the universe makes them available to us, and we've come to accept our human limitations. However, trusting the universe to take care of the person you love is much more difficult, especially if they're working in dangerous circumstances. That's where the greatest diffi-culties lies. We all want to protect the people we love, and we'll take matters that are beyond us into our own hands to try and make sure that we don't lose them. In doing so, we risk losing ourselves, and our way of loving can transform from a gift into a curse. We may become so afraid that we have no life of our own at all, just fear. So, in our ef-forts to protect others, we may end up among the living-dead ourselves. That, in fact, was Rashbir Dulku's story."

Laila's eyes searched mine over her cup of tea.

"Knowing this keeps us humble."

I nodded. I understood the concepts, but I always had trouble knowing how to fit them into the framework of the so-called 'real' world. Most of the time, it all sounded ludicrous to me. The random-ness of our gifts seemed just completely random, and without any rhyme or reason, at all. And, no matter how many times something auspicious happened to me at just the right moment, I never quite trus-ted it, because, just as often (or so it seemed to me), that serendipity wouldn't be there for us when we needed it the most. It was hard for the realist and pragmatist in me to accept this so-called 'giftedness' was somehow valid, and putting your trust in something so unknowable had never made much sense to me, notwithstanding the number of times I'd been forced to do it.

"What kinds of cases do you investigate?" I asked Laila.

"We, like you, specialize in cold cases. Last month, however, we took a case that was only a few months old. A business tycoon with connections to high-up government officials claimed that his daughter was kidnapped and had disappeared without a trace."

She held a plate of sweets out to me.

I chose a round, golden ladoo.

"When we found the woman, she told us a different story. She said she had fallen in love with someone who was the same caste as she was, but from a lower financial status. He was a clerk in her father's office. When the girl told her father she wanted to marry him, he was enraged. He told her he would not have his daughter marry someone who would drag the social status of his family down. And if she did marry the man out of her own volition, he would have both of them killed. To prove he would make good his threat, the young man was fired, then hired thugs beat him up and left him unconscious in an alley. The girl became frightened for him and broke it off for his sake. But, in time, they both realized it was no good, they had to be together.

"They planned their escape, while she played the dutiful and obedient daughter. Her father began to believe he'd finally talked some sense into her. He recommended a more suitable boy. She went on a few dates with him to society parties, and, eventually, she even became engaged. No one caught onto the charade. Then, one day, she just disappeared, like a breeze through a tree. Without a trace. Her father's people looked everywhere. The police were stumped. When we got the case, she'd been gone less than a year. There were few clues, so we had to use our special senses and powers. We found them living in Delhi, where, it seemed, her young man had secured an alternative identity, and an excellent paying job in a company competing directly with the father's."

I put my empty cup and saucer on the table.

"What did you do?"

Laila poured a second cup of tea for us. "Harshad and I resigned from the case. We were brought in to find a kidnap victim. As there was no kidnapping, we were within our rights not to divulge any information that would put the young couple in danger."

She sighed.

"Being a very powerful man, the father offered us a rather large sum—a bribe. Huh! What do we need with his money?"

I smiled. Trying to bribe a Nomad would be like trying to bribe the water in a river not to flow downstream. As far as I knew, there'd never been a Nomad who'd been turned.

Laila paused. She glanced over at the statue of Maha Kaali balancing on one foot, and mused, "Even in this modern day and age, some Indian parents think they own their children. They believe their children are in the world only to make them look good. They've forgotten our true Mother, who will one day destroy their ego's grasp on the world."

I raised an eyebrow. "Don't think it's just Indian parents, Laila. There are many parents like that in America."

Harshad's voice came from down the hall. "Am I interrupting? I hope not. Elanna, sorry, but I had to have a bit of meditation time. I hope you don't mind. Now, perhaps, you'd like to be shown to your room?"

I looked up and squinted. It was Harshad's voice, but he looked different again. He didn't seem so tall. His face was serene, and not in the least animated. He was wearing a white cotton, kurta pajama now, with a white hoodie.

I didn't know what to say.

"You look different. Wearing all white, like me."

Harshad spread his arms, and looked down at his outfit. "Yes, by George, I think you're right. This is my secret, mythical persona. You, on the other hand, seem to wear your mythical persona on the outside, even in public." He raised his hand and asserted, "Now, I don't think that's always wrong, but at times, you do rather look like Storm of the X-Men."

I folded my arms. "Hmm. Well, I wear varying shades of white, you know? And, besides, I live in New York City, where wearing all white can still be considered *sort* of 'normal'."

He smiled before heading out to the kitchen to get a jug of water from the refrigerator. I was still getting used to the idea that this was the same man I'd met at the airport.

"You may have a point. Or two." he said, as he walked back into the living room. "But do you really want to walk around wearing all white in a place where everyone else will be wearing such vivid colors? People will think you're a widow, or Death Incarnate, or some strange kind of American sadhu. Around here, you can wear a rainbow, or a hat with a parrot on it and nobody will bat an eye. But all *white*? No, I think you'll have to loosen your presentation up a bit, Ms George."

I laughed. The idea was tempting. I guessed I could try it.

"Why not?" I said. "Would either of you be in the mood for . . . a shopping expedition?"

"No, no, no!" Laila interjected. "Beeji sent a photograph ahead of you, and gave me your sizes, suggesting we pick some things up for you in advance. I hope you won't mind."

"No. Of course not. Just tell me what it cost, so I can pay for it."

"No-no-no-no-no-no-no! You can't pay for it," Laila tutted, "it's a gift from Beeji!"

"That woman. I'll have to buy something nice for her when I get back. She won't like it, but this time she goes too far. . . ."

The outfits Laila had chosen for me were beautiful: a parrot green, mid calf dress, with yellow and red embroidery around the neckline and cuffs, a soft pink chiffon sari, and so on. There were some colorful, western style outfits, too, most notably a blue, embroidered cotton tunic with black Capris.

After looking over the clothes, I took five thousand rupees from my purse and pushed it into Laila's hand.

"*No, no*, what are you doing? It wasn't that much," Laila moaned.

I closed her fist around the money. "You've got to take it."

"No. It's too much, it only cost four thousand rupees—oh, *damn*."

"*Hah*. You see? You've got to take it all now because I must give you something for the extra expenses of putting me up."

"A thousand rupees?" wailed Laila.

"You're right, it's not enough." I reached into my purse, pulled out two thousand more rupees, and pushed it into her hands.

"That will have to do until I get more cash."

We wrestled properly for another few minutes; then, finally, after much huffing and puffing, Laila gave up and reluctantly took the money. She blinked. "You're as good as any of our *desi* people at this, you know."

I smiled as I pushed my hair back from my flushed face. "I've argued with the best. Beeji can force anyone to keep her gifts or money. I've learned there's no use arguing with her, and, these days, I just take everything quietly."

"But, you insisted I take the money!"

"Yes. But she's not here, is she? Oh, I know, it's not like I won fair and square."

Laila sighed. "Beeji isn't going to like this. . . ."

"Tell her to bring it on."

"Very well. Getting back to the investigation, we'll be able to access all the resources of the Mumbai chapter headquarters. If we find anything, or anyone that needs to be examined, or incarcerated, or say, we need to perform some tests, we can use their facilities."

I looked at her puzzled.

"We? What do you mean by 'we?' I thought. . . ."

She smiled broadly. "Oh, didn't Harshad and I inform you? We'll be working closely with you on this case."

Dammit.

Of course they hadn't told me; they knew I'd balk at the idea.

Before I could begin to mouth my objections, Laila spun around to face me. Her energy was sharp.

"Remember, Elanna, the Mumbai organization, too, has been rocked by these goondas. Our poor Arti."

I closed my mouth. There was nothing I could say.

I nodded my agreement.

Yes, poor Arti. Poor Suraj. Simyrn. Saramma. And many others. Poor Indra.

Laila smiled and nodded demurely.

"It may take some getting used to, your working with us as a team, but do you know what I think?"

Her bright, oval gaze met mine.

"I think we're *all* going to succeed . . . magnificently."

The Teller of Secrets

I remember the next morning.

I awoke to a symphony. Of birdsong. Cooing, cawing, cawking and squawking, above the hums, beeps, and din of traffic:

> *Tweeet*
> *Nee-nee Nee*
> *Twitter-Tweet-Tweet*
> *Pibble . . . Fatter-twatter whifft*
> *EEEE-aaaa*
> *Eek-eek quipper whaaA*
> *Hr-r-r-r-r-r-r-r-r-r-r-Ack*
> *Tweet tweet ji-ji-ji-ji-JI*
> *Diddle-iddle-iddle*
> *Nct-nct*
> *Hr-r-r-r-r-r-r-r-r-r-r-Ack . . .*
> *Diddle-iddle-iddle Bwaaa*

I opened my eyes. Warm green walls. Fragrances. Air warm and poignant in my nostrils. Tropical. I looked around the unfamiliar room. A colorful print caught my eye; many Krishnas dancing with his many gopis, all his cow-herd girls. I knew the story from Hindi mythology, but I liked it best when Beeji told it. I smiled, recalling her animated voice. Her twinkling eyes. Her tone sometimes serious, sometimes entertaining. I sighed. Beeji was right; the telling of a story is often more important than the story, itself.

I continued glancing around the room.

My eyes fell on a few bright peacock feathers standing upright in a vase near the door.

Then I remembered.

This was *Mumbai*.

I was in Mumbai.

My eyes wandered round the room more freely. Near the foot of the bed, two ivory statues were set on a carved wooden dresser. Shiva The Destroyer sat in lotus pose, looking straight ahead. Unwavering. Meeting my gaze. Behind him at a respectful distance, Hanuman the Monkey-headed God stood, both regal and mischievous. Both figures were silent, as absorbed by the morningsong as I was.

I rolled over and watched the sun rays streaming in through the window and forming four bright squares on the floor. There, in one of them, I saw the shadow of a single bird. I got up out of the bed and walked over to the window. A lone Dorango was perched, solemnly, on the feeder just outside. The little black bird cocked its head and gawked at me for a moment; then it went back to imitating every sound it had ever heard. I watched him for a while; I listened to him, as he recounted every tale he had ever known, recollecting almost every single story on the planet. He knew everybody's business.

He reminded me of Minoj.

He was The Broadcaster.

The Teller of Secrets.

A Trickster.

A silver-tongued devil.

The Deceiver.
An army of bandits. A raging fire.
Run.

I shook my head vigorously to clear away the little bird's gossip. I took in a deep breath. I yawned and glimpsed my watch as I picked it up from the night table.

"10 A.M? What?"

I was flabbergasted.

I rushed into the ensuite to throw some cold water on my face before I bolted out the bedroom door, still wearing only the lightweight white-cotton pajamas Laila had provided for me. I hurried down the hallway, rubbing my eyes, and scratching my head, as I stifled a yawn.

Then suddenly, I thought I could hear *more* strange sounds.

I stopped, abruptly in mid-yawn, to listen.

Down the hall in the living room, voices were squabbling. An unfamiliar male voice droned on at length. Then another male voice offered some words, before a female voice jumped in rather passionately. Their tones became hushed, then rose to a cacophony, each voice wishing to be heard above the others. Meanwhile, out in the hallway, I was still trying to find my bearings. Trying to decide.

Should I go in?

Should I stay out?

Maybe it's a secret meeting?

"Would you care to join us, Elanna?"

What?

I nearly jumped out of my skin; I spun around to my left ready for a fight.

Laila, who had just appeared out of nowhere, was standing right next to me.

"Oh, did I startle you?" she retorted, with a smile.

I tried to smile back. "Don't worry, Laila, I'll get used to it."

In her living room, after she'd offered me a nice, cool glass of milk soda, Laila introduced me to four people, whom she'd met many years ago at a Religious Studies seminar; dear old friends from her University days.

Two men. Two women.
Mark, a Portuguese-Indian-Catholic-Christian.
Fatima, a feminist. Formerly Muslim, now Baha'i.
Gurdev Kaur, a woman Sikh-philosopher.
And Ram, a perpetually-displaced Dalit.

Their cadences lifted and fell in waves:

". . . But that doesn't matter. All religions have failed when it comes to the plight of the true indigenous peoples of India."

"Not true. Sikhism is without hyphens. The Guru ji's said there is no Hindu, no Musselman, no man and no woman, no higher or lower caste. All are equal in the creator's eyes. There is no need for dualities."

"Yet today, most Sikhs are second only to Hindus in their observance of the caste system. They oppress and exploit the Dalits regardless of what the Guru ji's have said."

"That is true. Yet we're not the only ones who've lost the core of their faith."

"Ah, true-true, and the Christians of many varieties haven't fared any better. There are still hardly any Dalit priests in the churches."

Ram managed a stiff smile. "I tell you, no matter how each religion declares humanity is equal, they cannot wash the uncleanness of the Dalit away. We can't be successful or be a leader in the community without other Dalits seeing us as betrayers of their ancient position. All sides wrinkle up their noses at us. Only Islam accepts us, and we can worship in the mosques, but we worry that we Dalits among the Muslims are becoming more and more enslaved by our own idealization of Islam."

"True-true, Ram, but what is lower than a Dalit? *Hu-u-u-h?* A woman. All through history, men have taken away her power until she doesn't know any better. Now, a woman can't even succeed without everyone thinking she's a lesbian."

"Truly spiritual practices require that women be free of such bondage."

"Even the most liberal and knowledgeable of all the religions, Hinduism, has lost its way."

"In order for organized religion to succeed, there must always be a 'them' and an 'us'."

"The populace has given power to priests, Vedics and religious leaders, over and over, throughout all of history. And they use that power and position to create a society that suits *them*. Period."

"They do what their original texts call an 'abomination' and make it prescribed ritual."

"A good way to enslave people is to add a little God to the mix."

They all turned to me, standing in the doorway. "We'd like to hear what you think, Ms. George, so please tell us. . . ."

I looked back at them and wondered. Up to that point, they hadn't been paying any attention to me, at all. Or had they?

"Um. . . ."

"Yes. You must tell us what you think, Ms. George, as a Westerner."

I bit my lip. "Certainly, things must have been worse before Mahatma Gandhi. At least, Gandhi must have drawn attention to the plight of the Dalits?"

Ram winced visibly.

Mark rolled his eyes.

Gurdev Kaur and Fatima stared at each other.

"Gandhi?"

"Two words. Poona Pact. Google it."

I shifted uncomfortably under their glaring stares.

Ram exploded.

"Dalits needed the Poona Pact. We needed a separate economic system from the rest of Indian society because they don't really want us."

The others stared at the floor.

I studied Ram; his eyes were angry and moistening. Then, I felt something deeper in him, as he was transported away and an ancient spirit spoke.

"This was our country first. Our very own bountiful, big, beautiful and wild mother. Our desh gave birth to Gods and Goddesses; they taught us how to live, love, sing and dance; they even taught us how to fight. We welcomed all manifestations of the supreme in any fashion that came to us. And they came. They came, saw and were enthralled by our Great Woman's bounties. But soon, they realized she could be a volatile lover. They didn't like her unruly times. Rains that washed everything away. A sun that drew out every drop of sweat. They saw her abundance and took it. More came and kept on coming. Aryan, Chinese, Moguls, Turks, Greek, Persians, English—all claiming little bits of her at a time. But she–she always had more and more. Generations came with eyes and stomachs full of want that never seemed to fill. Kings fought to claim her riches from other Kings who'd fought and claimed the riches from other Kings. Always another. Greater and more powerful. We watched them come and go, and stay; the blood of men, women, and children soaked her ground for centuries. Now? Now, when people think she's half the woman she once was, they want to leave her. Leave her with her depleted soil and tourist-y temples. Let them go. They will never find another that matches our wild and generous Mother. We are still here, Matha ji, still for you."

Someone sighed. Everyone looked up.

"Such a shame," said Harshad.

"Just one of the many shames," Fatima replied. "Remember there are the other 'low caste' members of our society. Women."

Ram rolled his eyes.

"Well, it is a blanket statement but the state of women's rights, even as they stand in the western world, is a laugh. In this country, it's just plain criminal. The sooner one can rid themselves of their daughter, the better, no? To tell the truth, most people would prefer a boy even today, including the Dalit families."

A rising level of mumble and grunts filled the room.

Laila muttered. "Huh. At the end of the day, even a slave may have some time to themselves. A woman? The more she does, the more she must do. It's unending. We have to stay vigilant to correct this for the women of the future."

She glanced over at Harshad.

He blushed, as he stood up. "Would anyone care for a milk soda?"

In a blue room. In a bungalow. High on a cliff overlooking a particularly rough section of the Indian ocean, Christine shudders for one last time. She glances over to her left where Sanjay's breathing is slowing to a steady rhythm. He paws at her and pulls her into him. She allows her body to be wrapped into his. Their arms, legs and other body parts meld, hot from the recent sex and the torpid Mumbai summer heat. Soon they'll be unconscious to the world.

She was oblivious to me. This was new in my experience of Christine. Most nights, even when she was asleep, I could feel her there, aware of my thoughts and responding with her own, whether I wanted her opinion or not. I was glad to have my own thoughts completely to myself for a time.

I sighed, as I tried to recall events that went beyond the thick wet-stickiness of their bodies. Beyond the rooms, beyond the 'life' that I was forced to live with Christine, beyond the days, weeks, months I'd been trapped in this body.

I was tired. Somewhere, during a particularly euphoric moment in their lovemaking, I saw Sanjay take the form of a nagh. Christine jolted us back into the bedroom immediately, but I couldn't be sure it didn't see me.

She's kept me pretty much hidden up until now. Mind you, Christine is adept at hiding, and she has a lot to hide. She rarely lets a thought come to the surface of her mind. She shoves all her insights, affections, and memories aside as soon as they hit her consciousness.

"There's no time for regrets," she always says.

She spends her time looking for bigger thrills so she can forget her past, whatever it held. At least that's what I suspect, although she scoffs at me whenever I ponder it.

"What do you think you are, a shrink? You're nothing but a weird, para-psycho freak lost in the cosmos."

I didn't let her get to me. She couldn't deny she was acting differently this time. She wasn't winning this conquest. It was as if she wanted to lose, just let it all go, simply go along with things. It was as if going along with things for her was the biggest thrill yet. Sanjay plays her for all she's worth. Christine's taken in by his heady, aggressive charms and devastating good looks; he has a lure that she's never come across before, and her heart beats so wildly at times, it's hard for her to stay conscious of her actions.

That's why I'm worried I'll be found out.

I have to concentrate and remember who I was, or I could lose myself to this existence forever. Christine only wants the glitz. She doesn't care much about every day things that are beautiful. Like a field of flowers. A walk beside an ocean. A cup of coffee with someone you loved.

"What?"
Wait a minute.

... 'with someone you loved'...?
. . . someone you loved?

Yes, it's true, I *did* love someone once.

But who? What was his name? What did he look like? And, if he loved me, why am I here?

I begged for clarity. A face. A smile. Warm brown eyes. Carmel skin. A handsome look. A strong, loving voice.

"Elanna?"

RICKY?

No, wait a minute.
Is that right?
'Ricky?'
Was that it? . . .

'Ricky?'

I meditated on the name:
Ricky

Rick
'Rakesh'
RAKESH!
The Moon.
Ricky.
Oh my God!

Now, I remembered.
Damn.
I only wanted this to be over.

In Laila and Harshad's living room, that same afternoon, Laila was pouring me a second cup of tea. I let my mind drift back to the Bollywood Planet, to the exact moment when Rajesh Sharma's ghost leaned over and whispered something in my ear. Those whispers began to form words. I struggled to hold onto them as they faded fast, and now I strained to remember, still baffled by what they could possibly have meant.

Seated in a large, comfortable armchair across the room, Harshad was staring at me intently. In my distracted state, his gaze was penetrating.

"Elanna, tell me, exactly what happened in the Bollywood Planet."

I felt the color rising up in my face.

"Ex-cuse me?"

"Yes, of course, I've read all the reports. But I wanted you to tell me in your own words."

I hesitated. I was surprised and embarrassed. But his intense gaze pinned me down. I let my mind go back again to that night. I saw Rajesh Sharma, standing there in the middle of the room, his visage flashing with glee, scheming even more mischief as he leaned over to whisper in my ear. I'd closed my eyes. Then I heard the words. He spoke them in Hindi, but somehow, I'd been able to translate them into English.

"One Body. Two Souls. One is a lamb."

I stopped dead.

What?

Had I said that out loud?

I looked around, feeling a little distracted and embarrassed. Harshad was staring at me. He repeated the phrase back to me in Hindi.

"Ecka vyakti. Do jivan. Ecka bahera ka baccha."

Finally I replied.

"Exactly, Harshad. Ecka vyakti, do jivan, ecka bahera ka baccha. 'One body, two souls. one is a lamb.' Those were the exact words Rajesh Sharma's ghost whispered to me that night in the Bollywood Planet, just before dawn, just as he unmanifested. When I came out of the vision, I remember an overwhelming urge for a slice of apple pie. Then, the last thing I recall is taking a bite out of that pie."

I cleared my throat. "After that, it's a blur. For the next few weeks, I was very disturbed, and all I experienced was a chaotic blend of events, sensations, remembrances, desires. Most of the time, I didn't know if I'd ever get back. I had to fight incredibly hard to hold on to my sanity, to have any sense left of the so-called 'normal' world at all."

"Amazing." Laila was studying me carefully. "What do you think Sharma meant by that phrase?"

I sipped my tea and thought it over. "I'm not sure. I did notice Rajesh Sharma looked very much like his illegitimate son, Suraj Amir. In fact, at times I thought they could have been twin brothers, but that would be 'two bodies, one soul,' wouldn't it? On the other hand, Suraj was the kind of person we all tend to view as lamblike."

Laila picked up a tea biscuit. "Parables are never easy to interpret."

"True. Rajesh might have been referring to the Bhujangen and its ability to possess people. That's another theory, I suppose."

Laila smiled grimly. "I suppose so."

"Still, it could have been Suraj, considering how badly he ended up, almost like a sacrificial lamb."

I shrugged.

Laila stared at me.

Harshad raised one eyebrow. "Sorry to have brought it all up, Elanna, I must have been unintentionally attuning to your thoughts."

Was he now? Well, this was becoming . . . more than just a little embarrassing. I looked around and began to feel impatient again. I managed a terse smile. "It's all right, Harshad. What I really want to know is, when do we get on with this? The two of you must realize, I'm very anxious to bring some people to justice."

Laila replied with a terse smile of her own. "Yes, Elanna. Of course, of course, you're right. We're just as anxious as you to bring this case to a satisfactory conclusion, and so is every other operative in Mumbai, because we've suffered a terrible loss of our own. But we must be patient. It could prove far too dangerous to move quickly. There's too much potential for the kind of distractions that would be yet another person's undoing."

Then, she smiled again, a little more relaxed now. "Besides, it is much too hot to go out during the day. Arrey, to go shopping in this heat would be too much of a chore, much less ferreting out powerful, psychospiritually-endowed evildoers."

I gave her a curious look.

She met my eyes, as her smile got wider.

"Fortunately, Elanna, the big fish we're seeking only come out at night."

Sanjay has an urgent power as well as animal magnetism, and he demands everything from Christine whenever they have sex. She digs her fingers deep into the bed as his cruel and gentle hands dance on her skin, kneading out every possible response. He's well-versed in technique, and has a deeper hunger than even Christine, who is insatiable herself, and relentless in her taking.

I can still feel his mouth all over her body, the way his tongue laps up her salty sweat like a cat at a milk bowl. From her face, down her throat, between her breasts, over her stomach. When he reaches between her legs, she writhes like a live wire. Her hips lift up to meet him. His tongue plunges in and drinks her.

I have to pull myself out of these memories; they're like a bad, bad dream.

The sun had almost finished setting by the time Laila, Harshad, and I had formulated a plan. We began as soon as we'd finished our second cup of tea, with Harshad laying out a row of five profiles from the Nomad data-banks across the width of the widescreen TV in their living room linked to his laptop.

"These five are considered to be the top Bollywood Dons."

I bit my lip.

Four men. One woman. Various ethnicities.

"Vijay Verma."

"Omi Shukla."

"J.D. Phagura."

"Ajit Premnath."

"Sholeh Shah."

Each photo had been taken at a distance but the Nomad's high-tech surveillance equipment served us well and the subjects were captured in fine detail. I noted that three of the five were surrounded by a light purple-tinged border in their photograph, a standard Nomad practice for denoting a person believed to have at least one significant, para-psychic ability. Not that it really mattered to me. I could see them for what they were: paranormal thugs, psychic bullies, ethereal warmongers. Thanks to whatever Laila had done with her powers the previous day in the Jeep, my abilities to center in and sense things were back now, and better than ever. So, I wasn't paying much attention to how dangerous my opponents could be.

I studied each face individually as Harshad zoomed in on them. Then, it occurred to me, despite the more obvious physical and facial differences between them, that there was an underlying sameness to all these individuals. An equivalency. Or something, perhaps, along the lines of a shared aura.

I asked Harshad to go through each photograph again. This time in full-screen view.

Then, I saw it.

It was the eyes. All five faces wore a similar, blank and calculated expression. Under closer inspection, the distinctions between them became blurry, as compared to that one overwhelming similarity. The same stone cold, vacant stare in each eye.

"Pretty scary looking," I said.

Harshad responded, almost reverently, "That they are, Elanna . . .that they are. All of these people are extremely dangerous. Many of our best operatives have lost their sanity, and some their lives, trying to bring only one of them to any kind of accounting. There is powerful jadhoo around each of them, thick walls of many kinds." He shook his head as he set down his laptop and looked over at me. "It gets worse, you know. There are others who operate even above the level of these five. Those people have been completely untraceable, and we don't have any idea who they could be. In fact, it's unlikely that anybody besides themselves knows for sure. Probably, even the Dons wouldn't be able to tell us who the top-top players in the game really are, even if we could ever get one of them to talk."

I bit my lip. "Wow."

Laila leaned forward. "Yes. Our prey is extremely elusive. Powerful and influential on many levels. All of them are extremely savvy to our most clever psycho-para-spiritual maneuvers too, and we've lost several of our top operatives in an effort to get the merest whiff of just one of them. So, clearly, we won't be able to start at the top and work our way down."

She frowned.

"But double dealing our way in on some lower level won't be a piece of cake either. These Dons, you see, employ many 'gifted' people of their own, and some of them also possess unique powers themselves. With all of these factors, combined with the political clout of the cartel, they've been unassailable. Even by our organization. Regular law enforcement agencies won't touch them, of course, and no one in the higher branches of government ever seems to have quite enough authority to force them to answer even the simplest of questions. This strategy has kept them essentially unapproachable for years. . . ."

Her eyes flashed.

"Up until now," she added.

She offered to refill my cup of tea.

I held out my saucer.

We spent the rest of the afternoon reviewing Nomad

documentation on the cartel. Photographs, statistics, movements of many groupings of Bollywood-mobs, gangs, goonda's, supposed cartel members, directors, producers, stars and starlets. Many names and faces and places went by. Charts and diagrams outlined the various organizational structures by which the cartel might possibly be organized, according to the many theories put forward over the years by Nomad criminologists and researchers. We'd discussed plan after plan, sometimes getting excited when we believed we'd found a way in, before discovering some gaping and deadly hole in each of our schemes. The bits of information from all our sources were racing madly around in my head as I tried to contemplate some further possibilities. With each failed plan, each flawed scheme, my despair was growing, my fears of never solving this case were looming larger, and all our ideas became riskier and more and more radical, and sometimes even outrageous, as the odds just seemed to stack up higher and higher against us.

I was getting tired. My head was starting to pound.

But I couldn't give up.

Not for Simryn's sake.

Finally, only a few moments before 6:00, Harshad put ten new profiles up on the widescreen. Six men. Four women. Many nationalities. Five columns across, two rows high. I blinked at the screen and tried to focus, but by now, every face I looked at was starting to seem pretty much the same.

I stifled a yawn.

Harshad suppressed a yawn of his own. "These are some of the 'rogues,' the freelancers, quasi-outsiders, and the wildest members of the mob. These ten are considered the least well-tracked mobsters in the entire cartel but, believe it or not, some of them are also considered to be among the most promising goondas . . . maybe even future Dons, themselves."

Then Harshad bit his lip, as he highlighted two of the figures and brought them up into full view. "But these two? No way. These guys are far too over the top. In fact, these are possibly the two most 'out-there' figures to ever be involved in the cartel. Neither of them even bother trying to be inconspicuous, or mask their involvement in mob affairs. Now, let's face it, that might make them among the easiest marks, too. But it's believed that they're both thought of as extremely unstable among the mob's higher-ups. Neither is widely-trusted. So let's forget about these guys. We don't really think either of them will be around much longer. They'll probably be taken down soon enough, if not by us or a jealous lover, then by the cartel itself, and after that, everyone associated with them will become persona non grata in mob circles. We might, however, try to target one of these other eight, who are at least a little more steady players."

He clicked again on both those profiles and made a move to delete from our view.

Then, something inside of me lurched.

"NO, WAIT!" I blurted out.

What?

Why was I screaming?

I turned to look at Harshad and Laila. They were gaping at me, startled by the urgent tone of my voice. But what could I say? At that point, I was as confused by my outburst as they were.

I hesitated.

I glanced around, and caught my breath.

I studied the screen.

"Who's that guy?" I finally said, pointing out one of the doomed mobsters.

"No, Elanna, he's far too out there," Laila interjected.

I bit my lip.

"I just wanna know who he is."

Laila sighed.

"Okay, very well, Elanna. His name is Johnny; 'Johnny Akkhara,' as they call him, which might be translated 'Foolhardy' or 'Reckless'. Like his moniker suggests, Johnny's believed to have been involved in some of the wildest, most outlandish schemes the Cartel ever dreamed up. International corporate influence-peddling at high levels and vast amounts of money laundering; hypnosis and manipulations of key commanders during critical military operations; drugs and psychically-enhanced honey-traps for major politicians and bureaucrats; disappearances of important government officials or their family members; unexplained onsets of mental illness by key figures in the world's justice systems or legislatures, and so on—as well as some other almost incomprehensible escapades that were well past the fringes of sanity. Johnny's also a major recruiter of younger goondas and goondis from the streets, and among Bollywood's desperate hopefuls. Meri bhath suno, Johnny's a dangerous man. Unpredictable too, they say."

I noted the purple-tinged border around the photograph.

Johnny *Reckless* huh? A paranormal with a penchant for recklessness? Of course, that's just how he'd be. Dangerous. . . . Unpredictable. . . .

Something told me this was our guy.

I flashed Laila a look.

"Laila, you know it already. There's something about him. We've got to find him."

She stared at me, incredulously.

Harshad furrowed his brow.

I took in a deep breath. "Look, he's the one we want and you both know it. You should know how this goes. You're both familiar with intuitive *leaps*, aren't you?"

I studied them. They should understand, they were Nomads. But it appeared they didn't quite trust me, yet, not entirely. Not after the affair in the Bollywood Planet.

The pair of them considered my argument.

I waited.

Finally, Laila spoke. "Very well, Elanna, let's see where your flash of intuition will lead us, shall we?"

She bit her lip, again, as she studied Johnny's portrait. "The nice thing about Johnny is he's an extrovert. He's out on the town almost every evening looking for fresh talent. So he shouldn't be particularly difficult to find." She frowned. "Hmmm, but where to start?"

She snatched up the laptop and began to dig into what we knew about Johnny; the data, the stats, the sightings and hangouts, the lists of all establishments he frequented. After a time, her tap-tap-tapping came to an end. And Laila looked up, smiling.

"Here," she said. "This is where he'll be tonight."

A high-resolution photograph of a five-star luxury resort in the Juhru Beach area appeared on the widescreen. "The Extemporaneous Glorious Gate Hotel" was massive–and pink. Seven stories high and twenty suites in diameter, spread across many acres. The doorways arched to a point, evoking a Persian feeling that was enhanced by the gold-painted pillars that stood before the building. Laila clicked on the screen to provide a bird's eye view of the hotel, situated beside a deep lake that weaved in and out among the trees and the golf course. She clicked again. Inside, the rooms spoke of simple luxury. Two bedroom suites with full accommodations and modern kitchen; dark wood furniture with red throw rugs over beige carpeting; king sized beds with gold and red ornate bedspreads; prints of water-bearers or gods and goddesses hanging on the walls; Buddhas and decorative vases on plinths and shelves. But the shot that interested Laila most was of the dining room: opulent, creamy pink walls, round roomy booths, large windows taking in the distant, city-lit harbor.

"It's called the Dhonni Maach, the Rich Fish. A gourmet Bengali restaurant, highly regarded among the Bollywood elite and high-roller hopefuls for it's rasmali."

Laila glanced over at me.

"What do you think, Elanna?"

She'd gone with her gut, and I approved.

I gave her a simple nod.

At that moment, out of the corner of my eye, I caught a glimpse of Harshad. I noticed him staring at Laila, wearing a deep frown before he felt my attention on him and turned away. He'd tried to hide it, but it was too late. In that brief instant, I'd seen his look of doubt and trepidation, and felt his despair. Yes, he was as anxious as anyone to go after the bad guys, but that meant Laila, his wife, might come under fire. Be exposed to powerful, unpredictable enemies and dangerous situations, and possibly forced to endure Lord-knows-what kinds of subtle energies and influences.

I turned back to study Laila. But I didn't need to pick up on her vibe to see she was pumped. Her face was flush with adrenalin. No, there'd be no talking her out of it now.

She's a Nomad, too, Harshad, I thought; she chose this life of unpredictable danger, the same as you and I.

I bit my lip, as I looked down at the floor.

Damn.

You see?

That's why I've always hated working with partners.

7:30 PM.

Harshad had gone into his bedroom to spend time in deep meditation, while Laila and I got dressed for the evening. I was focusing on disguising myself. I did my hair up in a French braid and stood in front of the mirror. I applied a little rouge to my cheekbones and chose a rose colored lipstick. I tilted my head and smiled, ready to play the soft and naive American tourist. As I stepped out into the living room, I was surprised to see a man in a black silk suit with sunglasses, a tall, brawny man with a bald head and thick neck.

"My goodness, Harshad," I said, "that is an apropos persona."

"Thank you," said a deep, raspy voice.

Laila popped into the room a moment later wearing a simple mid-thigh black dress. Her hair appeared to have been cut into a short bob. Her body moved lithely and subtly under the dress, like a would-be starlet out to crash a party. Her eyes flashed daringly. Her reserve and demure mannerisms were nowhere to be seen. In fact, she hardly seemed like Laila, anymore.

"What's so different about you?" I asked.

"It's the wig," she said.

"No, it's more than the wig. It's your demeanor . . . or something."

Laila smiled as she studied me, head to toe. "You'll need a much better disguise than that. I have just the thing." She pivoted like a supermodel and disappeared into their bedroom. She sashayed back carrying another wig. A brown one this time. "Try this on. Remember, the people looking for you will know exactly who you are and precisely what you look like."

I peered into my bedroom mirror, while Laila helped me adjust and style the shoulder length hairpiece, using some hairspray to set it in place. Then, she turned me round, and employed a black eye-liner to draw a mole just below the corner of my mouth.

"There," she said, "that ought to do nicely. "

I turned back to the mirror, and drew in a sharp breath. Laila was right; someone else was looking back at me.

"That's not me. Those aren't my eyes."

Laila smiled indulgently. "You're right. It's not the wig."

"Then what?"

"A-hem. . . ." The sound came from behind me.

I turned around to see Harshad, leaning against the side of the bedroom door, and wearing a wide grin.

"It's me. I'm cloaking you."

"Cloaking me? Who am I supposed to be, Harshad?"

"Who are you supposed to be? Interesting question. That often depends on who is looking at you."

I turned again to study my reflection in the mirror. I inhaled deeply. After closing my eyes, I carefully grounded myself and removed the wig; then I opened my eyes and looked back up in the mirror again.

There I was.

Now, there's a useful trick, I thought, as I glanced down at the wig. I'd never encountered such a powerful cloaker before.

Harshad smiled, widely. "Indeed, Elanna, there are only a few of us who have the ability to cloak. In public, people never see me or Laila in the same way twice, unless I wish it. And, as you've also seen, I manifest an even rarer ability to mask a person's vibrations sufficiently to deceive even other, gifted people."

"At least the two of you seem to have a grip on what you can do, Harshad. You two seem, well, almost normal in comparison to me."

Laila caught my gaze in the mirror. "We are what we are, Elanna. You've been given more to handle than most. And, so far, it seems you've been able to handle it."

"Yeah, that's what they keep telling me."

I sighed, as I put the wig back on. Then, I turned once more to examine myself in the mirror.

Another stranger's face was looking out at me. But this one was different. The glint in her eyes was dark. Foreboding.

I winced . . . at the sight of her.

Laila flashed a knowing smile.

"You see? With a little help from Harshad, you won't look a thing like Elanna Forsythe George."

A wild thought occurred to me:

But what if that is me, the real me?

I shook it off, as I spun round to face Laila.

"Come on, Laila, what are we waiting for?"

Johnny's Reckless

9:00 P.M. LATER THAT EVENING.

Relief from the heat at last.

The Dhonni Maach was chic.

The three of us sat at a table overlooking the lake outside *The Extemporaneous Glorious Gate Hotel* in Mumbai. We perused the menu in the busy restaurant. I sat across from Laila and Harshad trying to look relaxed while appearing engaged in inane conversation. I had to admit Laila and Harshad were better at keeping up appearances than I was.

We ordered some wine and appetizers.

The place was filled with the rich and elite. Harshad pointed out some of the famous and not so famous Bollywood stars, as well as some well-known business people from Mumbai. I recognized a few people from the Bollywood Festival in New York. There was the handsome and very charismatic Davinder Bains, one of the top-top leading hero/romantic leads in Mumbai. Sonny Pradhna, an up-and-coming archetypal villain character actor that all the top Bollywood directors were vying for. Rambir Mankesh, a leading financier, was having dinner with Noor Chand, a woman who was famous for playing evil, overbearing mother roles. I recognized another man sitting a few tables away. He'd had a minor role in Meri Dil Ka Tara as Vinod Kumar's very businesslike manager.

Harshad answered my curiosity. "His name is Shami Jahan. He plays many small supporting roles. It seems he's always there, present in every movie, lurking somewhere in the background. He'll likely never get any larger parts, but he gets paid well enough and is left alone by the media, mostly, so he doesn't have to cope with much of the undesired attention."

"Like some Hollywood types," I replied.

The strong silent ones that ground a scene. As Shami Jahan ordered his dinner, he appeared much the same as his character in Sharma's last movie. Stoic. Staid. Not much fuss. The people he was with seemed to be very much like him. Harshad told me they were partners in a business venture. Jahan had major shares in JTL International, a heavyweight biotechnology company based in Mumbai.

The musical quartet on stage was about to begin their second set when I sensed a presence behind me. I resisted a strong urge to turn and look. Finally, on the edges of my peripheral vision, I spotted the hostess leading two men to a table on the other side of the restaurant.

"There's Johnny Akkarah, " Harshad whispered. "I don't know who the other man is."

Just then, Laila got up. "You'll have to excuse me, I've got to go to the rest room."

As I watched her walk across the room, Harshad launched into a silly story about a time when he was in Hyderabad and saw someone who looked exactly like his mumi, his mother's older brother's wife. "I hadn't seen her in so many years, and I got so excited that I wasn't listening to what my intuition was telling me. I wasn't thinking because, I mean, who else could it have been? So I ran up and put my arms around her shoulder."

Harshad laughed.

"Oh my God, you should have seen the commotion. The woman's voice was not like my mumi's, for one thing. She screeched on and on about how she was going to call the police because I had tried to rob her of her idjit. I mean, she flatters herself, the woman was over sixty. I tried to calm her down and explain the situation, but she was causing such a scene that I finally had to dash around a corner and hide behind a dumpster. Of course, when the police came they couldn't find the strong and tall man the woman had described, only a thin, elderly vagabond sleeping on the ground."

He chuckled a little more at his recollection.

I smiled as I lifted up my glass and took a sip of wine. I gazed around absently. I noticed Laila standing beside Johnny's table, leaning right in next to him.

Like a fly on a wall.

Good job, Laila, I thought. I wondered what juicy bits of information she'd be able to dig up.

Suddenly Harshad burst in on my thoughts. His voice was loud and brash. "Now, Bahana, please stop beating around the bush. Tell us, what exactly did you do to our friend Rakesh?"

"What?"

I nearly spat out my wine.

I glared at him.

He leaned in closer to me over the table and whispered abruptly. "Sorry. I don't mean to pry into your personal business, but I had to capture your attention."

My 'attention'? Why? To remove it from Laila? Well then, he'd succeeded. I hadn't allowed myself to think about Ricky even for a moment since I'd left New York . . . well, okay . . except for maybe a moment or two.

I let out a ragged breath. I was shaking.

Then, I realized something. I hadn't told Harshad or Laila a thing about Ricky. In fact, I hadn't mentioned Ricky to them at all.

Before I could find time to frame a question, Harshad answered it. "Don't you realize that Laila has been close friends with Rakesh's sister ever since childhood? When you vanished for all those weeks,

Laila spent a goodly amount of time on the phone consoling her friend. Her bhaji was in pretty bad shape you know."

"I know." I said, "And that's why I had to end it."

Harshad didn't blink.

I bit my lip. "He's not like you, Harshad. You don't lose it every time your wife goes out of your sight."

"No, but it's something we work on continually and still argue about sometimes. Over time I've had to . . . adjust, let's just say, but the truth be known, if it were up to me, she'd be staying home more often."

I grimaced. "It doesn't sound easy."

"What doesn't sound easy?"

Laila's voice behind me.

What?

When'd she get back?

Harshad turned round to face her, seeming unperturbed, as if appearing out of thin air was a normal thing to do. "Ah, well . . . you see, I was just talking to our friend here about what it's like being . . . in our business."

Laila rolled her eyes. "Oh, that."

Harshad smiled. He seemed tired as he reached out for her hand. "Tell us then, what you've been up to, oh brave woman warrior?"

She smiled back at him and shook her head. "Oh, nothing piyara. Let's just go. It's suddenly gotten very boring in here."

Inside their vehicle, Laila was more talkative. . . .

"The younger man with Johnny appeared to be an Associate of some sort, someone who's trying to work their way up in the cartel. But I didn't catch his name. While I was there, Johnny received a phone call from a woman named Rita, but I didn't hear much of that conversation either."

I gasped out loud, as I leaned in closer to the front seat.

"Rita? Could that be Rita Chawla?"

She wrinkled her brow. "I don't know. Even when I leaned in closer, I could only hear snatches of their conversation over the phone. But then I started to feel a psychic interference, as if someone had an inkling I was there, so I got out of there quickly before either of them had a chance to discover me."

Harshad shot me a pained look.

I winced. "I'm sorry, Laila."

"Chalo, teek ha. It's all right. It's part of our job. And yes, I suppose it could have been Rita Chawla on the phone. Rita is especially infamous for her natakas, her performances, as an interfering stage mother. Her public outbursts around her daughter Karishma's career are legendary."

"So what else did you learn?"

"They're going to 'Transcendental' tonight. That's a nightclub downtown. Very hip. It sounded like they're planning to meet some people there. 'Higher-ups', they said. So, Harshad, we'll want to be very careful, because the people they were talking about are linked to senior government officials, who are quite close and influential even within our organization."

She paused.

"And Rashbir Dulku is going to be there too," she added.

Harshad reached across, squeezed Laila's hand, and smiled yet another tired smile.

"Good work, my little mole!"

The heat of the day had finally ended. The Mumbai streets were busy, cooled down by the evening ocean air. Harshad weaved the car through traffic, gliding effortlessly in and out of tight spots. I gazed out the window. In the evening light, the temples, hotels and restaurants stood out like castles in a Gothic fairyland tale. People grouped outside well-lit venues. Young couples walked hand in hand. Young men and women hung out in groups, out on the town. The breeze coming in through the open car window was heaven, a relief from the heat for a few hours.

Harshad drove on toward Juhru beach. The great city seemed to rise out from the waters of the dark Indian Ocean as we neared the coast. We turned into the parking lot of one of the buildings.

Palm trees stood about tastefully around a brightly lit fountain,. as spotlights strategically highlit the name just before the walkway.

"Transcendental"
"Mumbai's hottest, most exclusive new nightclub"

Men and women in groups, as couples or solo, walked to and fro, around the vicinity of the building. Bees at a hive.

Inside, the joint was hoppin'.

Mumbai's well-to-do, Bollywood's hopefuls and some up-and-coming mobsters were milling about in the lobby, putting lessor pretenders to shame. All dressed to the nines. Ready to party. People shouted out loud. Some stood at the bar posing; others strutted past. Some high-fived and laughed, caught up in the throb; while others looked suitably bored. We scanned the crowds for Johnny and his Associate, or any sign of Rashbir Dhulku.

Laila bit her lip. "I suppose we should mingle."

Once inside the main dance area, we went our separate ways. Each of us swept a different direction. We were caught up by the bass-y rhythmic thump of the pounding music into the various swellings of the crowd. Blue light patterns danced over the stage while a white strobe light pulsated haphazardly at the center of the dance floor. Men and women hopped and bopped; they jumped, gyrated and spun. The flashing lights and the sounds of instruments and vocalists pounding out East-meets-West styles of fusion, and probably some drugs too, lowered everyone's inhibitions.

I found myself in the thick of it.

I danced.

Like a droplet in an ocean.

Others danced.

Around me.

With me.

Then away.

Men danced as if they'd lost their souls, offering themselves up to the women. They waved their arms and stomped their feet. Women struggled to free themselves, grasping at a life they were convinced their mothers secretly craved.

I kept my eyes open.

A few men danced with me, but then moved on. They'd tried,

but they weren't what I was looking for. Across the room, I glimpsed Laila dancing with a short and stocky man in a black silk shirt and beige pants, a potential mark. Someone touched my arm. I turned to see a huge, menacing man with a thick neck, who seemed out-of-place. The strobe-lights bathed him in his polite and well-groomed attire. He got up close to me and a shiver of fear ran right through me.

I wavered, feeling unsure of what to do. I was considering whether or not to reach for my gun when I realized with some relief that it was only Harshad in a disguise somewhat similar to the brawny persona he'd had on for most of the evening. He crooked a thick finger at me to follow him, and we weaved our way through the crowd to a corner of the lobby. He lit a cigar, and blew a big puff of smoke in the air, before he reached for his wallet and handed me a wad of bills.

"I must go. Business calls. But, anything you want, my darling, it's on me."

Then he made his way out of the lobby.

As I looked around, wondering what that was about, I noticed Johnny Akkarah. He was standing only a few feet away. Looking right at me too. I stared back at him, then realized I was still holding Harshad's large wad of bills in my hand. I tucked them away, beside the revolver, in my little purse.

When I looked back up, Johnny was standing right in front of me, not two feet away from my face.

I let out a gasp.

It *couldn't* be!

I flushed at the familiarity of his features.

The same eyes.

The same lips, except they weren't wearing a disassociative smile.

Up close, I suddenly realized why I'd been drawn so powerfully to that photo of him. Johnny Akkarah was the spitting image of Suraj Amir. The same dark eyes. White teeth. The same, graceful way Suraj carried himself. The same smooth way of gesturing. All of his features were almost exactly the same.

Was Suraj gone then?

Was this a possession?

I recalled what Suraj told me in Buffalo: he had a maternal half-brother in Hyderabad; but, the thing was, Suraj also looked so very much like his biological father Rajesh Sharma. Furthermore, Sharma told me himself that his wife, Sheila often accused him of sowing more oats than Johnny Appleseed. All the while, inside myself, I could feel my heart thundering. Johnny's presence was rather heady.

I had to remember why I was there.

For Simryn.

And, sure, maybe this guy looked just like Suraj, but without all his twitchy, annoying neuroses. *Still, no matter how sexy Johnny Akkarah appears to be, he's still the bad guy*, I reminded myself,.

Johnny let a flicker of a smile play across his lips.

"You seem far away, Miss. . . ?"

"Ah, my name is . . . Marla."

I could feel intense heat from his eyes.

"Marla? Marla who?"

"Your name first."

He smiled. Charm oozed from every pore. I could feel myself becoming a little more unsteady.

"Oh, yeah. Sorry. I'm Johnny, Johnny Sharma."

Sharma?

"Ah, hi there, Johnny. I'm Marla – uh – Smith."

"Hey, Marla, do you wanna dance?"

I found myself nodding like a damn school girl.

What was this?

Watch it, I told myself.

Johnny led me deep into the dancing, mingling crowd. When we got close to the sweetest spot in the middle of the floor where the throb-throb-throbbing of the various vibes in the room came together at their most intense point, he grabbed me round the waist and pulled me into him nearly knocking me over. As we danced, he peered deep into my eyes. I tried to catch my breath. I was surprised by his sudden embrace.

His body was hot, wild, and muscled.

My head spun. My heart raced.

What? Why? How?

A sly and sexy smile lifted the corners of his lips. His eyes sparked with glee before he loosened his hold. He stepped away but his gaze still penetrated me. The boom-boom-boom of the music caught him up and we danced, arms capturing the air, legs stepping high, hips gyrating in all directions. The beats tossed us around like rag-dolls; wild and out of control. My heart throbbed seeming ready to leap out of me. Johnny moved in close, his body coming up almost flush against mine. His scent was sweet and warm. I don't know what to tell you. I never felt quite like that before. I longed for him to throw his arms around me and pull me in all the way. I could feel my own limbs getting heavy with . . . with . . . with. . .

With what?

With . . . desire?

Yes, desire.

The plain truth was, I wanted Johnny.

About 2 AM, Johnny led me off the dance floor and out into the lobby. "What are your plans for the rest of the evening, Marla?"

I leaned against him holding onto both his hands. I lifted my gaze up to hold his. He seemed amazingly beautiful.

"I don't have any plans," I confessed. "I could go home. But maybe I don't want to . . . just yet."

He thrilled me with his ingenious smile once again. "Sure, doll."

Yeah, I was thrilled when he called me that, but then I cringed, recalling that Gary Dhami had used that exact same term.

"I've got an idea," Johnny said. "Just give me a little while to take care of some business, then we'll find somewhere else to go."

We walked through the lobby and around the corner of the dance club. A large, brutish goonda guarded the door, but as soon as he saw Johnny he stepped aside and let us through. The heavy door thunked close behind us. We stood together for a moment before we could see a light peeping through an ornate, paisley curtain hanging down to the floor at the dark end of the hallway. I tuned into the sound of voices, murmurings and occasional shouts.

I was about to ask him where we were going when Johnny put his hand on my arm. "Just follow my lead." When we got up to the curtain,

Johnny pulled it back and walked in, tall like a gunslinger entering a saloon. I followed. We entered a modest but illicit gambling den: only one roulette wheel, and a few spotty blackjack and poker tables

As soon as we walked in, another man looked up at me from a table, and caught my eye. It was Johnny's Associate, the younger man I'd seen with Johnny at the Dhonni Maach. I felt his gaze rising and falling, up and down, all over my body.

Then, he raised his glass to me and winked.

I could feel the color rising up in my face.

As I got closer, I noticed that the Associate looked very much like Johnny.

So, he too, reminded me very much of Suraj.

I looked away.

Johnny brought me over to a blackjack table close by. As I sat there counting my chips, I scrutinized both Johnny and his 'Associate'. I sighed. I was, as one might say, caught between a rock and a hard place. There was Johnny but also his Associate. Now I could gaze into Johnny's daring eyes, and also flirt with his Associate in only a slightly 'disinterested' manner. It was turning out to be a very sweet situation.

The dealer drew my attention to the game. I placed a bet and then looked back over at Johnny.

He smiled.

"Do I know how to show a woman a good time, or what?"

I smiled back at him. "You get my vote."

He met my eyes.

I looked away.

He coughed. "Look, doll, I'll be back – I promise – but first, I have to take care of some business."

With that, he walked away from our table.

I frowned peevishly, and stared at my chips.

When I looked back up, I noticed that Johnny's Associate was gazing at me, thoughtfully, from his own table across the room. I sighed, and immediately returned my attention to the game.

The dealer meted out two cards to each player. On my right, a man with a mustache was smoking a cigar. His concentration was beginning to waver. The woman on my left was fidgeting nervously;

she fingered her chips agitatedly with one hand, while lifting up the corner of her cards with the other.

'Nine of Clubs'
The hole card sits next to it.
The fidgety woman's cards read:
'Three of Diamonds'
'Ten of Clubs'
Thirteen.
I had:
'Two of Hearts'
'Nine of Clubs'
Eleven.
The man with the cigar next to me had:
'Ten of Diamonds'
'Ten of Clubs'
Twenty.
The woman on my left taps on the table.
"Hit me"
'Seven of Hearts'
Twenty.
"Hold"
Now it's my turn.
I tap.
'Ten of Diamonds'
Twenty-one.
The man on my right raises an eyebrow.
He taps.
'Nine of Clubs'
The dealer draws for him.
'Five of Clubs'
Fourteen.
Another card:
'Nine of Clubs'
"Dammit."

I looked up. The Associate's gaze had caught my attention.

I smiled.

Just a little.

Johnny didn't return that night. I was getting angrier, but I still waited and watched for him. I'd played about twenty games, varying my bets. I won some, lost some, then I hit a winning streak. By the end of the night I was up close to RS225,500. The dealer was getting nervous, so I tipped him and gathered in my winnings. I was still looking around for Johnny when I heard a silky smooth South Asian male voice just behind my right shoulder.

His breath caressed my hair as a shiver goes up my spine.

"Hey, I couldn't help but notice what a great blackjack player you are. Be careful, or people will think you're a cheat."

I batted my eyes at him. Once.

"Why would they think that?"

His eyes narrowed.

I leveled him with a scathing look.

"Look, I don't know who you are but I don't take to being called a cheat. So expose my ruse, or walk away. I'm not here to lose, you know."

A humor-filled glint touched his eyes. "Now Miss, don't be upset." He gestured to the stool next to him. "Sit down. Let me buy you a drink."

I gazed at him with disdain. "Fine. Vermouth."

He hailed the bartender and ordered drinks.

"What's your name?" he asked, pulling out a cigarette.

"Why is it that men here don't introduce themselves first, before they ask a woman for her name?"

He smirked. "Quaint American tradition, that. . . ." He lit his cigarette and sucked at it until it caught fire.

"It's called 'having manners'."

He scowled.

"Vah, I've never seen a woman with such a sharp tongue before."

"You seem to bring it out in me."

He glanced up sharply.

I lifted my glass to my lips. "To us."

He stared at me. His eyes were brooding, calculating and cool, and I was trying to be so cold, so cruel, but inside, something deep in my soul kept rebelling, "No, no, no, no, don't. This man is delicious."

My heart was beating faster.

The Associate smiled his sardonic smile.

"Oh, and by the way, Miss, in case you're wondering, Johnny-bhai won't be back tonight. It's just like him to a leave beautiful gori woman stranded somewhere, abandoned there all by herself."

He finished his drink, and walked away.

At that point, there was no other choice but to get up and leave. The euphoria of flirting with two beautiful men was wearing off. What was this? I wondered. I'm acting like a goofy teenager who'd just discovered boys. The big goonda at the door checked me out, eyeing me up and down as I made my way back into the main area.

Immediately, I saw a man rushing towards me. My heart leapt! Was it Johnny? Coming back for me? No. It was only Harshad in disguise. Then suddenly, I snapped back to myself, 'Oh, my goodness, what am I doing?'

Harshad rushed over and grabbed me by the arm.

"Bhan ji, where have you been? I've been looking for you everywhere. Come on now, it's long past time to go home."

He dragged me along roughly until I nearly stumbled and almost fell over. Then I wrenched myself away from him, spun around, and stared with my eyes full of anger and amazement. He grabbed both my arms, pulled me in violently, and held me tight against his chest.

"Harshad," I whispered brusquely in his ear, "what the hell are you doing? I'm not supposed to be your daughter."

"*Suno*, Elanna, something or someone has been able to penetrate my illusions. We've got to get out of here now!"

He turned and dragged me roughly through the after-hours crowds, while waving his arms dramatically and shouting pedantically at me as we went along. At the car, Laila was ready in the driver's seat with the engine running. She launched us into traffic as soon as we jumped inside.

Laila locked the front door of their apartment, then she headed out into the kitchen, "Would either of you like a glass of ice-water?"

"Yes, thank you Laila." Harshad replied, removing his shoes. Then he stretched out on the sofa, laid his head back and rubbed his eyes. Very shortly, Laila reappeared with two glasses of water. Harshad sat up only long enough to drink his down in one gulp. It was obvious that he'd been deeply shaken. He was trying to appear stoic, but I knew he'd been vulnerable. On the drive home, Laila had asked me where I'd been and I'd told them about the 'secret' gambling room. The rest of the ride had been quiet. Harshad was keeping silent, and I knew enough not to press.

After he'd been lying on the sofa, very still, for five long moments, Harshad sat back up again. He was looking more lucid now, and soon, he began to tell us his story.

"After I slipped you the money Elanna, I was milling around mostly outside the building, and keeping most of my focus on the cloaks and maintaining the three of us in disguise. I didn't dare venture very deeply inside the place; and, when I did go in, I tried to stay close to the lobby where it was quieter and I could concentrate better. I spent quite a lot of time hanging around outside the lounge, sipping on a drink and making small talk as necessary. Then, at about 1 am, I began to sense that someone or something was trying to penetrate my thoughts, and I started finding it difficult to concentrate. Keeping that force, or whatever it was, out of my head was a great distraction. Around two o'clock, I spotted Rashbir Dulku standing not too far off from me in the lobby. He didn't seem to quite know exactly where I was, but I could feel his presence there; he was trying to penetrate my thoughts and locate you. I attempted to maintain my center and keep him away from me, with some success. But the most disturbing thing was, I had no sense of where Laila was, or you either, Elanna, so I decided I'd have to risk going out on the dance floor and find the pair of you. Then, when I finally spotted Laila, I insisted immediately that we locate you and get the hell out of there. It was getting too difficult for me to maintain our disguises, with Dulkhu pressing in, and so many other people and distractions milling about."

Harshad let out a heavy sigh and ran his fingers through his hair.

I noticed, now, that his hulking, thick-necked persona was disappearing, and he was beginning to look a lot more like, simply, himself . . . if such a thing was possible. "I'm sorry," he said, "we had to retreat, Elanna. We decided the only thing we could do was wait for you outside, even though we had no idea when, or if, you'd be coming out."

A shiver ran up my spine. "I don't understand. I thought your cloakings were impervious to other's abilities."

"I know. I mean, I don't know, but perhaps, Dulku was able to adapt?"

Damn. That only confirmed my assertions about working as a paramystical. You never know what, if, or when something will go wrong.

So what should we do now?

Harshad answered my thought. "I'm sure the problem is only temporary. I'll just need a bit of time to recover. Then we can make a new plan."

Yes, take a little time, I thought. I could certainly understand that. I can't count the times my own powers have been shorted out after exposure to an enemy vibe, or after I'd fallen into some strange, alternate realm. When I'm working, it seems like I spend most of my time in recovery. Then, as I studied Harshad more carefully, I noticed he still had that strange look in his eyes. Something else must have happened. There was something he hadn't told us yet.

"Yes, more did happen, Elanna. I didn't want to mention it until we were safely at home. It was very bad. When I was trying to look for you and my senses couldn't locate you, it was as if I'd gone completely blind."

Laila spoke up. "This affair has certainly turned treacherous enough for us all now," she said.

I met her gaze. She wasn't smiling. She looked scared.

"We'll have to slow down. We need more precautions, better planning and less rash moves."

What?

What did she say?

Slow down?

Not a chance.

With Simryn's rapist-killers still out there somewhere?

I could still hear Simryn screaming.

They've cut or torn off all her clothes now. She's naked. Arms pinned down by her sides with two men holding them. Another ugly face leers at her and hovers above her. It sneers. Full of glee. A knee inserts itself between her knees. She fights, as they try to force her legs apart, but they're too strong. She's about to scream again. Then, her survival instinct kicks in and she thinks better of it.

No! She's about to faint. Her heart's pounding much too hard. She'll just go limp. She'll just let them do whatever they want to do with her.

Now, I hear another voice screaming:

"NO-O-O-O-O-O-O!"

What?
Whose voice was that?
Was it mine?
Yes.
Dammit.
It must have been.

All I could hope for, now, was that Harshad and Laila hadn't heard me.

I took control. I refocused on my breathing until I found myself back on the couch. I pushed away the horrific flashback and re-centered myself. Now, my only chance was that I hadn't screamed out loud this time, and totally ruined my chances of staying on this investigation.

No way, I told myself, there's no way I'm letting anyone take me off *this* case, under *any* circumstances.

But, in that moment, Laila was preoccupied with Harshad. And clearly, he wasn't in any shape for reading my mind. Now, there she was, sitting right next to him, on the couch, rubbing his neck and arms tenderly, and looking very concerned.

"Did you hear what I said, Elanna? We need to use a lot more caution. We must reconsider, reassess this entire situation carefully and reflect on all its dangers. We can't afford to be so reckless any longer."

Clearly, the haunted look in Harshad's eyes a moment ago had affected Laila deeply.

I turned away from her, and looked over at Harshad. I caught his eye. "Harshad, you said something else happened too. Now tell me what it was."

He met my gaze. "Yes, Elanna, there's more to tell. Something else was there with Dulku. I don't know what it was. There was something with him, yet at the same time, so much larger than him. An incredibly strong, almost incomprehensible psycho-spiritual force. Its vibrations were terrifying. I just stood there, barely able to move, or think, or even blink in its presence. Then, something flashed in my mind. I saw an Asura with three goat heads hovering above us on the dance-floor. All the heads were swinging wildly about the room spitting fire and blood and venom. Soon, hot blood was dripping down all the walls, and the venom was seeping into every person near Dulku, so I knew I had to get us out of there. I'd never seen nor felt a dark presence quite so vividly before."

Laila gave me a cautioning glance.

I leaned back in my chair.

Hmmm, what was this? A new entity had appeared on the case. Was it the Bhujangen? A similar being? I didn't know. Then something else occurred to me. Why on Earth would anyone put something like that inside an already-powerful paranormal? It was a chilling thought. How could any one person ever hold on to so much psychomystical energy in one place, at the same time?

Wouldn't they just . . . entirely dissolve?

Sanjay's gone out. About an hour ago, he simply got up out of bed, showered, and left. He didn't say a word to Christine. I have no idea where he went or when he's coming back. Christine senses my agitation and laughs, telling me she has it all under control. What? Under control? Who? Christine? The girl whose entire life is dedicated to chasing her addictions to powerful people, money, thrills and sex?

Believe me, I wasn't reassured.

She just yawns like a satiated kitten, and falls asleep, waiting for his return.

Back inside Harshad and Laila's apartment, the three of us spent a week planning and preparing for the next move. To ease the pressure on Harshad, we decided we'd have to enhance our physical disguises and work on developing the characters we would assume during our next attempt. Harshad would spend his time in meditation to repair his aura, strengthen his resolve, and seek out a stronger spiritual cohesion. Meanwhile, Laila and I would meet with local Nomad officials to ensure a backup squad was in place around whatever establishment we would frequent. They'd be ready to nab Rashbir Dulku before he could ever get inside.

Sanjay comes back a few hours later, and wakes Christine up with a kiss. She pulls him into the bed and they make love again. Afterwards, she gets up, wraps a bed sheet around her slender body and heads for the shower. I moan at the pressure of the steaming water against my skin, trying to imagine all Christine's sins are being washed away.

"Stop it 'Lana, you're such a drama-queen," I hear her say.

I sigh to myself. It's hard to find any peace.

After her shower, Christine comes back into the bedroom wrapped in a towel. The maid had been through to make up the bed. A new black evening dress is laid on top of the fresh, indigo bedspread. Sanjay is standing across the room looking out the window with his hands behind his back.

"I took the liberty of shopping for a few things you might need. I hope you don't mind."

"Thank you, Sanjay," she says.

"I'll leave you to get dressed." He begins to walk away, but then he stops and turns back to us. "Oh, and you'll be joining me for dinner tonight with a friend."

She looks at him. She knows it's not a request. But doesn't protest.

He turns and walks out the door.

"Huh?" she thinks. She wouldn't take that from any other guy.

She couldn't abide a man who tried to treat her like his 'Bitch' any more than one who catered to her every whim. But, this time, it's different somehow. Sanjay's gotten under her skin. He's wild, dangerous, and spooky in sharp, handsome packaging.

"What do you think, 'Lana?" Christine asks, as he shuts the bedroom door behind him. "What kinds of plans do you have in mind for our dearest Sanjay?"

What? What could she possibly be talking about?

I was in shock.

She's never asked me about a thing before.

She sighs and runs her fingers through our hair. "It doesn't matter. Whatever fix I get us into, in the end, you'll have to get us out. I'm only here for a good time, you know, not a long time."

She pulls the new black panties up over her slim legs and slips the skimpy black dress over her head. She walks to the full-length mirror to admire her profile; she turns left, and then right.

"Exquisite, isn't it? Look darlin', I love adventure, but I have no delusions about who's really in charge here. Just let me know what you want me to do, 'Lana honey."

She turns to look over her shoulder at herself in the mirror.

I notice she has a really nice ass.

On the third day, the three of us began to incorporate a set of ancient breathing exercises, 'I' statements and visualizations. We envisioned mystical shields around us and spoke complete ownership over all our thoughts and our vibes. Mornings began with rigorous yoga followed by hours spent in silent contemplation. Each afternoon we practiced taking on a different persona, examining and adopting the inner structures of people we knew or public figures. We'd embody each new personality as fully as we could in intentions, mannerism and voice. By the fifth day, I was beginning to understand the abilities and perspectives of a chameleon. From there, I ventured out to create a new person. Traits, smiles, idiosyncrasies, likes and dislikes, a history to support her existence. I believed I'd acquired the ability to create shifts in my bearing and personality on command. By the evening of the sixth day, I'd developed a daring and powerful new persona with undeniable magnetism. I stood there in front of the mirror and watched her emerge. Soon, I'd be able to sustain her for hours.

I was ready.

Christine's turned out splendidly in the black dress when Sanjay comes back. I disappear into a corner of Christine's mind as he lifts her hand to his mouth. He raises his eyes to meet hers, and I draw back even further, just in case his gaze penetrates too far.

Christine smiles, and closes the distance between us.

They exit the bungalow and walk out through the garden. Sanjay opens the passenger door to the black Volvo coupe. Christine slips in. He shuts the door behind her and walks over carefully to the driver's side. He starts the car without a word and backs out onto the street. We ride in silence for a time. The air conditioning feels crisp and cool on Christine's skin.

Finally, Sanjay speaks. "You haven't told me very much about yourself, Christine."

She turns, peering at him over the edge of her dark-mirrored sunglasses, but says nothing.

He grunts. "We're quite the pair of chatterboxes, aren't we? I wonder what we're both keeping quiet about?"

Her reflection on the windshield smirks as the car continues through the city.

"I like it quiet, honey. What's so important that people need to talk all the time?"

"Not much, I guess."

He glances up in the rear view mirror before changing lanes.

"Precisely," she says as she pulls out a cigarette.

He produces a gold-plated lighter, flicks it open and presents the flame. Christine puffs the cigarette to life. The first blast of nicotine runs through her body, soothing our nerves.

The rest of the ride was alive with quietude. Christine takes in a breath. The air conditioning feels good on her skin. She's spent a great deal of her life driving in air-conditioned cars, being the daughter of a Don and the wife of two husbands in 'the Business'. Both were dead now. Dominick was found floating under a bridge;

Lance's body was discovered in the trunk of an abandoned car where no-one would ever have found him at all, except he got to stinking pretty bad in the hot afternoon sun. Neither of them knew the value of keeping their mouths shut. Christine was alive because she did.

She gazes out the window as they drive past countless South Asian people suffering in the afternoon sun. She's always known the greatest truth in life.

There were people with.

There were people without.

Simple.

Christine always made sure she was one of the people in the cool, air-conditioned cars.

She pulls out another cigarette and puts it in her mouth. Automatically, Sanjay reaches out once again with the lighter.

"Would you like me to drop you off where you live to pick up anything?" he asks.

She shakes her head. "I travel light, Sanjay."

He smirks. "I guess a woman who moves around so much from one man to another doesn't need much baggage."

She turns and blows her smoke right into his face.

He blinks. And coughs a little.

She sighs and rolls her eyes.

"Now, why'd you have to go and ruin a perfectly good time, Sanjay?"

FRIDAY, 7:30 P.M.

Once again, Laila had ascertained Johnny's destinations for the evening. To enhance our disguises, Laila and I decided we'd both dye our hair. I chose black. I'd selected a shimmering red, close fitting, sleeveless mid-calf dress with matching red shoes. I looked at myself in the full-length mirror. My eyes went down over the curve of my breasts, to my waist, over my hips and down towards my shapely calves. I smiled with satisfaction and went off to the bathroom to put on my make up. Black eyeliner brought my eyes forward. Black mascara lengthens my unassuming eyelashes. Matching red lipstick embellish my lips. I pouted seductively. My cheeks adopted a deep blush I did not feel. I turned around and took a last glance in the mirror, before going back into the living room to wait for Laila and Harshad.

'Yeah,' a voice called out from deep inside of me. 'There's gonna be some trouble tonight. And I'm gonna be the one with the biggest tiger's tail in my hand.'

Harshad walked out of the bedroom in a new guise. This time, a small mustache with platinum wire glasses. He wore a camel brown suit with a dark shirt and a gray tie.

"You look like a computer programmer today. Quite Nerdy-Chic," said Laila, appearing right beside me.

Harshad smiled. "I'll be the nervous guy standing out front who's too shy to go in. Do you approve, Elanna?"

I was caught between a compliment and a giggle.

"Sublime will do." Harshad quipped.

I tilted my gaze to one side. My eyes wandered from Harshad's nerdy head down his chic-suited body and back up, stopping at the slight bulge in his pants.

The voice inside me purred.

At the next red light, Sanjay pulls out a gun, points it at us and indicates the door.

Christine glares at him. "You're not serious."

"Sorry, doll. But we both know there's more going on here between us than meets the eye, don't we? Don't try to deny it, I can feel it, even if I can't quite figure it out. There's something about you, something inside, that's so katharnak, so dangerous."

The black Volvo coupe drives away, leaving Christine and I stranded on the hot, sweltering street.

"You're on your own kid," she says to me.

Then, she's gone.

Damn bitch.

Back in Laila's guest room, I grabbed a shawl and had one long last look in the mirror. Out of nowhere, Laila appeared next to me. We stared at each other, then back in the mirror, each assessing the other in her seductive finery. She laughed, breaking the fatally-awkward silence. I studied her carefully. Her hair was cinnamon streaked. She wore a deep cyan dress with spaghetti straps. She'd scooped the hair up and pinned it with a barrette on one side letting it fall off to the other side of her head. She looked wonderfully sensuous.

"I think you'll be pretty difficult competition for me tonight, Laila," I said. "I'll have a hard time keeping their attention with you around."

Laila winked. "Sometimes competition is good."

"Hah," I replied. "Is that how it's going to be?"

"Hmmm, kiya gal ha? Aren't you up to it?"

She smiles coyly.

I smack my ruby-red lips. "Bring it on, sister."

The voice inside me laughed.

After Christine left, I wandered the streets of Mumbai for many hours, not knowing who I was. I could still feel all Christine's compulsions and afflictions echo inside me as I tried to fight off the urge to join a line of women in a red-light district waiting for an opportunity to earn money for their families. My memory is spotty. But I remember men strolling past our lineup, eying the women up and down. One man nods towards an attractive woman whose male relation leads them into an alley. A few of the women look after them. Some are annoyed at not being chosen. Others, younger ones, looking relieved. Some of them hadn't even reached womanhood yet, only children.

Then I heard a rattling sound.

I turned around.

A decrepit invalid rolls past me on a flat cart pushing himself along with his hands. Another disheveled man, with wild gray hair, limps along behind him, trying his best to keep up. He turns a crazy-eyed face around to look at me. His madness leaps out at me; I feel like I never want to breathe again.

My head reels, and I shake it wildly. Vigorously. I moan loudly.

The man stares at me. His eyes widen. His mouth falls open. He scurries away. Limping as fast as he can.

I stare after him, wondering what to do.

A woman's voice calls out at me from somewhere: "NO, there's too many. There's nothing you can do for them, it will only drive you crazy."

I wondered who that was? Then, a name popped into my head. "Laila." Yeah, I thought, I think I do remember a 'Laila.' But what good did it do? It wasn't enough. Like half, or so, of an equation. Incomplete.

I focused intently, standing there, in the midst of all the other women in the line-up.

I fell into a meditation.

I samyana'd on the name:

Laila.

Laila, Laila, Laila, Laila, Laila.

I pondered it. Like a koan.

Then, I sang it:

> *"Laila Majnu do badan eck jahn thay."* (Laila and Majnu, two
> souls as one.)

"No, no, let me think, not Majnu."
'Laila
and
. . . Harshad!'

Who?

I looked up and down the lineup. I really didn't know. All I had was a couple of names. But that was enough. It was a clue. I left the lineup of women and started down the street. I walked and walked around Mumbai for many more hours, passing through many districts, waiting for my mind to clear, trying to piece together all the bits of information I needed.

Like 'Who Was I?'

Finally, a faint glimmer of an idea occurred to me: Christine used to call me Lana . . . Lana. . . .

'Lana'?

I rolled the name around in my mind:

Lana, Lana, Lana, Lana, Lana.

Lana.

Lana?

Lana Who?
Lana from Havana?
Lana Banana?
Lana Eats Manna?
What?
No, I do not.
You don't?
No-o-o-o-o!
Are you sure?
Yes.
But . . . isn't that your name?

> *"Lana Lana bo Bana*
> *Banana fanna fo Fana*
> *Fe fi mo Manna, LA-A-A-N-A"*

NO-O-O-O-O.
No, Daddy, that's not right.
(I stomp my foot.)
My name is E-E-E-E-Elanna!
By four A.M., it had become clear to me. I knew who I was. I was Elanna Forsythe George.

It was some hours later, well past dawn, and a little before 9:00 A.M. by the time Laila buzzed me into her building. When she opened the door to their suite, her eyes grew big as saucers.

"I know," I said. "I saw my reflection in the glass windows of your lobby."

She looked down into my right hand. "Where'd you get that?"

I looked down, too, at the Browning GP135-B revolver I was clenching there.

"Ah, I don't exactly remember."

That was true. I didn't know where I got it. But I was pretty damn sure it'd helped me out in some difficult situations.

'Ya Devi Sarvabhuteshu, Branti Rupena Samsthita'

[Translation: Hail Goddess, who reigns over us in the form of confusion.]

It took Laila a while to coax the revolver out of my hand.

After she'd finally locked the weapon up in a drawer, she led me by the hand into an unfamiliar living room, then scurried back out into the kitchen. There was a sound like water pouring. I looked around at where I was. Where was I? Was I back? Was I back from somewhere else? My eyes fell on an ominous statue of the fearsome goddess, Kaali Ma sitting next to the stereo. Its eyes flashed! I took in a sharp breath. – Were those eyes blaming me? Who gave them the right to judge?

Was it my imagination?

I shook my head.

That's when I heard a key twisting in a lock. I leapt to my feet and spun.

"Laila!"

A man standing in the doorway had stopped and was staring at me. My heart was racing. My jaw clenched. I watched him wild-eyed and got prepared to rip him apart. But he just stood there, staring at me with what I believed to be revulsion, and his mouth hanging open.

Then I felt a softer touch on my arm.

Laila, with a jug of water and a glass.

My mouth was as dry as dirt. I'd never wanted water so badly.

The man, who by now had entered the room, was standing close by. It suddenly dawned on me: he must be named 'Harshad.' However, I couldn't recall ever knowing anyone named 'Harshad.'

Harshad?

What did he look like?

Suddenly, I caught a whiff of myself.

"You know," I said to the strange man, "I'm pretty scummy. So, I think you might wanna put something down on that sofa before I sit on it."

I watched as he quickly brought a clean sheet out from a closet and spread it out over the sofa. After I sat down, Laila poured me a glass of water. Then another. And another. And another.

I drank and drank and drank and drank.

Then I collapsed.

At some point, they must have woken me up, and I managed a hot shower and a few bites of food. After that, by what must have been mid-afternoon, I found my way back into their guest room, fell down onto the bed there and slipped into a dark, dreamless sleep.

I don't know how long I was sleeping, perhaps for a few days, or maybe it was a few weeks. I awoke only for such brief periods as it takes to use the washroom, or get a bite to eat.

And I wouldn't say a word . . . not to anyone.

Then, one morning at breakfast, I told some of my story to Laila and Harshad. I recollected the tales of Christine and her songs, of Bara Banta, and of Sanjay the goonda, the high oceanside bungalow, and the streets. But, trust me, I didn't go into details. Nausea kept quelling up inside me at the thought of ever sharing such subject matter.

Yes, it's true.

I had some things to sort out.

The question that wouldn't leave my mind was why Sanjay'd blown Christine off like that. Did he just get sick of her? Had he sensed my presence and known something was wrong? Or . . . maybe it was the nagh?

Another morning, at a later date, Laila was pouring me a second cup of tea.

I let out a huge sigh.

A voice came to me, unexpectedly, from across the table.

"Would you like to talk about it now, Elanna?"

He was staring.

I bit my lip.

I pondered for a moment, then sighed again.

I shook my head.

Harshad's face was always changing and unreadable but, at that moment, I could see, he was . . . perturbed. He'd been patient with me for long enough.

He started talking, on and on.

". . . so, you see, Elanna, after you dashed so madly away on that Friday night, we had no clue what happened to you, nor any concept of where you could have gone. The Mumbai operation searched every-where. In fact, the spectral-specialist division even brought in a consult-ant with an ability to contact people in many places in, ah, 'the beyond,' so to speak, in case you'd. . . ."

"Harshad, take it easy!" Laila barked at him.

He pursed his lips. "Oh, of course . . . I'm sorry."

I waved his apology away. "No. It's fine, Harshad. It's our job and we can't afford not to talk about it. I'm ready."

"No, no. Laila is correct. We should wait a while longer. I just wanted you to know that we did do all we could to find you after that night. I don't know what happened. Just as you were getting into char-acter and about ready to go out, it seemed that something changed in you. I was just bringing the car round the front of the building for you and Laila when you suddenly shot off and ran away. We tried to chase you, but you were very fast. The strange part of it was, I couldn't pick up on any of your vibrations at all. Neither could any other operative here in Mumbai, nor even the special para-psychic 'trackers' we brought over from America; we exhausted all avenues."

I lowered my eyes. "Sorry."

Laila touched my arm. "It's not your fault."

I nodded at her reassurance.

"The experts in our organization believed you may have absorbed some of Harshad's ability to cloak, and that might have been an entirely intuitive response on your part. You may have been protecting yourself on a completely subconscious level against the deadly, psychomystically-enhanced assassin who was on your trail."

I shook my head. "How long ago was that?"

"Oh, about six months," Laila said.

I let my fork drop with a clatter and covered my face.

"S-six months? I had no idea. . . ."

Harshad's tone softened. "Easy. You didn't do any of this willfully. We know your gifts are difficult, so powerful and unpredictable. It doesn't matter. We're just glad to have you back with us."

I smiled at him. "Yes. I'm quite a survivor, aren't I? I just seem to have a knack for it."

Laila frowned.

Then, she mumbled, ". . . well, that's more than we can say for Rashbir Dulku,"

"What?"

My jaw dropped open.

Harshad eyed Laila carefully for a moment. She gave him a sidelong glance.

He considered, then breathed out heavily and sighed.

"Dulku's . . . gone," he said.

Laila pursed her lips.

I stared.

"Gone? What do you mean by 'gone'?"

Harshad's face was full of reluctance; he was unsure how much I could handle.

I frowned. "Just give it to me straight, Harshad."

He bit his lip.

"Four days after you disappeared, Elanna, two of our Mumbai operatives discovered a body in an alley – or perhaps, I should say, a mound of ashes that somehow still clung together, in the vague shape of a body. In any case, it was very strange. We thought, at first, it might be you, so we commissioned some tests. Eventually, they found some small traces of DNA, which turned out to be, not yours, but Dulku's."

What?

My head reeled. I slumped back in my chair. That night after the wild scene at Transcendental, Harshad related his harrowing tale of Dulku and the frightening entity that emanated through him and controlled the dance floor, wrecking havoc from an energetic realm. Dulku was already a powerful paranormal, and the energies of the Bhujangen, or whatever they'd put in him, must have proven too much. I felt a chill pass through me. My hands gripped at the sides of my chair. Damn. They'd used Dulku like a suicide bomber. He was just another throwaway minion; another chamcha; another useful, psychospiritually endowed, netherworldly *sap!*

I eventually managed to calm myself down.

But it took more than a few long, focused breaths.

When I looked back up, Laila was staring at me. "What can you tell us about this 'Christine' entity, Elanna? Do you think that she might still return someday? Perhaps to look for Sanjay?"

I contemplated. "No, Laila, probably not. Christine was a very strong personality, very calculating and cold, but her role was to get me a look inside the Bollywood machine, and she's already succeeded at that. The only thing is, I almost wish that she'd have stayed a little longer, so I could have learned more."

Harshad eyed me carefully. "You said she was the child of a Russian mafioso. And those people are like that, calculating and cold. They have to learn to live by their wits. So you could be wrong, don't underestimate her cunning. But, in this case, I somehow doubt she'll be coming back. Something tells me, you're probably right."

"Yes. Probably."

I shuddered, remembering the long hours of enduring Christine's cold, sexual abandonment.

"What's our next move, Elanna?" Harshad asked.

"I don't know, Harshad. Right now, I only want to sleep."

I found my way into the bathroom to bathe and then shower. It really didn't matter how many times I washed myself, I could still never cleanse my body, mind and spirit from Christine's vices. An hour later I toweled myself dry and walked back to my bedroom. After I'd donned the nightie Laila had left out for me, I lay wide awake. I was utterly exhausted, but unable to find sleep. Finally, I got up, unrolled my yoga mat, and performed a few simple asanas, breathing deeply. But echoes of the past few weeks pushed through my mind, despite my efforts, and soon, my body was shaking from the shame. I tried to put it all out of mind but, finally, I broke. I yanked a pillow off the bed to muffle the sobs and sat on the floor, crying and rocking myself, trying to find comfort, somehow.

I hated my abilities!

I hated being a prisoner in someone else's body.

I didn't choose this.

I hated how it always happened like that.

Out of nowhere. Without warning. With no permission.

Then, there I was, again, watching, feeling, and being with Christine, as she gave and took sexual pleasure with Sanjay. I was feeling like a little girl in a closet, peeking out through a crack in the door. I had to remind myself that I was no longer experiencing those things, that I was out of there. My body ached from the mixed feelings of terror and the hunger for masochistic pleasure, yet there was nothing for this, but to just let it go. Let it go. Like everything else before this.

Eventually, I fell asleep on the floor, still hugging the crumpled, now wet pillow.

It was 3 A.M. when I woke up. My eyes were nearly swollen shut, and my head pounded. I got up and went into the kitchen and got a glass of water and went back into my bedroom. In the middle of the room I set out some candles and a stick of incense. I sat down on a pillow to meditate, breathing in slowly, holding the breath, then letting it out calmly. I kept breathing and focused intently on the candles in front of me. Despite my aches, I closed my eyes and entered into a deep state of relaxation and timelessness.

I inhaled gently

– held the breath

– and let it out slowly.

After a time, my heartbeat slowed to a deep calm. My mind became still and clear as a starry night. I opened my eyes, just slightly, to meditate on the flickering flames of the candles.

Deep contemplation.

Detachment.

Timelessness.

Bliss.

I was on a vast and empty plane. This time, familiar constellations appeared in the starry sky. Each twinkling star was calling my name. It felt . . . familiar somehow, unlike the times when I'd faced Anil Negendra as the Cobra entity in Buffalo, or when the Bhujangen had possessed Officer Rudy. No, this was something entirely different. Although it was extremely quiet, I felt as if I could hear all of life flowing through in its busy-ness. Almost in song. A holy hymn. Rejoicing, praiseful voices.

And then, something else. . . .

CHING . . . CHING . . . CHING!

A sound like . . . ghungaroos on a dancer's feet.

I waited.

The sound got closer.

"I AM THAT I AM," a disembodied voice says.

I was fully alert, now. From whence that voice came, outside or inside of myself, I couldn't tell you. My eyes darted around the room. A chill went up my spine.

"DANCE WITH ME, CHILD!"

I jumped up off the floor.

"Ah, sure, all right."

A warm wind was blowing mysteriously throughout the room, whistling and gathering the mist together. The mist was whirling and swirling, as if wanting to take a form. Finally, a figure began to emerge. Legs, an ample body, a head. As the misty image became solid, I started to see a womanly shape. Her skin begins to get dark. Then darker.

Darker than dark.

Darker than soot.

She stood there, unmoving, with her back to me. A red full-moonlike fiery halo begins to appear behind her in the room. As my eyes adjusted to the new brightness, I began to see her more clearly. Then, I realized the woman's skirt was made up entirely of dismembered human arms.

I jumped back.

"WHAT'S THE MATTER, CHILD?" the voice asks. **"DON'T YOU KNOW WHO I AM?"**

She turns to face me. She spreads her arms. All eight of them.

My insides exploded with sublime terror.

In two of her four left hands, she was holding a sword and a three pronged trishula. In her top right hand she had the freshly-culled head of the demon Raktabija. The demon's blood drip-drip-drips into a skull-cap held in a lower right arm. She smiles and takes three steps towards me, causing the horrifying garland of infant skulls around her neck to jangle and stir.

TUD-ITY TUD TUD! TUD-ITY TUD TUD! TUD-ITY TUD TUD!

She stops right in front of me, and punctuates the event by pounding the ground, hard, with her *trishula*.

THUK!

I thought I was going to be sick. I stepped backward as far as I possibly could, until my back was up against a wall. Then, I realized that wasn't a good place to be, so I started inching towards the door, while still keeping my eyes fixed on the hideous apparition.

I turned the nob. The door wouldn't budge.

Damn.

The ghostly female-figure watches me. Her head tilts to one side; her black-black lips smile widely. The whites of her eyes flash with madness. Then she opens her mouth as if to speak and red blood pours out over her dark lips onto her black-black chin. It drips thickly onto the infant skulls around her neck, and from there, dribbles down on the ground.

Nice, I thought, a little fearfully.

She BOOMED.

"I AM VIRGIN, MOTHER AND CRONE.

"I AM CREATOR AND DESTROYER OF ALL."

I swallowed.

The Dark Mother, the Mother of Time, *Maha Kaali*, was standing right in front of me. She was staring right at me. The whites of her eyes were frightful.

I shuddered.

She leans in close, smiling with blood-soaked glee. . . .

"ANYONE WHO DANCES WITH ME WILL HAVE NOTHING IN THE WORLD TO FEAR, FOR I AM THE MOTHER OF TIME AND I AM MORE TERRIBLE THAN ANYTHING OF THE FLESH.

"AREN'T YOU AFRAID?"

Kaali Ma's eyes become slits, as she steps forward and opens her mouth.

A hot flame shoots out.

That awoke me from my state of frozen terror. I jumped back and slapped myself all over to put out the fire. The smell of singed hair and clothing filled my nostrils. Kaali Ma smiled.

"DANCE WITH ME, MY CHILD.

She lunged forward and swung her sword. The blade nicked my arm.

Quickly, I covered up the wound with my hand. "*OW*, Mother. Watch what you're doing with that thing, *damn it*!"

She swung again, but by now, my adrenaline had kicked in and I dodged easily. Her blade whistled by.

"HA! SO YOU ARE READY THEN."

Her arms spread out again. She stands there, staring at me, looking like a ginormous spider. Eight feet tall. She steps forward and swings again.

Alerted now, I ducked. She swung again. Then again. Again and again. She tracked me around the room, swinging her sword while waving the severed head of the demon in front of my face to taunt me.

"SURRENDER, CHITI DEVI. SURRENDER YOUR MIND, BODY, SOUL. SURRENDER ALL YOUR ATTACHMENTS, ALL YOUR LONGINGS."

With every breath I'd dodge yet another blow. I pivoted, jumped and dove out of the way, but sometimes I wasn't fast enough and she'd cut me. It went on and on. Hours. Days. Months. Maybe years. Every time her sword cut me too deep, I'd be sure I was done. This was it. I couldn't fight anymore, I was too wounded But then, something inside would rally and I'd dodge yet another blow. There were many times that I was down on the floor, spent and bleeding, just wishing for it to be over, *now*.

But then, I'd hear that dark, terrible voice again:

"GET UP, GET UP AND DANCE!"

I'd have no choice but to drag myself up and the attacks would begin anew. Centuries and millenniums passed as I jumped, rolled and ran, desperately dodged the ruthless, endless blows. Then finally, some-where on that dark, ethereal plane, I felt the last of my resistance ebb away. There was no fight left in me. I stopped and stared into the Dark Mother's face, and then . . . it happened. We danced. The room dissolved. The dance itself was formless. Inexpressible. We danced for a long, long time. Or, maybe it was just a few minutes. I don't know.

When we had finally stopped dancing, the Dark Mother moved in close to me, and smiled her blood-drippy smile. The sound of her voice was softer now, almost compassionate.

"I AM THAT I AM, LITTLE ONE. I AM CREATOR AND DESTROYER. I AM MORE TERRIBLE THAN ANYTHING IN ALL THE UNIVERSES, AND YOU HAVE DANCED WITH ME."

"No problem, anytime," I said.

The Great Mother grinned. She turned away from me with her skull necklace *thud-thud thunking* as she went. Then, she stopped. She looked back over her shoulder at me and spun around.

"AND YET, YOU WILL NEVER SOLVE THIS MYSTERY."

What?

It took me a moment.

Then I remembered.

"Simryn . . . !"

I swallowed.

"What, *no*? What are you saying, Matha ji? I have to, I promised."

"NO CHILD, YOU WILL NOT SUCCEED. THE JOURNEY IS NOT FOR YOU."

Kaali Ma blinked. Events from the past, future and other places flashed before my eyes. Backward-forward. Forward-in-back. Sideways-in-time.

I'm in the middle a huge lotus flower, floating above a clear, blue lake. The Mother of Time stands next to me, enjoying the wonderment of the day. The sun is shining and a mild breeze is blowing through luscious green grasses, caressing the leaves of an ancient bodhi tree that is thriving not far from the shore of the lake, as Maha Kaali turns to face me.

"I AM THAT I AM, LITTLE ONE. I AM VIRGIN AND CRONE. I AM CREATOR AND DESTROYER. ON EACH PETAL OF THE LOTUS IS A PATH TO A POSSIBLE REALITY. CHOOSE A PETAL, NOW, SO YOU MAY SEE."

Countless lotus petals are swirling about our feet. I stepped forward onto the nearest one. Everything in all the universes immediately began to revolve, and I was going in a circle.

I'm whirling and swirling, sighing, flying, stumbling and falling; leaping and spinning; dissipated and dissolving.

Each time I stepped out onto a new petal, I would travel through time, space and free will to a new destination. But the journeys always came to a dead end, and I was never able to solve Simryn's murder. Then Maha Kaali would blink, and I'd find myself back in the center of the lotus flower. Still, I wouldn't give up, I'd refuse to quit.

I'd try another petal.

And another.

And another.

But I could never find a solution. Many times, I'd end up back in New York with all my energy, and my resources exhausted. At the end of one journey, I was utterly numbed, and so severely depressed at having failed to solve the mystery that I stayed inside my apartment for years and never took on another case. On some possible paths of existence, I ended up psychotic and hallucinatory, unable to find my way back from other realms. On many threads, I was killed. Sometimes, my body parts were found in garbage disposals, at the bottom of cliffs, in the trunks of abandoned cars or spread about in various locations. Petal after petal brought new scenarios, but never an answer. The last petal I tried sent a chill through me. I was psychically-enslaved by the cartel, and had been placed in a trance, with all my energies and aware-ness channeled through a group of *Bhujangen*-possessed individuals, and the entire Nomad network was being destroyed.

I cried out.

"NO, Ma!

"I can't let it happen this way.

"There has to be a path.

"I've got to find Simryn's killers."

Kaali Ma just stood there. Solemn and serene, she shook her head.

"NO, LITTLE ONE, YOU SHALL NOT SUCCEED."

Her voice echoed continuously throughout all the universes. The whites of her impenetrable eyes stared out pitilessly at me from inside her dark face. She raised her sword high in the air above me. I just stood there, resigned to the inevitable. There was nothing more I could do for Simryn; everything I could ever do had already been done. Flashes of light blazed over and over, as Maha Kaali swung her sword, and I screamed in shock and horror while the Mother of Time cut off my arms, my legs, and, finally, my head.

Then, everything went white.

I found myself back in Laila and Harshad's guest room, sitting in lotus position on the floor in front of a spent, sandalwood incense stick, and many, many, cold candles. I took in a deep breath and opened my mouth. Praises began to fall, without my willing it, like little jewels from my lips.

"Oh, thank you. Thank you, Mother of Infinite Compassion.

"Jai. Jai. Matha ji. . . ."

The words of the prayers came to me in English, Sanskrit, and many other languages and ancient tongues. I opened my eyes and everything was the way it had been before. I stood up slowly, I stretched my limbs. My body was on fire. I glanced around the room. My eyes stopped at the peacock quilt on the bed. The embroidered peacocks seemed to dance with their sequined eyes reflecting the vivid colors of the rainbow. I closed my eyes and shook my head. When I opened them again, the peacocks had stopped dancing, but their eyes still seemed alive.

I was feeling exhausted, thirsty and (understandably) somewhat whacked out. I stumbled out to the kitchen, took a cold jug of water from the fridge, and poured a tall one. I was doing my best to exercise control, but I drank it down in one gulp, quickly. I poured another and took it back to the guest room. I gulped that one down, too. Sweat was pouring from my entire body. I toweled myself dry, got into the bed, and hid beneath the now-still eyes of the silent peacocks.

At some point, I finally fell asleep.

Strange images. One by one. Unfamiliar. Situations playing out fast. It was my life. It wasn't my life. I couldn't tell you. I jarred awake. It was 4:30 A.M. Fear like a blanket was dropping over my entire life.

It took a long, long time to calm me back to sleep.

Rakhi: The Thread of Brother-Sister Bonding

When I woke up the next morning, the dorango outside my window was singing a new song.

> *Toorrr-a-looor-a-loorrrrr*
> *bak-bak-bak-baaaaaas*
> *Cheetee-lit-it Cheetee-lit!*

I opened my eyes and stretched out in bed.

Somehow, I felt . . . different.

> *Moo-la-moooo! Moo-la-moooo!*
> *Chala-gee, chala-gee. . . hrrrrr-hrrrr!*
> *Ht-ht-ht Ht-ht-ht Ht-ht-ht*

At peace.

> *K-k-k-k-k-kaw K-k-k-k-k-kaw li!*
> *Aaaah-gee Aaaah-gee Bch-bch-bchaou!*
> *MiYA-mit Mia Mit-mit-mit*

The green walls of the guest room enveloped me. For the first time since I'd been in Mumbai, I felt at home. It was strange. The morning fragrances didn't seem foreign or poignant to my senses. As if I'd always known the sound, smell and taste of Mumbai. I turned to watch the sunrays falling through the four-paned window making the familiar bright elongated boxes on the floor. Dust particles danced merrily in the rays of sun, reminding me of Ricky's bedroom. I smiled. Perhaps, when this was over, I'd see what could be done about me and Mr. Chandra. I grinned at the prospect. Then I gave myself a gentle admonishment: *Now don't go thinking too far ahead; you've got far too many problems here to solve.* I kicked the quilt off me and grabbed a shawl up from a chair next to the bed. Feeling thirsty after my fretful night's sleep, I headed down toward the kitchen for another drink of water.

Outside in the hallway, I heard familiar rousing voices. I smiled. It was Ram, Gurdev, Mark and Fatima, still embroiled in debate and engaged deeply in their fervent discussions. So it must be Thursday, I thought as I sat down quietly on the stairs and listened in, while their voices drifted out animatedly from inside the kitchen nook.

"Yes, yes, that's obvious. My parents would think I was a heretic and, naturally, they'd be upset. I've eaten pork in the past, however, just so I could get over the notion that I'd be damned by Allah for it. But I will say that pork is terrible for one's health and that's likely why we're told it should not be eaten. Beef is much better. However, we're prohibited from eating that here. It seems cows, bulls and buffalo have more rights on the streets of India than human beings."

"Edicts, schmedicts! Eat whatever you want to eat, I say."

"Even if my religion allowed beef eating, I wouldn't do that. I can't bring myself to eat any kind of flesh."

"What about the flesh of a carbooja?"

"Cantaloupes, yarrh? Don't be silly."

"Sorry, yaarh."

"What's the point of having strict dietary restrictions for any other reason than one's health? I don't want to be perceived as someone who is 'only trying to make a statement.' I want a deeper understanding of my faith and to get past outward definitions. I want to know what is at the core of my faith. What is at the core is the common goal of all spiritual practice? To love God and your neighbor. Common decency, my friends, and common sense!"

"Do your parents know of your conversion from Catholicism to Syrian Christianity?"

"No. All they know is that I have an 'unreasonable answer' for every misconception they have about everyone and everything else. It makes them furious. But then, I have an answer for most misconceptions other people have about everything else, too. Hell, I have many misconceptions myself. People should be in it as deep as they like, but being 'spiritual' doesn't mean one can be ignorant or judgmental of other faiths. That totally defeats the purpose."

"Well said."

"Of course, I know most of you are on board, but that statement would do nothing but convince the world we are nothing but a roomful of heretics."

"Yes, Jesus was labeled as 'heretic' when he was alive, and he would definitely be labeled one again if he were here now. He'd be standoffish, outspoken, unruly, and hang out with 'the wrong crowd'—just like the first time. I don't see that the second coming will be any better. He will try to pull down the boundaries between people and many will push them right back up again. No matter how much he demonstrates, over and over, that we must stop being so rule-bound and truly live life, people always seem to prefer to run back to their white-washed tombs."

"Ahhh. See how removing common sense from spiritual life has created such monsters? Fundamentalism brainwashes people into performing such atrocious things in the name of God."

"Then people will demonize everyone associated with those

'fundamentalists.' Just look at what happened in America, look what happened when the Twin Towers went down, and now everyone is suspicious of anyone who is Muslim. And the people who demonize Muslims are usually fundamentalists themselves."

"Bas karo, yaarh, it's so depressing."

"Nine Eleven, what an ominous date. Nobody will forget that. The media coverage. . . ."

"Yeah, it's a good thing they decided to do it in September and not in July."

"Why is that?"

"Are you kidding? Americans would be hitting the panic button every time someone said they were going to the 7-eleven."

"Those are run mostly by Muslims, aren't they?"

"Okay, yaarh, that was just plain stupid."

"Sorry."

"Yes. I'm sorry, yaarh."

I couldn't help but laugh.

"Uh oh, I think the American is up."

I shook my head. It was always interesting to hear what people say when they think they're alone. I remember how Beeji said she was going to pack up and move back to India because Americans didn't know that Bombay had changed its name to Mumbai. "It has been since 1997!" she lamented. After a while, she calmed down. "What to do? I love living here in New York."

The conversation in the next room continued without me.

"As an immigrant in India, I find I have loyalties to both my maternal and adoptive country. As much as I don't want to live in Afghanistan, it hurts when people say things about Afghanis here."

"There is probably no one in this room who is an original Indian, except maybe Ram here."

"Yes, that's a definite 'maybe.' And so what if it is true? Do you think they'll give us the recognition. Not a chance."

Hmmm, interesting. I, myself, of course, had never taken much interest in my background. I had an aunt who was obsessed with her connection to the Duchess of whatever-whose-it in England. The duchess had a sister, Elizabeth Harrington, who moved to Boston in 1836 with her husband, Martin Taylor, who was a Banker. Aunt Lilith and my mother, are the fourth cousins with Elizabeth's granddaughter-in-law, Chelsea Taylor. I never bothered to understand this, but Aunt Lilith was interested in little else. She didn't realize she had her own life to live and make history with. She couldn't see past it. Then, there was the story about a painting of the duchess. After Chelsea Taylor died a childless widow, and left everything to charity, there was an estate auction. Lilith had made quite a show of out-bidding another buyer. She spent a little more on the painting than was reasonable, and her husband told her so. But, in the end, they threw in the coat of arms, too, and she was thrilled.

I thought that was just plain weird.

Just then, Laila came out of the kitchen with a cup of tea for me "Good morning Ela. . . ."

"Good morning, Bhan ji," I said.

I stopped at the sound and put my hand to my throat.

That wasn't my voice.

Laila froze in mid-motion. Her eyes widened. The cup she was carrying hit the floor with a splattering crash. She covered her mouth with her hands. She gaped at me and pointed to my arm. I lifted it up and looked. It was a lovely, light caramel brown.

I got up and ran down the stairs to the full length mirror in the foyer. I stopped just a few feet away. My heart was thumping; I closed my eyes. The fear crept into the pit of my stomach.

I wasn't ready for this.

I told myself to get a grip. Whatever it was, I'd deal with it. I looked down at the ground before I took the last couple of steps to stand in front of the mirror. Then, I opened my eyes. I gazed at the light caramel, brown-skinned feet reflected in the mirror, followed the shapely calves to slim thighs that disappeared under my nightgown. My eyes went straight up to my face, and, suddenly, I lurched back a step.

It wasn't me!

I swallowed. There she stood. Exquisite and beautiful. A South

Asian woman with long silk-black hair that fell down past her hips. Gora gora rang; soft caramel skin. Long, slim neck and sharp, classic features. Her almond-shaped, dark oval eyes peered back at me. She bit her lip, as she looked me over, too.

She was very young.

Eighteen, perhaps.

It was my body breathing, my heart beating, but it was no longer under my control, just as in so many cases before. I watched as the young beauty fell to the floor in shock. I couldn't believe it. She was shaking and crying uncontrollably.

And me? I was very tired. I didn't think I could take another shift like this, just then.

With all the compassion and sensitivity I could muster, I told the girl to get a grip on herself. But it only made things worse. She started crying even louder. Then, when I looked up from the floor and back into the mirror, I saw Ram, Gurdev Kaur, Fatima and Mark come rushing out of the kitchen, with Laila standing right behind me, staring at me, dumbstruck.

"Elanna. . .?"

I wiped my eyes. I opened my mouth to speak, but the voice answered for me, "Nahee, mera nam Rakhi Chand hai."

What?

NO.

It was ME.

Elanna!

From across the room, I could hear Ram's voice, fallen to a whisper. "Rahki, that's such a beautiful name." His eyes were growing softer and wider as he gaped at her.

I turned around from the mirror and glared at Ram. His gaze was alight with awe. His face shone. I glanced over at Mark, but he was equally dumbstruck. Then I saw Harshad come strolling out of the kitchen, but even he stopped dead in his tracks and stared, his face becoming as flush as the other two.

NO. It was ME. Elanna!

I protested, but could feel myself being pulled back further and further inside this new being.

"Bhagvan Raksha karae," whispered Laila. "Rakhi Chand, please tell me. Is Elanna also inside there with you?"

Rakhi nodded and sniffled. "Hanji, and I'm afraid of her."

Laila looked puzzled. "Why are you afraid, Rakhi Chand?"

"Because," she answered, "I don't know what she might say next."

"Oh," Laila said, "you mean because she's a little outspoken?"

"Yes!" howled Rakhi Chand. "I'm afraid she won't know when to keep quiet, Bhanji. I don't want to get in trouble with my elders!"

Things were becoming clearer. My dance with Kaali Ma had not taken me away from fear. No, instead the Mother of Time had thrown me even more deeply into what I feared most: obsequiousness and dependence. To be powerless; to not be in control; to be unable to speak up for myself. Would I be forced to be subservient to others? At that moment, I could do little about it, even though I was doing my best to keep present and mindful, there was nothing I could do but wait. I soothed and calmed myself and tried to tune into Rakhi Chand's consciousness that was whirling all around me. Her thoughts were very wild. She was very emotional and high strung. Her vibes were ricocheting and rebounding all over the room.

It was too much.

"Would you please calm down?" I shouted at her. "We're not going to get anywhere by. . . ."

Rakhi Chand covered her ears and cried even louder.

I bit my lip and shut my mouth. This wasn't going to get us anywhere. I decided to concentrate on some full and gentle breathing. It turned out to be the right thing to do. After Rakhi Chand calmed down a bit, Laila asked her if she wanted a cool drink. She nodded. Soon, she had a nice cold glass of water. She gulped it down, quickly, and Laila poured her another one.

Myself, I was wishing for something a little stronger at that point.

I contemplated the situation. I guessed, for now, I'd just have to wait. Patiently. And, Lord knows how well I don't do patient. I found myself wishing I could hit someone. Rakhi Chand threw the glass of water against the wall. Well, it made me feel better, but Rakhi began to cry all over again. "I'm sorry. I'm sorry, Bhan ji. I couldn't help myself. She's angry . . . I want my Bibi ji!"

"Where is your mother, Rakhi Chand?" Laila asked her.

The wailing stopped a moment, as her thoughts cleared up.

Then she began to cry again. "I don't know, I don't know! Who is my Bhapu ji? Who is my Bibi ji? I don't know. I don't know the place where I came from, even though I can see it, feel it. . . ."

The clouds rolled in. I took cover. The storm rocked Rakhi's mind and body. There was nothing I could do but wait for it to be over.

It took a few hours longer until Laila, Gurdev and Fatima could calm Rakhi down, at all. They also needed to try to communicate with me, so I had to keep my cool and be sensitive to Rakhi's fragile state. Her emotions were like the sea during a storm. As much as I wanted out of this, I didn't dare lose my temper and kick it up again. (And hence, I learned another level of patience.)

We discovered that Rakhi could remember sights, sounds, times, events and descriptions of 'a place' with people whose names she remembered. She could remember stories of what happened in her childhood, but could not name her mother and father. The school she attended was a private Catholic School.

"My father believed in the best education for me, whoever he was. All I know is that he worked a lot and was away so much. My Bibi ji was always home, always taking care of me." Her kaleidoscope of childhood memories poured out like a soliloquy from a Bollywood B-movie.

Then, all at once, it occurred to me.

I remembered the words Rajesh had spoken back at the Bollywood Planet. . . .

I couldn't believe it.

How could this possibly be?

"Ecka vyakti. Do jivan. Ecka bahera ka baccha."

My eyes got wide, and I spat, "THAT BASTARD!" . . . Sharma'd knocked me up!

There was silence in the living room, as all the women stared at Rakhi.

"It wasn't me," Rakhi pleaded. "It was the American woman. I would never swear like that."

Brahman: The Abyss

It came as no surprise that Rakhi Chand loved Bollywood movies, especially the ones made by Rajesh Sharma. One day, when she and Harshad got to talking about movies, she jumped up and asked him to put on some raga-hop. I could feel her feet pounding the ground in tight rhythms that got louder, then softer. My arms came up in front of my face. They opened and closed like a gate as Rakhi snapped her fingers, and clapped her hands, then she began to perform the dance of our lives.

She was a genius!

I could see by the look in Harshad's face that he was amazed and impressed. Laila stood clapping in time and sang along with the music coming from the CD player. Rakhi's body spun as her hands wove intricate movements and patterns everywhere. Her feet kept up complicated, precise rhythms. Eventually, I shut my eyes because I was getting dizzy. Then it was over. At a dead stop. Harshad and Laila were whistling and clapping very loudly.

"Vah, arreh vah." Harshad said. "Maza agiyya ha, Rakhi. You are so gifted. Where was it you said you studied?"

Rakhi pouted. "I told you before, I don't remember. . . ."

Then she began to cry again.

I didn't know how to convey anything to Harshad and Laila from inside Rakhi's body. It seemed the only time Rakhi would speak my words was if they were inappropriate. Like a child would.

"Dammit."

Rakhi apologized, profusely.

It took a couple of weeks before Rakhi could hone in on what I was saying. Communication between us and with Harshad and Laila was becoming easier. Rakhi and I struck a deal: I'd stop being so blunt and not say things that would make her look bad; while she, in turn, had to try to think clearly and not have so many emotional break-downs. It was a relief that her English was perfect. She spoke Hindi quite well too, and knew a lot about history and culture. But she had no idea where she'd learned any of it and didn't like to be pressed about her past. She'd just get upset and start to cry again.

After a time, Harshad and Laila stopped asking those questions. It was a good thing, too, because my nerves were getting so jangled by her outbursts. Sure, I'd cried in my life, but enduring that kind of un-bridled emotion on a constant basis? It was harrowing. Rakhi would start to cry at the slightest provocation. She was constantly annoyed by one thing or another, and she would get temperamental over the tiniest of things. She'd be aggravated by any small noise, by every peep that anyone made, and she always wanted everything just 'so'. But worst of all was when she cried over her sappy movies—of all things.

At times, I couldn't take it anymore. I'd begin to yell and scream at the top of my lungs for someone to get me out of there. Of course, those outbursts always made Rakhi uncomfortable and embarrassed but, what the hell, at least I felt better.

Excuse the pun, but why should I be bottled up?

One day, I decided it was time she got over it. I started to say everything I wanted to say, and even more, just to let her know how I felt. I'd belt out my favorite rock songs and play air guitar just to annoy her. I practiced my karate and got into my most difficult yoga poses, then shouted out complex chemical equations at the top of my voice. I took over with all my might, convinced soon she'd be at my mercy.

But, no, she retaliated.

She'd listen to her insipid Bollywood hits and mind-numbing bhangra tikka tak hip-hop fusion music turned up as loud as possible. She'd stand me in front of the mirror and wiggle her hips in a provocative and uncomfortable way, just to taunt me, while simultaneously exposing her midriff and cleavage in one of those skimpy blouses that I hated seeing her wear.

Harshad and Laila stayed up until dawn one night trying to hammer out a workable truce. Rakhi was not to watch sappy movies. She'd have to find better quality movies to watch, with better plot lines. Harshad volunteered to select some half-decent Indian flicks for us. Rakhi, for her part, couldn't stand the more real-to-life forensic shows like CSI, so I'd have to settle for action-adventure alternatives like The Matrix. Rakhi would also cut down on too many sweets, and I'd cut out eating meat.

Sure, fine. Dal and rice would have to do. But I'd have nothing to do with eating okra.

She wouldn't drink wine either, although I sometimes desperately needed some to relax.

Sure, fine.

Another time, we were up all night arguing about which side of the bed to sleep on. I wanted to sleep on my back; she wanted to be on her stomach. We tossed and turned incessantly. We just couldn't make it work. We fought on and on like two siblings on a road trip. I'd complain if she put too much sugar in her chai, and she wouldn't ever drink Earl Grey tea without cream or sugar.

I was a prisoner and sometimes the only way I could get anything was to make a lot of noise. Harshad and Laila tried to go on with their lives around the whole melding experience, but it must have been awkward. There were arguments, temper tantrums and tears, and at times we even resorted to name-calling. It all came down to this, I wanted my body back and she just wanted me to get lost.

Can you imagine?

"I was here first," I shouted.

"Maybe you think you were here first, but this is my body." Rakhi glared as she folded her arms against her – uh – my – I mean – our chest.

By the end of the month we were exhausted. Our voices were strained from the bitter battles. But it was no use. We couldn't get away from each other. We lay on the sofa all day and all night. Laila would throw a chaador over us at night, because we wouldn't go back to our bedroom. Somehow, the living room was a more comforting place.

The nightmares were bad.

Flashbacks of memories she knew nothing about. People's faces. Situations. Feelings of being unvalued, overlooked, pushed and criticized and abandoned. Helplessness. The winds howled inside her and the darkness settled. Fear. Lots and lots of fear.

I cried out.

"Okay, Kaali Ma, I get it, I've been arrogant." I'd never grown up knowing what it was like to have my parents tell me they wished I was a boy instead of a girl. If they ever thought anything like that, they certainly didn't ever express it.

More memories came in stomach-churning waves.

Threats, spoken and unspoken. Anger withheld. Her joys and dreams dashed as only dreams of wanton women. Obedience and fear was the marking of a good woman. The terrible waves came and came. Then, one night, they finally overtook me and I succumbed. I let them take me out to sea. I couldn't fight it anymore. I needed rest.

That is how the White Devi drowned.

And me?

I was stranded in the middle of a vast abyss, too tired to pray for anything.

Rakhi wakes one morning to the smell of chai. Laila is gently stroking her sweat-covered forehead. She rolls over and her swollen eyes look up into Laila's concerned face.

"Rakhi? Elanna?" Laila asks tentatively.

Rakhi's still shaking. She sniffles. "Laila bahn-ji, Elanna patha ni kitha ha."

Laila frowns. "What do you mean you don't know where she is?"

Rakhi puts her arms down and pushes herself up to sit against the sofa. "Raath aukha nangiya si."

Last night was very difficult. . . .

For the last few weeks, Rakhi and I had battled bitterly over the presence of will in the body. That night, her life-force broke forward and overwhelmed me with the force of a tsunami. It rose up, crashing at everything inside of me. I was tossed and battered. I knew Rakhi didn't do it on purpose, it was more like an energy coming through her and adding to the already-confused mix. I cried out to her and tried to help her, but we were lost in the darkness and the waves.

I didn't know what was coming, but I knew I couldn't do anything to get out of its path.

". . . I could see her fighting and struggling. I called to her. For hours and hours, I heard her fighting. She screamed at me to make it stop. But I couldn't. It just came and took over everything. It was three o'clock in the morning when I felt her go silent."

Rakhi shakes her head at Laila. "I don't know if I feel her anymore. But I don't hear her."

"Mein takhi, aackhi, murrhi paiy han, bahanji."

Rakhi's tired of crying and cannot cry anymore.

Laila wordlessly goes to the kitchen, brings back a glass of water and holds it to Rakhi's mouth. Rakhi drinks with what strength she has left and falls back into darkness.

I don't know how long I was flung about in the dark waves, barely keeping my head above water. I called her name over and over. I did not swim anymore. I was carried by the chaos. I shut my mind to it all and thought of nothing, hoped for nothing and waited for whatever evil would come on me now. Waited and wondered if this would be the one that finished me. I almost hoped it did. In fact, I was hoping beyond hope that it would. The images came on me like angry visitations of apparitions, ancient and unforgiving. There was no real sustenance except the lightning that flashed across the sky to reveal the completeness of my destitution. No land. No ships. Just the broken remnants tossed around me. In brief, blinding flashes, I saw pieces of the life I had built. My home, my job, my friends. I was too tired to mourn them. I reasoned that I'd lived a good life, and decided I would be at peace with that, and that would be my company, as I lay here in this void.

So, I watched as the light revealed them all, and thanked God for them all. But then, it changed. A bolt lit up the stormy skies in waves and I screamed. I could no longer see the pieces of the life I'd built up. The light became merciless. Around me floated the wholeness of the things I had not achieved. The things I had not experienced. Regrets. Dreams unfulfilled. Love not acquired. The things I'd put off in life. The pictures I'd had in my head during my childhood of the family that I dreamed of. The brothers and sisters I craved. The family holidays and outings I longed to take with my parents. Then, the light revealed my mother, chiding me for not being a big girl when I really just wanted her to hold me and tell me I didn't have to go to boarding school. I was seven years old. Three years later, I greeted the news of my parent's eventual and civilized divorce with expressionless acceptance. The Cold White Devi was born.

Cold cases? No. Stone-cold dead cases. Who else but a corpse with a fierce will to live could solve them?

I was lost in the abyss for an eternity.

CUT CUT C-U-U-U-T!

A month later, when it began to look like I was never coming back, Rakhi moved out of Laila and Harshad's apartment. They asked her to stay and tried to keep her under wraps so the Nomads could maintain a close eye on her, but she refused. Her argument was simple. She was, as best anyone could tell, an adult now, so she had a right to find her own way in life. Even if she'd just manifested out of thin air only a few weeks ago, she must still have a karma, a destiny of her own.

A destiny that was hers alone.

Not mine.

Yeah. Fate had sure dealt her an interesting card.

But, yeah.

Of course.

Don't worry.

. . . She'd keep in touch.

. . . and that was the last Harshad and Laila would see or hear from her for many months.

That left the pair of them in a sticky situation. How would they explain what happened to the American Nomads? What about Ricky, Beeji, and Captain Stewart? Or my mother? Would anyone believe their bizarre story? How would the Nomads react?

They called Beeji.

On the phone, Beeji's adamant. "Just leave it to me," she says. "I will say that Elanna went for a swim in the Indian Ocean one day and didn't come back. That way, when she does emerge, we will simply say she lost her memory, or something."

But her voice is quiet, and not as animated as Laila has always known it to be. Is Beeji struggling with her doubts? Laila pauses fot a moment before giving voice to those doubts.

"But, Beeji, what if Elanna doesn't come back?"

Beeji's voice on the phone becomes more emphatic. "No, no, no! Don't cloud your mind with doubts, Laila. Elanna will be back, mark my words. Until then, we must simply pray, perform puja, and the Goddesses will hear us and strengthen her, wherever she is."

Laila hangs up the phone. She turns to Harshad, who's standing right next to her, and listening intently in on the conversation.

He gathers her up in his arms.

Her voice shudders. "It's . . . not anyone's fault, I know, but I wish I knew what to do."

He strokes her hair. "I'm sorry, Laila. After that night, I couldn't sense even a little bit of her anywhere inside Rakhi. As best I could tell, she wasn't there at all. She was gone. It was pretty much like she . . . died."

Laila gazes up at him; her beautiful, almond-shaped eyes are full of tears. "Piyara, we must do what other people do who don't have our abilities. We must keep faith."

Enough!

I'd had enough of this.

I put my hands up over my ears to keep out the silence and shut my eyes against the light. I took a deep breath and squeezed every

muscle in my body to cork up the noise inside me. I held my breath
and waited. It only made the noise rumble louder, then louder. Feet
stomped like an army on a march. The shouting became cries of women
and children cowering in fear. I held it in longer and longer until it was
time. Then, I opened my mouth and the scream came forth like a
lightning bolt. The bolt streaked across the sky and shattered the
darkness. Then, the sky splintered and fell into the water like black
glass. Behind it stood a huge sun, shining bold and hot. Everything
melted away like a bad dream and I sank to the bottom of the blue
ocean. All the debris of my life, all good and bad, was left behind.

It's gone.

I can't see anything anymore.

I can't hear anything.

I'm alone.

Now, I notice the sounds in the silence beneath it all, the vibrations
behind all life—overpowering it. Sounds of elements. Winds. Waves.
Growing vegetation. Crackling fire. Nature and animal sounds. Howling, growling, barking, mewing and chirping. They all come together at
once, around me, just like that dorango outside my window.

> *Shhhhhhhh-wah! PaashA! Fwaaarrr-SHA!*
> *Hnnnnnn. . . hnnnnnnn. . . .*
> *Ooh-AH AH AH Ooh-ooh AH AH AH*
> *RrrrAOUOO*
> *Nggggah*
> *RrrrAOUOO*
> *Ta-tik-i-tik-i-ta-ta-ta–*
> *Tik-i-ta-tik-i-ta. . .*

Then, the lights come.

What? Wait a minute. Something's wrong.

Those aren't the lights I was expecting.

Those are spotlights! Bright white and hot!

Then, I heard the music. (Oh no! . . .):

Dhoom! *Dham! Taka taka TA.* **DHOOM! DHOOM! DHOOM!**

A-tinga linga linga linga-tinga linga–tinga linga
A-tinga linga linga linga-tinga linga–tinga linga.

> I feel movement. Movement.
> I'm moving. . . . (moving. . . .)
> Spinning.
> My arms reach and flail. I'm jumping up at the Moon.
> No, wait.
> I'm flying.

"Z-O-OOOOOOOOOOOOOOOOOOO-O-O-O-M!"

Suddenly, a man's voice broke the spell. . . .

> "CUT CUT CUT! NO NO NO—"

> What?

"You there! Yes, you on the stage! Eck minute, suno. Wait just one moment, please."

I shielded my eyes from hot lights that washed everything out. Footsteps walked steadily toward me. I squinted out of the lights at a shadowy male figure emerging from the darkness outside the glaring circle of light. He stops a few feet away from me. He stared at me with a bemused look for a while before he spoke

"Look, Babe, whoever you are. You're wonderful. You dance like a devil and a devi at the same time. Your style is captivating. You have masti. Aphrodisiac. And I've never seen anyone shimmy quite like you. But Babe, listen. Listen carefully, okay? Please, please, please, darling, try to stay inside the markers we set out so we can film you. This isn't a live audition, you know. And the producers, directors and backers, the ones you really need to impress, aren't even here today . . . samajae?"

He's waving his hands around wildly and emphatically as he talks, looking like he's ready to tear his hair out.

Finally, he lets out a very deep breath, turns away, exits the circle and merges back into the darkness.

Then, everything dissolved.

Lights flash all around me, again. Red-yellow-green – GO lights!– Sparkling, jewelry-box city lights. Traffic sounds and people talking.

"Any idea what it is?"

"Nahee. Just the usual cattle call."

"Ah . . . ."

I look around and notice I'm in a line up. At the front of the line I see a sign, but someone tall is blocking my view, so I step to the side where I can see it clearly.

It reads:

Golden-Lion Productions
AUDITIONING TODAY:
Chorucs dancers

Walk ons

Minor Speaking Roles

Line Up Here

And suddenly–POP!–a camera flash goes off in front of me.

I'm blinded.

Everything goes dark.

Now, I'm squinting into lights again. . . .

This time, it's a ridiculously overlit, full Moon shining out at me over the pounding waves of an ocean. Cool air is blowing my hair around. I can hear the whirring of machinery around me. Voices muttering. But inside, I feel a serene kind of quietude. I listen for the cue; the fifth bar at the beginning of a melody. I lift my arms. They feel angelic.

My fingers form doves, peacocks, fish. I watch them dance around me. I lunge to the side–step–pad the ground in syncopated rhythms.

> *Tah tiki-ta!*
> *Ding-a*
> *Tey . . . TAH TAH*

I lift my heart up to the night sky and capture its essence. My body manifests movements, as dictated by the melodies.

The dance is basic.

Instinctual.

Natural.

Easy.

I'm flying again.

The moon smiles as he watches me dance. I thought I heard the applause of millions in the roaring surf. The stars overhead sparkle. I thought I saw a name somewhere in the nightscape.

I look up and gaze into the moon's full face.

I smile back at him.

"CUT-CUT-CU-U-U-U-T!"

My eyes almost rolled to the back of my head.

Now what?

I shielded my eyes, again, from the blaring moon, and listened to the sound of approaching footsteps.

Six.

Five.

Four.

Three.

Two.

One.

A man in horn-rimmed glasses steps forward into the moonlight. He stares at me for a long time, then he shakes his head, as if in wonder, and smiles. He turns and begins to yell. Quite loudly.

"Oh, Sakander Ji, are you awake up there? Oi! What's wrong with you? Yaar, we have to keep this shot from running over budget, aab I will not get my bonus, and my little girl Leela needs braces and my wife is breathing down my neck to buy her a vacation home in Goa. Now, please, just try to keep a spotlight on her."

With that, he stomps out of the circle of light. Back out into the darkness.

I'm swallowed up again.

By now, I'm wondering about all these dreams.

Or *was* I dreaming?

". . . CUT-CUT-CUT!"

Another stage.

More hot lights.

This time a man with long curly hair carrying a placard has barged into the circle. His movements are emphatic, impatient.

"Deera what are you doing here?" a voice says from outside of the lights.

The man with curly hair blusters. "Where is Feroz? He needs to fix this right now. Something must be done about this outrage before any more filming resumes, samajae?"

The man in the horn-rimmed glasses enters the circle of light once more.

"Okay, what now, Deera. What's the problem?"

The man holds up a huge placard with a collage of many arms and many legs in shades of red, orange, and gold.

Come see the Greatest
DANCE! DANCE! DANCE!
EXTRAVaGANZA
"BOLLYWOOD STORM"
Featuring: Khuram Dharma & Shiela Amin
and Introducing the Latest, Greatest, Newest, Dance Sensation:
Rakhi!

I'm astonished!

I blink and look closer.

Deera glares. His eyes are bulging with accusation. "Problem? What's the prob. . . .? What's the. . . ? Just look at this! Her name is not nearly big enough. Rakhi has real talent, and she's going to be much bigger than anybody else in this movie. Who's Khuram Dharma? Huh. Just a stock handsome prettyboy. And Sheila Amin? Flavor of the month, and she wouldn't be here at all if she wasn't someone's chacha-muma's patheeji-pharnji. But we all know that gristi relationships do not a film make, don't we? It's indisputable that neither of them can dance, and it's my client who's bringing all the masti to this movie. Bollywood Storm is guaranteed to be an enormous blockbuster, it will make millions, and I will not stand by and allow a client of mine to be put at disadvantage by a pack of thieves, nahee. So, go tell Feroz, I want this situation remedied immediately!"

The man in the horn rimmed glasses looks up at the moon. His eyes roll. "Look, Deera, you know as well as I do that Feroz isn't here. He's in New York all week talking with the backers, but I'm sure he'll be ecstatic to talk to you as soon as he gets back. Now, please, stop being such a khotha and get off my set—and let me make my film!"

I'm swallowed up again, as the darkness descends on me.

The next time the lights come on, I'm on a beach. I put my hand up, shielding my eyes from a hot sun that's pounding down on me. I squint hard to see better, but I can't make out anything more than just an ocean that seemed to stretch out to infinity just in front of me. I could hear the sounds of the surf striking the rocky shores off to my right, just beyond the small stretch of sand that I was lounging on.

Suddenly, I sat up with a start. Somehow this landscape looked familiar. I spun around. That bungalow up on the cliff looked quite familiar too; I was quite sure I'd seen it before.

Then, I realized I was feeling sensations that I hadn't felt in what seemed like forever. I'm alive and warm, and, yeah, it feels good. I sigh. I close my eyes, and put my head back resignedly against the chaise lounge. I'm lulled to complacence by the steady pounding of the surf.

"This is the life," I hear myself say.

Time passes.

Then, I hear a male voice calling out to me, from somewhere amid the waves.

"Urrey, Koorhia! Hey, you there, up on the beach. Who are you? The most beautiful and sexy woman in Bollywood?"

I squint my eyes against the sun to see a muscular, dripping wet male figure in a bathing suit emerge from the ocean and move steadily towards me.

I recognized him.

I bit my lip.

Damn.

I couldn't believe it!

Sanjay?

As he got closer, I noticed that even his usually sullen and clipped expression seemed somehow improved. He looked, in fact, like he was. . . smiling? And rather widely and openly, too. He stops three feet away and looks me over, up and down. My panic at that moment had a palpable tone. How did I end up here? Was this a dream? Was I lost in some alternate reality? Sanjay didn't even seem like the same man.

Then, he spoke. "Ah my most beautiful Parvati devi. You are the most beautiful vision this beach, the ocean and the sky has ever beheld before. You are so radiant, the sun pales in your presence and the moon is on the other side of the world, hiding enviously, biding its time, until the moment comes when it can shine its moonbeams onto your path."

What?

This had to be a dream.

That's not the real Sanjay.

Then suddenly a different mood came over him. Ah, here comes the real Sanjay now, I thought, as his face begins to contort into an arrogant scowl.

He sneers a ever-widening sneer. "All the same, darling, remember who made you what you are, piyari. And I could break you, too, don't you forget."

With that he reached out and pulled me abruptly to my feet.

Then, from somewhere just slightly askew from the center of my consciousness, I thought I could hear a female voice responding:

"No, no, no, silly. If anyone made anyone, it was me that made you. And don't you forget that, mera jhan."

Rakhi giggles and gives Sanjay a playful push. Taken by surprise, he stumbles. He staggers backwards, then trips and tumbles awkwardly on his rear end. He looks around, startled, confounded, and confused. As he gets back on his feet, his tongue's hanging out awkwardly. Now, his expression alters again as he looks up at us, abashed. "I'm sorry, Rakhi, I don't know what comes over me. But, listen, just don't ever pull something like that in front of my friends, okay?"

He springs forward and there's only a shadow of his darker mood still hovering somewhere, as he steps in closer and tilts Rakhi's face upwards. He peers deep down into her eyes. The sight of him, the sharp, familiar, and handsome terrain of his face, the feeling of his warm breath on our skin all seemed, well, quite sensual, as Sanjay's arms encircled Rakhi's waist and pull us in close to him.

He lowers his face to hers.

I take in a breath.

But at the last moment, Rakhi turns her face away before I could taste his lips.

"Opho, look at how late it is, piyara. I have to take a nap and do my yoga. Would you be a love and pick up a few things for dinner from the vegetable stand? Come, help me pack up all this stuff."

She's already released herself from his embrace as she bends to pick up her beach bag and towel, then she straightens up and looks at him, expectantly.

He sighs. But complies.

It's dinner time and Sanjay's sitting across the table from us enjoying the meal that Rakhi cooked for him. He smiles, hungrily and greedily, and at that moment it all came back to me. All of it. Everything he'd ever pulled with Christine.

My mind turned suddenly cold.

I decided I'd have to try reasoning with Rakhi.

Look, I know who this man is. You should have seen what he pulled with Christine.

Christine? Who's Christine? I'm not Christine, whoever she was.

Christine was a woman Sanjay dropped like a two-bit hooker on the streets of Mumbai, in nothing but a skimpy, black dress, as if she was a cheap piece of meat that'd gotten a bad smell. He'll do the same with you when he's finished, too. We need to make a plan. I can't waste this second chance. We have to get information out of him that will lead me to the murderers of Simryn Gill.

Listen. I'm glad you're back and all, I'm glad you made it. But this is my life, not yours.

I'm just saying. . . .

Say whatever you want, this is my life, and I'm in control. So we're going to do whatever I decide.

Rakhi glances over at Sanjay, whose lips are smacking loudly as he chews. "Kamal ha," he says, "this is so-o-o tasty! Homemade dahi, zucchini masala dosa, salad with mango dressing. Where did someone as talented and koobsooriti as you learn how to cook in so many styles? Goan, Punjabi, Gujarati, Rajastani, Tamil Nadu. The spices are so fresh. And the tastes. . . ."

Rakhi smiles. "You know me, Sanjay. If I want to do something, I'll just do it."

Sanjay smiles back at her and returns to his dinner. "Thank goodness for that."

See? He's eating out of my hand.

The old 'a way to a man's heart' theory, huh? Mark my words Rakhi, one day he'll get tired of your cooking and you'll be gone. You have no idea what you're dealing with; this is much bigger than you and Sanjay. Tell me something, do you even know what he does for a living?

Sanjay? He's a businessman.

A 'businessman?' Let me give you some words of advice, you silly little fool, I knew this man before you were even manifested, and he's nothing but a two-bit Bollywood gangsta and a prettyboy loser. He's dangerous and callous, and, doubtless, he'll just turn up dead one day, like they all do. Do you really understand what you're playing with here? The Bollywood mob is not fun and games, you know, and on top of that, Sanjay's not even really just Sanjay. He's got a nagh, the darkside-spirit of the Bhujangen, living in him. Take a closer look. Can't you see it, feel the serpentine presence? Wake up, little girl!

Rakhi studies Sanjay as he continues to wolf down his meal.

A nagh. Is that why he's a little grumpy sometimes?

Grumpy? No, you stupid child, it's much more serious than just a little grumpy.

Rakhi had had enough of me. She sighs resolutely and glanced around. I noticed Sanjay's bungalow had changed. What was it? Hmmm. There were no visible improvements. Nothing had been re-painted and all the furniture was the same, the same kitchen table, chairs, the same sofa in the living room, the same pots and pans that Christine had spent hours scouring, but somehow the place seemed different. It felt, somehow, like a home. It had a strong feminine presence.

Damn.

I had a real bad feeling about this.

Later on that evening, Rakhi lifts her head up from Sanjay's chest and gazes up at him. He runs his hand through her long black hair, his body is hot with passion. She moves her hand down past his abdomen. He moans. She leans over and kisses him before she rises up on him.

She soars.

Like wind above mountains, over the valleys and through trees. She rustles corn and wheat fields. She flies until she comes to rest on a cool grassy plain. She lies there, emanating joy.

Then, she saw it.

The nagh.

I could feel its fierce, otherworldly will trying to possess her.

Rakhi begins to sway. Back and forth. Side to side. As if responding to some distant song. The nagh begins to move in sync with her, hypnotized. Rakhi spreads her arms, inviting it in. The tongue flicks as if longing for a taste. The nagh moves in closer and they continue to sway and dance. Rakhi reaches her hand up and pats the cobra's head before moving down beneath its hood. Her fingers curl round its neck while her other hand slides down its body almost to the tail. She lifts the slithering entity from Sanjay's mind and drapes it around her neck. It tries to recoil, but Rakhi's humming and cooing soon relaxes it. It's eyes close and the nagh falls asleep.

The apparition fades and disappears.

Sanjay opens his eyes as if from a trance. He looks up at Rakhi in startled wonder. "My God. Who are you? Are you a sorceress? A Jadhioorani? Is that why I want you so much?"

Rakhi smiles. "I'm no Jadhioorani, my darling. I'm just a woman who loves you."

He frowns. "I'm not sure which is more frightening."

Sanjay sighs and pulls Rakhi down beside him. He wraps his arms around her and buries his face in her neck.

She listens, as his breathing becomes steady and content.

Soon, he's asleep.

'Oh my goodness,' I said to myself.

The next morning Sanjay drove Rakhi to her chic Bachelorette apartment in a hip section of Navi Mumbai. She spent the day doing her yoga practice and taking care of her bills and household needs. Me? I was orienting myself to being 'alive' again, so to speak. I looked around the space. Rakhi had done well for herself. She was eating healthier and being frugal and responsible with her money. For lunch we enjoyed a nice bean and pasta salad she made. She even had a cup of tea, no milk or sugar. I was quite surprised, but being who I am, I couldn't just leave it alone.

Where did Sanjay go?

To work, I suppose.

To work? Doing what? A hit for the Bollywood mob? Or, maybe he's a drug kingpin? Come on, Rakhi, he must have told you something.

That did it. Rakhi stopped listening to me entirely. She got up, went over to her stereo, cranked up her loud, obnoxious bhanghra-hop music and kept it cranked up for the next several hours.

My stars, I thought, some people can't take any criticism.

Mid-afternoon, Rakhi got a phone call.

A familiar voice comes over the phone. "Rakhi, darling, how are you?"

"Deera, what's happening?"

"Lots, babe, lots. Listen, I've been able to set up a session between you and Raj Balru."

"The dance instructor? Why? I can already dance more styles than everyone else put together."

"Of course, darling, of course, you're an absolute genius. You're a wealth of talent. But I just want an assessment of your abilities. Then, if it seems beneficial to your career, we might enroll you part time in Raj's school just for the prestige. He doesn't just work with anyone, you know? Besides, there's nothing wrong with improving on perfection."

Rakhi sighs.

"Oh, all right, Deera. When do I see him?"

"Tomorrow morning. Eleven o'clock."

"Sure."

"That's my babe. Has Deera ever steered you wrong? Show up, and knock 'em dead!"

Then, later on that afternoon, another call.

"Oh, hello, Sanjay-jahn."

"Rakhi, would you come to dinner with me tonight at the Dhonni Maach?"

"I'd love to, but I've got to be home early because I've got an important appointment tomorrow."

"I'll get you home early."

"Will you drive me tomorrow?"

"Of course. Can you be ready for dinner by six?"

"Yes, piyara, I'll be ready."

"One more thing. It's a business meeting. So dress up nice and sexy. That always helps nail down a deal."

Rakhi's grip tightens on the phone receiver. After she hangs up, she sighs.

You know, Sanjay's such a sweet person, but there are moments when. . . .

When . . . he's a total pig?

Rakhi purses her lips, but says nothing. She simply gets on with her daily routines.

I got the silent treatment for the rest of the afternoon.

Sure, fine.

At Dhonni Maach, that evening, Rakhi was sipping a glass of wine when Johnny Akkarah walked in.

I nearly choked.

Rakhi began coughing.

"What's the matter?" Sanjay asked.

"Um, nothing, the wine went down the wrong way."

I'd forgotten all about Johnny. I hadn't seen him since that night at 'Transcendental'. When I was inside Christine, I hadn't seen him at all. Of course not, I reminded myself, Sanjay never took Christine anywhere.

As Johnny sat down at our table across from me, I had a lot of mixed feelings, but he was still gorgeous, and I couldn't stop my heart from racing.

I bit my lip.

Rakhi laid into me.

Johnny's a dog, and he goes through women the way a drunken sailor goes through cheap wine.

What about Sanjay?

Sanjay hasn't done anything like that since I've known him.

Nothing like that, perhaps, that you know of? Here are the facts, my naive child. Sanjay's bad news, and someday, he's going to dump you just as unceremoniously and ruthlessly as he dumped Christine. Mark my words, it'll happen, a bad tiger will never change its spots.

Rakhi's eyes roll.

No, he won't dump me. I don't give it all away at once, like Christine did.

I swallowed hard.

I didn't know what to say to that.

As we waited for our dinner guests, Sanjay's phone rang. After a cryptic exchange he got up from the table, seeming a little distracted. He started to walk away, rather absently, but then turned back to Johnny. "Johnny-bhai, I have to go out somewhere. Stay here with Rakhi until I get back, will you?"

Johnny's eyebrows raise. "Sure, yaarh."

"Thank you, yaarh. See you in fifteen, doll."

Rakhi winced a little.

Once Sanjay's out of earshot, Johnny looks hard at Rakhi. "You must be setting a new world record."

Rakhi's eyes narrow, but she keeps quiet.

"I keep wondering how long it'll be until Sanjay gets tired of you. I know him, he's my brother, after all. He likes his women wild. His sexual exploits are infamous. Legendary. The fires burn bright but they don't last long. Even before that trashy American woman came along, he'd had a steady diet of one-night stands or week-long trysts at most, for years."

Rakhi's gaze is cool.

See? I told you. He's a dog. Just barks and barks all day long. Don't try to compare him to Sanjay. Johnny's not anything like Sanjay, even if they are brothers.

I was flabbergasted.

You mean they really *are* brothers?

Haan. Why else would I put up with him?

Rakhi turns her attention back to Johnny. I study him closely. He's still wearing that same wide, disinterested smirk he had on the last time I saw him.

"What was the name of that insane-assed, sex-crazed white woman? Oh the stories he used to tell about her, how she'd keep him cooped up in his bungalow for weeks and weeks."

I cringed.

It's true Rakhi, I heard about. . . .

Rakhi clears her throat. "I'm sure we all have a past, Johnny Bhai."

"Vekho, I'm not your brother."

Johnny jiggles his now empty glass. The ice clinks loudly.

"My glass is empty, Rakhi. Would you do me a favor and fill it?"

Rakhi leaps up and walks abruptly away from the table.

In the Ladies room, she studies herself in the mirror, and carefully wipes the tears away from her koobsorit, kohl-lined, almond-shaped eyes.

I could feel her heart breaking, just a little, perhaps for the very first time.

Rakhi's mood was sullen, as Sanjay drove her home that night.

Sanjay's sitting on the couch in her bachelorette apartment. Rakhi comes out of the adjoining kitchenette and hands him a bourbon. He takes it from her, angrily. He's not himself. He looks annoyed, almost sinister.

"I'm going to be away on business for a few days, Rakhi. So, Johnny-bhai has volunteered to drive you to your rehearsals next week."

"Sanjay, I can take care of myself. I don't need Johnny to drive me around."

Sanjay leaps up.

His eyes flash.

He grabs Rakhi harshly by the arm.

"Ow, Sanjay, stop it. What are you doing?"

"These last few months have been . . . fun, darling. You're a nice little package, but it's-s-s over now, Rakhi. I regret that I have to let go of you s-o-o s-s-s-soon, but we s-s-s-s-till have tonight."

Rakhi's heart crashes to the ground. I could feel her waning.

"No, Sanjay, don't. . . ."

His grip tightens on her forearm.

Her knees buckle. She goes limp with despair.

That's when I stepped in.

I raise myself up to Rakhi's full height and meet Sanjay's eyes.

I sneer. "Take a good look, Sanjay, and tell me, who's playing whom, hmmm? Now, if you'll excuse me. . . ."

I shifted my weight, pivoted backward, and dropped away, easily freeing myself from his grasp. Then, I stepped back to assume a 'Tiger' Weng Chun fighting stance.

Sanjay's lips pucker. He crouches very low, and begins to hiss-s-s. "Who do you think you are, *Brussssssssss Leeeeeeeee?*"

I hear a sound . . . like. . . .

On the ethereal plane, Sanjay stands before me. His eyes flash with anger. His head turns to one side with a loud snapping sound. His body becomes long and thin. His face narrows. His eyes turn black, the black of nothingness, and nothing reflects out of the void of them. Fangs appear in his scaly, serpentine mouth. His snake-tongue flickers in and out. He coils and hisses. He's ready to attack.

I slow my breathing, finding its source.

"Just. This."

The Bhujangen sways menacingly, back and forth, trying to hypnotize me with its gaze, but I stay alert, and hold my ground. I can still hear the everyday world all around me.

The traffic outside.

The ticking of a clock.

The whirling of a ceiling fan

The buzz of electricity hissing through a light bulb.

A spider rubbing his legs together on its brand new web in the corner ceiling

The nagh lunges. I move, grasp the snake below its head. It writhes angrily, trying to escape, but I've got it. I swing it around by the tail a few times; I close my eyes and focus.

"This snake. In a cage."

The Bhujangen hisses and struggles, but I don't relent.

Finally, it stops.

In the cage, the nagh shrinks and shrinks. It turns pink before it grows white fur all over its body and sprouts soft bunny-ears. I open the cage and lift it out.

I smile, tenderly, at the cute, little rabbit sleeping in my arms.

Rakhi lay the sleeping bunny down on the sofa-bed before she staggered into the bathroom, and splashed some water on her face. She looks up, and studies her reflection in the mirror.

"Thank you."

No problem.

When we got back into the living room, the rabbit had disappeared.

Sanjay was laying curled up in its stead, sleeping peacefully, and looking lovable and innocent. My eyes roll as Rakhi's soft sweet gaze looks down at him.

Your relationship is doomed. Men from the underworld are hardened.

She doesn't reply.

We should call the Nomads and have him put away.

"No!"

The spell you evoked last night had only a temporary effect Rakhi. Fighting evil is never easy, you know.

But Rakhi's staring off into space; her expression is unreadable.

Okay. WHAT-ever. I'll take it from here.

What do you think you're going to do? Cuddle him to death? Reform him? *Awww*, such a sweet story. But, sadly, it will never happen. That never works. In eradicating bad guys, one cannot afford to be so soft and sweet as you. . . .

"Oh, shut the hell up!"

You get the picture; some things never changed between me and Rakhi.

The next morning Rakhi was singing a soft melody to herself as she made breakfast. She hears Sanjay rousing himself on the sofa-bed. She turns in time to see him get up and stretch. He notices her watching him and literally hops, skips and jumps over to her. She takes a step back, not knowing what to expect.

He smiles, a charming and precocious smile. "Namaste, Rakhi. It's such a beautiful morning."

She blinks.

He gathers her up in his arms. "What's wrong, piyari, you look like you've never seen me before?"

She frowns. "I'm sorry. I think I'm still trying to get used to how amazing you are."

His eyes become solemn and serene, as he gazes into her flawless, beautiful face. He picks up the tune he just heard her singing in the kitchen, and begins to hum it, sweetly and ever-so-softly, as he gazes ever more deeply into our eyes.

Then, somewhere amid the swirl of all the universes, I thought I could hear the violins starting up.

. . . as Sanjay begins to sing.

> *Mere dil ne soonia, jaan ne Mana*
> *This morning. . .*
> *It was like I saw you for the first time.*
> *Are those stars in your eyes?*
> *Did the sun borrow your smile?*
> *Hmmm Mmm Mmmm*
> *My heart has heard. My soul now believes*
> *This morning . . .*
> *I opened my eyes, threw open my arms*
> *It's like we just met*
>
> *But how could that be*
> *when you've been here with me*
> *Mere Dil ne soonia, jaan ne Mana.*
> *The world is cold, the world is cruel*
> *I don't care now, cause I'm in love with you.*
> *My love is not a rose, no-no!*
> *I am tired of all the thorns*
> *Mere chandri Jahn Rakhi.*
> *My heart has heard, my soul now believes*
> *Mere dil ne soonia, jaan ne Mana*

He was about to kiss Rahki, full on the lips, when the doorbell rang. . . . .

Sanjay stops. Leans his forehead against hers and rolls his eyes. "*Now* what?"

But his mood rebounds quickly. He's smiling widely again as he bounces to the door, and he swings it open with a flourish.

"AH-ha-ha Johnny-bhai, aiyo, aiyo!"

Johnny looks perplexed as he steps in through the door. He studies Sanjay carefully before turning towards Rakhi with both eyebrows raised.

"Urrey, what did you put in his chai? He's jumping around like a kangaroo."

Sanjay smiles at him even more brightly. "I don't know how to tell you Johnny-bhai, but I woke up this morning and realized just how wonderful life truly can be. Now, I just want to sing and dance and. . ."

"Well, don't. Remember, you have an important meeting this morning. If you leave right now, you might have time to go home and change."

Sanjay looks down at his watch. "Aiyee, you're right."

Johnny turns to Rakhi. "Are you ready? We're supposed to be at the dance studio by eleven."

Go with him Rakhi. Do it for me. Just this one time.

No way. I didn't agree to this. And I'm not going to go anywhere with that pig.

Look, if I hadn't stepped in last night, you and Sanjay would be in pretty bad shape, by now . . . so, you owe me.

Hmmph. Okay, just this once.

Outside Rakhi's apartment, I nearly gagged.

Johnny drives a baby-blue, 1955 Cadillac El Dorado convertible, with tail fins and white-wall tires; the kind of car where the leather upholstery hugs and holds you close. We were in a pimp-mobile. To top it off, he plays loud, bad, American rock music throughout the entire trip, and drives at breakneck speeds, with his left elbow continually hanging out the driver's side window.

What was I thinking?

I don't know . . . what were you thinking?

Shut the hell up.

Now, Johnny starts shouting loudly at Rakhi, his voice rising up high above the raucous KISS song, 'I Was Made For Loving You,' that's blaring out over the Cadillac's sound system. "What was up with Sanjay this morning? He seemed so . . . happy, or something."

"I don't know what you mean, Johnny-bhai!" she shouts back with equal fervor. "He always seems happy to me."

"Last night, he told me he was dumping you."

"Oh Johnny-bhai, that's our Sanjay, he's such a kidder!"

From the driver's side, Johnny shoots us a sidelong glance. "I told you before, Rakhi, I'm *not* your brother."

The rest of the trip was spent in silence. The sights and scenes of the Western Express Highway whirled by as we headed north of the Mumbai film-city complex. Johnny steps on it. I can feel the wind blowing my hair around, as he dodges precariously in and out of traffic, accelerating and decelerating constantly, with dramatic flair.

Rahki doesn't even blink, as Johnny hangs on a hairpin spin to veer into the parking lot of a small strip mall, somewhere in the northern section of Mumbai. A bold, black-and-blue lettered sign painted on a large, second-storey window above us clearly indicates we've arrived.

MASTI is a MUST at
Nataraja Dance Academy
Bollywood's Most Famous and Best Dance Studio.
All Eastern and Western Styles
Forget the Rest.
Expect the Best.

In front of the mall, Johnny's baby-blue Cadillac screeches to a sudden stop. He vaults out over the driver's-side door and makes his way straight to the studio door. Just outside, he glances back at Rakhi.

She stares at him, petulantly.

"What are you waiting for? I'm not your naukhar," Johnny calls out to her.

She purses her lips and throws open the door of the car. Johnny saunters in just as Rakhi catches up behind him. She stops the door, just before it slams shut on her face.

She's keeping quiet, but I can tell, she isn't happy.

Sorry, but, as they say, all's fair in love and war.

. . . Just *can* it!

Rakhi, Natrarani

I'm flying again.

In a large dance studio with two adjoining walls wrapped by mirrors Rakhi's running, jumping and whirling through a solo audition.

She's passionate.

She's reckless.

Suddenly, she stops.

Loud bhangra-hop drumbeats are crashing down as if from out of the sky. They come to a crescendo, then diminish to silence, reaching a momentary, and only temporary, resolution.

And, thankfully, the butterflies in my stomach have stopped lurching, even if it is only for a moment.

(I quickly offer up a prayer of thanks. . . .)

Then, the electronic drums started up again, only this time they're even louder.

Their relentless rhythms are. . . .

CLANGING

BASHING

(. . . at my brains.)

Rakhi suddenly turns, runs and lunges. Her movements are aggressive and elegant in response to the rhythmic thudding.

This is her music.

She breathes it.

RATTA-TAT-TAT-TAT TATTA-TAT! TAT-TAT-TAT TATTA-TAT-RAT!

. . . Machinegun-like beats.

Precise.

Spasmodic.

Thrilling.

Now Rakhi's poised and ready. I catch a glimpse of her in the mirror. Her arms whirl and swirl. Her stance is like a mountain.

She's elegant.

She's aggressive.

Rakhi runs, leaps, and falls. Then she rolls away.

(I'm beginning to feel nauseous again.)

Then, she freezes. We're on her feet. Gazing round. We're keeping still . . . but I can tell she's holding herself in.

Anticipation.

Subtle change.

Response.

Twa-a-a-n-n-n-n-g.

A sitar played by human hands blends in a softer feel for a moment.

But Rakhi's not fooled.

She smirks. A trace of whispery amusement crosses her face.

Then suddenly, she's proven right.

A scream arises.

A thundering *"ARRRRRRHHHHHHHHHH!"*

Rakhi responds to the electronically enhanced howl by bolting low over the floor; then she dives, hits the ground lithely, spins and twists in one spot. She's up on her knees, looking around. She gets to her feet with the stealth of a soldier in battle, lifting her arms straight overhead, with fingers outstretched; Virabhadra emerging from Earth to answer Shiva's call.

She flies toward battle.

She enters the fray, spinning-spinning-spinning. Arms stretch out on each side of her like twin blades. Heads roll, left and right. Blood from asuris and asuras soaks the ground. Screams from the evil ones on all sides arise all around us. They flee in terror.

(To tell you the truth, I couldn't help feeling proud of her.)

Now, Rakhi's crouching low. Watching.

Hoo Ha!

Hoo-ha!

Rocks to the left and to the right.

Hoo Hoo Hoo.

Lunge like a panther. LEAP at the sky. Lands one foot. SPINS. Stutter-step to a stop-hop. Wham! Right! Left! Right-Right-Left.

It's . . . dazzling.

It's . . . dizzying.

(I'm definitely feeling nauseous.)

The music surges. Pounding pounding pounding. Harder. Louder. Faster.

Booweeeeee-eeeeeeeeey. BooWISHA-wom-wom-wom-wom-wom. . .
TWHAP

Rakhi's cool. Under control. After one final spin she lands on one foot, kicks at the sky with the other.

Ba-boom-BA . . . Ba-boom-BA . . . Ba-boom-BA

Mercifully, the last beat falls, and Rakhi pulls herself into Tadasana. Feet together. Palms folded at her heart, she takes a long calming breath. She gives thanks and bows.

"Lakh, lakh Shukhria. Merbhani. Jai, Jai Matha ji."

. . . CLAP-CLAP-CLAP-CLAP-CLAP-CLAP-CLAP!

Rakhi looks up and studies the man walking towards her. He stops a few feet away before tossing her a towel. She wipes the sweat from her face and then whips the towel around her shoulders. The whirling ceiling fans begins to cool the sweat on her dance gear. The man stands with arms folded across his chest. He raises his index finger to pursed lips. A pensive pose.

"Hmmmmm," he mutters. "Yes, yes, yes, interesting indeed, Miss Chand, quite interesting. I especially enjoyed the melange of styles from which you drew, and I couldn't help but notice the elements of samba and rumba that you've blended into your banghra-stomp-hop with, of course, a few strokes drawn from our own classical raga traditions, and not to mention the pervasive influence of the American free-style throughout. I also saw the subtler and more esoteric elements drawn from the various forms of our subcontinent's metaphysics. It's a very demanding style, isn't it? It requires such deep commitment, so much concentration, the invocation of an almost dhyana-like state, and still to be so very physical, so passionate and athletic, and, of course, so provocative . . . so very daring."

Yeah. Right.

The man's name is Raj Balru. He's the proprietor of this dance studio. He'd been rushing over to introduce himself, preening and fawning immediately over Rakhi, the moment we'd come through the doors. I'd recognized his type right off. A sycophantic, smarmy, duplicitous character if there ever was one.

Watch out for him, Rakhi, I told her, he'll promise you the sun, the moon and the stars. But he won't deliver.

Natch!

Now Raj takes a few steps back from Rakhi . . . .
One.
Two.
Three.
– Ooops!
(He stumbles, and nearly topples over, but recovers.)
Four–Five.
Stop.

"Hmmmmm."

He studies her again. This time with extreme pensiveness.

"Hmmmmm."

She stares back at him. Her face is blank and expressionless.
I tried to interject some humor.
What portions do you think he likes best? Thighs, rump, or breast?
Not funny.
Raj's smile grows wider. "Congratulations, my dear, I've never seen an, um, untrained dancer with such a remarkably well-honed physique and lines."
"Untrained? Who says I wasn't trained?" Rakhi snaps.
It was then that Balru turned his attention to Johnny, who'd been staying cool, standing a small distance away with his back up against a wall.
"Uhhhm, yes, but, as you know, dancing in Bollywood films does require quite a lot of sophistication, and don't get me wrong, my dear Mr. Akkarah, she is already quite good. Still, I think she could have . . . even more of it. We could take her talent to an exceedingly high level. Here at Nataraja Dance Studios, we are exceedingly

particular about which dancers we will teach and allow to represent us in the film industry. A dancer must have talent, of course, and the right body, the flexibility, strength, and so on and so forth. But it's more than that, too. We are looking for that certain something, that je ne sais quoi, that uncommon drive, which can deliver the kind of passion and ability directors have come to expect from dancers who've come through our Studio. And, fortunately for your Miss Rakhi, I believe she does have the potential to possess those qualities, if she's willing to work hard."

The man finally turns back to look at Rakhi. "Do you understand, Baetee?"

Rakhi glares.

Raj's mouth stretches out into a fatherly grin.

He nods. "Good."

He turns back to Johnny. "Next, I will have to see how she works with a partner."

He claps his hands.

A suitably handsome, lithe young man in dance gear enters the room. He stands next to Rakhi, poised and ready.

Raj steps back, waving his arms expressively as he retreats.

"Take her in your arms, Turan. Rakhi, I want you to lie back in them. I want to see your vulnerability. An exposed heart, a kind of love offering to the Gods. Do you understand?"

Rakhi rolls her eyes as she turns to her partner.

Turan wraps an arm around Rakhi's waist. With his free hand he guides her arm back over her head. She leans back in an arch, her braided hair tumbling onto the ground.

I look up, with startled wonder, into the man's practiced, passionate gaze.

The music begins. Slowly.

Turan brings Rakhi up to standing. His face only inches away. Our bodies respond, undulating in a lovers' tango. Free and gentle at first. The softness eventually gives way to the siren call of the horns. Turan's warm breath caresses her face. Rakhi leans in.

The maracas come in. Edgy and demanding.

The bongos *dhoomp-da-bhoomp . . . dhoomp-da-bhoomp.*

As the violins call, Rakhi falls into a swoon. Turan lifts her up again and spins her around. The horns surge – she puts her arms around Turan's neck, leaps up, and wraps her legs around his waist. He spins her around. She falls back and spreads her arms out. They spin together like a top.

I'm flying . . . flying . . . flying . . . flying.

After a while, Rakhi gathers herself up in his arms and Turan stops spinning. The drums deepen. She looks into his eyes and caresses his face. He's a lion amongst his pride. He's the One. The chosen. The Alpha-Male. He's taking, holding, possessing, molding, melding.

Lines blur.

Now, he's gyrating against her.

She consummates with equal force.

She can do this.

She *loves* doing this.

I gasp for breath, dizzy from the motion sickness, ready to beg Rakhi for mercy.

But then, the music exploded all around me. . . .

Turan drops Rakhi to her feet, turns her around and spoons up against her.

I can feel the hot thrumming of his pulsating hips.

Rakhi breaks away.

He grabs her and pulls her back in. She stamps her feet – pushes him away. Her arms swing wildly. He steps back. His hips swivel in rock-steady rhythm, waiting. She can't stay away. Rakhi moves in shimmies up and down against him. It's gettin' all hot and sweaty.

Turan's look is fierce.

Rakhi's eyes are wild.

They're both crazy.

. . . And it's a kind of crazy that ain't ever gonna stop!

HOP!

Thump-a-dump
Thump-a-dump
Thump-a-dump
Thump-a-dump
Thump-a-dump!

A female singer moans and trails off. . . .

> *"I can't help it*
> *Help it*
> *Help it*
> *Help it*
> *Help me. . . ."*

. . . just as the ground drops out from under me again.

(I'm flying . . . flying . . . flying.)

I caught a glimpse of the three of us in the mirror; Turan's got Rakhi lifted high up in the air, then he drops her.

She flies down between his legs, and I tumble down with her.

At the last possible moment, their arms link. He pulls her back up. And tosses her away. . . .

Rakhi spins and lands on her feet. She turns and glares at Turan. I feel a tigress rising up within her. Wild and indomitable. Turan dares to meet her gaze. They freeze. Wild eyes caught up, bound by primordial forces, an unbreakable challenge.

They're poised
Ready to erupt.

But then, the music changes.

A roaring-20's American tune jumps out of speakers.

Jitterbug!

TAH-TAH-TAH-TAH . . .
TAH-TAH-TAH-TAH. . .

"Arrrripha!"
I can't catch my breath.
It goes on and on. They fuse every possible style—Latin, hip-hop, modern, Eastern, Western—breathing hard, sweating hard, coming back for more. Delivering with every ounce.

PAH-PAH-PAH-PAH!

Then, it's over.
They're collapsed in each other's arms.
They're . . . Hot . . . Wet . . . Spent.

(I finally get that breath.)

Balru's clapping brings them round. Rakhi and Turan stand up and bow.
Balru steps forward. "Thank you, Turan."
I glanced at Turan from the side. The dancer nods and frowns, and glances darkly as he walks away.
Raj Balru turns to Rakhi, purses his lips in a most serious contemplation, and finally, he delivers his rhetoric. "My dear, there are many ways to get to the top. You are an up-and-coming star in this industry, there is no doubt, and, although you are indeed a most remarkably talented dancer, there is only so far you can go as a remarkably talented dancer. You are still a bit raw – a little flighty – and will need to learn to discipline that impassioned, but unruly wildness with precision. More technique is required, more savoir-faire, more elegance, more ease in the execution. I believe you will also benefit with some acting lessons so that you can move into speaking roles. At Nataraja Dance Academy, we can give you all of that. And, who knows, my dear, if you work hard, you might even be as famous as Pratema Shivapati one day."
Rakhi bites her lip.
Who? Pratema Shivapati? Ye bak-bass kiya ha?

She's well-known dancer. I saw her once. She had a short, lead dance part in a nightclub scene during Meri Dil Ka Tara. She wasn't half bad.

Meh. Okay.

Balru continues.

"Yes, yes, yes, well, Pratema's only one of hundreds of successful filmi-dancers who've come through here. You do realize that, don't you, my dear? Nataraja Dance Academy has paved the way for many, many, many, many girls like you."

Girls like Rakhi? I thought. If he only knew. . . .

Raj pauses. He's got his 'considering the situation more carefully' look on. He shakes a finger at Rakhi.

"Vekho! The truth is, I know what you're thinking—and yes, I totally agree, you are far more talented and have more masala than the vast majority of garden-variety type dance-starlets. But to get a top-top reputation in the Bollywood filmi-industry takes something very, very special, so you must understand that you have to know someone to be someone. Then, there is the other myth that you have to be someone to know someone. But in any case, don't you forget that you also need a great deal of knowledge. You need consciousness of the variety, the different types of styles, the fashions and trends. Here, we can show you how to refine your techniques and add subtleties. You must be able to please the critics too, my dear!"

He stops and peers.

"So . . . the question, Baetee, is this. Do you want to put in time and work to use Nataraja Academy's vast dance teaching knowledge and resources, including, of course, our vast lists of industry contacts?"

Rakhi blinks.

Balru turns and walks away a few paces before he stops. He turns round to face her.

"I will take that to be a 'Yes'. Good decision. Now I'd like to see how you interact with multiple dancers." Balru turns and claps his hands three times.

A troupe of four males jogged out onto the studio floor. They took up positions around Rakhi.

North.
South.
East.
West.

Balru smiles. "Rakhi, my dear, these are the Upadhyay brothers: Ami, Pumi, Rama, and Chand. They trained here, and have gone on to very successful careers, both as chorus dancers and sometimes even lead dancers in many fil-lums. But don't be mistaken, oh, no-no-no-no! They know their stuff, they've got the styles. They can dance up a storm using nearly any dance-form that was ever known on this planet. In fact, so could their father, a renowned Kathak dancer in his own right; and his father before him taught the Odissi classical style to royal princes. Their mother, also, was a queen of the Bharatnatyam classical. So, you see? Their family have been dancing in Bollywood for generations. Indeed, even before films were being made, their family were dancing the traditional classical styles in the courts of kings and queens all over India, and they come from a long line going back . . . why, going back for centuries. That's quite a pedigree, don't you agree? Yet, even they are here, training to master more modern, American styles, and this demonstrates exactly the kind of prestige this studio can muster, that we can lure such endowed, enduring dancers . . . samajae?"

Rakhi manages a little smile.

Raj sighs. "Very well, Let's see what you can do."

He turns to Ami, Pumi, Rama, and Chand. "I'll need a depiction of a sort of Chaos, of Impassioned Movement. I'm looking for a sense of Overpowerment from the men. A competition. A compulsion, really, a need to possess."

He turns back to Rakhi.

"And you? You are the object of their wanting. A Helen of Troy, if you will, the desire of many. Do you understand, Rakhi?"

Rakhi smiles. Knowingly.

A bass guitar *thumple-thumple-thumples* out from under a snare drum.

A slapback-echoed guitar nails a riff.

It's the 60's, Bollywood style.
A dhol joins in.
Shoo-wop meets Hindi-pop.

Dhoomp sha-da Dhoomp-dhoomp sha-da! Dhoomp sha-da Dhoomp-dhoomp sha-da

Ami leaps forward and wraps Rakhi in his arms. She looks up over her shoulder at him. He has a look in his eyes. Lust. Rakhi pushes herself free. Pumi then grabs her from behind and lifts her up above his head. I feel myself hover above them all. I look at the reflection in the mirror. Rakhi is poised as if in flight. When Pumi puts her down, she runs, but Rama and Chand cut her off, try to corral her.

She dodges, turns, and runs back. The high hat *tinga-mingas* as the trapped maiden tries to escape. But the guitar comes back in, echoing the hungry howling of wolves.

Now, she's surrounded. Ami and Rama grab hold of her arms and legs. They're swinging her, wild and wide, from side to side. Up and down. They swing her high and let her fly. She lands in Chand's eager waiting arms.

She looks at him.

He leers.

She struggles.

She breaks free, and cartwheels away from him, but before she's able to regain her balance, she's trapped again. Surrounded. They move in. They push, pull, prod and toss her about.

Their faces whirl.

Rakhi's getting dizzy. Disoriented.

I watched as all four dancers pull at Rakhi from every side. Eight hands holding her tightly.

Suddenly, she starts screaming.

Her arms swing and she lunges in all four directions, pushing all four men away. One after another, they stumble back. Rakhi crouches and recoils. Her eyes flash with anger.

Then she runs the nearest dancer and. . . .

THWA-A-A-A-K!

She slaps Rama's face. Hard.
Rama, astonished, topples over to the floor.
He stares up at the ceiling, wide-eyed with astonishment.
(My mouth falls open.)
The music continues.
A singer sings: *Shoo-wa bop bop bop. Bop. Bop.*
Rakhi towers over Rama. She's glaring down at him hard; her mouth twists into a panther-like sneer.

Pumi, oblivious, still lost in the dance, moves towards her. Rakhi spins round to face him, ready to strike again. But Pumi stops dead, frozen by her fierce gaze. He sees his fallen brother at her feet and scampers backwards toward the far corner of the studio.

From behind, Ami spins Rakhi round to face him.

T-H-W-A-A-A-A-K!

Her left hand comes around and slaps him hard. Her right follows.

T-H-W-A-A-A-A-K!

The dancer stares. Aghast.

Rakhi steps back and crouches, glaring up at him. She moves like a cat. Flowing. Lunging. Her hands cross in front of her heart as she spins around. She lifts her right leg in the air as she lands, her arms spreading apart gracefully for balance; the kick flies like a viper.

Ami's eyes google. His mouth purses in shock and horror. *"Omigawd, that kick was for real."*

Ooo la! I thought. He caught that one right square. That's a great place to aim a kick, Rakhi, if you can land it.

The dhol player takes a solo.

Ratta-tatta-tatta-tat. Ratta-tatta-tatta ta. Ta doonga duppa duppa dauppa DOONG.

Ami groans as his entire world whirls in ever-enlarging realizations of nausea and pain. He's almost out on his feet. His knees buckle. He implodes and collapses the way a sub-standard skyscraper built on bribery will when the Richter scale hits nine.

He joins his brother Rama on the floor.

Writhing in agony.

By now, Chand and Pumi are clear on the idea that the dance is over. They run like hell to opposite corners. Rakhi stomps out of the room, angrier than anyone I've ever seen, snapping up her warm-up jacket on the way out.

The door bangs hard behind her.

PW-WHAAA-AM!

Sweet, I think.

I watched as everyone else in the room tried to gather themselves. Rama held his cheek, looking dazed. Chand's confusion turned into a scowl. Pumi was hauling Ami off the ground and half carried and dragged him into the next room. Balru stood apart looking away from everyone, brooding as one hand scrubbed his chin vigorously.

I wondered. What had gotten into Rakhi? Was it the dance? Did she get carried away? Was it something the men did? Was it something familiar about the men that triggered her? Maybe. But, of course they have similar features, after all, they were all brothers. I pondered each man carefully, looking for any signs of hidden malice or duplicity, wondering if any or all of them could be more than they appeared to be. But I found nothing. Or nothing unusual at least.

So, if it wasn't something about one of the men, then what? I wondered.

Then, it hit me.

As I looked around at all four dancers.

"Oh, four of them . . . all at once . . . of course. . . ."

I pondered that for awhile.

Then, something else occurred to me.

"Wait a minute, Rakhi's gone. She's not even in the studio anymore. But I'm still in here."

So, at that point, I wasn't inside Rakhi anymore.
When'd that happen?
How'd I miss it?
I thought about the last time I'd been viewing the scene from Rahki's perspective. It was somewhere during the last dance that I'd found myself standing, pressed into a corner of the room, watching with the rest of them.
Wow. Really?
What was going to happen next?
Where was I now?
Was I back in my own body?
I looked down at my hands, but there was no sign of me.
No sign of me in the mirrors, either.
Damn.
All that was left of me now was some kind of disembodied apparition.

Meanwhile, as I was pondering my own loss and confusion, Raj Balru had sufficiently recovered from the shock of the scene we'd just witnessed to make a move.
After silencing the music, Raj skulks up to Johnny, who's been staying impassive, leaning up against a far wall, throughout the entire scene.
Raj puffs himself up with a heavy sigh. ". . . Oooohhh, yes, yes, yes, Mr. Akkarah, it is very much as you said. She IS a willful one, isn't she? Yes, definitely. Much too stubborn, too full of herself, for her own good. Ha ka na? But don't worry about it. No-no-no-no, not at all. There won't be any repercussions over this incident. Deera and I will smooth everything over with the Upadhyay brothers. Offer them a plum role in return for their silence or something. They'll be glad to take it too, they are good guys."

Raj sighs loudly again now, clearly exasperated.

Now his spleen vents.

"But . . . that young girl, what are we going to do with her? A very daring dancer, to be sure, but the way she acts? Baparray! If she doesn't smarten up, I predict it will be many, many years indeed before she gets anywhere in Bollywood, and I am usually right. Would you tell her this for me, please?

"Vekho. Tell her, if she doesn't want to waste her life dancing silly little improvisations in tiny, artsy-fartsy, avant-garde theaters in front of, at most, a dozen or two people or so, for a bunch of elitist snobs who think they're oh-so-ahead of their time. You know, the ones who call themselves the 'nouveau cognoscenti.' Hah. Such boorish posers. Damn their wine-sipping, beef-supping souls. Yes, tell her this for me, please, that if she doesn't want to end up there – and she really ought to take my word for it and be pretty damn sure she doesn't – well, then, she'd better start listening to sensible people . . . like *me*."

Johnny looks at him, still impassive. He shifts from one foot to the other while shoving a cigarette into the corner of his mouth. He stands there. Motionless and non-responsive

I was still staring into Johnny's blank face when the room began to dissolve.

The next thing I knew, I was back in the car, back inside Rakhi.

"Well, that was fast." I thought.

Right away, Rakhi made it clear she was in no mood to talk with me. I tried to reason with her again.

Well, why are you giving me the cold shoulder? I know you felt something. Don't you realize yet that you can't always walk away, or just kick someone who triggers you 'where-it-counts' whenever something happens? That won't solve your problem, and you're going to have to face up to it sooner or later, aren't you? That must be why I came back, Rakhi. I can't close this case alone. You and I must work together to find out who was behind the murder of Simryn Gill.

There was no response at all.

She keeps staring out the side window.

Inaccessible.

Like a locked room.

She broods at Johnny as he comes walking out of the studio. He stops, briefly, to light the cigarette that's still hanging from his mouth. "That was some performance," Johnny quips as he gets in the car. Look, I'm no expert, but I don't think pulverizing a bunch of students is the normal thing to do if you want to enter a prestigious dance academy."

"Funny, who said I wanted to enter it? This is nothing but foolishness. I can already dance circles around any of them, so I have no need of either Balru, or his stupid, insipid opinions."

"Yeah, I think you're right. More dance lessons aren't going to get you to the top. In my opinion, Raj Balru is a waste of our time and money. And, besides, he makes a lousy pundit."

Rakhi gave him a puzzled look.

"Don't worry, you had to be there. As for contacts, I have plenty. I'll arrange for you to meet all the right people."

Johnny starts the car.

"Listen, I'll arrange to take you out for dinner and introduce you to someone who can really help you get connected. This woman knows every director, every producer and everyone who is anyone in Bollywood."

Rakhi's mood is still sullen; she stares straight ahead. "I'll think about it."

"You do that, think about it, but make sure you don't blow her off like you did Balru. This woman can make or break both you and your career."

"Yes, Johnny-bhai."

Johnny takes a final drag from his cigarette before snuffing it out. "I told you before. Do not mistake me for a brother, Rakhi. By the way, I need to stop by my bungalow before I drop you at your apartment."

"Sure. Whatever you say, Johnny-bhai."

After parking in front of a seaside bungalow, several miles down the beach from Sanjay's, Johnny walked over to the passenger's side and opened up the door for Rakhi.

She glared at him. "I'll wait here if you don't mind."

Johnny smiled. "Well, I'm going to be awhile. I have to make some of those important phone calls on your behalf. You don't want to just sit out here in the heat, do you?"

Rakhi got out of the car. After Johnny closed the door behind her, she stepped up beside him.

"Okay, let's go in. But don't think you can get away with bad behavior with me, Johnny Bhai."

"Wouldn't dream of it, doll. Wouldn't dream of it"

Once inside, Johnny led Rakhi into the spacious, modern living room. He indicated the white leather sofa before he strolled over to the bar to pour himself a bourbon. "What would you like to drink, Rakhi?"

"Water."

"C'mon, don't you want a real drink?"

Rakhi rolled her eyes. "No. I just had a strenuous dance work out and I need to rehydrate."

"Right, okay. I'll be back."

Johnny went into the kitchen. A few moments later he brought their drinks over and sat down next to her on the sofa. "I put in that call to my contact. I've arranged for us to meet her Friday night for dinner at 7 P.M."

"That was quick," Rakhi said, as she accepted the cool glass of water.

"Well, in the end, it's not the number of people you know, it's the ones who can deliver that matter." Johnny smiles as he sits down on the sofa. He pats the empty spot between us. "Come and sit a little closer, Rakhi, so we can talk."

She doesn't move.

Johnny smirked. "What's wrong? Where's that Tigress that just kicked the asses off four men? Look, you must realize that I don't mean you any harm."

Rakhi glanced over. She was about to say something when. . . .

Suddenly, it's like I'm seeing Johnny all over again, for the first time.

His eyes flash!

He's exuberant. Wild with abandon.

He laughs. . . .

As his laughter fades away, I stare up at him in wonder. I found myself falling deeper and deeper into his eyes. The room suddenly brightens. A cool breeze soothes my skin, as it ruffles Johnny's hair a little. I look back up at him again—I'm envisioning his figure in a beautiful beige, red and gold embroidered sherawani chooridar.

He looks quite dashing.

I bite my lip.

My hand goes out to his smooth, handsome face. His skin is warm under my touch. His gaze holds mine. My heart thumps, then beats faster. He steps in close and wraps his arm around my waist. He gathers me up. We stand for a moment in an embrace. He lifts my arm and spins me into a silent waltz. There's no music, but Johnny leads me with confidence in a sweeping Viennese Bouree. I feel as if I'm dancing on a cloud.

His eyes sparkled with . . . something.

What? (I wonder).

I smile up at his deep rich brown eyes, enjoying the smoldering, still-bridled passions of our bodies. I swoon, overcome with . . . with . . . with. . . .

With what?

I don't know.

At that moment all I wanted to do was to taste his lips.

Deeply.

But then, an annoyed female voice clattered in my head, shattering the illusion. . . .

"O Pho. Aap kiya kartae ho, Johnny Bhai. . . !"

My world rocked. Everything stopped.

What?

Once the clouds had dissipated, I looked around and realized that I was still in Johnny's bungalow. Johnny was lying there half sprawled out on the floor, half clinging to the couch. Rakhi was standing over him, glaring down. Obviously, she'd just released both of us from his charms and embrace, with a certain amount of prejudice.

She glares. "Take me home now, Johnny Bhai."

Johnny's gaze narrows a bit.

"Aacha pher Rajkamari-a. Your wish is my command. Chalo ji. Let's go."

Johnny dropped Rakhi off at her place, close to 7 P.M.

"Remember, I will be by for you Friday at six. Be ready."

She nodded as she got out of the car, still too angry to speak to him. He drove off with a roar, as Rakhi made her way into her building.

In the elevator, she was fuming.

I told you, Johnny's a dog.

He could be worse.

Yeah, you wish.

Rakhi walked out of the elevator and pulled her keys out. As she entered through her apartment door, her jaw dropped open. The place was full of flowers of every color: roses, carnations, marigolds, pink and white daisies. The fragrance surrounded us and enveloped the senses. I watched as Rakhi wandered into the middle of the room looking around. The room resembled a meadow on a mountain plateau with various wildflowers as well. There was even a vase of sunflowers by the window.

"Sanjay?" Rakhi whispered.

"Rakhi!" came the reply, as Sanjay stepped out from behind the front door. He was wearing a light beige kurtha and khaki-colored pants. There was something different about him.

Rakhi let out the breath she'd been holding. They both stood still, enchanted.

The music began. A flute from the East. A violin from the West. A santoor padded by softly.

Rakhi stands there still as a doe, uncertain of whether to flee or stay.

"But, I thought you were away on business?" she says.

"Business? Oh yes, business. Well, I decided I didn't want to do that, so instead, I went to see my mummy. She was very happy to see me, of course, and then I told her that I had some very good news for her. You should have seen the look on her face when I told her I would be bringing her bahoo home to meet her soon."

The flute and santoor smile together and twitter.

"Sach?" Rakhi responded, her eyes round with delight.

Sanjay reaches for her hand and kisses it. "Haan, sach. I hope that's okay. You do want to marry me, don't you, Rakhi?"

Rakhi bites her lip. "Yes. Yes, of course, I do."

Sanjay looks elated. He gathers her up in his arms and holds her closely.

And me?

I found myself standing invisibly behind a rubber tree plant in the corner of the room.

I didn't have to guess at what would happen next.

The violins lift and swirl . . . as Sanjay begins to sing his heart's avaaz:

> *Koosh Koosh Man Ho giya–thusi duso ji kiya ho giya?*
> *Something's happening. Can you tell me what's going on?*
> *This morning I woke up and found I was alive.*
> *Thusi duso ji, Kiya ho giya?*
> *Can you tell me what's going on?*
> *I saw your face like it was the first time,*
> *my heart skipped a beat and fell in line.*
> *I'm alive, I'm alive. Please tell me what's going on?*

Rakhi steps forward gracefully towards him, her arms outstretched, as she lifts her own voice into song:

> *Man Dusdi hoo kiya hooa*
> *God got up this morning and decided it would be so*
> *Don't ask, don't wonder*
> *It's the miracle of love*
> *Don't ask, don't wonder*
> *It's a miracle*

Sanjay sings:

If this is a love, it's more fragrant than all the flowers
and God should fill this world with only your image
I'll be your Lord Krishna and you my Radha ji

I stood watching from the corner as they danced, gazing into each other's eyes.

At that point, I knew I was losing my grip on Rakhi.

Rakhi sings. . . .

Meinu hor kosh naihi chahi da ha
You are my sun, moon, stars
You are the ground under my feet
And I need nothing more than that

As the song was finally nearing an end, Sanjay lifted Rakhi up in his arms and carried her to the sofa, humming as he went. I was still standing there, unnoticed, as he lowers her to the cushions. When his lips found hers, I tried not to pay attention; I tried to find something else to look at. Finally, I turned around to face the corner and attempted to distract myself from the sounds of their smooching, breathing, and giggling.

That's it, I reckoned. It looked like I'd have to find another avatar, or manifestation, or whatever. This one had been swept off her feet and, by the looks of it, Rakhi would probably soon be giving up her dreams of fame and fortune to become Sanjay's love-bug, make him roti, chapati, or some other kind of sub-continent flatbread, and bear him many children. Probably all sons.

And with Sanjay, of all people. Christine's ex!

So what was I still doing there, standing in the corner like a voyeur? I should get out, that'd be the only decent thing to do. But how? And if this is how it was all going to turn out, *why* was I ever brought back from the void in the first place?

Dammit.

No, wait. Hmmmm. There must be a reason. There must be a way. Otherwise, I would never have arisen from the abyss and would have been spared the embarrassment of . . . this.

Just then, I heard Sanjay get up, turn off the lights, and then return to Rakhi. I stood there in the dark, still wondering what to do, and trying not to listen to all the lip-smacking, moaning, and groping.

Yeesh.

After a time, I noticed something odd. The sounds of the lovers were getting softer, quieter, and echoing off into the distance. But it was more than that. It was like someone had turned the volume down on the entire world. When I turned back around, I could see no trace of the lovers, not even an outline in the darkness. Nor, for that matter, could I find a trace of anything else that had been in the room. In fact, as best I could tell there was nothing; nothing to hear, nothing to see.

Wow, I thought.

There I was. Utterly and completely alone.

In total darkness.

Total silence.

I watched and watched as the darkness grew deeper and deeper. And deeper still.

The silence was deafening, too.

I waited and waited for something to happen.

Like something always did . . . eventually.

But, no.

Not this time.

This time, there was nothing.

Nada.

Not a sound.

I looked around for one last time, holding my breath as long as possible.

Nope. Still nothing.

I breathed out. A very heavy sigh of relief.

Makhan Singh to the Rescue

The darkness I found myself dissolved into was . . . very still.

I was liking it, alone there in the dark, wherever it was. The softness and silence of the place allowed me to drift over time as one does, you know, when one has found that spot, the sweet space in meditation where every thought, every distraction is gone and all that matters is the Now. That magical point where every sound, sight and feel in the universe comes to light all at once, especially in the darkness.

I was thoroughly enjoying it. Every sensation that had ever been, seemed to be flowing through me disinterestedly, spontaneously, and without effort.

It's going to be especially delicious here . . . in this perfect stillness, I thought.

The temperature's not too bad either. And the air smells good, too.

I was quite sure I'd be content there for quite some time.

Perhaps an eternity or two?

(After all, I'd earned some rest, hadn't I?)

Then, from out of nowhere, a spotlight popped down on me. It was bright and blinding. I covered my eyes up at the intrusion.

"What the hell?"

I wondered what was coming next.

Was I going to be interrogated?

I waited. Anticipating.

The silence, however, just kept lingering.

Oh my goodness, I thought, as I found myself hoping God wouldn't judge me too harshly.

The silence just seemed to linger . . . on and on.

Until, finally. . . .

"Aap Simryn ka chetha nahee reha?"

A man's voice sounded out from somewhere in the darkness.

What? I thought.

Who was that?

And why was he accusing me of forgetting my Simryn?

Just then, another spotlight popped on. It beamed down intensely only a few yards away from me. In it stood a tall, elderly man with a beige turban wearing a matching kurta and pajamas with red, black and gold mojan on his feet. He was leaning lightly on a cane. His long white beard shone around pink lips. His eyes sparkled as he smiled at me.

"Who are you?" I asked him.

"A storyteller."

"A storyteller? I thought you were here to interrogate me."

"Ah, sorry," the old man said. "I must have been caught up in the – uh, melodrama."

My eyes rolled up. Just what I needed, another ghost with an unlimited budget. "Okay, just try to keep special effects down to a few tasteful ones, will you? It'll be much more effective that way."

"I'll try."

"And I suppose your story has something to do with Simryn?"

"Ah!" he said, waving his finger at me.

"Right, I know, I know. I've got to listen."

He smiled.

I took in another deep breath.

And sighed.

He begins his tale:

"There was a war that was the beginning of many, many, many wars. It started a long, long time ago when a man thought that he had discovered the divine . . . and that's all I'm going to say about that."

"What? Well, that was quite short."

"What did you expect? It's filmi-noir. Oh, there's far more, but I feel it's more appropriate to show than to tell, don't you?"

"It's your story." I retorted.

He smirked.

I glared.

He raised one arm out in front of me. "Touch my sleeve."

"Your sleeve? You've got to be kidding."

"No, I am not kidding."

"Isn't all this just a little . . . cheesy?"

The old man smiled at me, apologetically. "Sorry."

I glared again.

He waved his arm in front of me one more time.

Great.

But what other choice did I have?

So, I touched it.

I wasn't prepared for what would happen next. Visions flashed past me fast. Existences. Journeys and their forks in the road. (You know, the usual). Then, time accelerated, faster and faster, until I began to feel a little sick.

Then, **BOOM!**

I admit it, I passed out.

When I came back around, I was in a place with bright sunshine and the birds were singing. I'd just realized I was in some kind of meadow when I felt a firm hand reach out and touch my shoulder. "Are you okay, Baeta?" the old man asked. I looked up. He was hovering above me, crouching down there in the grass next to me. I glared at him, as I rubbed my head.

"What was that? Chitty-Chitty-Bang-Bang?"

"I'm sorry, Baeta. I will try to be gentler next time."

The old man extends his arm to pull me up and I look around.

We're standing on a slight slope in some tall grass bordering a roadside. The land around us is quite flat with only a few rolling hills. And the day is extremely hot.

"What do you see here?" the man's voice asks.

"Just a long hot dusty road."

The man's voice grunts as he glances around. He taps the ground with his cane a few times, and suddenly we're surrounded by many people of all kinds. Both men and women. And children. Livestock, too. Horse-drawn wagons and bufflao-drawn carts carry families and their possessions. Some are riding, while others follow behind on foot. Some are Jaghirs, Subhedars, or Zamin wallae – politicians, soldiars, and landowners; others are mere servants and farm helpers. But they all have something in common, a sullen look of exile.

I covered my face up with a scarf against the dust as they passed us by. "What is this? Why are we here?" I asked the man.

He doesn't answer, but just keeps looking into the crowd. All around us goats are bleating. Cows moo. Children shout whine and cry.

Then, I saw her.

A dust-covered little girl wearing a dirty, worn sulvar kameez, was walking behind her mother, holding desperately onto the fabric of her dress, trying not to get lost. Her hair looks like it hasn't been combed in days. She turns her head and looks right at me. Her bright eyes nudged something inside me, a sense of familiarity. And, though she was definitely upset and bewildered, I saw a look of determination in her eyes.

"Wait, is that Simryn?" I asked the old man.

"No," he said, as he put out his arm.

I glared at him. My eyes demanded an answer, but I could see there would be none, so I reached out and touched his sleeve.

And, once again, we were gone.

I don't like talking about the next scene at all. Even as an experienced forensic scientist, I was deeply affected by the sights. The first thing I can remember is the horrid smell of bloated bodies in the heat. Honestly, I'd never seen the devastation of out-and-out war. I cursed the quiet wind that blew and stirred up the smell of death. I covered my face with my hands, shutting out the images of the lifeless, fly covered bodies around me. My legs buckled, and I found myself on the ground, retching. Then, I felt the old man's hand on my shoulder.

My heart lurched and thumped loudly.

"*Why* are we here?" I moaned as he helped me up to my feet. I remember every second of standing there among the decapitated and mutilated bodies. Nothing stirred, except the black flies that buzzed around them and landed on their gaping wounds.

"Why? There's nothing here. No hope at all. Nobody's left, only dead people."

The old man's eyes were stoic but not unsympathetic. "Please, be patient."

Then, I heard something. I didn't know what it was at first, but slowly it became clearer. It was the sound of a child crying out weakly somewhere nearby. My heart throbbed as my eyes darted around.

My gaze pierced the man. "There's a child alive in here somewhere. We've got to find it."

He didn't say a thing. He just bit his lip and nodded again, and took in the entire scene, until his gaze fixed itself in a particular direction. I turned to see what he was looking at. Then I spotted another, younger man in a dark blue turban and khaki uniform, making his way unsteadily through the carnage, and covering his face with a cloth, and heading toward the spot where it seemed most likely the cries were coming from.

"Oh, thank God," I said.

The man bends over and picks up the small child and straddles it on his hip. I peered in to get a closer look. It was the little girl I'd seen in the previous vision. I watched as the man tucks the frightened child's head against his shoulder and covered her face with the cloth that he'd used to cover his mouth and nose. He quickly carries the little girl back through the gauntlet of dead bodies. I catch my breath and turn to my guide. The old man stands, watching the scene, seeming unaware of my presence.

I caught his gaze.

"Who are you?"

"My name is Makhan Singh."

"Why are we here?"

After a long moment, he turned to me. He seemed tired, but managed a smile anyway. "All in good time, Baeta, all in good time."

With that, he held out his arm, and, one more time, we popped out of existence.

In the next scene, I found myself standing in a dark room with a window. Through it, I can see the moon hovering above the building across the street. Outside, silhouettes of people walk by in the night, and although it is dark, there is much loud talking and confusion. I looked over at elderly Makhan Singh, who was standing right next to me. The moon revealed some of his features.

"We're in Delhi," he says.

As my eyes adjusted to the dark room, I could see two cots placed on opposite sides. They're both occupied.

Makhan Singh speaks.

"The man decided to head to Delhi. During dangerous times, one meets many extraordinary people, and, thankfully, many of them were extraordinarily good. Throughout the journey the girl was very weak, but somehow he kept her alive. Because he had to, you see. She was all that kept him from succumbing.

"When they arrived in Delhi, they were among the hundreds of thousands of peoples displaced from their homes by the Partition. Fortunately, he found a place for them to stay quite soon, even though it was only a one-room hovel near a busy street. It was a palace compared to the conditions we had already lived through. Now, we had a safe enough place to live, and I could start to rebuild our lives from there."

I looked at him. "You. You were the one who rescued her."

"Haan," he said, confirming his slip.

Back on the cot in the dark room, the little girl whines in her sleep. She tosses and turns, then begins to struggle and thrash around. Finally, she bolts straight up.

"*Maaaaaaa!*" she screams.

From the other cot, the young Makhan Singh stumbles across the room. He finds the other cot and gathers the frightened child in his arms to comfort her.

The old Makhan Singh shook his head.

"That poor child had nightmares for a very long time. We all did, but her condition was worse. She didn't speak for a long, long time. I remember this room well. How I could see the moon and watch the people on the street. Most of the night I was alert, planning what I would do the next day. Who I would see about a job or our needs. It would seem that I'd just fall asleep and she'd wake up screaming. My heart would jump into my throat. With my eyes half closed I would find my way in the dark to her munji. She'd push at me and hit me very hard sometimes, but I'd hold her until she stopped struggling. There were many nights I'd fall asleep there with her."

"After much caring and gentleness, she did begin to speak, but it was clear she'd forgotten everything about who she was. The only time she 'remembered' anything was in her dreams. People shooting guns, running. Shouting. It didn't make sense to her. She didn't even know her own name. I'd been calling her 'baeta' ever since I found her. In my busy-ness, I didn't even think about it. Then, one day, I asked her if she wanted a name. She picked it herself. "Muna," she said, with such seriousness. I still can't help smiling. I asked her why she wanted to have that name. She didn't know. She just liked it, and I decided that it was good enough. I was without anyone and so was she. So, when I could afford it, I registered her for school as Munjinder Kaur, my daughter. And she, after seeing the example of all the students in her class, called me her Papa ji."

In the moonlight, I could see Makhan Singh's eyes glistening.

"It's time to go," he said.
He put out his arm.

In the next scene, we're standing on a very busy street. It's sunny and the mood of the day seems bright. Makhan Singh and I begin walking south down the street.

"Just a bit further, around the corner."

Soon, we came upon it. . . . An event. A street scene. We spot the young Makhan Singh playing an Indian flute with great fire and ability. Another man is sitting on the ground playing a dholki and singing. His voice sounds incredible. I see Muna, seven years old, singing and dancing. She smiles vivaciously, as her arms and legs fly about expertly. Her gestures are precise, her eyes expressive and charming. An audience stands around in a circle and watches, clapping in time and smiling. When she finishes her performance, the whole crowd applauds and Muna puts out her little pink scarf for people to put money in her choli. I had a good look at her. By now, she's become a sharp, intelligent, cunning young street hustler, and extremely determined.

The old man, Makhan Singh, is smiling quite brightly as he stands next to me.

"We made a nice life for ourselves in Delhi, you see. We had many friends there, people who didn't have a family or roots to go back to, other people like us. I remember how we all used to get together and play music. It would cheer our hearts. I was good at making flutes and playing them, and I had a friend, Abdul Khabir who played a dholki and sang. Such an avaaz he had. Our neighbors joined us with a few instruments or clapping and singing in chorus. Muna danced with some of the women, and we found she was very good. Her smile would melt anyone's heart. She was a great little performer. At the end Muna would walk around the circle holding out her little pink chuni. People would put a few annas in her choli, with which she bought food and items for children less fortunate. After her nightmares subsided, she had become a most cheerful child."

We watched and listened to the praise of the spectators. Finally, we watched as the young Makhan Singh picks Muna up, places her on his shoulder and they make their way home, chatting and smiling. I thought about how nice it must have been, and just how wonderful I'd felt on that summer vacation in Niagara Falls with my parents when I was five years old.

I sighed, deeply.

"Oh, she had such natural ability," the old man said, "and I began to wonder what kind of people she had come from. People here are very particular about that kind of thing, you know, which is why I never told anyone how I'd found Muna."

He put out his sleeve.

I listened one more time to the sounds of the happy, busy scene, before we began to dissolve once more, back into the shadows.

Now we're standing in what seems to be a sitting room. The younger Makhan Singh is older now, probably around forty. He's sitting next to another man around the same age. Across from them at that table sat another man and a woman.

The old Makhan Singh turned to me.

"By the time Muna was of marrying age, life was going quite well. I had my own business and Muna had completed her schooling. It was time to look for a life-partner for her. We had a comfortable but modest home, and I was connected well enough socially. A friend of mine told me of a family that had a son that would be suitable for my daughter."

We turned back to the scene, just as the young Makhan Singh began to speak to the couple.

"Yes, it is true that I've been both mother and father to her. My wife? *Absoss*, regretfully my wife died a few years after Munjinder was born. That was even before the war broke out. My daughter and I escaped with our lives and left everything else we had back in Lahore. Our land, her birth documents, everything we owned. It's been just father and daughter ever since then."

I turned back to Makhan Singh, feeling puzzled.

The old man glanced over at me, before returning his attention to the scene.

Just then, a young veiled woman walks into the room with a tea tray. She carries the chai tray with grace and sets it on the table between the four people, then walks back out of the room, quietly.

The man sitting next to Makhan Singh leans forward to the couple. "I think it will be an appropriate match. The girl's lineage and status appears to be equal to your dhan khani. I have seen her habits and abilities. She's educated. She can cook, clean, and she's very well spoken. She is also Makhan Singh's only child."

The elderly Makhan Singh pondered the scene, his voice sounding melancholy. . . .

"*Haan*, I remember thinking that all they could talk about was how well she would suit their son. No one talked about what they would offer her, or how they could make her happy. But I kept all this inside myself, thinking perhaps this was perhaps the best I could do. It'd work out, I told myself. I agreed to their modest-enough dowry request, and we spent the next two months in preparation.

"We had no family connections at all, just our friends. But we held the customary two weeks of celebration and invited all the friends we made in Delhi. Her girlfriends scrubbed Muna's arms and legs with turmeric on the days of her miya. They sang traditional bholian, danced, stained their hands with henna designs, and for two weeks people came and feasted."

Makhan Singh reaches for my hand again, as the world dissolves into images:

Women scrub turmeric on the mitiyar girl's arms and body. Henna designs on arms, hands, legs, feet. Dancing. Singing. Food and sweets. More singing and dancing for everyone except the bride. She watches as they celebrate.

Then, at last, the day comes.

She waits, dressed in red and gold.

The veiled groom arrives on a white horse.

The ceremony begins. They sit together for the first time.

Her father takes the end of the groom's long red scarf and puts the larh in his daughter's hands.

Four lavas.
The bride and groom exchange marigold garlands.
A shared cup of milk with jaggeree.
Her tearful father putting her in her dholi to journey to her "real home."
The nerves of the suhag rath, the wedding night.
Husband unveils his wife for the first time.
"Munjinder Kaur and Ranjit Singh. . . ."

A daughter is born. Another beautiful girl.
Sparkling eyes. Curious fingers and limber limbs.
Mother sings.
Baby laughs.

I found myself again, standing alone with the old man.

"They called her 'Roopa', and she was, as you see, a beautiful vision. She grew under the love and pride of her mother and her family. She learned to walk and began to run around the house. And, just like her mother, she danced like a mischievous cherub. I remember how she smiled when I came to visit. Everything was good at last. I thought I'd finally succeeded in rebuilding our lives."

The vision of Muna and the baby dissolved into the darkness. Only Makhan Singh and I remained now, standing alone in our respective spotlights. I looked at him, as he leaned heavily against his cane. He hesitated a long moment before he spoke again. . . .

"One day, my Muna's nightmares returned. I don't know why. She never told me. The pieces of the life I had constructed for her fell apart. Ranjit Singh was very concerned, but the rest of his family were suspicious. There was nothing he could do. Munjinder's background, her lineage was . . . "questionable." When I went to see them and tried to do something, anything, about the situation, Muna's mother-in-law turned and railed angrily at Muna's father-in-law. She screamed on and on about how she could be anyone's child. She even voiced her suspicion about a man and an orphan girl's possible relationship."

Makhan Singh stops and looks at me.

"I have no reason left to tell any lies from where I am now, so you see the truth as it was. My Muna was a beautiful child, and that weak, frightened child had given me hope. In return, I nurtured her and gave her a life, and in that way, I found mine. As a woman, she had attributes most other women envied. She was smart and resourceful. She brought such joy things into her in-law's home. But it didn't matter after that day, she was returned home to me with Roopa. No amount of talk or gifts of money could change their minds. My grief was heavy. I thought I'd done the best thing for her. Truthfully, however, I can't say I was entirely sad. No, I was angry. How dare they treat my daughter as if she was suddenly 'blemished'? How were they damaged? They didn't deserve her—nor my beautiful granddaughter. Their son didn't have as much character in his whole body as Muna had in her umgali, her finger, and I told her that many times."

"But Muna grew bitter and angry from the loss of her husband. She had fits and blamed me, her old father, for everything. As the years went on, and I grew older, her anger gave way to depression, and she was often hospitalized. I went to see her when I could, but I was left to raise Roopa on my own. Roopa also was a brilliant child. There were times when I felt lost and broken over Muna's condition. Then Roopa would come sit in my lap and put her arms around my neck. '*Nana ji*,' she'd say, 'I want to *dance*. Play your flute for me.' As much as my heart wasn't in it, it would eventually cheer me. Slowly, we returned to a somewhat-normal life. I worked to raise Roopa and put her through school. She had a keen interest in dancing and the world was settling down more. I paid for all the dance lessons she desired. Then, when she was sixteen, she wanted me to take her to Bombay to become a dancer in the surging Bollywood film industry."

"By then, Muna had become a permanent patient in the hospital. She was too immobilized by anger and fear to care if I came or went. So, after much persuasion, I agreed and took Roopa to Mumbai. We found a nice little apartment close by the studios and lived modestly. Those days reminded me a little of my earlier days with Muna. I went with Roopa when she auditioned for dance troupes. She immediately caught the eye of many directors, choreographers, actors and production managers. They all wanted to give her parts in their movies, front and center in the dance troupes. There was talk that she could be in line for bigger dance parts, maybe even a female lead someday. She got bigger and better dance roles all the time, sometimes working in three movies at the same time. Soon, she was making enough money to have her own apartment and an agent to take care of her needs. Despite my better judgment, I let her persuade me to go back to Delhi. I had wanted to go anyway. I was missing Muna, and from what I'd learned in a friend's letter, she was deteriorating."

"It was during the shooting of her fifteenth minor movie role that she met him, the young, handsome and debonair, your would-be director Rajesh Sharma. It was love at first sight, and the first time for her. It would also be the end of her career. That was when Simryn was born. She had a determined little cleft in her chin, just like her grandmother's, and when I was anywhere near her, she'd always look up at me and laugh or goo-goo contently.

"You see, Rajesh fell head over heels in love with Simryn, just like with every child that came before and after her. Everything Rajesh loved was inappropriate. Everything he loved was something that his image, his status or his wife, Sheila, took away from him."

Just then, Makhan Singh glanced to his left. Another light appeared right beside him. A woman, sitting on a hospital bed, appeared in it. Makhan Singh looked at her, a little stoically at first, then just a touch of a smile appeared on his face. He hobbled over to the woman and sat down on the bed next to her. She looked up at me. The dark circles under her eyes made the whites of her eyes stand out, but her skin was fair, and still quite beautiful, despite her age.

"This is my Muna. She is much older now," he said.

He put his arm round her shoulder.
She turned to face him.

Makhan Singh finishes with his story.
"When Simryn was a baby, I took her to see her grandmother.

Muna was known for her outbursts, and the doctors warned me about letting her hold Simryn. But when she saw her, Muna held her arms out for the child. I couldn't deny her that. She spent the whole time kissing and cooing her. She'd been deteriorating, despite everyone's efforts, and so I took Simryn a few more times after that. But there was nothing anyone could do. Muna died when Simryn was almost three months old.

"When Simryn was two, Roopa married her Amar Singh Gill. He was a fine man. He showed a lot of pride and interest in all of Simryn's successes. She loved science, history and mathematics. He bought her a magnifying glass and as a toddler she used to go about the house inspecting every little thing. When she got older, she wanted a chemistry set, which Amar gladly bought her. She'd spend days looking through the microscope at everything from dirt to bugs. And she had that one thing in common with both Roopa and Muna, she loved to dance. Especially for me, her old Nana ji.

"When Sinryn was seven years old, Wahe Guru called me home. After I was gone, there was no one to encourage her to dance, except Rajesh, who only came by about once a year on her birthday. So, as Simryn grew, she forgot about dancing. She was in her first year at college when Rajesh asked her to audition for that film."

I stood watching the two of them as Makhan Singh and Muna rocked gently in each other's arms.

Father comforting daughter.

Daughter comforting Father.

Yeah, I thought, I guess there were always the little things. . . .

Smiles.

Tears.

Words.

Sighs.

Makhan Singh looks over at me. "You know, Rajesh was a rascal, but he had a good heart. In spite of his mistakes, he always tried to do what he could to fix them."

Suddenly, all the spotlights popped off, and Makhan Singh and Munjinder were gone.

Just. Like. That.

I'm all alone in the dark again.
'What was that for?' I asked myself.

Then**—BOOM!—**I'm somewhere else.

This time, I recognized the place. I was standing out in front of Laila and Harshad's apartment in Navi Mumbai. I looked at the traffic in the road and the people on the street, felt the cool warm air on my body. I looked down at myself. Yes, I did have my own body back. But the strange thing was I had on that same sari that I'd worn at the Bollywood festival that night in New York; the white, pink and blue one with the gold svastik embroidery.

I was puzzled.

I won't kid you, I was glad to have my body back. But why now? And *why* was I wearing that sari? What did it mean? I decided to go for the obvious. Go inside and talk to Laila and Harshad, then get in touch with Beeji and the Nomads so I could figure out my next move.

I walked up to the entrance of the apartment building and punched in Laila and Harshad's code, and waited.

Almost immediately, Harshad's voice came over the speaker-phone:

"Elanna, get in here. Quick."

My heart began to thump loudly.

I swung open the glass door, as he buzzed me in, and made a dash for the elevator, and hit the UP arrow a bunch of times. Harshad's voice had been urgent. Something strange must be going down. My nerves were edgy. When the elevator doors finally opened up, I barged through them and immediately hit the '5' button. I was concentrating on slowing and controlling my breath, trying to maintain some poise in this baffling situation.

The numbers above the elevator doors lit up. . . .

One.

Two.

Three.

Four.

Five.
Stop!
I squeezed through as soon as the doors began to open. Harshad was already standing in the hallway, waiting for me, holding open the door to their apartment. He yanked me into the suite, roughly, by the arm as soon as I reached him, and slammed the door tight behind us. He shook me.

"Elanna, near the entrance of our building, did you see anyone? Was anyone there?"

"What? No!"

"For the past several months, the whole Mumbai chapter has been under seige. We've been very heavily attacked on many levels. We're doing all we can to cloak ourselves and blend into the woodwork. Appearing out in the open the way you just did could prove very dangerous to us."

I looked at his face. I'd never seen Harshad so edgy. A bolt of fear and dismay shot through me, as I wondered if something might have happened to Laila.

Harshad put a finger to his lips. "Don't you even dare *think* about her."

That's when I realized.

Damn.

It was me!

I'd blown their cover.

Harshad dragged me, unceremoniously, into their guest room. He shut the door behind us and stared at me hard. "The dark ones will be looking for you, and I definitely don't want them to find you in our house, so hide in here; I'll go try to find Laila."

Then he dashed out of the room, full of urgency.

Hide, did he say? But where? I looked around for a place. In the closet? No, too confining. Under the bed. Yes. That would do. I grabbed the black quilt with the embroidered peacock from on top of the bed and pulled it on around me to conceal, as best I could, my bright white, pink and blue sari with the golden svatsik. Then, I dropped to the ground, slithered under the bed, and curled my legs up into my chest in a fetal position. I focused intently. After a time, I thought I could hear otherworldly sounds coming up the elevator shaft from the lower floors of the building.

Knocking

(Voices)

Shouting

(Feet running up stairs)

The guest-bedroom door flies open.

(Four dark figures entering the room.)

Then, I passed out.

I floated for a time in a darkness; then I began to see visions. Faces hovered above me in the room, and I could hear hoards of angry beings. I saw and heard all their thoughts. Inwardly, I knew all their motives. Every being was like a bubble, and, as I passed through each bubble and came out the other side, I knew all their guilt and their innocence, and each time I wondered if this would be the one that destroyed me. I felt savagely drained by each experience, but I could see no other choice; so I continued, passing through being after bubble-being. Each had a face that seemed clearer and clearer to me as I passed through it. I traveled through face after face, another after another, until all the faces finally began to blur. When I could no longer distinguish one face from another and each being I encountered seemed to have the same face as the last, I began to feel the pain of each face, searing me continuously. How long could I go on? I'd only heard four pairs of footsteps enter the room, but, by now, I was sure, I must have walked through many thousands of faces.

Then, just when it seemed as if I'd passed through the face of every possible being in all the universes, I finally fell down. I collapsed; I lay there, utterly exhausted, but still wriggling around impotently. Then, as I struggled to get to my feet, I saw something new. On the ceiling, in the corner of the room, a black mist was hovering above us, in a vague shape. Startled, I jumped up and realized immediately that I was surrounded. Now, everywhere I turned, above, below, left, right, there was nothing but black mist. I put my hand to my throat. I was choking. I tried to cry out for strength and struggled to breathe, but the mist was sapping my energy. My spirit was waning. It would soon be too late, I thought, and within this vision, I could see no escape; so I gave up. I gave in. I accepted my impermanence.

Then

KABOOM!

Three flashes of light manifested in front of me and blew the dark mist away. I looked up. As the lights emanated intense energy, the dark mist began to dissipate. Slowly, I started to feel strengthened and healed. I tried to see what the lights were, but I couldn't tell. All I knew was their benevolent glow. My body, mind, and spirit lifted and relaxed. I could sense the multiverses expanding. They grew and grew and grew. When everything had grown as large as possible, it all began to deflate again, like a balloon. The contraction accelerated and continued to accelerate, until, suddenly, it collapsed into a single, subatomic particle.
Then

TH-WUMP!

"*Now* what. . . ?"

When my eyes reopened, I was in a green meadow. A blue sky stretches overhead. The air smells clean and breezy. I notice I'm sitting on a swing hung from a huge old oak tree. I feel the texture of the braided rope in my hands and smell the hemp it's made of. I look out around me at the flowers by a stream, decorating a nearby hillside. I feel my feet on solid ground. I use them to push myself on the swing a little, enjoying the gentle movement. I close my eyes and take in the warm, spring air. It was obviously too good to be true. But, oh well. . . .

I imagined I heard a mandolin playing, with notes as quick and plucky as the day. A long baritone note played by a flute sailed by.

I lean into the swing, pump my legs.

I want to soar and meet the sky.

I pump harder, and faster.

A dhol player suddenly appears on the ground in front of me, keeping rhythm with me as I push up and pull back. I get higher and higher, then, when I'd gotten just about as high as I could, I could feel hands behind me, helping, pushing me even higher. I looked back.

It's Sanjay.

He's laughing, and singing an old, Indian nursery rhyme:

> *Choothae, Mathae*
> *Umb Pakhae*
> *Carboojae Katchae*
>
> ------
>
> *Swinging on a swing*
> *The mangos are ripe*
> *Cantaloupes are not*

I turned around to see Rakhi's brown toes pointing out in front of me, reaching up into the crystal blue sky.

Then, Sanjay begins to spin the nursery rhyme into a new tune of his own:

> *Mere dil diya Rani*
> *Mere sawadh mitti banni*
> *Je thoom na hai –Tho–meinu makhan jasa dhil kethon*
> *mil na si?*
>
> ------
>
> *You are the Queen of my Heart*
> *You are my sweet song*
> *If you did not exist*
> *How would I have this heart of sweet butter?*

Now, I hear Rakhi's voice singing out in response from inside of me:

> *Meinu chooth nayhi bolina atha ha*
> *Qiyoo shoti moti dook sathatae ha*
> *Ma nahi qoyi Rani ja banni ha*
> *Man Makhan ki dhil kasi banathi ha?*
> ------
> *I am not in the habit of lying*
> *Why, the smallest hurts make me sad*
> *I am not a Queen, nor a sweet song*
> *How can I make anyone's heart turn to sweet butter?*

When his turn comes up again, Sanjay sings out once more with great passion:

> *Tu ha mere Chandari*
> *Tu ha mere Suraj*
> *Tu ha mere Poorab aur Putcham,*
> *Tu ha jo ha mere jan*
> *Je thoom na ho THO meinu makhan jasa dhil kethon mil*
> *na si?*
> ------
> *You are the moon*
> *You are the Sun*
> *You are East and West*
> *You are what is, my soul*
> *If you did not exist*
> *How would I have this heart of sweet butter?*

'Oh brother!' I thought.

I was thankful when the song was over. Sanjay had stopped pushing me by now, and the swing was beginning to slow down, when I felt vigorous hands behind me, and suddenly, the sky lurched up in front of me again. I looked over my shoulder. It's Ricky. His strong arms are lifting me higher and higher. But there's no smile on his lips, no joy in his eyes. And he's not singing.

Why *not?* I wonder.

What's wrong?

Doesn't he like to sing? Is he the only Indian person in the whole world who can't carry a tune?

I let go of the swing, flew off into the sky, and, as the wind whistled around me, I turned my head to look back. I could still see Rakhi swinging on the swing, with Sanjay pushing her. But Ricky's no longer there. He's gone.

Sanjay starts to sing again.

> *Tu ha mere dil diya Rani*
> *Tu ha mere sawadh mitti banni*
> *Thoom ho–tho–mere makhan jasa dhil ha mila*
>
> ------
>
> *(You are the Queen of my Heart*
> *You are my favorite song*
> *Because you exist–that's–how I have a sweet heart like butter.)*

The song faded, as I flew further and further away, across valleys filled with harvest, cantaloupes, watermelons, wheat and vegetables. People dressed in colorful clothes are singing and dancing after a plentiful harvest. I kept flying over the mountains, over many lands and a vast, vast ocean. It seemed endless. Finally, I saw land, but I don't stop flying. Then, I reached a huge range of mountains, cresting far beyond my vision, high up in the sky. I veer up and go over them. On the other side are deep, lush valleys, vast acres of trees, and bountiful, wide meadows.

Then, I found it.

A field of buttercups. No, not just any field of buttercups; the perfect field of buttercups. I descended from the sky to land on solid ground and looked all around me. There was nothing but quietude, punctuated with the sound of birds and the breeze rustling the tall grasses. Butterflies and bees fluttered and buzzed from flower to flower.

I took in a deep, soothing breath and held it for a long time. I couldn't believe the huge sky above me, the huge expanse of space with not a soul close by. But the most beautiful thing was the rolling, yellow blanket of buttercups. That did me in. I shuddered and a tear rolled down my cheek.

I promised myself, one day, I would return to that place.

Then, suddenly. . . .

AR-R-R-A-A-A-A-N-N-N-N-N-N-G-G-G-G-G-GG!!

I'm jarred awake by the sound of an alarm clock.

I opened my eyes, and looking around, I found myself once more, back in Rakhi's bachelorette apartment. I rolled over on the bed. Then I heard Sanjay's familiar snoring in Rakhi's living room on the other side of the partition. Oh, thank goodness, I thought. At least, I was back somewhere that made *some* sort of sense. I got up, pulled a blanket on around me, and walked into the bathroom. Then, I turned on the light, and looked up into the mirror.

> Rakhi's standing there, gazing back at me.
> She smiles widely.
> "Hello. It's good to see you."
> I stare.
> Ah, it's good to see you too, Rakhi.
> "So-o-o. . . ."
> So what?
> "So, tell me something . . . who was that other guy pushing you on the swing?"
> You and I had the same dream?
> "Yes."
> Oh? Well, okay, that was Ricky. Rakesh Chandra is his real name . . . but all his friends call him Ricky.
> "'Rakesh', huh? And what do *you* call him? Your most precious jhan chand piyara dearest?"

No, Rakhi, it's not like that, we're just friends.

Rakhi shakes her head, vigorously.

"Nuh-uh-uh!"

What?

What are you trying to tell me, Rahki?

But Rakhi says nothing more. She only smiles back at me, knowingly, from the mirror.

Rita: The Truth

Six nights a week for the past three years, the jazz-raga-fusion singer Meghana Prasad, and her band, have entertained in the smoky lounge of the Roshan Asima, an exclusive members-only club and restaurant on the southwestern outskirts of Mumbai. Many of the Bollywood elite wile away hours there, being soothed by her smooth voice as they await tables, or the arrival of guests. At this moment, the band is nearing the end of their first set.

Meghana cradles the microphone in her left hand, standing center-most on the small, dim spotlit stage; she's looking sultry tonight, with her backing band now sounding the opening strains of yet another steamy ballad. Her pink lipsticked mouth puckers up, and after a few bars she raises the mic, waiting for her moment. On the last beat of the twelfth bar, she enters in.

Kiss-kiss-kiss
Kiss me all day long

I long for you in the morning
And all day long

Kiss kiss kiss

(A saxophone echoes the dreamy, dramatic melody.)

Sunset is my savior
For I know my love will be savored

Kiss kiss kiss

(The curvaceous brass horn squeals and calls out)

Kiss kiss kiss
Kiss kiss kiss me all day lo-o-o-o-o-o-o-ong

Meghana hits and holds a high note. Her breath is calm and smooth. Her dynamics are under control as the saxophone sails across the room with her; two lovers in a passionate and forbidden embrace.

They don't want to.

But they can't help it.

So they. . . .

Doooooo wap-wap-wap!

Across the room, Rakhi's sitting in a corner booth with Johnny Akkarah. She's decked out in a brand new evening sari from one of the finest boutiques in Mumbai.

She glances up at Meghana. "That singer, she's not bad."

Johnny, cool as ever, wearing his dark sunglasses even in the half-light of the lounge, says nothing. He takes an expressionless drag on his cigarette. "You think so? Seems to me like if she were any good, she'd be more than just a lounge singer by now."

Rakhi smirks.

As if responding to Rakhi's insight, Meghana sparkles.

> *Kiss kiss kiss*
> *Ooooh, I don't want the spotlights*
> *Don't wan' a million hearts' delights*
> *I just want you to hold me each and every night*

Her eyes go out to Johnny as she steps down off the stage. Behind her the saxophone is still crying out, warning her, pleading with her to come back, but she just keeps on strutting. She walks right up behind Johnny and taps him on the shoulder. He bolts up, removing his sunglasses with one deft motion before he spins around, ready for anything.

Meghana just smiles, as she lifts his chin up with a finger and looks deep into his eyes.

> *Oh, oh what I'd give*
> *What I'd sacrifice*
> *Just to feel your body next to me, loving me tonight*
>
> *Kiss kiss kiss. . . .*

A titillated piano tinkles.

. . . and the disembodied saxophone gives it one last, desperate try, before fading away.

(Spurned.)

Now, Meghana takes a single step back, while raising one arm up in confession, as Johnny just sits there, basking in her glow.

> *Kiss-kiss-kiss*
> (*lallalooloolalallooo*. The lonely saxaphone sighs)
> *Kiss-kiss-kiss*
> (*hissity-hissity-hiss*. The high hat spits)

Kiss-kiss-kiss
(*ba ba ba ba ba booo-ooom-mmm.* The tom-toms solo)
Kiss-kiss-kiss
(*binnnnmg.* A tiny triangle thrills)
Kiss kiss . . . kiss-s-s-s-s-s-s

Kiss kiss . . . kiss-s-s-s-s-s-s

Kiss kiss . . . kiss-s-s-s-s-s-s

Kiss kiss . . . kiss-s-s-s-s-s-s

It goes on and on.

Until finally, Meghana's voice walks away like a whisper, as the song closes.

A long moment of silence followed.

Then. . . .

. . . clap clap . . . **clappity clap clapclapclappity clap** . . . clap clap. . . .

A light scattering of applause floats across the room, mingling in, here and there, with the quiet levels of conversation, and barely audible above them.

Unflappably, Meghana saunters back to the stage, where she flashes a wide and appreciative grin. "Shookhria. Meribhani. Thank you! I'll be back right after I get my break."

FRIDAY, 8:43 P.M.
Johnny had shown up at Rakhi's apartment, promptly at six that evening, all dressed to the nines in an easy, minimal, moody black turtleneck with matching pants, and a brand new silver-gray jacket. He'd

brought Rakhi here in a vintage, yellow Lamborghini Aventador coupe tonight, instead of driving his beloved, baby-blue Cadillac pimp-mobile. Clearly, he was eager to impress. We'd arrived at the Roshan Asma right around 7:30, and, ever since then, we'd been waiting expectantly in the lounge, eager to be summoned by whomever it was that Johnny had arranged for Rakhi to meet that evening.

As we waited, Johnny was becoming even more nervous. All evening long, his eyes had darted around behind his dark sunglasses. Indeed, he wasn't even noticing any of the pretty girls, whose gaze might happen to linger on him as she walked by.

Now, he fidgets with his cigarette, anxiously.

Rakhi clears her throat.

Johnny starts to look at her, then he glances around, pretending to be intrigued by some other minor event somewhere else in the room.

Just then, the hostess walked over to our table.

"Ah, sir, yes, Ms. Chawla will see you now."

Ooooh. Rita Chawla, just as I suspected. Be careful, Rakhi, Rita Chawla's the one I've been warning you about. Remember what I've been telling you, and be very cautious.

Huh? Kiya?

Weren't you listening to me this afternoon? Rita Chawla is an extremely powerful and dangerous woman—and whatever you do, don't lock gazes with her. Don't look her in the eyes.

Oh, stop worrying so much. Whoever she is, I can handle her.

Sacred Mother, I thought, boy, is she ever overconfident.

Yes, and thank you for that vote of confidence, now would you please stop bothering me?

The hostess led us through the dimly lit dining area. Large windows along the walls reflected the likenesses of people as they dine in their cozy candlelit settings. Outside, beyond their reflections, lay a magnificent view of the city lights dotting the night-scape. The lights of a few boats and ships blinked as they moved slowly through the harbor.

In the furthest corner I could see Rita Chawla reflected in the window. As we got closer I saw she was engaged in a conversation with a man and a woman standing at her table. They were absorbed in conversation, but it was hard to make them out clearly. Rita made a dismissive gesture with her finger and the pair relaxed. They unfroze. They began to fidget and shift around.

I recognized the man.

Rakhi, that's Asif Salam, the actor who portrayed Vinod Kumar in Meri Dil. . . ."

Yes, I know who he is. Who's the woman?

At that moment, perhaps by serendipity, Salam stepped aside so I could get a good look at his female companion.

Oh my goodness, Rakhi, that's Lila, Karishma's so-called image consultant. What's she doing here? Be very careful with her, too.

Rakhi rolls her eyes.

Give it a rest, will you?

Okay, *don't* listen to me, then. See where it gets you. . . .

As we approach her table, Rita looks up. Her reflected gaze in the window meets ours just for a moment. As Johnny greets Rita and Asif Salam, as the maitre d' pulls out a chair for Rakhi. Once everybody's settled, he informs us that our waiter will be with us shortly, and takes his leave.

Meanwhile, Rakhi gets her first long look at Rita.

She certainly appears elegant and sophisticated in that sari, even if it is at least a decade too young for her.

Clearly, Rita hadn't changed much.

Don't let appearances fool you, Rakhi. Don't let her take you by surprise.

Ji. I have her M.O.

I could feel Rita's presence. Her command. Chin tilted upward. Features sharp. Her eyes move expertly. Taking it all in. Examining everything and everyone.

As she continued her muted conversation with Asif Salam, I studied her lavender-colored sari. Its intricate burgundy and black, vine and leaf design enhanced her still-striking form. A gold pendant hung about her neck. It's rich, old-world design was veiled, tactfully, by the pallu of the sari. Her long hair was up in a chignon, the same elegant style she'd worn at the Bollywood Festival in New York. At that point, Rakhi took in a deep breath, and I inhaled some of Rita's exotic perfume.

I had to admit she looked beautiful, and yes, elegant and sophisticated. I studied the way she interacted with Salam with her small and
barely-detectable, but poignant gestures. The quiet way she conversed;
the spark that revealed so much.

"... but now, my dear Asif, I have some other business to attend
to, so we'll have to continue our dinner conversation later. Please, be
sure to call me."

The actor hesitates. Then, a smile pours over his handsome lips.
His eyes linger on her.

"Thank you, Ma'am. I will await your call."

Catch that?

Yeah. Like 'get a room.'

Asif shakes hands with Johnny and their gazes lock. He smiles at
Rakhi as he put his palms together in 'namaste.' Before Asif walks
away, he casts Rita one final, long and lingering glance.

I don't know what it is, Rakhi, but when I saw him at the festival
in New York, he wasn't so . . . vacant.

Never mind that, did you catch the way Johnny's acting around her?

I watch as Johnny stares blankly at Rita.

Yeah. There was something going on all right.

Rita tilts her head towards Lila. Lila had seemed edgy the
whole time, and I wondered why. She clears her throat abruptly before
she speaks.

"Yes, in any case, ma'am, I will carry on and get going on the
plans we've been discussing. Call me if you need any help."

Rita seemed suddenly impatient. "Yes, and thank you, Lila. We'll
talk later."

After Lila walks away, Rita eyes Rakhi intently. She looked her
up-and-down.

"Hmmm. So Johnny, this is one of your promising, up-and-
coming young starlets, am I right?"

Johnny's attention snaps back.

"Oh, yes, that's right."

He clears his throat.

"Rita, I'd like you to meet Rakhi Chand.

"Rakhi, Ms. Rita Chawla."

Rita nods and looks into Rakhi's eyes.

(I looked away.)

"A-hem," Johnny coughs. "Ah, Rakhi's already making quite a splash on the Bollywood dance scene."

"Oh, yes. So I've heard. She's won a leading role in a dancing movie that's due to come out next summer, is that correct?"

Rakhi puts her palms together. "Namaste. It's a pleasure to meet you, Mrs. Chawla."

Rita's eyebrow arched. "Well, Johnny, she is well-mannered. Her English sounds impeccable too. Can she also speak Hindi?"

Rakhi smiles. "Hanji. Mein Hindi, Punjabi, Urdu, Gurjarati aur Tagalore bhi bholti hoo."

Rita's tone holds a smirk. "Hah. Teek ha. It does help if one has command of various desi languages and dialects, but, as Johnny alluded to, they say you're actually a dancer, and as such, you shouldn't expect to get too many speaking parts in films."

"She's hoping to eventually appear in acting roles as well," Johnny retorts, with a touch of timidity.

Rita blinks, looking slightly bored. "Well, my dear Johnny, that may be a longer road than expected. I heard about the scene at Mr. Balru's dance studio earlier this week. Ms. Chand will have to realize that to get a starring role in films, a woman needs softness, femininity, allure. Those are the qualities that will endear someone to the acute sensibilities of the Indian public. She needs to become much more refined and subtle. . . like my Karishma."

Her gaze narrows.

"Perhaps, Ms. Chand, you'd eventually be better suited for the 'second female' type of role. You know, a character part. Of course, those roles require quite a bit more than merely being multilingual and being able to dance well, but admittedly, you are uncommonly beautiful and do have a certain . . . how shall I say this–a certain overt and aggressive presence? You might have enough sex appeal, therefore, to be suitable for that sort of role. Do you know what I mean? The 'bad girl' roles. The woman who titillates all the men. Helen's 'dance of the wanton woman' characters in any number of nightclub scenes, for in-stance. Or the tossed-in nach-girl parts in so many, many movies. Yes, you might do well as that stock character, the woman who always goes too far and, regretfully, but also repeatedly, gets what she deserves. . . ."

You're right. She's a real bitch.

Told you.

Rita leans back.

"Now, let me tell you how it really is, Baetee. The Indian public are fickle, and they love to heap praise on their good girls. But the reality? They all secretly come to be entertained by the sultry, sexy bad girls. Of course, they won't ever admit it, but we desis know our sex-appeal and only want to see the best and hottest women in those roles."

"So what, or whom, must one do to become one of those 'best and hottest' women, Mrs. Chawla?" Rakhi asks.

Rita's eyes widen. Mockingly, she turns wide-eyed to look at Johnny. "Oho! She is a bold one, isn't she?"

Rakhi leans forward and looks straight into Rita's eyes.

"Excuse me, ma'am, but Johnny does not represent me. Nor am I one of his 'wannabe girls.' He offered to introduce me to you and that's all. So, please, when I am in the room, address me directly."

Ooooooooch!

Rita glares at Rakhi for a moment. Then, she looks away.

"All right Miss Chand. Let me put it to you as clearly as I can. If you want to be one of the best and hottest, I suggest you learn how to exude a – a certain advanced sense of sensuality. If you want to be a Bollywood bad girl, you'd better learn the simple truth that there are some things you cannot always fake. Remember, it's not just what you know. . . ."

Rakhi and Rita's eyes meet. Their gazes lock.

I could hear the hissing, the rising, the. . . .

Rakhi, don't do that, look the other way!

Stay *out* of it.

"Very well. As you say, Mrs. Chawla, who then will I have to 'get to know'?"

Rita blinked. "My dear, I said nothing like. . . ."

"No, of course not. You wouldn't. No one ever does."

Rita sits back in her seat, arms crossed and pondering, until, finally, she speaks up. "The unfortunate fact, my dear, is that you're right, that is the reality of Bollywood. Of course, if you think about it from a director's point of view, why would he take a chance on untried talent? How can he be sure of what you could deliver onscreen?"

"How many wrinkled old producers, stars or directors did your daughter have to, you know, 'get to know' before she broke in to the business?"

That did it.

Rita's cool demeanor cracks; her eyes widen.

"No-no-no, my dear child! You have to understand, Karishma's case is entirely different. She has a great deal of training. She also has the history, the Bollywood lineage and pedigree. You see, I acted in films myself when I was young, and Karishma's father was a business-man and a prominent financier of films and other such ventures. My daughter lives and breathes the same air as the greatest actors of our time, and has done since she was very young."

. . . and yet, she still can't act.

Touché.

Rita's eyes flash even wider, trying to penetrate Rakhi.

Rakhi shrugs it away. She's not having any of it.

"Mrs. Chawla, the best and worst kept secret in the entertain-ment industry is that unknowns, those new to the industry, have to 'pay their dues.' But make no mistake, I am not like most of those kaboothri's. I'm not some naive pigeon. I don't have any desire to sell myself out or play snakes and ladders games on Bollywood casting couches. You see, I don't really need any of this."

Rita purses her lips.

Rakhi holds her head high.

Johnny sits between them, nervous as hell.

After a long silence, Rita finally speaks. "Yes. I see where you're coming from. I can understand how most young hopefuls come with such ideals. You're new to this business, Miss Chand, and, at first, everyone thinks they can make it on their own. Many, many like you come here to gain their fortune, many of them without lineage or appropriate background. They just pop out of thin air and then disap-pear just as quickly, like little flashes in the frying pan, so to speak. Let me tell you my dear: few, if any, succeed for very long, very few indeed."

She sighs. Resignedly.

"Paar, certainly, if you feel you can accomplish something without any help from me, or anyone else apart from that inexperienced manager of yours. What's his name, Deepa?"

"Deera."

"Yes, yes, of course, my dear, 'Deera'. Well then, all I will say for now is . . . *bonne chance*, good luck."

Rakhi smiles, as she meets Rita's gaze again. "I have something better than luck, Mrs. Chawla. It's called 'a destiny'."

Rita's eyes are blazing like hellfire.

I could feel it, her gaze trying to penetrate me. A sound like. . . . Like . . . ? Sensations. Everything dissolving. Another plane. An empty plane. Another sound, a sound like. . . .

"Opho, snap the hell out of it."

TH-W-A-C-K!

My consciousness snapped back into the room.

Thanks.

Don't mention it.

I looked back over at Rita. The fire in her eyes had cooled somewhat, but now her lips were curling up into an unsightly snarl.

"You may have a destiny, Miss Chand. But you'll never be like my Karishma. You'll never be a good girl."

Rakhi blinks. Unmoved.

Rita goes on. ". . . and just who the hell are you, anyway? No one here in Bollywood ever even heard of you before your big coup on Bollywood Storm. Just where did you come from? The fact is, my dear, that even now, none of us have any idea what kind of rock you might have crawled out from under."

The silence that followed lingered. I noticed Johnny had slunk way down in his chair. He seemed shaky, out-of-place, as if he were wishing, desperately, to be someplace else, anyplace else. I didn't blame him. Neither of these women was giving an inch.

Finally, Rita's demeanor softened. She unfolded her hands in front of herself and, once again, smiled a large, warm and welcoming smile.

I didn't like the looks of that.

"Oh well, choro gaal, let it go. Let's just agree to disagree, shall we Ms. Chand? We are in the same business after all, and we'll likely be seeing each other around. So, we ought to try not to harbor any ill feelings, don't you agree? I'll tell you what, I'm throwing a party for my daughter Karishma tomorrow evening. It's the annual bash for her birthday. I know this won't be much notice but, still, I'd like to extend to you a special invitation. Please come! This event will give you a chance to make some connections, mingle a bit, as they say."

Rakhi nods.

"Yes. Thank you. I'd be delighted to come, Mrs. Chawla."

". . . Rita."

"Rita, very well. Thank you."

"You're more than welcome. And, by the way, please bring Sanjay. It would be so nice to see both brothers in the same room again."

I could feel Johnny becoming even more tense.

"I'm sorry – ah – Rita, but I prefer to keep my business and personal relationships separate."

Rita raises one eyebrow. "Very well. Whatever. Bring whomever you wish, then."

The waiter reappears at our table. After he places their drinks before them, Rita raises her wineglass.

"To good girls," she says.

"To destiny," Rakhi replies, as she takes a long sip of her deep, red wine.

To Simryn.

The drive home was extremely quiet, at first, with Rakhi watching the Lamborghini's headlights revealing the road as Johnny spun in and out of traffic. The Mumbai evening air was warm, so Johnny had taken the top down. The wind was whipping through Rakhi's long black hair. However, I could tell something was wrong. Johnny seemed . . . tense; he wasn't his usual cool and arrogant self.

A few miles further down the highway, Johnny speaks up. "Let's face it, Rakhi, you are either a very brave woman, or a very foolish one."

Rakhi looks over at him. "Whatever do you mean, Johnny-bhai?"

He glances disdainfully in her direction. The moon reveals his handsome face. He sneers and returns his gaze to the road.

But he couldn't keep it in.

Five minutes down the road, he bursts forth, spewing out angry words:

"WOW, you know? It's like you're really not afraid—'of anyone'–'or anything'—at all, ever.

"Aapda koyi paravaha ni ha? Aren't you ever concerned for your own safety?

"Like—what? Are you crazy or somethin' . . . ?"

Rakhi's gaze is cool. "What is it you think I need to be afraid of, Johnny Bhai?"

Johnny's eyes widen. His boot hits the accelerator, hard. The Lamborghini lurches forward. We speed up. The lines on the road flash by faster and faster and faster.

Now, we're in overdrive.

WHA-A-A-A-A-R-R-R-N-N-G!

Johnny's not showing any signs of slowing down. Rakhi looks straight ahead. Her long black hair whips wildly all around us. A corner looms into the headlights, coming up fast. Johnny spins into it narrowly, sliding into the wrong lane. There's a car coming. Wheels screech. One side of the Lamborghini lifts right off the road. It comes crashing down with a thud and jostles us around.

Rakhi straightens up in her seat and looks at Johnny. He keeps accelerating, swerving between traffic, in and out, scornfully glancing at Rakhi as he goes.

Another corner. This time the car careens around it, then spins sideways and skids into the opposite lane. Right into the path of oncoming traffic. We're out of control.

Other cars SCREECH to a halt.

Horns BLARE.

Johnny wrenches the steering wheel and jars the Lamborghini into the proper lane, just in time to avoid the nearest oncoming car. The coupe veers and fish-tails before settling back down in the left lane. Johnny hits the accelerator, again, and we're off, racing back down the highway.

Rakhi grits her teeth.

Johnny's seething.

He shouts out some more:

> *"Aren't you AFRAID, Rakhi?*
> *"WHY aren't you afraid?*
> *"I'm gonna drive us BOTH off the road RIGHT NOW.*
> *" You're gonna die out here on the highway tonight . . . with me!"*

Rakhi holds on. Eyes wide. Looking straight ahead.

We all stare death in the face.

Suddenly, Johnny slams on the brakes. The car spins and fish-tails again, then slides and swerves amid the thinning, late-night traffic. It comes to a stop in the middle of the lanes. The smell of burning rubber fills all our nostrils, as Rakhi looks around, and I thank the gods that no one hit us.

I could feel Johnny grab Rakhi's shoulders and shake her, with his voice full of angry desperation:

> "What's wrong, Rakhi?
> ". . . *WHY* aren't you AFRAID?"

Rakhi looks over at him and holds his gaze.

"Why would I be, Johnny-bhai? Your life was in danger, too. Let's face it, you weren't going to crash this car. You're too scared to die, yourself."

Johnny glares. He's looking very, very angry.

He pauses just before he releases her.

His head slumps on the steering wheel.

He's trembling.

Finally, he looks up and sees all the cars maneuvering around us, blaring as they pass. Voices shout out windows. Fists shake. Horns are honking.

Johnny speaks up again, sounding tired now. "Do you think this was bad, Rakhi? This ain't nothing. You don't have a *clue* about Rita."

"She doesn't scare me, Johnny-bhai."

"Take it from me, she should scare you. Do you know what you did back there? You blew her off! Now, she may have looked as if she took that lightly, but trust me, Rita Chawla never takes things lightly."

"Yes, Johnny-bhai, I know that." Rakhi sits back in her seat. "Now, please, take me home."

I could sense Johnny's cool stare attempting to pierce her with its power and grasp at her essence. But Rakhi keeps still, keeps staring straight out the front windshield, showing no signs of fear. Not even so much as a blink. Finally, Johnny gives up. He turns aside, grabs the wheel, rev's the Lamborghini, and maneuvers it back into traffic.

The rest of the ride home was spent in silence. Broodingly quiet.

When Johnny pulled over outside of her building, Rakhi stood up in her seat and vaulted out over the passenger's door, not bothering to wait for the door to be opened.

She smooths her sari. Then, she looks back at Johnny, and winks. "Thanks for the happy joyride, Johnny-*bhai!*"

She made her way toward the entrance of the apartment. The evening air in Mumbai was still quite warm, but I could feel her shivering, just a little.

To tell the truth, I was so proud of her, I could have burst wide-open.

Harshad: The One Who Laughs

SATURDAY, 5:00 PM, ON THE EVENING OF KARISHMA CHAWLA'S CELEBRATED BIRTHDAY BASH.

Rakhi's getting ready to rumble. . . .

Sanjay's sitting on the sofa in Rakhi's tiny bachelorette apartment. He flicks on the television set. A set of clipped and polished female voices fill the room:

"Now it's time for KWOL's on-the-scene entertainment reporter – everyone's favorite celebrity gossip insider – our very own, Ramala Premnath!

"Yes, indeed, Indu ji. It will be a very busy Saturday night here in Bollywood, and, as you can see, I'm here out in front of the Super Gold

Celebrity Max-Theater, where the long-awaited premiere of mega-superstar Amandeep Khan's latest film, 'Bhujanga Bola' – 'The Snake Whisperer' – is scheduled to premiere this evening at seven o'clock. Meanwhile, across town, at the Grande Ballroom of the Taj Lands End Hotel, Chauvi Arrh Productions is putting on a birthday bash for Karishma Chawla, one half of Bollywood's newest and hottest couple. Along with her husband, Bobby Nihal, hundreds of Bollywood's stars and personalities, directors, producers and actors of every genre will be there, in attendance, to help Karishma celebrate her 23rd birthday. As always, it promises to be a well-attended event, so thank your lucky stars if you've got an invitation. I have a feeling it's going to be a very magical evening for many of Bollywood's biggest and brightest. Don't you agree, Indu?"

"Yes, Ramala ji, it's the kind of event that we all wish we could attend, just to watch the dramas unfold. As we've seen in past years, a thousand hopes and dreams are forever hanging in the balance. Those in the know have been getting ready for this party for many months, and, like I said, thank your lucky stars if you've got a ticket."

"Indeed Indu ji. I'll definitely be there on the scene, to speak with some of the greatest celebrities in Bollywood as soom as they step out of their limousines, and you know I won't be afraid to ask the hard questions, don't you? So stay tuned! For KWOL Entertainment News, this has been Ramala Premnath in front of the Super Gold Celebrity Max-Theater in East Navi Mumbai. Now, back over to you, Indu ji."

"Thank you ever so much, Ramala ji."

Behind the Venetian blinds that set apart her bedroom, Rakhi studies herself in the mirror. She smooths her hands over a new sleeveless, sapphire-blue dress; she looks classically beautiful.

Good choice, I thought to myself.

She's applied a soft midnight and neelum blue eye shadow over surma lined eyes. Just a hint of burgundy blush. A warm plum lipstick to finish. She's wearing a diamond on a gold chain so fine, that when she put it on, it appeared to hang in thin air, as if embedded just below her collar bone. A matching pair of delicate crescent-moon diamond earrings completes the look, which is offset so elegantly by that deep blue dress. Now, she drapes a sheer white-gradiating-to-sapphire-blue chuni around her shoulders, veiling the sparkling pendant.

Just then—*ding dong!*

The doorbell rings.

Rahki smiles. This is the moment she's been waiting for; that's the sound she's been anticipating.

Sanjay calls out from the living room: "No, don't stir, my darling, I'll answer it."

Rakhi smiles again, indulgently, as she hears him bound to the door and come to full stop with a cute hop. The door opens with a loud cr-e-e-e-ak.

"Why, Johnny Bhai. Namaste. What a pleasant surprise!"

Johnny grunts.

Sanjay's voice smiles broadly. "Aiyo, betto! Sit. What would you like to drink? Scotch Whiskey? Rye? Carrot juice?"

Johnny winces. "Uh, no. If it's all the same with you, Sanjay, I'm only here to pick up Rakhi."

"Acha, Johnny Bhai, I will call her,"

Sanjay turns around to see us standing behind him.

He catches his breath.

"Ah, there she is, Johnny Bhai. I envy the fact you'll be gazing on her radiance all night. I trust you will watch that no harm comes to my precious flower?"

Johnny scowls. "Look Sanjay, I don't know what this natak is about, but I am not amused. Aap nu kiya hoya yiaar? You act as though this–this woman–has removed your brains and your balls at the same time."

Sanjay's dejected.

Johnny brushes past him. "Bah, what-EVER."

Rakhi's indignant. "What are you doing here, Johnny Bhai?"

Johnny stops and stares at her with fierce eyes.

"What am I doing here? What do you think? I'm here to drive you to Karishma Chawla's party, you know, the one Rita so graciously invited you to, yesterday."

Ding dong!
The doorbell rings again.

Once again, Sanjay bounds to the door, and swings it open.

A man with a thin mustache is standing in the doorway, wearing a chauffeur's uniform.

"Your limousine is waiting, Ms. Rakhi."

"Thank you, Charlie." Rakhi strolls past Johnny. "Oh, Johnny Bhai, I'm so-o-o sorry if you had the impression I'd be going with you. You see, my agent—Deera?—well, he and I made other arrangements. We thought I'd make a better impression if I showed up in a limo on my own, and it might open up more doors if people see me as . . . unattached?"

Just outside the door, Rakhi turns to Sanjay and smiles indulgently.

"Don't work yourself too hard, my pet."

Sanjay brightens. He lifts her hand and kisses the inside of her palm.

"I await your return my love, mere maheebooba."

Rakhi smiles graciously and turns to the driver. He steps aside to allow Rakhi through.

I can sense her laughter.

Did you see that? Johnny's jaw dropped like a mule overburdened by a ton of bricks.

Serves him right, the schemer.

The driver guided the baby pink limousine through traffic to Juhu beach. Mumbai's eclectic landscape had always intrigued me. Bungalows were becoming a rarity, as modern sky-high buildings and condos were springing up from the ground. Still, amid all the modern living and technologies, there were the disadvantaged, the broken, and the utterly lost. Millions and millions of them, in fact.

You know Rakhi, I've been to many of these kinds of grand events. They're always the same. Look around you. Do you think those 'rich'n famous' Bollywood bobble-heads have it better than any of those people outside, living in their hovels, biting and scratching their way to the top? Think again. There's a level of abject bitterness and hunger in the pit of those complacent and well-fed stomachs too. Mark my words, you won't find any beauty there.

Rakhi turns away from the window.

Give it a rest, will you? You're getting on my nerves.

Yeah, well. . . .

Rakhi shakes her head, exasperated, and looks back out the window. She isn't listening.

Okay. I'd let it go. For now.

The baby pink limo pulled up in front of the roped off, red-carpeted entrance of the Taj Lands End Hotel. A young valet steps forward to open the door and extends his gloved hand to assist Rakhi elegantly out of the vehicle.

Don't show them too much leg, Rakhi. They don't like that kind of thing too much here.

Oh, shut up.

Okay, I will, but don't say I didn't warn you.

A toned and shapely thigh emerges from the limo as Rakhi steps out eloquently onto the red carpet.

Heads turn.

Onlookers gasp.

Rakhi looks absolutely stunning in her deep sapphire-blue dress and matching stiletto heels. The crowd behind the ropes suddenly falls quiet. A murmur runs through them. They're not sure what to do. They want to start swaying and screaming, but – kamala ha! – how can they when they don't even know who she is?

"Ye sundarati kaun ha? Yes, she's beautiful – but who is she? – where'd she come from?"

"Maloom nahee, I don't know. Why you asking me?"

The crowd continues to murmur as Rakhi starts down the red carpet. Then, a tall, lanky super-model-thin woman in a sparkly red dress approaches us. A man carrying a video camera follows close behind. A few feet away, the woman turns to face the camera.

"And three. Two. One . . ."

"Ramalah Premnath here for KWOL Enterainment News, and we are at the Taj Lands End Hotel talking to Bollywood's latest, newest, greatest, most sought-after dancing sensation, Rakhi!"

Rakhi looks at Ramala with an amused glint in her eyes.

That TV woman. She's got a really funny voice.

Maybe, but pay attention. Mind your words, Rakhi, these people are sharks.

Ramalah smiles an extra-wide smile. "Rakhi, it seems you've created quite a stir in Bollywood lately. As a complete newcomer on the scene, you've managed to land a scene all to yourself in the long-awaited dance-movie extravaganza, 'Bollywood Storm'. And even though your film isn't finished yet, the word is that your scene is going to be very hot. Everyone in Mumbai and, in fact, the world can't wait to see it. But, if you don't mind me asking, how exactly did someone, who's virtually unknown to the movie public, ever manage to secure a role like this?"

Rakhi's gazes at her, quizzically. "I suppose they must have liked the way I danced."

Ramala tilts her head. "Yes, I understand, but certainly you must have, uh, known someone who recommended you for the role? A director? A producer? A mentor? Was there anyone who helped you achieve this breakthrough?"

"Actually, no."

Ramala bites her ultra sparkling-red ruby lower lip.

"Rakhi, let me be blunt. There's been a lot of talk going around in some circles of the film industry. You see, no one, anywhere, seems to know who you are or where you are from. Is that something you'd like to share with your public today?"

Aha, see the teeth?

Rakhi smiles indulgently.

"Er, no, not really."

Now, Ramala purses her lips.

"Oh, I see. But could you tell us, at least, what made you become a dancer? Did you always dream of being a filmi-dancer, even when you were a little girl?"

"No, no, no, you see, I was never a little girl."

"Aha! I do see. You mean to say your parents, whoever they were, were so poor and so obsessed that they pushed you and pushed you? Oh, how unfortunate, you poor dear. You never really had a chance to enjoy your childhood, did you?"

"No, that's silly. I don't have any parents."

Ramalah's eyes widen. "Oh, then you're an orphan?"

Rakhi's exasperated. "I didn't say that either."

Ramala's baffled, and a little irate. "Very well, Rakhi, is there anything you might like to say to your budding public tonight?"

"Yes. I hope everyone who comes to see the film enjoys my dancing. I'm having so much fun."

Ramala blinks. "Ah, thank you, Rakhi."

She turns to her cameraman. Smile back up to full force.

"Well, ladies and gentlemen, we may not know who Rakhi is, but the world is certainly waiting with baited breath for her premiere dance performance in 'Bollywood Storm', the upcoming extravaganza that's scheduled to be released in early Navambara; now, back over to you, Indu ji!"

After the cameraman slowly lowers his camera, Ramala's smile wanes, just a little. Her eyes dart around until she spots a man getting out of the limousine behind us. A soft, faint flicker of a sneer crosses her face. "Rajnesh, look over there, it's Davinder Bains. He always gives a good interview, let's go!"

Rakhi continues down the red carpet, smiling, and waving at the people.

I had to ask. . . .

Ah, Rakhi, your interviewing skills are rather . . . um, raw, aren't they? Didn't Deera coach you on how to present yourself to media?

I told her the truth, didn't I, what more does she want?

The truth? My goodness Rakhi, forget about the truth. The truth may have a place somewhere in this world, but not here. This is a media event, and the truth isn't all that important here. It's the way things *look* that's important, see? In an atmosphere like this, a thing isn't what it is, it's what it looks like, or what it seems to be, you understand? Listen carefully, I'm only telling you this because, if you don't wise up pretty soon, they're going to make mincemeat out of you.

Amid all the shouting and pushing, a particularly bold photographer pushes and shoves his way to the front of the line.

He raises up his camera.

"Rakhi! Miss Rakhi! Gimme your best smile. This one's for. . ."

Rakhi stops and smiles at him. He takes aim.

His camera snaps and pops like a mad thing.

That does it.

All the paparazzi pounce.

Dozens of them enter in, shouting and shoving, each competing with every other viciously for her attention:

"Rakhi . . . Rakhi . . . Rakhi. . . ."

"Rakhi, your movie isn't out yet, but we all already adore you."

"Rakhi jahn, smile for us darling! "

"What do you mean 'who's she?' She's. . . 'Rakhi'."

"Yeah, yiyaar. Every man's dreamboat—"

"And every woman's nightmare, HAH!"

"Now making her way gracefully up the red carpet we see the newest, hottest sensation. Here comes Miss Rakhi. And, ooooh, how stunning, how komi, she looks in sapphire blue; so provocative, so katharnak."

"Show us some moves, Rakhi!"

"Haan, let us see some of those dance steps that set Bollywood on its ear."

Rakhi's looking around, somewhat bemused.

> Her heart's beating faster.
> She smiles cautiously for the cameras.

> See what I mean? A little overwhelming. Isn't it?
> Yeah, a little.
> She looks around at the scene a little more, just as another horde
of reporters descend on her, trying to get the scoop.

Rahki's bombarded.

> Eyes pop
> Smiles spread
> Sneers appear

This is Rakhi's big moment:

> *"She's so-o-o-o-o. . . ."*
> *"She's IT, yaaar."*

They're certainly paying attention to you now, Rakhi.

> Why wouldn't they?
> True.

Rakhi's The Latest.

> The Greatest.
> The Newest.
> The Up-and-Comer.
> 'The Kid.'

> *"DING-DING-DING-DING-DING!"*

After the din dies down, Rakhi carries herself with grace the rest of
the way up the red carpet: a single, modest blue gem among the many
simmering-glimmering flashes of glitz and gold.

Inside the lobby, I recognized some of the people I'd seen in New York at the festival. Rakhi smiles graciously at each one when they meet her eyes. Some smile and nod. Others look past her, preoccupied.

Don't worry, Rakhi, they're just too cool for school.

What are you talking about? This isn't 'school,' we're at a birthday party.

Oh, never mind, it was just an Americanism.

Hah, I knew that, I was only pulling your leg.

Rakhi followed the sign in the lobby to the venue where Karishma's birthday party was being held. She paused just inside the entrance. Although lights were dimmed, the room glowed with golden balloons, streamers and silver stars suspended from the ceiling. I looked at the far end of the ballroom and saw a stage with a lone microphone. A huge six-tiered cake sat on a table in the middle of the room. Above it all, a huge banner read:

– – HAPPY BIRTHDAY KARISHMA, ## INDIA'S DIL KA TARA! – –

I studied one of the tables placed along the walls. The candles, napkins, and dessert trays were all decorated in gold. Gold and silver confetti was sprinkled over the white table cloth. Beautifully designed platters of delicacies, h'orderves and snacks are stacked up high, strategically. The aromas are beginning to make Rakhi's mouth water.

The place is filling up. Big stars mill about, meeting and greeting, shaking hands, hugging, kissing cheeks. Smiling. So happy together. A few, special photographers are also present, to capture these memorable, magical moments to be shared, later, with the world.

Afterward. . . .

A Terse Nod.

A Tight Smile.

A stubborn chin.

A Frown. A Sneer.

WHAT-ever.

Rakhi feels a hand on her shoulder. She turns to see a familiar, expressionless gaze meet with hers.

"Well, fancy meeting you here, Bhabhi ji."

"Sister-in-law? You finally got the idea, Johnny-bhai."

Johnny shrugs. "What can I do? I tried. Now, since we let you make your grand entrance alone, the way you wanted, how about you let me introduce you to a few people?"

"I don't know."

"C'mon, this is a Bollywood schmooze fest. I saw the way you handled yourself out there with the press. You've got some things to learn before you can woo them like the big stars do."

Rakhi shrugged. Still, in spite of herself, somewhere inside she's stirring with excitement. "So, who do you know, Johnny-bhai?"

Johnny smiles. "Ahhhhh, the ice queen is star-struck."

Rakhi smirks. "Teek hai, baba! Lead the way."

Johnny takes hold of her arm, as they move in among the throngs. "First thing, Rakhi, this is a Birthday Party for Karishma Chawla, and it's not the place to play 'Little Miss Dancer.' These people do not take kindly to wannabes.

Rakhi stops dead and glares at him. "For your information, I do not seek attention, Johnny-bhai."

"Wait. Look over there," Johnny says.

I turn to see Bobby Nihal, Karishma Chawla's now-husband, walking toward us. As he got up closer, the actor caught Rakhi's eye and held it.

Rakhi bit her lip. She seemed to melt inside.

Wow, I thought, that look was certainly longer than seemed proper.

Rakhi smiled, seeming a little taken aback.

Then, he winked at her.

Never mind Karishma, I wonder what Rita would think of that? Karishma?

Johnny spoke up as soon as Bobby was out of earshot. "Well, there goes Mr. Bollywood himself, the poor bastard."

"What do you mean, Johnny-bhai?"

"Just watch."

I turned to see Bobby Nihal walk over to a young and

handsome looking man and shake his hand. The two men walk off together toward the fruit-filled buffet table, chatting as they went. We continued watching as the men stood, side by side, gazing at the spread. Then, Bobby Nihal reached around the other man's shoulder and gave him a playful squeeze. It seemed innocuous enough.

Johnny raised an eyebrow. "You wouldn't believe the kinds of things some people will do to get to the top."

Rakhi looked over at Johnny.

He nodded. "No, I wasn't fooled, not even for a minute."

Yeah, I thought, I supposed that I, too, must have known something wasn't right when I read about Karishma's engagement to Bobby Nihal in the paper, the morning after the Bollywood festival. All of that had seemed just for show, too, just like that wink.

The two men laughed animatedly as they filled their plates.

"Yep. Gotta love this business. There's always more than meets the eye," Johnny said, as he looked around the room. "And oh, look who's here, Rakhi, it's your buddies."

Rakhi turned to face the ballroom entrance.

Three lithe, long legged, light skinned beauties had just strolled in together. Shoulder length, auburn dyed and streaked hair. Identical light beige, Covergirl base over tired skin. Rose blushed cheeks. Bright pink and silver eye shadow above dull khol-lined eyes. Must-be-kissed pink lip gloss on thin, humorless lips. Each woman was wearing matching baby-pink tops and very short shorts.

They stop.
They pose.
They pout.
(WOW.)
Other women look on.
They smirk and sneer.

Then, suddenly, I'm back in the hallway on the fifteenth floor of the Bollywood Planet:

As I step forward, four pairs of khol-lined, hopeful, doubtful eyes follow me.

I stare down at the door. I think I see four shadowy female shapes all undulate at the same time.

Whispering. Whispering. Whispering. Whispering

Sighing Sighing Sighing. Sighing.

Trying to see *beyond beyond beyond beyond* . . . .THIS!

In the dark of night. . . .

A single woman in pink snaps her fingers and points straight ahead. On cue, all three of them toss their hair back and strut away into the crowd, simultaneously. Three pairs of baby pink heels clickety clickety clack against the polished marble floor in the Taj Mahal hotel's Grande Ballroom.

Rakhi cringed.

Who are they? I asked her.

They're known in the business as 'Miss Pinkie and Her Girls'. They were chorus dancers in some scenes in my movie. It's strange, but none of them can dance and all three are clumsy, pushy and arrogant. They're so self-centered, they kept disrupting all the shots. I don't know why the director ever put up with them.

Maybe they made a pretty good foursome with him?

Oh, barf. But that might explain it.

Their arrogance?

Sure. Whatever.

You don't care?

Bingo.

The three women milled about together, looking straight ahead with their frozen, super-model death-stares fixed downwards. Miss Pinkie sees us. She steers the other two toward Rakhi, hands on hips. Glaring, sneering into our eyes. Just as they are about to pass by, they all turn away in unison:

"*Hmmmph.*"

I watched Johnny's eyes follow their wake of long legs under jiggly pink bottoms.

"Hey, Rakhi, you got to be pretty stiff competition to warrant that kind of attention. Otherwise none of them would even bother to give you a dirty look."

"Well, that is good news, isn't it Johnny-bhai?" Rakhi said sarcastically.

Johnny smirked. "You, you know, are something else."

I was caught off guard by his sudden charm.

Rakhi smiles a little, in spite of herself.

That's when I noticed a short, balding man standing a few feet behind Johnny. His arms were folded as he held an unlit cigar between his teeth. His gray hair crept up through his black sideburns. His eyes are riveted on us; he seems completely enthralled by Rakhi.

I wonder what he wants?

I don't know. Maybe he just knows quality talent when he sees it?

Rakhi leans in towards Johnny. "To your left. Who's the man in the dark blue suit sucking on a cigar?"

Johnny catches sight of the man in his peripheral vision.

"He's a big-time Bollywood producer for Chauvy Aarh Productions, Rakhi, and apparently, he has an eye on you."

Eyes fixed on Rakhi, the producer walks over. He stops and looks her in the eye before his gaze moved quickly around her face, down her throat, over our bare shoulders, then, without any trepidation, into our cleavage. They linger there a bit too long for my liking before making their way down her waist, over her hips, down to her legs. Finally, his eyes shoot back up to meet our gaze.

Rakhi blinks.

That letch. I should smack him.

Yeah? I'd like to see that.

The short, balding man moved the cigar around with his teeth.

Then, he grinned. "Namaste, Johnny, and who is this *fan*-tastic young creature?"

Rakhi's annoyed.

She crosses her arms. "Didn't your mother teach you that it's not polite to stare?"

The cigar in the man's mouth droops a little, as the smile on his lips begins to sour to a glower.

His eyes get narrower. "Don't you know who I am, young lady?"

"No, and I don't care."

Startled by her insolence, the big-time producer withdraws his cigar and glares before he abruptly walks away.

I could hear Johnny's throat clearing loudly. "Kamala hai. What? Are you crazy, Rakhi? Don't you want to know who that man is? He's one of the most influential producers in Bollywood."

Rakhi isn't moved.

"I don't care. It doesn't give him any right to insult me."

"Hey bhagavana, ye jiddi gadhi nal kasa bahana pagiya? You're about as stubborn as a mule. What do you think this is? Do you think all these powerful people are here to cater to you? Sure, you are a budding talent and you're off to a good start, but you won't get much further by being arrogant and uncooperative like this."

Rakhi stiffens. "Look, I didn't ask for your help, and I'm not going to be nice to people who disrespect me, Johnny Bhai."

"S-h-h-h-h-i-t! Don't ever call me that again, especially not here. Dammit, I need a drink!"

As Johnny abruptly steered Rakhi toward the bar, I couldn't help noticing how heads were turning. Rakhi was unperturbed. At the bar, Johnny ordered a glass of water for her and a double scotch whiskey, neat, for himself. Rakhi gazed up at the mirror behind the elaborate bar as she waited for him to finish. For the first time since she left her apartment I was aware just how stunning she appeared, absolutely radiant and vital. Her eyes were alive. Her visage glowed. I felt in awe. Then I saw the throng just behind her, also reflected in the mirror. Some were leaning together, staring vacantly at Rakhi and whispering among themselves. Others threw furtive glances. An older woman sneered her jealousy over her glass of champagne. The male she was accompanying, however, had a different kind of a look.

Did you see that, Rakhi? It figures. You're the new girl in town.

No, it's more than that. You're the hottest, greatest sensation that's going to hit Bollywood for a long, long time, and that, essentially, is like painting a bulls-eye on your own forehead. They'll be out for blood soon.

What are you talking about? I haven't done anything to them. Why would they want my blood?

Because they're *jealous*?

Oh, wow. You must be really off your rocker. They don't even know me.

Oh, my goodness, you've a lot to learn, little girl.

Rakhi shakes her head and turns to Johnny. I caught a quick look of vulnerability flying across his face as he pushes a glass of water into her hands.

He looks back to study the crowd.

"Shall we mingle?"

After they'd stepped back into the crowd, Rakhi was introduced to some of the more well-known actors and actresses. Johnny stayed close by as they worked the room, smiling, nodding. Out of the corner of her eye, Rakhi spotted Miss Pinkie and her Girls moving quickly from one star-studded group to another, talking animatedly to anyone and everyone. Some people frowned. Some winced and took a step back. Others just walked away. It was sad. They didn't even know that all the people knew all there was to know about their . . . indiscretions. They had lost and they were desperate, if a danger to themselves, mostly; more causalites of the Bollywood machine, like Christine, and many others.

Suddenly, Johnny grabs our arm. "Look over there. See who's just walked into the room?"

Rakhi turns.

Johnny hisses in her ear. "Get it? Even the biggest stars have to stop by here to pay their regards, no matter how busy their schedule. Do you understand now how truly powerful Rita is?"

She gasps.

The room had gone utterly quiet.

People could hardly believe it.

"THERE HE WAS."

"IN THE FLESH."

In that moment, it seemed the whole world was holding a communal breath. The violins did a swoon. A flute fluttered. A sitar resonated.

THIS WAS HIM.

The Biggest and Greatest Superstar Bollywood Had Ever Known. . . .
The One. The Only.

MR-R-R. . . AMANDEEP. . . K-H-A-A-A-N!

Amandeep Khan moves towards Rakhi and I with lithe grace, command, purpose and charm. His way parts miraculously through the crowd.
    Heads turn.
    Mouths gasp.
    Women gyrate.
    Men sputter.
    We watch as he progresses through the hall.
    He's smiling. He waves. He stops to shake people's hands. His big, beautiful brown eyes scan the enchanted crowd, until his gaze happens to fall upon Rakhi. In that moment he halts, as if he can't believe his eyes, and even the background music seems to leap up a little, starts to rise a bit, increases in fervor.
    Khan stares at us.
    Rakhi takes in a breath.
    Okay, to tell the truth, even my eyes widened a bit. I mean, everybody knew who he was, Amandeep Khan: 'The Most Beloved Leading Hero In The Whole History Of The Indian Silver Screen'. It didn't matter where you were from. Everyone in India loved Amandeep. He was their Best Friend. Their Son. Father. Husband. Their First Love. His Tall Smooth Look, His Smile, was now washing over us all, and we felt shy, helpless, and doe-eyed.

Yet, somehow, in that moment, it seemed that Mr. Amandeep Khan only had eyes for Rakhi. He makes his way swiftly through the crowd and stops dead in front of her. His cologne catches up and envelopes our senses.

His soulful brown eyes hold onto ours.

"I'm sorry, Miss, but I don't believe we've yet been introduced."

Khan's gaze moves through us, lighting fires wherever they go. I can feel Rakhi's body falling into a slow seduction. She begins to imagine herself next to him, if only for a moment, in a field, cavorting in a surfeit of wildflowers, then walking close together, singing, holding hands, smiling. He gazes deep into her eyes as he lays her down on the ground amidst the wildflowers, and. . . .

Snap out of it, Rakhi!

Huh? Oh, yeah. Thanks.

Amandeep's slow and easy smile was excruciating and dazzling. Rakhi's heart was beating almost out of control. Okay, I could understand that, but somehow I knew there was some other thing involved. Something was wrong. Something was up with that.

Hmmm.

Rakhi takes a slow, deep breath, before she presents her hand to the Mega-Superstar. "Hello, my name is Rakhi. It's a pleasure to meet you, Mr. Khan. My boyfriend and I have enjoyed so many of your movies on our lazy, off-day afternoons."

Mr. Khan raises an eyebrow. "My, Johnny, she does have a radiant presence, doesn't she? Why, she's an absolute breath of fresh air."

"For now." Miss Pinkie snipes a remark from behind Khan's shoulder, then casts another seething glare at Rakhi as she and her girls pass by. I could feel the anger; the desperation, the echoes of a lost past, a wasted life, a used and abused youth.

Once again, I found myself sojourning back to the fifteenth floor of the Bollywood Planet:

> . . . sounds of bodies inside, whisperings, sighings, quiet moanings.

The darkness begins to fill up with sounds, like the ebb and flow of the waters of a delta, rising and falling, in and out, in rhythm.

Tittering, Tittering, Tittering, Tittering.

Crying, Crying, Crying, Crying.

The room was dark now, moans of rapture, heavy sighs.

He gazes deeper and deeper into my soul.

I shivered once more. With some bitterness.

Khan, of course, is entirely oblivious to Miss Pinkie's plight. His attention is fixed on Rakhi now. When he speaks, his voice is an attempt to make love to all her senses; the rhythms of his admiration are slow and easy.

"Yes, of course, of course, I've heard of you, Rakhi! Everyone in Bollywood says you're a fine, talented young dancer, and I believe with your spit and fire, daring beauty and sensational body, you could even be my next number one leading lady. Just picture it. We could do Action/Drama/Adventure films with many, many beautiful song and dance numbers. Oh, yes, you could be the *yin* to my *yang*, Ginger to my Fred Astaire, Rekha to my Bachan. Oh yes, yes, ye-s-s-s, yes-s-s-ss, we'll be the next big dance-roman-s-s-s-ce couple to set all of India on fire. They'll be thirsting for news – of us-s-s-s, deare-s-s-s-st, Rakhi."

Wow! I thought.

Even Rakhi, the unborn devi-child, who was usually so unimpressed with everyone, was susceptible to these superstar charms. Under the influence of Amandeep's powerful sexual mojo, combining now with the emerging force of the nagh coming up from inside him. I could feel her knees beginning to buckle, just a little.

Steady, I reminded her.

Wha? . . .what?

Keep steady.

Oh, haan, thank you.

Finally, Rakhi speaks.

"But – Mr. Khan *ji* – what about your *wife*?"

Khan's suddenly unnerved.

"What? What about my wife? What do you think you're talking about? I've always been a faithful husband, and good provider for my children, Miss, and you can't always take everything you hear in the media so seriously. It's a business, you know. It's what we do for a living."

Rakhi smiles. A little weakly.

"Well, ah, as you may recall, Mr. Khan, I already have a very nice role in a fine, upcoming movie called 'Bollywood Storm' that's already in post-production."

Khan smiles a little wider. And winks. That, in combination with his expensive and sophisticated cologne, and his vibe, was making everything a little heady, even for me. I, too, began to hang on his words and feel as though I might faint.

"Rakhi, my love, I know we can get you in on more than dance spots. With your poise, your athletic abilities, and that fiery tongue of yours, I bet we could get you in the front door for much bigger things."

He reaches into his coat pocket.

"Take my card."

Rakhi glances at it.

"Call me, Miss Rakhi, and we'll make a date of it, shall we? With my influence and connections, we could get you plenty of speaking parts. Smaller roles to start, of course, as goes without saying, but with the passage of time and your abilities, the sky's the limit, my dear."

Rakhi's smile is faded.

She receives the card from his hand and glances down at it. "That all sounds–uh–interesting, Mr. Khan. I will take your offer under consideration, and, perhaps ask my agent to get in contact with your people at some point in the future?"

She tosses his card nonchalantly into her purse.

It snaps shut.

Ka-lip.

The sheen of Amandeep Khan's superstar smile has dulled

significantly. His fingers go subtly up to the knot in his sleek-silk tie. He tugs at it, in a plain gesture of frustration and embarrassment, before he turns to speak to Johnny. The soft seduction in his voice has waned noticeably, too.

"Yes, well, of course. It's wonderful seeing you again, Johnny."

Before he exited, he turned back to Rakhi, one last time.

"We'll definitely talk another time, Miss Rakhi," he said.

With that, he stalked off into the crowd.

I watched as Johnny's face gaped after the big star's back. He swallows; then he turns to face Rakhi. He looks baffled.

"Meinu mardala ha. You're killing me, Rakhi! It looks like you went and shot another opportunity to make an influential connection all to hell. I don't know what to do with you. Of all the bevakuphi. . . ."

Rakhi blinks.

"Fine, you can take care of yourself, then. I may see you later, but now I need a drink."

"Sure. And don't worry, Johnny-bhai, I'll be fine." Rakhi says.

Johnny pauses. A look of consternation passes over his face.

"Ye-ah."

After Johnny walks away, Rakhi looks around, and realizes that almost everyone in the building is staring at her.

Do you see what just happened, Rakhi? Does that make you realize how vicious and cow-towed these people can be? Ever since Khan walked away in a sulk, no one, not one of them, has even made a move to speak with you.

Hmmm. Yes, there is something up with that.

We both pondered the situation.

Then, suddenly, all the lights in the room began to fade. As the light grows dimmer and dimmer, everyone looks about, not sure of what was happening. Finally, a familiar voice comes over the loud speakers:

"Good evening to you all!"

A large spotlight hits the stage and reveals Rita Chawla, dressed in a stunning, sparkling gold and coral red sari, standing at the podium. Her hair, pulled together stiffly in an up-do, is held by a very generous spray of baby's breath. She smiles her signature cool and regal smile.

People stopped chattering, except for a few awkward voices that quickly, realizing their mistake, sputtered away to a courtly silence.

Rita stands in that silence for a moment, before she looks around the room.

"Thank you, thank you, everyone, Well, today's the day, and I'm so glad that everyone here has taken some time to help me celebrate my daughter's janam din. It's so hard to believe that my beautiful child is going to be another year older. It seems like only yesterday we were all here celebrating her last birthday!"

A loud and long applause issues from the crowd. Rita stands on stage, hands clasped together in front of her, a smile perched on her lips. When the quiet returns, she continues.

"Sayada sabhi maluma hai. Perhaps most of you know that many good things have happened for our Karishma. She's been working hard this year. Kaphi mehanata pesa keetha. As a result, three of her movies will be ready for release this summer. What an accomplishment."

A round of applause goes up, timely and dutiful, then it peters off.

"Yes. Over the years, I've seen so many blessings come to me. First of all, a mother's duty and faraj is that her daughter be married, teek ha? Now, I know these days are modern and children have their own mind about such things. I must say I was very, very surprised when Bobby Nihal proposed to Karishma at the New York festival last year. But, Karishma veiled this little faux pas by including me in the decision. What could I do? My joy, meri sukha ananda, has always been dependent on my child's happiness, as it is the same for every parent, hanna?

The crowd murmurs its approval.

Oh, good Lord. It's the same spiel as in the New York Times article.

Rhetoric has little to do with originality.

Touché.

Rita continues.

"Karishma's sadi to Bobby Nihal, Bollywood's newest, most sought-after leading man, was perfect. They have similar ideals, similar goals. And they look very, very sweet together, don't they? Well, enough of a doting mother's pride, would you please help me congratulate Bollywood's enduring sweetheart...my daughter...Karishma!"

On cue, a wave of applause arises from the crowd as they await the guest of honor.

Where's Karishma?

Over there.

From behind the curtains, stage right, Karishma emerges, striding gracefully, waving to the now appropriately cheering-and-whistling crowd. Her long, silky hair sails behind her as she makes her way to center stage. At the microphone, Rita kisses her, then steps aside to join with everyone in applauding her. A chorus of song takes form as soon as the din of the applause dies down. Karishma looks classic and appropriately radiant in a short sleeved, mid-calved, baby-blue sequined dress. She smiles while the crowd begins to sway and sing and Rakhi steps in closer, as the anthem begins:

> *Happy Burrday to you*
> *Happy Burrday to you*
> *Happy Burrrrrrday dear Kar-i-sh-ma-maaaaa*
> *Happy Burrday to-o-o-o-o-o yo-o-o-o-ou*

Rakhi looks around. Flames from flicked lighters scatter throughout the darkened ballroom, like ships in Mumbai Harbor. Karishma stands and waves, then puts her hands together in Namaste, while they continue to cheer.

"Thank you! Thank you, everyone. Merebhani. Shookriah."

After a few more moments of cheering, the room quiets down.

Karishma stands quietly, appearing modest and unmoved.

Then, she begins, "Well, time does fly by, just as my mother said, doesn't it? It seems not so long ago I was here thanking all of you for showing up to my last birthday party!"

A murmur runs through the crowd.

"Yes, it has been a busy year, and I see so many familiar faces out there tonight. I've met so many people in this industry. It's amazing how many people know me. So many of you have worked with me, at one time or another, throughout my career. Since our wildly popular movie, Mein Kooshi Nahi, went over the top in ticket sales, Bobby and I have been committed to working non-stop to bring you quality entertainment. Just last week, we were at the Taj Mahal, shooting scenes for one of my upcoming movies, Mithuna Premakahani, Gemini Love Story, in which I play the double-role of a poor peasant girl who works in the wheat fields, and of her twin sister, who lives the life of a nach girl in the Emperor Shah Jahan's palace at Agra. The dhoom-dhaam dance scenes will be shot at Zakir Rose Garden in Chandigarh, which will stand in for the Shah Jahan's gardens in Lahore Pakistan. It will be a beautifully shot and cinematic movie, and I know you're all going to enjoy it very much, *so don't miss it!*"

The party-goers again erupt into cheers and whistling. Karishma smiles, patiently waiting until the last of the applause falls into silence.

"Well, I see a few people here I would like to thank. First, Shitarr Pathi Parvati, the director of both these films I've mentioned. Your vision and faith have challenged me to become a better actress. I would also like to thank my mother, and all the people at Majarani Productions for their hard work in bringing the best of the best entertainment to India, and the world. As you know, Bollywood has become widely popular – all over the world!"

The last part of her speech is nearly drowned out by the sudden rise of whistling, shouting and clapping.

"So, again, I want to thank my mother and Lila, my special consultant, and the caterers for arranging this bahuta barhiya birthday bash for me. Lila, what would I do without you?

"My, everything looks fantastic, and the food smells simply sumptuous. Again, let me thank you all for your well wishes and, of course, any gifts and donations you might want to make to Tigers and Tusks. Last year we were able to raise enough money to complete the forested compound, shelter for more than thirty tigers and provide a safe haven for many, many more elephants!"

A sharp roar of applause fills up the room, then again, it dies away.

Karishma looks out thoughtfully over the crowd. "I really do appreciate you all coming to my birthday party, and I hope you all have a very nice time. Dig in. Enjoy."

With that Karishma walks over to her mother and gives her a hug. Then she exits to the left, down the steps, through the crowd of well-wishers. She moves expertly from person to person, smiling, shaking hands, thanking them.

Then, as she got closer, I finally saw it.

The strain in her eyes.

A deep quietness.

The look of a prisoner who'd accepted her fate a long time ago. Even in New York, Karishma had seemed to have an air about her that was a little old for her age. Now, I watched the smooth crispness of her greetings. When she reaches us, Karishma smiles and is about to put out her hand to Rakhi. She stops mid-way, looking surprised. Puzzled. She withdraws her hand, and speaks hesitantly.

"I'm sorry. I know my mother invites people that I don't know to my parties, but for some reason I feel as if we've known each other . . . somewhere?"

Rakhi pondered that. "Perhaps we have, Ms. Chawla."

Karishma brightened. "Call me Karishma, I'm not really that formal. What's your name?"

"My name is Rakhi. Your mother invited me to your party only yesterday."

Karishma smiled. "Yes, of course, of course. I've heard of you. You've been making quite a splash on the scene. It's a privilege to meet you, Rakhi."

"The pleasure is mine," Rakhi said.

Karishma glanced around the room, and sighed. "Perhaps, we'll meet again one day, but right now I need to attend to my guests. Then, I'm going up to my room to lie down."

"Tired?"

"Hmmm?" Karishma murmured absently.

"I was just saying that you seem. . . ."

"Oh yes, one does get weary of being the center of so much attention all the time. Oh, I know, and I don't mean to sound thankless, but. . . ."

Rakhi nodded, "No need to explain. Being in the public eye, twenty-four seven. . . ."

"Well I do love it. I mean, who wouldn't? I love the work, the fans and I love the movie industry. It's just. . . ."

She glances up.

". . . it always feels like I'm at work, you know? Being 'up' all the time?"

"Yes. I'm beginning to know what you mean." Rakhi glances around.

Karishma smiled. She looked as if she was about to move away, but then, she stopped and looked us right in the eye.

"I like you, Rakhi, and I hope, some day, we could be friends."

Rakhi nodded. "Yes. That'd be very nice."

Karishma's smile waned. "Very well. As a friend, my first duty is to warn you to watch out . . . for my mother."

Rakhi nodded. "I know."

Karishma bit her lip. "Good luck. And who knows? Someday, we may get to make a movie together."

"Perhaps we will. Thank you, Karishma."

We watched as Karishma walked into the clamoring crowd. Pinkie and the girls giggled and preened for her as she stopped to say hi.

All around us the smiles seemed to get wider and wider. Soon, the room was so bright with them, there was nowhere to hide from the glare. A quiet, sickening hissing seemed to be emerging amongst the murmur of the glitzy crowd. Rakhi suddenly didn't feel so well. She looked around for Johnny, but could not find him anywhere. She searched the room and spotted a quiet corner where there wasn't too many people, where the smiles weren't so bright. She walked through the crowd hearing snatches of conversations:

"What do you think?"

"Another boring birthday party for Little-Big-Miss, eh?"

"Yeah. But what are you going to do?"

Rakhi's trying not to listen, but what's she going to do, shut everybody's mouth?

"That director, Shitarr Pathi Parvati. Ji, he's got the influence."

"Yeah, I auditioned for one of his flicks.My sister knows his best friend, see, so I got the part. But then they lowered the rate."

"You're kidding, yaar?"

"No yaar, I'm not. Well, I told my agent there was no way I would take a role under the rate."

"Listen yiyaar, you know what they say about men who get roles with that director?"

Yeah, sure. But a man needs to eat, yaar. . . .

Rakhi walks past. Not wanting to hear. Not wanting to see. After all, all of this has nothing, nothing at all, to do with her.

She doesn't want to be like these people.
   No. She doesn't want any of this shit.
   She only wants to dance!
   Just then, out the corner of Rakhi's eye, I saw someone I recognized. It was the-man-with-the-suit-and-tie, the actor from 'Meri Dil Ka Tara.' He was sitting in the darkest corner at a small table, staring off into space. He looks down at his glass of brooding, dark alcohol. He throws the rest of the pak back and smacked his lips. His glassy eyes search the hall for a waiter. He sees one, and points his free hand at his glass, thus indicating he wants another.
   He was so . . . drunk.
   So unhappy.
   So vacant.
   No, no, no, not at all like his triumphant character near the end of Meri Dil Ka Tara, who's ecstatic after he's won Geeta's heart.
   For some reason, tears begin to sting in Rakhi's eyes. She puts her hand up to her throat and looks around for somewhere to hide. She weaves her way through the crowd toward the ballroom exit. In

the lobby, she hurries down along the hallway. Finally, she finds a private washroom.

She tries the handle.

It won't give.

She stood there looking around, breathing deeply to try to ease the increasing pressure. She didn't even dare think about it. A few minutes later, an extremely made-over starlet emerged from the room. Her khol-lined eyes were glassy and wide. She pressed a pink nail-polished finger against the side of her nose and sniffled and wiped.

Rakhi gapes.

The woman smiles. A gargantuan smile. "He-he-ya! Nice party, eh darling? Say, do you want to try some of my nose candy? My boyfriend gave me enough to share. Want some?"

I could tell where she was.

"Um. . . no. Maybe another time?"

She frowns as she leans up against the wall. "Look, these parties are always so-o-o dull? They go on and on and on. Oh c'mon, it'll be a lot more fun afterwards, I promise. And, maybe then, we can be be-e-e-st friends, hanna?"

Rakhi bites her lip, rushes past the over-giggly woman into the bathroom and slams the door hard.

Inside, she leans back against the other side of the door, and breathes raggedly.

"What's *wrong* with these people? This was not what I envisioned. This is not what it was supposed to be like. It's supposed to be about doing beautiful things, and I don't want this. I don't want any of it. All I ever wanted to do was dance."

Is that what you thought life was about, Rakhi. Dancing? Come on, why do you think you're here? Why do you think you and I are together in this one body? Have you ever wondered?

Rakhi walks over to the sink and looks at herself in the mirror. She shakes her head.

"No. Because you're not real, and I am. So what I say goes. Why can't you ever accept that?"

I stared at her.

Sure, okay. But if you have everything under control, why are you standing there being so unhappy?

Hot tears are pouring down her cheeks. She wipes them angrily away.

Remember what I told you on the way over to this party, Rakhi? These events are just what I said they are, a bunch of scared and desperate people scratching and clawing. And none of them are any better than any person living in a hovel, even if these rich people aren't selling their bodies, and their children's bodies, for quite so cheap.

She glances away. "I don't know about any of that. All I know is that I want to dance. I just want it to be beautiful!"

I paused.

Yes, and the way you dance is beautiful, Rakhi. Breathtaking. People really pay attention. But do you know what? Dancing's not the real reason you're here. You're here because of Simr—

With that, Rakhi explodes, glaring straight at me in the mirror.

"You're about to say the real reason I'm here is because of Simryn Gill, aren't you? You're crazy. There never was such a person. And if there was a real 'Simryn Gill' somewhere once, still, what does it have to do with me?"

What did she just say? What's it got to do with her?

Okay, that did it.

There was never such a person, huh? Uh-uh. You better believe there was a real Simryn Gill. She had a real life and real plans. Simryn danced in a movie once, too, you know. She had a mother named Roopa who was a great dancer and was in a few movies herself. Simryn's father was Rajesh Sharma, a big Bollywood director who seduced countless women, including Roopa. But, luckily for Roopa, she married a man named Amar who loved Simryn and raised her as his own. Simryn had a nani too, named Muna, who lost her whole family during the war of Partition when she was four years old, and if a man called Makhan Singh hadn't happened on her, the only survivor of the slaughter of an entire village, then there wouldn't have been a Simryn. And you don't know this either, Miss 'Oh-I'm-Rakhi-an-island-unto-myself' but Muna was also a great dancer, too, much like you. And none of this is made up from some lame movie or dubious fantasy life either!

Now, what about you, Miss Rakhi-Oh-I'm-So-Invincible?

Who are you, anyway?

Who was your mother?

Who was your father?

Where, or what, did you come from?

Can you tell me *that* much, at least?

Oh wait, don't tell me, I remember now. You didn't have a mother or father, did you? In fact, you never were a child. You weren't even born, you just popped up into existence one day . . . in my body! Have you ever thought about that and considered what that might mean? Have you ever wondered if, after it's all said and done, you might be the one who's not actually 'real'?

Rakhi's enraged. She pokes her finger at her image in the mirror and pounds at it rhythmically.

"Not real, hey? Look again. Still not real? Dekha bhala karana. Have a GOOD look."

She slams the mirror hard with her fist.

WHAM!

A huge crack appears in the mirror's smooth, reflective surface. Tiny splinters of glass splay through the air on either side of us, as Rakhi glares her insolence.

"Dekha? Did you see it? That was pretty damn real, I'd say."

I waited, not saying a word.

She kept staring at me Strands of long, black hair stray haphazardly over her face. She rubs her fist tenderly.

Okay, Rakhi, fine. Let's just say, for one moment, that you're the one who's real. After all, you are in command, aren't you? Sure, fine. So, just go ahead, be real, and deny every little thing. Simply ignore the fact that you popped into existence one day, only – oh, whenever that was – and then deny what happened the other day in Raj Balru's dance studio with those four dancers. Yeah, tell me something, if you didn't know anything about what happened to Simryn, what was that all about? Why'd you react so strongly, huh? Don't tell me you don't have any memories, because I'm the one who's in here with you, remember? I'm on the inside, so you know that I know that you know that you can remember lots of things, even if all you ever do is sublimate. Maybe you can lie to yourself, but you can't lie to me. I know you pretty well. In fact, I'm pretty sure, I know you better than you know yourself.

For a moment, a shadow of fear crosses Rakhi's face.

Well, that's a first, I thought.

She hesitates. For an instant, she bites her lip.

Then, another mood catches up with her, and she leans forward, taking me on eye to eye in the cracked mirror.

"What? You think you know me? Then why don't you ever listen to me? *Suno!* I've told you over and over, I've never heard of this, this – 'Simryn' – person. I never met her, I don't remember her. This is my life, and I all wanna do with MY OWN LIFE is DANCE! Samajae? GET IT? GOT IT? GOOD. I don't care about this—'Simryn' person—and I never WILL.

"I. . . . JUST. . . . DON'T. . . . CARE!"

She turns away from the mirror. Eyes wide. Fuming.

I sighed.

Listen Rakhi, everyone has a mission in life, and you're here to serve justice. Your job is to get us inside the Bollywood scene so we can finger Simryn's murderers. Understand? If you want the truth, Rakhi, here it is, Simryn Gill is the real reason you're here in this world.

The shaking begins deep down inside Rakhi.

Her voice trembles.

"No, that's not true! This is my life and I'm not going to let you ruin it with your crazy, crazy fantasy."

It's not a fantasy, Rakhi. Think about it. What's the first thing you can remember?

"G-get out. Leave me alone."

MAKE me!

"What did you say? *Make* you? . . . O-kay . . . That's it . . . We're *done. . . .*"

There's a shift. We're on the ethereal plane and all the dualities are dissolving. It's neither light nor dark, here, and Rakhi's a she-wolf howling at the Moon, while a lizard looks on. And there's a never-moving, always unrelenting, pitiless Sun beating down on us. Forever and ever. Amen. Rakhi's alive! She cries to all the universes, announcing her arrival, as she struts purposefully toward a sign that says 'Exit'.

> *Clickita clackita clickita clack*
> Her footsteps echo.
> *Clackita clakita clackita click*
> Only a few steps
> *Clickita clackita clickita*
> Prettygirl blue steps.
> *Dhoom-a-daka-laka-laka-dhoom-D-H-O-O-O-O-M* steps.
> Almost-comic **Ka-B-O-O-O-O-O-O-M** steps.

Then
CR-E-E-E-E-A-A-A-K!

The bathroom door's wide open, and Rakhi's looking back at me with stone-cold, khol-lined, almond-shaped eyes. She smiles. A demure smile.

She waves:

"'Ta ta. . . !'"

And

BLAM!

She's gone.

And me?

I'm all alone in the dark again.

"My eyes, my eyes, I can't SEE!"

Suddenly, an angry mood hits me, and I started to scream.

"*R-A-A-A-A-K-K-K-H-H-I!*

"*YOU YOU –*

"*Silly, foolish, double-crossing little she-dog.*

"*YOU – YOU–*

"*Stubborn, ungrateful, pin-headed, little brown, bitch-puppy, fool-monger.*

"*YOU.*

"*YOU. . . .*

"*YOU. . . .!*"

When my rage had subsided sufficiently, I began to wonder where I was, and I found myself still in the bathroom, still standing by the sink, and staring blankly back at the still-vibrating door that Rakhi had just slammed.

Damn, I thought.

What was I going to be now? Would I be an invisible ghost again? Would I have my own body back?

I took in a very deep breath before I turned to look into the mirror.

Yikes!

There I was.

In the flesh.

Pale.

Pink.

As vulnerable as the day I was born.

Absolutely butt-fucking naked.

I threw my hands and arms up to cover my intimate parts, and stood there with my mouth gaping open, like an embarrassed version of Botticelli's Venus.

The gravity of the situation kept hitting me over and over.

Like a gong.

There I was, sole heir to the prestigious, Bostonian 'George' family fortune, descendant of the sister of the Duchess of Who-knows-where Lady 'What's-it' from England, standing buff effin' naked in a swank bathroom of a luxury hotel, smack in the middle of New Mumbai, without having so much as a clue where to find even a shred of decent apparel, and without, as far as I knew, a single soul on this entire continent who gave a fig about me.

(Okay, I was feeling a little sorry for myself at that point. So sue me.)

Look at me, I don't even have a tan!

What in the world was I going to do?

I started fuming. "Damn you, Rakhi, I'll get even with you for this."

Then, as my eyes darted around the room, I began to wonder what I could use to cover myself up.

Toilet paper?

Hmmm, no.

Paper towels?

Then, I heard a tiny creak, and turned to see the bathroom door beginning to open.

I leapt at it!

From the other side of the door, another woman was pushing and shoving hard against me.

"Hey, kaun ha, what gives? I need to go. Let me in."

I won the struggle, slammed the door shut in triumph, and locked it. I leaned back against it, and slid sullenly down to the floor.

"Dammit," I said aloud, "dammit dammit dammit damn."

After some time spent sitting there alone, with my back up firm against the bathroom door, my fuming was transformed into brooding. Hmmm. Whatever Rakhi was not saying was definitely revealed in her reaction. I wondered if her conversation with Karishma had left Rakhi's heart heavy. She'd seen that life as a Bollywood celebrity was not always all that it was advertised to be. Or, at least, it hadn't turned out so in Karishma's case. I glanced around at the beautifully-tiled, pink walls, the opulent sink and the state-of-the-art toilet, and began to wonder how long I'd been sitting there in the nude, with the air conditioning blowing away. I was getting cold. I also wanted very much to go home.

"I miss New York," I said to myself.

Then, I heard another loud knock on the door.

"Ah. I'll only be a moment longer."

The knock came again. Even louder now, more insistent.

Damn.

"Could you please wait for just more moment?"

A chesty, heavily accented old woman's voice responded. "Elanna, daravaja kholo, open up the door."

Needless to say, I was taken aback.

What?

How?

The voice spoke up, again. "Elanna, open up quickly now, Baetee, it's me!"

Me?

Who?

Who was 'me'?

Who could possibly have known?

But, somehow, I knew. . . .

"Harshad?"

I couldn't quite be sure, so I got up, and unlocked the door. I opened it only a tiny bit, just enough to peek, and looked out with one eye to see a matronly and slightly plump, older woman, who was standing there, all alone.

"Harshad," I whispered, "what are you *doing* out there?

"Let me in, Baetee."

"What? No, Harshad. I've got nothing on. I'm naked in here."

"Yes, I know. And I've brought you some clothes."

"Clothes? How. . . ?"

The old woman's eyes narrowed, as she peered at me intently through the small crack in the doorway. "Believe me, Elanna, when I'm cloaked as a woman like this, I don't – well – I don't care about such things in the way men do. You must also realize that, even when I'm myself, I only have eyes for Laila."

I blinked. But I didn't budge.

She sighed.

"Listen, I'll keep my eyes closed, okay? Think about it. Consider carefully. What other options do you have?"

I considered. The old budhi was right. I was in a sticky situation.

'Very well, Harshad. But keep your eyes shut tight, will you?"

"Yes."

I opened the door, only a little more, barely enough to let in a package.

"Are your eyes shut good and tight?"

"Yes, they are."

I reached out and grabbed the damn clothes.

Laila: The Dark One

After I snatched the package out of the old woman's hands, I pushed the bathroom door shut in her face and locked it up tight. Then I locked myself in the stall of the swank private washroom in the Taj Land's End Hotel and tore open the brown paper package. I pulled out a deep indigo dress decorated with a few flowing lavender sequined flowers, with matching shoes and underwear wrapped inside. I got dressed quickly, then realized the dress was, well, ill-fitting – somewhat too small in the waist, and much too big in the bosom.

Oh, well, I thought, perhaps Harshad is just a guy after all.

Then, I heard his old woman's voice speaking at me through the door. "Are you ready in there, Baetee?"

At that point, I figured there was nothing else I could do, so I let the old budhi in.

"Harshad, what's going on?" I asked her.

The plump matron smiled and tossed her long mane of dyed-back-to-black hair over her shoulder. I couldn't help but notice that the party dress she was wearing was rather youngish.

Harshad spoke. "I must explain as quickly as I can. The Mumbai operation is still at war with dark and evil forces, but it's going rather well. The balances seemed to tip in our favor after you appeared that night. So now it's time for us to return the favor."

"How did you know where I was?"

The old woman shushed me impatiently. "There isn't enough time to explain everything. I can't stay long, because Laila and the Nomads need me desperately."

"Very well, Harshad, thank you for the clothes. Goodbye."

"No, no, no, Baetee. Not quite yet. First, I must fill you in on some very important information that Laila and I stumbled upon this afternoon, at the Dhonni Maach, when we spotted Rita Chawla, Johnny Akkarah, and another man named Amandeep Khan, all engaged in deep conversation in an opposite corner."

"Amandeep Khan? The actor?"

"Ji haan. Not only a brilliant actor and a mega-star but also one of the most powerful paranormals around Bollywood. He is also, of course, as we know now, deeply involved with the Bollywood cartel."

"Of course."

"At once, Laila decided to engage in a little psycho-espionage. It was risky, but I had to go along with it. After all, no one has been able to garner much information on the nature and location of these incomprehensible dushmani forces that are bombarding us from the psychic plane. She only managed to eavesdrop for a moment before the three of them began to feel her presence. They became un-comfortable and went silent, but she did manage to discover some things that are, at least, as pertinent to your case as to the Mumbai organization's plight. At that moment, Rita, it seemed, was making quite a fuss over our friend, the up-and-coming young banghra-dancer, whose star seems to be hurtling straight over the top."

"Rakhi," I interjected.

"Who else?"

The old woman stopped and looked around, even though it seemed almost certain that we were alone.

"Elanna, their game plan is to tame Rahki, and try to direct her talents to their advantage. They want to ensure she will only get movie roles that have been especially groomed for her, and will only dance in scenes that are carefully laid out, by them. Thus, they hope to make sure ensure that Rahki never reaches her full potential, and never threatens Rita's daughter's success. Here is what Laila heard Rita say:

'We must be very careful. She is too wild. Much too impulsive. Too charismatic and too vibrant. She must not be allowed to go on in that way. In recent years the public has been giving these 'bad girls' too much sympathy. We've allowed them to find their ways far too deeply into our hearts, in spite of their moral flaws. And, therefore, this 'Rakhi' phenomenon must not go unchecked, and Rakhi herself must never be allowed to achieve anything more than a superficial veneer of stardom. Why, if that young woman ever acquired any real power in Bollywood, it could prove disastrous for us all.'

I mulled over the information. Yes, this was all turning out to be rather simple. Rita was merely an extremely bitter and excessively paranoid stage-mother who wanted to cripple all the young artists, thereby ensuring that her daughter Karishma would have little competition. That way, she hoped to keep her daughter at the very top for a prolonged period. And, towards that end, she was willing to nip Rakhi's future in the bud, turning her into yet another of those safe, watered-down, tamed, predictable, so-called Bollywood 'bad girls' who never really dance a step not carefully laid out for them by the established filmi-industry. Of course, it all made sense now. It couldn't have been more clear. And, even dear old Johnny Bhai was working against us, going so far as to even betray his own brother's fiancée. In that moment, somehow, those things seemed incomprehensible, and in fact, almost unthinkable to me.

"Nasty," I muttered.

Harshad agreed, immediately. "Yes, very nasty indeed."

I considered him a bit more closely, feeling slightly disturbed by the 'old Bollywood-madam' disguise he'd put on: some aging and haggard ex-starlet, one not even famous enough to play 'The Mother' role anymore.

She looked back at me, pathetically. She seemed almost like a long-past expiration date on a milk carton.

I bit my lip.

"I don't think it would ever work, Harshad, do you? Rahki would never allow herself to become a weak, insipid, superficial, Bollywood-authorized version of herself."

The Bollywood madam shook her head, vigorously. Then, she hesitated, and her eyes narrowed, as she leveled me with a cold, hard stare.

"But there's more, Baetee."

I swallowed.

This couldn't be good.

"What, Harshad?"

He frowned. "If Rahki will not acquiesce to their wishes, the Bollywood-cartel is willing to resort to extreme measures. Just before the three of them began to sense Laila's presence and forced her slip back into the spaces between time, the last thing Laila heard Rita say was:

'. . .if she refuses to comply, we'll deliver her to the Upadhyay brothers to do as they wish with, as long as they agree to carefully dispose of the body, afterwards.'

So, I thought, our very own Johnny-bhai was turning out to be, not just a cheap Bollywood pimp, but a would-be murderer to boot.

I bit my lip, again.

Damn.

"Thank you, Harshad," I said. "for showing me some of their cards. I'll know better now how to play mine."

I could feel Rakhi's anguish welling up inside me; her dreams and aspirations, her talent would be crushed, and Rita would turn her into more of a nobody than if she'd never manifested. At that moment, I just wanted to see her win, and I wished I had given her more encouagement instead of always blowing my stack. I decided, right then and there, that if we ever worked together again, I'd make sure she'd get to dance her way and also have the recognition she deserved. But how would I ever get her on my side now? Why would she want me around after we'd railed against each other ever since the day we began inhabiting the same body? Sure, I'd laughed at her little-girl dancing dreams. And she'd turned her nose up at my pursuit of Simryn's killers. We hadn't gotten along very well, had we? And I hadn't helped the situation. But I knew, after all, there had to be something deeper than any that between us . . . didn't there?

Harshad interrupted my broodings. "I have to leave you now, Elanna," he said. "but Laila and I will be in touch with you soon, I hope."

Then, he changed, but this time it wasn't his appearance. Instead, the old woman's demeanor altered dramatically. She began acting out, gesturing like a pushy buffoon, while speaking in a loud, rough voice, preening and staring:

"Oh my *gawdh*, my dear, oh my gawdh, are you absolutely sure your name isn't Channo Malak? O-Pho! As a young woman—she was my sister's neighbor's cousin's youngest child, you know—well, she was so-o-o-o-o beautiful that whenever she walked down the streets, in our pind, everyone would just drop everything they were doing just to stare at her—even the women. And you, my dear. Well, I admit it's amazing, but true nonetheless—you look just like her. Why, you're her absolute spitting image!"

The budhi paused.

"*Acha ji*, I'd better go, before I end up eating somebody's joothi. Aagarh!–namaste."

She walked over to the door. But, just before she went out, she spun back around to me—and winked. Then, she clapped her hands three times before she crossed over the threshold of the bathroom door, and closed it tight behind her.

Harshad was gone.

I stared after him.

What?

What was that?

A *natak*?

Then, something else occurred to me, and I smiled as I spun back around to look in the mirror.

A pair of khol-lined, almond shaped eyes were looking back at me. Two glossy, cherry-red lips were curving up into a big, saucy smile.

I smirked one more time.

'Just as I thought,' I thought.

In the mirror, a brand new, ravishing South Asian beauty was smirking back at me. The ill-fitting, deep-indigo, party dress I'd put on earlier fit now, like a glove, over her gloriously full, voluptuous curves.

My mouth began to water.

"Damn, am I beautiful!"

I couldn't help but laugh. It was a big, beautiful, lovely, saucy laugh.

"Thank you, thank you, Mahta ji."

Outside, in the main ballroom, the crowds were getting thinner. The gala was approaching that stage when only the hangers-on are still there; you know, the one still trying to score; those still looking to make the connections to find whatever it is that they believed they needed.

Fame?

Fortune?

Men?

Women?

Drugs?

Booze.

Attention?

"C'mon bartender, oi Yaara, just gimme one more. . . ."

Does it really matter what the poison is?

Maybe.

Or, maybe not.

In any case, I knew Johnny Akkarah would be there, languishing among the stragglers. He'd be nursing his wounded ego, and drowning his vague but growing fears of what Rita might do to him, now that he'd failed many times over with Rahki. And, of course, I was right. There he was. Standing alone at the bar, fingering yet another glass of bourbon, biting his lip, wearing his usual vague and expressionless gaze.

I made my move. Sauntering up slowly to the edge of the bar, I leaned in quietly beside Johnny.

He glances over.

"Who the hell are you?" he asks.

He's glaring.

I return his glare and stick out my chin. "I'm Channo. Hey, don't mind me. I'm just a little peeved at the moment. Some bevakuphi half-wit with a big cigar just told me I look like some pind walli chirrhi he used to fantasize about, back in some village somewhere."

Johnny sniffs. "Why didn't you tell him to go to hell, then?"

I pick up his unattended drink and finish it for him.

"I did."

Johnny's amused. His eyes get narrower. "So, you felt a need to come over and tell me this?"

I yawn. "Yeah, I needed the entertainment."

Johnny raises an eyebrow. He's beginning to look more interested.

I capture his gaze.

I brush a long strand of black hair out of my face.

"You know . . . these parties? They make me feel so restless, and I'm so-o-o bored."

He looks me over. Hard.

I stare back at him.

Our gazes lock. We're getting in sync. Both of us knows that the other knows, too. And both of us know that each of us knows what real power and real pleasure really are. And each knows the other one, too. Because we're the same. Yeah. We're the special ones. The wild children. The beautifully-endowed ones. The chosen. The privileged. And it's the kind of privilege that just gives us the Gawd-damned, carte-blanche, fucking-inalienable rights to just fucking be. . . .

Reckless.

Foolhardy.

And so damn drop-dead sexy.

"So. . ." Johnny says, as he stares right through me.

". . . So, you're bored, huh?"

"So. . . ?"

He smiles. A knowing smile.

"I think we can remedy that."

He reaches for my arm and draws me in close. I tingle at the closeness, as I look up into his dark face. He takes his time, his eyes are roving all over me. His gaze is becoming glassy, and I can feel his powerful presence, as he lowers his head to mine.

I shiver.

But then, he releases me, suddenly.

Now, we're headed for the exit. He's pulling me along. All the way out of the hotel.

I'm laughing.

"Oh, don't tell me we're just going to go back to your place. Take me somewhere where I can get some excitement."

Johnny stops dead. He gives me a look that I know would have turned Rakhi's blood cold.

"Don't worry, meri tathi jalabee, I see plenty of excitement in your future. Soon, you'll have more excitement than you know what to do with."

I tilt my head and woo him with a soft, pitiless gaze.

"Mmmmm, yes, I'm sure of it. Soon I'll be with other, more important men, climbing for the top. But before that. . . ."

I reach for his shirt collar and draw him in.

His eyes lift up to scan my face, chin to lips, lips to large, almond-shaped brown eyes.

". . . before that, let's go have ourselves one really good time, Johnny, while I'm still within your reach."

Johnny smirks breathlessly. "Yeah. That's what they all say."

Unperturbed, I move away from him. I saunter out through the parking lot towards his car. I felt my new body move with a sapenie ke thorr. Hips glide from side to side. I've got a promise in my stride. Yeah, Johnny's a tough case. But, I know. His guard's coming down. His temperature's rising.

I stop by the side of his baby-blue Cadillac and wait for him to open up my passenger door.

Johnny, hands on hips, drops his gaze to the ground and scans for the resolve he knows he doesn't have. Finally, he walks over in sweet resignation and opens up the door for Channo. I looked into his eyes as I lowered myself into the passenger's seat. He shuts the door and walks over to the driver's side. He got in and put his key in the ignition and kept his gaze straight ahead. I watched his profile, attuned to his internal struggle. After a moment, he started the engine. The headlights blared against the concrete wall right ahead of us before Johnny threw his stick shift into reverse. The car flew out of the parking stall and barely stopped before Johnny jerked the stick shift again. We accelerated forward, zooming towards the EXIT.

I throw my head back against the passenger seat rest, and sigh, as he spins out into traffic.

Johnny drove wordlessly through the city. I gazed out at the passing five star hotels. Neon signs. Sky-scraping apartment buildings. Busy red light districts. Eventually, the remaining cityscape dissolved into mountains and trees. The wind blew across my face. I took a breath. There was an ominous feeling in the warm and humid night-air. I sensed an energy building up inside Johnny like the promise of an oncoming monsoon. Then, Johnny swerved onto the same road we'd been down the night before, the same one he'd driven so recklessly while trying to frighten Rakhi.

"My guess is you've got something in mind?" I say to him, while staring innocently.

He doesn't say a word, just keeps driving.

Many miles later, we turn onto a dirt road through a jungled area and drive down a long, winding pathway, until we reach the end.

Johnny turned off the engine. We sat there in the dark for a time, saying nothing. I listened to the jungle noises, the distant sound of the swelling ocean coming in, easing the energies of the day. I contemplated the events, the anger, the frustration of it all. And now the presence of the moment. Within that quietude, I hear his voice.

"So, are you prepared for the most exciting moments of our lives?"

I look up in Johnny's face; I'm startled by his sudden vulnerability.

I swallow and slowly smile. "Can't *wait*."

Guided by his flashlight, Johnny led me to a set of gray stone steps descending, down and down, cutting a path through the thick jungle underbrush that hugged the mountainside. At the bottom of the steps we followed another long winding path leading further into the jungle, carefully choosing the correct forks. After a time, we came into a clearing overlooking a cliff with a view of the ocean. We were still pretty high up along the hillside.

We stood together against the rail and took in the expansive sandy beach and the surging ocean waves, spotlit by the full moon. It took my breath away. To the right, I saw the endless sparkling city-lights of Mumbai. To the left, a more sparsely lit shoreline with dark, shapely mountains reclining against the indigo sky. I turned around to look at the jungle behind us. Many trees, plants, and vegetation growing so close together. Their many limbs swayed in the wind, caressing each other. A holy and wild consummation.

"We're not there yet." Johnny's tender voice said.

I nodded, feeling the rising anticipation in my throat.

He led me down the flash-lit jungle path. It continued weaving back and forth, presenting more forks in the road, descending further and further down towards the beach. Then, finally, there we were on the white, sandy roaring beach. The full moon stood round above us, casting a haunting light on the rolling waves. Johnny was looking down along the shoreline. I followed his gaze to a bungalow.

He took my hand in his and led me across the virgin sand dunes, up the stairs onto an expansive veranda. The two-story bungalow appeared to be made of brick. As I stood looking around in awe of it's beauty in the moonlight, the breeze came and blew my hair into my face. Johnny turned to me and quickly pushed the strands back behind my ear.

I gaze up into his face.

His eyes meet mine, full of shock, wonder, and surprise. He leans in, places his hands gently on my cheeks and searches my gaze, as if looking for a way out.

But there is none.

Then, I heard his heart's song.

> *How many faces came and went without my consent?*
> *Safe in my cocoon, love never did bloom and obstruct my senses*
> *But now the real game begins*

I knew you were dangerous when you first walked in
Long soft black hair shimmering like the stars in the Milky
Way

At that point, I knew.
It was time for me to get to work.

Channo begins her dance; a snake charmer, playing a *punji*. Her body undulates at the whining, flowing, swaying, droning of the tune. I whirl around Johnny, my movements are steady but seductive. I can sense him weakening; his eyes are glazing over. A desperately hidden passion begins to emerge from his innermost being.

Channo stays with the dance and I'm completely aware that soon he'll be all hers.

Johnny collapses in utter defeat. From far within his song, he continues to reach out; his song from the most secret of places:

> *Mere dil de Devana*
> *Man behosh hogiya hoo*
>
> ------
>
> *(My heart's highest ideal*
> *I am losing myself)*
>
> ------
>
> *Whatever you decide to do to me, you may do*

I circle around him once more, still fingering notes on the invisible punji. My hips sway, hypnotically. Johnny's head lolls side to side, his eyelids are growing heavy. We sway together like that, until his eyes shut completely.

Channo stops dancing and drops down on her knees in front of Johnny.

I summon him from within. He concurs. He agrees. Here, in the mountains, amidst all this beauty, Johnny has decided to surrender everything in a most beautiful and sensual way.

With that, I moved in closer, reach into his chest and took his heart with my hands. It lay beating between my palms, trusting me, accepting of whatever fate I'd chosen for it. My own heart thumped with empathy until I couldn't hold it inside anymore, Tears began to fall. I let them come without inhibition. Then, without warning, a thunderous cry came out of me and flashed across the sky:

" . . . . **Johnny**
    ***Bhai*!**"

When my eyes were open again, I discovered that the heart I'd taken out of Johnny had become a Cobra. But there was a sweet quietness to it, and it was unlike any of the snakes I'd challenged before. Its visage held surrender of all earthly things, and my tears began to flow again, dropping freely from my already-dampened cheeks onto the cobra's scaly skin. It's mouth opened wide from unspoken pain before it went limp.

I stood there silent for a long time, not willing to let go of this creature that had given itself up to me so willingly. Finally, I lay it gently on the ground and fell asleep next to it, exhausted by the whole damn charade.

We must have slept all the next day because by the time Johnny shook me awake, the sun was setting. I sat up and looked at his face. It was different. His eyes and his demeanor were softer. I wondered what this incarnation of Johnny would be like.

"It's time for dinner Channo . . . um, Bahan ji. Come see what I've cooked for you."

I stood up and wondered at the change in him.

He turned and gazed deeply at me. "What is in the past is in the past, my sister. It was truly the desire of both our hearts that brought this to be. Did you know, when you called Bhai that my heart has always truly wanted a sister? And so, I want you to make it official."

I was aware of the ritual.

I went inside the house and found a pair of scissors in the kitchen drawer. I snipped off a strip from the hem of my dress and went back outside where Johnny stood.

"Give me your right arm."

I brought the torn fabric down around his wrist, and tied a couple of knots in it to secure it.

He looked up into my eyes.

"I am happier today than I have ever been my whole life, Bhan. I am ashamed of who I was before. I was a man who dishonored women. I hope God will forgive me for my multitude of sin. He has opened my eyes and given me a gift. Today, I have found a sister."

After dinner, we settled into the living room. Johnny sat on the sofa across from me, looking around at the Bungalow as if he'd never seen it before.

He began to tell me his life story. How he'd grown up in a poorer section of Mumbai, partly at home, partly on the street.

"My father was an alcoholic. Depending on what he had been drinking, and for how long determined if I played games with him, or ran out into the street away from him while my mother stood in the doorway so he wouldn't catch me. I would spend those nights wandering around the streets, or staying at the house of a friend."

"Wouldn't your father beat your mother instead?" I asked as I sipped some English Breakfast Tea.

"No," Johnny said. "My mother was my father's first and only love since they were children. He would never raise a hand to her. It was only when he was really drunk and upset about how his employer treated him that he would get angry, and vow that no one was going to mistreat his kid that way, and swear that he would make me tougher." Johnny sighed as he put his teacup down. "Don't ask me why he thought that giving me a beating would toughen me up. But, eventually, my mother found out what kind of drink actually made him crazy. He was fine with beer, whiskey and rum, but it was the moonshine from local illegal distilleries he liked. That stuff that was one hundred proof. One tablespoon would put an inexperienced drinker out of his mind. My father could drink down a good solid Pak or two. He said it made him forget what he did for a living."

"What did he do for a living, Johnny-bhai?" I asked.

Johnny looked out the window as if to retrieve the information from the dark night. "He folded boxes in a cardboard-box factory."

I frowned, and wondered if that would drive me to drink, too.

"I have no idea why he thought beating me would ever prevent me from being abused by somebody else. That was quite silly, really, but because I was out there so much I did learn quite a bit about the street. Sometimes, I slept in street alcoves, or under trees in the park, even though I had a bed at home. Not that it was much of a home. Only a little better than the shanties, where the prostitutes lived."

He drank down the rest of his tea before he continued.

"When I was seventeen, my father took ill and couldn't work for a few months. He begged his boss to let me take his place in the factory because we needed the money desperately. The bosses agreed, so I went to work there, but I didn't stay any longer than I had to. I wasn't passive enough to do the job. I kept talking back to the bosses whenever they'd come around and verbally abuse us. Then, when my father asked why, I told him I'd learned how to be tough from the lessons he taught me, just like he intended. He didn't approve of that, of course, but he couldn't say anything about it, either. I quit my job as soon as my father returned to work, and carried on with my habits of staying out at night and carousing. Now, I was doing it even when my father wasn't throwing me out. I'd already begun to make connections and money through various lucrative, illegal ventures."

"What kinds of illegal ventures?"

"A bit of trading in contraband and some influence peddling. But mostly recruiting, bringing beautiful young people, both men and women, into prostitution and getting those with special talents involved in the gangs and rackets." He stopped and looked over at me. "You see, all my life, I've always had a way . . . of seducing people, of bending others to my will."

"I know," I said.

I pressed on. "Tell me about your brother."

"My brother?"

"Yes, Sanjay."

"Wait a minute. How did you know about. . . ?"

"I, too, have my ways, Johnny."

For a moment he looked at me, incredulous and frightened. Then he shrugged and decided to go on with his tale.

"Yes, it's true. Sanjay is my real brother, even though he is not my mother's son. We had different mothers. Sanjay is my massi's baeta, my mother's younger sister's son. Massi died in childbirth when I was fifteen. That, I think, was enough to make my father even sicker. The long hours he had to work at the box factory was bad enough, but now he had two boys to support. Later, I found out I wasn't even really his son. He supported us, even though neither of us were actually sired by him. But, as kismit would have it, in the end, we learned that we do have the same father, after all."

I stared at him, wide-eyed.

What?

"Ji. Oh, yes, I remember those days, the period after Sanjay arrived. My stepfather would groan every night when he got home about how he would never be able to forget all those boxes, box after box, row after row of boxes, thousands of rows of boxes passing endlessly before his eyes."

Johnny put his teacup down on the table, got up and paced.

"It's no wonder my stepfather drank."

I stifled a yawn. I was beginning to find Johnny's sob-story a bit annoying. Okay, I thought, but so what? Johnny was turning out into just another hapless goonda with an 'oh-poor-me' story to tell, after he was caught in my trap.

Then, suddenly, something else occurred to me.

I couldn't believe it!

My mouth fell open.

After I recovered sufficiently to close my mouth, I leaned in towards Johnny. "Are you trying to tell me that you and Sanjay are both really the children of. . . ?"

He looked up from pouring himself yet another cup of tea.

"Yes. You are a very smart woman. I've never told anyone; it wouldn't have been safe. But it's true, Sanjay and I are both the children of. . . ."

I slapped my forehead and braced myself against the sofa. "Don't tell me . . . your real father was. . . !"

Johnny smiled, as he sat back comfortably with his tea. "Yes, that's right you see, our real father was Rajesh Sharma."

I fell back on the sofa in shock and disbelief.

Johnny went on with his story. . . .

"I discovered much later through reliable sources that Sanjay and I were only two of the many among Rajesh Sharma's offspring that he never heard about during his lifetime. Neither of us had known the truth of our parentage while we were growing up. Nor, of course, did my supposed-father. If it were up to my mother, none of us, and especially not my inebriated stepfather would ever have known."

"How old were you when you found out?" I asked, as I lay back against the sofa.

"I was eighteen when that can of worms was opened. One day I came home to find this well-to-do sophisticated lady standing outside our little shanty talking to my mother. My mother looked . . . scared. She told me to go inside the house but the woman put her hand out to stop me. She looked me up and down and remarked that I was the spitting image of my father, and that was it."

Johnny paused. "I stood there, puzzled because I thought I looked nothing like my father. Then, when my mother jumped in, begging the woman not to tell me anymore, I knew something was wrong."

Johnny got up and stuck his hands in his pockets before he continued. "I tried to follow her as she walked to her cab, but my mother grabbed me tight. I shook her off and ran after the woman's taxi as it drove down the street, but I couldn't catch up. I tried to get more information from my mother, but she acted like a deaf-mute. It didn't matter how strongly I demanded to know what it was about.

"You know, we didn't have much and I was already becoming a pretty good criminal, but meeting Rita Chawla was the beginning of my true downward spiral."

Ah, yes.

Rita.

I looked over at Johnny, and saw his eighteen year old self standing there with Rita Chawla at that critical moment in time.

"I was angry and bitter at my mother. She allowed my stepfather to throw me out on the street whenever he got too drunk, instead of throwing *him* out to sober up. Then she hid who my real father was from me. I had no choice but to find Rita. As my mother wouldn't give me any more information, I set out on my own to discover who I really was. I even left Sanjay behind without a backward glance. He was only three years old at the time. I was so angry, I moved to a different part of Mumbai and didn't talk to my mother or visit her for many years.

"Since my mother wouldn't even tell me Rita's name, I had no idea how to find her. So I got involved in one racket after another. I gave up looking for the woman and began to find ways to make the big money. I finally got a job as a dealer in Bara Banta. That was about three years after I left home. I'd worked there only a week when Rita walked in. She recognized me immediately."

I watched Johnny's eyes, as he envisioned the meeting.

"I couldn't believe my luck. By then, I'd given up the whole idea of finding my real father. I'd become my own man and didn't care who my father was. The one I'd lived with most of my life was an emotional flake and the other was not willing, or able, to come out and claim me. Huh. What did I need them for? I was still curious, of course, but I wasn't going to pursue it further.

"Rita didn't show much interest in talking about my father, either. Instead, she spent the whole night flirting with me, throwing long, smoldering glances at me over the Black Jack table. At the end of my shift, she asked me to accompany her to her car. Then, she asked me to ride with her to her apartment. Well, let me tell you, in those days, Rita Chawla was not only a sophisticated lady, but also a very beautiful woman, so let's just say I didn't need much encouragement." Johnny sighed and looked at his feet. "Yes, Rita was more beautiful than anyone I'd ever seen before, and I don't think I've wanted, or needed, someone so badly since. But soon, I also realized she had the darkest soul of anyone I'd ever known. . . ."

"So . . . even at that tender age, you could recognize her for the kind of woman she was?" I asked him.

Johnny took a sharp breath in and exhaled.

"Yes, yes, of course, but . . . it was like a bad drug habit, an itch that no amount of scratching will ever ease. No, there was more to it than that. It was Rita. She infects people. Rita is so powerful, that even those with great power and confidence in themselves end up doing what she wants."

I considered and wondered if Rita was only powerful with people who had a deep and unfulfilled need.

"How powerful is she, Johnny?"

A sad look came over his face.

"So very powerful. It is said she has *jadhoo* so strong, if she only thought that she wanted someone's head on a platter, it would be there by morning. She learned from powerful masters the art of snake-charming, so there would be no recourse for the crime, and that is because she is one of the most powerful ones, the *Naga Devatas.*"

I sat up, and remembered the presence of the Cobra in so many of my conflicts. It was never any other snake.

Johnny continued. "We are the humble worshipers who make offerings to her and the other Naga Devatas."

"How could that be? How could any person become a Cobra Goddess, so that other human beings would be forced to worship her?"

Johnny rubbed his eyes and shook his head. "We made love that first night when I escorted her home. It was incredible. She drew out the night, taking everything slowly and dangerously. I remember very little of what actually happened, except for the state of constant ecstasy. The only thing I do remember was the moment when she finally orchestrated our climax. I was staring right into her eyes when I heard the hissing. Then, I was hanging in limbo, hypnotized. When I finally climaxed inside her, it felt like I had left an essential part of me with her."

Johnny stopped and ran a hand through his hair.

"After that, whenever she wanted me, all she had to do was beckon with her mind, and no matter where I was, I would drop everything to come do her bidding. And the more times I came to do her bidding, the more I could not refuse. She was my Mistress, and she controlled many aspects of my life."

I bit my lip. "You said 'was'. Does that mean that you are free?"

Johnny shook his head and smiled. "Yes, it is true. I am free and my choices are now entirely my own. But I am also a marked man. Rita will know I'm no longer linked to her, and they will come after me in their good time." He sighed heavily. "I didn't ever tell Sanjay that I was in this business. It's a good thing that he didn't get involved. I made sure of that."

My eyes grew bigger; I was astonished. That, of course, was a out-and-out lie. I knew, almost as well as Johnny did himself, that Sanjay was a Bollywood badmash; a core bad-guy, immersed in it almost as deeply as Johnny was. But somehow, to cover up for his veer, Johnny had been able to resist the pull of the connection we'd made last night, the intense feelings of closeness brought on by the spell of seductive-empathy I'd laid on him, and he'd even gone so far as to to be able to tell me an out-and-out lie.

Hmmm, I thought. This was odd. I'd never heard of anything like that happening before.

But, by now, I could begin to understand. It had taken some time to get used to it, but if there was one thing I knew now about being a desi, it was that, when your family loves you, they really, *really* love you.

I thought about that for a moment. I felt slightly in awe of Johnny and Sanjay's relationship. I glanced over at Johnny out the corner of my eye, as I got ready to probe even deeper and drag the full truth out of him.

But, just then, his cell phone rang.

Rinnnnng. . . . Rinnnnng. . . . Rinnnnng. . . .

He flips it open.

"Hello?"

Within seconds, Johnny's face fell flat, and his eyes began to dart around. He was clearly very concerned about something; in fact, almost panicked.

When he finally spoke, his tone had a desperate edge. ". . . Chup karrkae suno, Sanjay. Just shut up and listen. Don't go back to your place. Put Rahki in a car and drive up here to the cabin. And don't stop to pick up anything along the way. I want you to go right now, and make sure no one follows you . . . got it?"

I stared at Johnny as he wiped his brow with the back of his hand, then turned to look at me.

"So it begins. The endgame."

"I know."

"They will try to destroy us in every way they can. You realize that?"

I nodded. "Yes, there was a man in Buffalo who didn't make it through the week, even in protective custody, after my battle with him when the Bhujangen was driven out from him."

"Anil Negendra? You are the person who took down Anil Negendra? How could that be? I was told the one who took him down was a gori woman. . . . Who are you? . . . You can't be. . . ?"

I stared at him, almost apologetically. "Yes, Johnny, I am Elanna Forsythe George."

Johnny blinked, and swallowed hard.

With a flashlight in one hand, Johnny led us along the trail to where he parked the car. When we reached the Cadillac, Johnny paced back and forth looking at his watch, waiting anxiously for Sanjay, and listening to the story I gave him of how I came to act, and look, the complete opposite of who I was.

"You hid yourself well, Channo. Oh, I mean, Ms George . . . ."

"Keep it at Channo, Johnny, that will do just fine."

"But, what about Sanjay? Were you involved in removing the nagh that Rita put in him?"

I looked over at him, and studied his eyes carefully.

"No." (I lied.)

"Then, how did it happen? How was that nagh removed?"

"Oh, I'll never understand why things like this happen the way they do. When I was confronted by Anil Negendra, his nagh became disoriented, and later, the Buffalo police found him whimpering in his cell, frightened and crying. He was a mess. I don't know what happened with Sanjay, but that nagh was very weak because Sanjay's girlfriend, Rakhi, was keeping it asleep most of the time. Then, somehow, it was transformed into a bunny."

"How do you know all this? No, wait, never mind. As Channo said, you have your ways."

Johnny mused. "This is all very interesting. Later on, I was turned into your brother. It's as if whatever feeling or situation we find ourselves in will determine what we must become. Negendra was under a lot of pressure to do away with the troublemakers. He was probably so scared of you that he turned into a big baby. As for Sanjay, the only explanation I have is that his sex-drive has always been somewhat, ah, 'over-abundant'. One time, this wild American woman was with him in his bungalow, and they screwed like rabbits for weeks."

I blushed and pushed the still-vivid memories of Christine out of my mind. Maybe that was true, but at that moment, I wanted so badly to tell him that he should be grateful that Rakhi always called him 'brother,' instead of asshole, like she so often wanted to.

Then, all conversation stopped, as Johnny and I waited. We both heard something. We strained at the hum of a vehicle coming down the dirt road, amid the sounds of crickets and the sudden hooting of an owl. The car was getting close. I began to get an eerie feeling. I could sense Rakhi's presence. Her fear. She was struggling. I could also feel Sanjay's thoughts. He was terrified for his life.

I turned to Johnny, just as we began to see headlights peaking out from between the trees. "I think we'd better make ourselves scarce, because Sanjay and Rakhi are not alone."

We ran over to the edge of the jungle and hid in its shadows, as the car came into full view, with its headlights sweeping all the way across Johnny's blue Cadillac. We moved further along the periphery until we were close to the dirt road. The car stopped, and the driver's side opened up. A large man stepped out. He pulled a revolver and made his way tentatively towards Johnny's car, waving the weapon menacingly as he went.

"It's a trap," Johnny hissed. "They've led the goondas right to us."

"Shhh. They didn't do it voluntarily."

I could sense Rakhi's state of mind clearly now. She was beside herself with fears about Sanjay's well-being. Her emotions were beginning to flood my sensibilities. I took a deep cleansing breath and pushed her thoughts away, back into a little corner of my mind.

"They're going to find out we're not in there fairly soon," said Johnny, "so I suggest we rid ourselves of them, as quickly as possible."

"I agree," I said.

Johnny had an idea. "You provide a distraction and I'll move around behind. You wait until his back's turned and I take him down."

All right, why not? I'd been bait before. "I'll start to make my move in thirty seconds. Will that give you enough time?"

Before Johnny can reply, I sense something behind me moving in from the dark jungle. I turn just in time to see a thick arm about to wrap itself around me.

I lunge, avoiding the goonda's grip while simultaneously delivering a vicious Karate kick to his midsection.

"GAARRUMPH!" a male voice groans.

I turn back to Johnny.

Three other men have him in their grasp.

One of them swings up his arm, holding a blunt object.

And

T-H-W-A-P!

Johnny stops struggling immediately and collapses to the ground.

I took a step forward toward the three men, determined not to let them take Johnny.

But then – POOF! – I just disappeared.

I dissolved into nothingness.

Oh no! I thought.
Not again.
Why now?
Dammit.

Bright stars flash before my eyes, like supernovas, before I find myself back in the darkness.

And even now, here, alone in the dark, I think about all the mistakes that were made, not only that night, but throughout the entire case. The trouble is, sometimes I can't even think straight. Ever since that day on the roadside with Martin Johnson, I haven't been able to think as critically as I did before. I long for the days when everything was based on fact, science, and logic. Once a crime scene is scoured, and all the witnesses have given their testimonies, suspected murder weapons are put in sterile plastic baggies, everything is dusted for fingerprints, items of clothing, hair, and DNA is collected. All that's left after that is the lab. Long white coats. Bright florescent lights. Microscopes, beakers and test tubes. If the process required isn't in the lab, all we have to do is send it out somewhere else to be tested. Science is interesting. It's satisfying. It's safe. At least in a lab, I wouldn't just dissolve into blackness right out of the middle of a dark jungle overlooking Bombay – er – Mumbai.

"Hello, Elanna."

"Laila, what are you doing here? Where are we?"

"Between the microseconds. Listen. I don't have long. Pay attention. Look over there."

In the distance, I heard faint music. Laila points to her left. We turn to see the dancers, each one dancing in his or her own spotlight. They dance toward us, with the spotlights moving with them, setting them out against the dark, ethereal plane. They groove to thunka thunka beats, as they come closer. They whirl and swirl. Wave and sway. Hands like peacocks and fish.

Laila leans in. "How many dancers do you see?"

I count.

"Seven."

"Are you sure? Look again."

I re-count.

"Hmmmm. Only six."

"Yes."

"But *why?*"

"Someday many more dancers will dance here. Just not yet."

"Many more? How many more? More than twelve?"

"Many more."

I gape at her.

"More than fifteen?"

She smiles.

"That's right."

Suddenly, dark shadows are swirling all around Laila. "I must go," she says. "The Mumbai chapter is still under attack. I must get back to Harshad."

Then, she's gone.

I'm all alone in the dark again.

What? I wondered.

What was that all about?

I stood alone in the dark and pondered.

Rakhi's Song

I don't know how long I was there, alone in the darkness.

But the dreams were wild. . . .

Land and ocean alive, bucking humans off it's back. Roaring turmoils. People fall into crevices, run from tsunamis. The sea is full of bodies, all of them terrified, stupefied. I see my own body floating there among them. I looked at my face. It was calm and soothed. I'm getting closer to the shores of Nirvana, or somewhere. Despite everything I've gone through. Yes, despite the many attacks of the Bhujangen-force in Buffalo and New York, despite nearly losing myself in unbridled and all-consuming lust after that night at the Bollywood Planet, and despite the months of intimately experiencing Christine's sexual exploitations in Mumbai, the thing I was afraid of more than dying was becoming a soul-killer like Rashbir Dulku.

I survived all that.

I'm okay.

Now, I hear bodies further out in the ocean beginning to scream and cry, gnashing their teeth and calling out for me to save them, too. The screams get louder and louder. I look back at myself on the ocean, but all I'm able to do is lie there, keep still and stay afloat. From the sky, I watch the others struggling against the magnitude of the ocean. The despair rings all around me as one by one I watch them go under. From where I am, floating above it all now, up in the air, I realize I can't help them; I don't know how to help them.

Finally, I'm the only one left, floating on the vast, blue ocean. I watch myself lying on its surface as on a lounge chair. I ponder my loneliness; I close my eyes.

The tears came. Oceans of them.

I'm awake and lying with myself on the ocean. I don't feel alone anymore. I smile, listen to the waves, feel the wind and taste the saltiness of the air, watching as the shores of Nirvana draw nearer.

Now, someone emerges next to me from beneath the clear, blue waters.

It's Simryn.

She smiles, as she stretches out beside me and reaches for my hand. I smile back at her. We float together toward the shores.

Talking.

Smiling.

Laughing.

Crying.

We're happy together.

It's perfect.

Then, I felt something trying to pull me under.

Simryn gasps and reaches for me. She holds on as I hover just beneath the surface. I can feel her pulling, trying to bring me back up, but whatever is pulling me is too strong. She fights and fights but a stalemate is the best she can do. Then–POP!–she's gone. She dissolved. The blue crystal ocean rushes in to fill the gap and there's nothing left but water holding me up where her arm was. I struggle and struggle against the pull, but it's no use, I'm going under.

I sink deeper and deeper, down to the bottom.

After a time, I felt myself moving in and around the dark spaces beneath the ocean. I could see everything and I heard everything. I felt the threads of Time moving over me, through me, and past me.

Time smiles.

We play.

We sing, dance, and tell stories.

I dream and dream and dream.

Then, I'm awake. In present.

Next thing I know, I'm being pushed into some sort of tunnel, moving towards a kind of hazy glow. My head's squeezed so hard that I think it might break; my arms press in against my body and everything is so tight.

"Somebody, please make it stop!"

At the sudden release my body began to throb. A bright light shines at me and I shut my eyes against it. Everything feels cold. I try to move. But I can't. In that moment, I feel the brutal sting.

SLAP!

"Again!"

"Wake her up!"

Men shout.

FWAAAP!

"UNGH!" My lungs sting sharply with the first intake of air. I feel dizzy. My mouth's as dry as cotton.

"Give her some water."

A thick hand forced my slack jaw open and soon a heavenly trickle of cool, wet liquid pours into my parched mouth. I gulped at it eagerly, trying desperately to replenish my dehydrated body. I smacked my lips after it stopped, still wanting more.

"Take off her blindfold."

Someone pulls my head forward and grapples with the knot at the back of my head. I squeeze my eyes tight against the sudden bright light after the blindfold is whipped off. It was a few moments before I could peer at the faces of the men standing around me. We're in some sort of cave. I can feel my head throb. I almost passed out from the pain.

Now, I hear a voice speaking out from somewhere inside me.

Hurts, doesn't it?

The voice sounded familiar.

I forced my eyes open and tried to get my bearings, but then I realized that I'm hunched over, sitting on some kind of hard surface with my hands tied up behind me. As my vision begins to focus, I look down at my feet.

They're brown.

High arches.

Perfectly spaced toes.

I heard the voice again.

'I said, it *hurts*, doesn't it?'

My head was pounding hard.

Mouth still dry.

It all starts to come back to me, sort of.

I gathered my thoughts together and shook the last of the cobwebs from my brain.

Yes, Rakhi, it does hurt.

The air around us felt heavy and dank. My skin felt surprisingly cold. I tried to sit up, but my hands were tied up behind me. A dull pain greeted me from my lower back. I raised my head up a little to see a tall, thick man standing in front of us.

He's a goonda, Rakhi says.

A what?

A heavy. A gangsta. Get it?

Oh yeah, right. I remember now.

The man sneers at us before he turns away.

We take a breath.

Rakhi, where are we? What's going on?

We're captured.

Captured? How? What happened?

They were waiting in the apartment when I got back from the gala. They already had Sanjay. They jumped me as soon as I walked in the door. They tied me up, put me in a sack and tossed me into the trunk of a car. They drove for some time and stopped somewhere. I thought I felt you close to me, but then you disappeared. After that, they drove for quite awhile. Then, when they finally stopped, they took me out of the trunk and put Sanjay, Johnny, and I into a helicopter, I think, and flew us here.

Where are we?

I don't know. We're in a cave. Somewhere out in the jungle, judging from the animal cries.

A cave out in the jungle? Okay, but if it's a cave, how does the light get in? That's not artificial light.

The light? I don't know.

I looked around and counted. There are about twenty people. Hmmm. No. Nineteen. All men. I studied their faces, but they still seemed blurry, out of focus. I turned my attention to the contours of the cave itself. It's huge. At least forty meters high. High above us, stairs were cut into a precipice on the left. At ground level, there were human figures carved in the rock face of the walls. Then, I look to the right.

Rakhi took in a sharp breath.

There it stood. A scaly twenty-metre tall Cobra carved into the stone. The jeweled nagh on its forehead caught the light from the unknown source. It sparkled and flashed. It towered over everything with its mouth wide open. The carved fangs were bared and polished, and the tongue flicked out over the open jaw. I looked up into its eyes. They were dark and empty, like the ones I'd seen in the vision I had at the Bollywood Festival.

I shivered.

In front of the giant cobra stood a platform with a stone slab. Ancient, rusty chains were spiked into the four corners of the slab. I didn't have to wonder. Admittedly, my background in Indo-archeology was spotty, but there wasn't much doubt we were in an underground temple built many centuries ago by some dark and undocumented Naghine sect who once worshiped here and performed terrifying human sacrificial rituals on that very slab. Probably at midnight.

How long until then?

The light that reflected in from somewhere outside the cave wasn't enough to let me know the time of day.

Above us, I could hear footsteps.

Rakhi looked up, as I strained to focus.

A heavy-set man in a white explorer's outfit with matching pith helmet strutted down the staircase.

Who's he?

I recognized him.

He's someone you don't want to know.

It was Robert Smith, the Aussie millionaire and wealthy proprietor of the international Mom & Pop Hotels chain; a Bollywood aficionado; and, like Sanjay and Johnny, another of Rajesh Sharma's unrecognized illegitimate children. But Smith's a little worse than that, he's also a multiple murderer. He's killed a lot of people. Among them, a nach-girl named Mona Prajapati, whom he met during a precipitous moment at the Bollywood Film Festival in New York City; an anonymous Indian-takeout delivery driver in Buffalo, NY; and my friend Simryn Gill's half-brother, Suraj Amir.

Robert descends the stairs, and comes over to stand right in front of us. He bends over, thrusts his sweaty, ugly mug right up close in Rakhi's face, and delivers a hard, cold, lewd smile.

"So, what'ta we got here?"

Standing up, he turns to face a thick-looking goonda, who is waiting behind him.

That's the one who's been slapping us. The fat one, Rakhi tells me.

Smith sneers.

"Tell Rita we've brought the girl around. Tell her to hurry up because the show's about to begin."

The thick man smiles a blunt smile, before he turns and makes for the stairs.

Smith turns back to study Rakhi.

"So, 'Rakhi,' is it? Well, I hear you're a pretty good little dancer, and, you know, I'm a pretty big Bollywood fan myself. So how good are you, really? Are you another one of those jiggly-tart Bollywood flash-in-the-pans, or can you *really* dance. Can you dance good enough to save your own life?"

He nods at two of his men, who are standing right behind him. Rakhi watches as they walk off to our left. Then, I see Johnny and

Sanjay across the cave; they're slumped over and blindfolded, bound up with the same thick ropes that we are. The two goondas remove their blindfolds and slap them around a little. The brothers start up, with their eyes darting around, squinting at the sudden bursts of light.

Smith jeers. ". . . hey, tell you what, sweetie, if you dance *really*, *really* well, well then, maybe, just maybe, I'll throw in the lives of those two no-accounts, too."

"Rakhi!" Sanjay cries out. "Are you hurt, my love?"

Johnny grits his teeth and snarls. "Don't touch her, Smith, or you'll live to regret it."

Smith's cruel laughter echoes around the cave.

"Oh ho, Mr Akkarah, there's a threat I'd like to see you make good on, seeings how you've been good for nothing, so far, during this whole affair. But, no, we're not going to hurt Rakhi, She's just gonna do what she does best, for us . . . she's going to dance."

Smith's gaze appraises Rakhi. "However, my dear beautiful one, if you don't dance the best that you, or anyone else has ever danced, you will die. And the pain, oh the pain. My, if your begging and screaming is anything like my dearest Mona's was in New York, then, ah—the pain will be exquisite."

Rakhi sneers at him.

Just then, another familiar voice echoed down through the cave.

"No, no, no, Robert, not this time. This time, I can't allow you your fun."

Rakhi looks up to see Rita Chawla, standing in a doorway at the top of the stairway, poised in a beige, floor-length priestess gown.

She poses.

She's about to make her grand entrance.

I watch as Rita glides gracefully down to the bottom of the stairs.

When she reaches the floor, she turns and makes her way toward us. I saw an image of a cobra embroidered on her beige gown. She was wearing a tiara with a golden cobra coiled around her head. Its hood spread wide. Dark eyes. Tongue flicking out. Identical to the one in the room.

She frowns at Smith.

"I'm sorry, my pet, but if I let you play games with this one, she will destroy you. And, furthermore, we have more important plans for her."

Then, she turns; her eyes fix on Rakhi.

She sneers.

"Elanna Forsythe George, *hah*! The Chiti Devi, herself. I knew it was you."

Pffffft—what? 'Chiti Devi?'

Ah, yeah, Rakhi, that's what some people call me. It's my avatar, sort of.

Hah! Oh, sorry . . . um, I didn't mean to laugh.

I said nothing.

Rita smirked. "When I heard of this 'Rakhi' phenomenon, how that starlet's reputation was rising so quickly, I knew something had to be wrong. That was why I arranged that little meeting at the Roshan Asima. It was Lila who whispered me your name, but I suspected it was you already. The way that nach-girl spoke, she was so—arrogant! Imagine, some puny, backward village-girl showing such disrespect to me? It was *impossible*."

Rita's eyes flash with even more disdain.

"It had all become quite clear. This 'Rakhi' was only you in some silly para-psychic cloak. Oh yes, don't worry, I'd become aware of your first attempt at disguising yourself as the Russian-American trollop. You got your hooks into our Sanjay pretty well. Our Indian men are so bholae, so naive, and you 'American' women have no scruples at all. We had a difficult time getting Sanjay out of your clutches. Johnny, yes—Rakhi—your very own Johnny-bhai, was waiting to eliminate you after Sanjay brought you out that night, supposedly for dinner. Yet, for some reason, Sanjay showed up alone, and claimed that you got away from him. He was adamant that he didn't know how you got away, but only a person of extraordinary power could have eluded me like that, without a trace, the way you did."

I stared at Rita, dumbfounded. I had no idea why Sanjay'd dropped Christine on the street like that. It was just plain weird.

Rita continued. "Ms. George, did you know that you've become extremely annoying? A true thorn in our sides. Did you really think you could negotiate the Bollywood maze undetected?

Well, no one can. Did you really think your little, bevakuphi disguise would get you in?"

She sniffs. "So, you appear in the ruse of a dancer, an ill-mannered child who expects to immediately receive whatever she wants. You cause scenes, create disruption and show such disrespect to the innate order of our nation."

I was tired of her bullshit. "Get off it, Rita, I know your game. You're out to destroy any woman who might be the least bit of competition for Karishma. I heard all those people talking at the birthday party, they're all afraid to try to compete with her. In real life, you're destroying your own daughter."

Rita crosses her arms and glares at me. "What would you know about me and my daughter?"

"I spoke to her at the birthday party and she warned me, as a friend, to watch out—for you."

Rita lunges forward, ready to deliver a blow. But Rakhi throws her head back and laughs. That stopped Rita right dead in her tracks.

"Ironic isn't it, Rita?" Rakhi speaks up. "You were so busy protecting your daughter from everything in the world, you didn't see you were stifling her greatest potential. That night, I saw the boredom and despair in Karishma's eyes."

Rita's seething. Her eyes widen. Lips clench.

But then somehow, she manages to compose herself.

"No, no, no, you saw no such thing! These are nothing but the defeated ramblings of a self-satisfied woman who thinks of no one but herself. My Karishma is happy in her duty to her country. But you? You've done nothing since you got here but grab, grab, grab, and take without asking. That is why India must eradicate the evil of wanton women like you, and so, for the sake of Mother India, we must end all this . . . quickly!"

Rita turns to Smith. "Watch her. I'll go prepare for the ritual."

She snaps her fingers. Most of the men follow Rita as she made her way up the stairs and out of the cave, leaving only Robert Smith, the thick goonda, and two others to guard us.

At the top of the stairs, Rita stops and looks back at us.

"Oh, and Robert, one more thing, stop worrying about that little *vesya* Johnny took up to the bungalow. If Lila hasn't found her by now, you can rest quite assured the jungle got her. . . ."

Then, she was gone.

At that moment, Rakhi was staring intently at the back of Robert Smith's head.

Rakhi, what are you doing? That's a dangerous man. Be careful.

Oh? Well, I guess a WOMAN'S got to do what a WOMAN'S got to do, right?

No, Rakhi!

Smith turns to face us.

He gazes deep into our eyes.

A quick and wicked smile spreads all over his face.

His cruel eyes gleam.

Sweat beads at his brow.

We fall into a vision.

I see Rakhi. She's descending a steep hillside, wearing almost nothing, only a provocative harem dancer's outfit. A wild breeze blows her long black hair away from her face.

I see Robert. He's walking boldly across a meadow. He sees Rakhi. His lust heightens and he runs towards her. His arms open wide, then wrap tightly around Rakhi's waist. She peers into his cold eyes and laughs. Her fingers dig deep into both his cheeks. Her wild, wind-blown hair veils her face as she kisses him. "Ummph!" he grunts. His eyes open wider and wider with surprise and delight. Then, Rakhi lowers him down onto the ground, and. . . .

And *what*, you ask?

Well, after that, just use your own imaginations, okay?

Back in the cave, Rakhi and I gathered ourselves. . . .

I'm sorry, Rakhi. I know that wasn't real exactly, but it was disgusting.

Rakhi says nothing.

She seemed far away. As if trying to rid her ethereal body of the horrid feelings and sensations.

I'm sorry you – ah – 'we' had to do that, Rakhi,

Rakhi's seething.

YOU were Christine. *You?*

She erupts. A vitriolic rage.

WHAT? No, it can't be true. That's gotta be impossible.

I swallowed.

Well, uh ... um. . . .

"What?"

Rakhi gasped out loud.

Let me get this straight then, what that 'Rita' person said a few moments ago is – ah – *the truth?*

Ah ... uhm, mmm, well, it is 'kind of' true.

'KIND OF TRUE'? What does 'kind of true' mean?

I swallowed again.

Okay . . . it's true, more or less.

'More or less'? Which: 'more,' or 'less?' – were you or were you *not* Christine?

I sighed. A very long sigh. It was time to own up.

Yes Rakhi. It's true, I was her.

Another loud gasp.

Her mouth fell open in horror and dismay. I could feel her eyes getting wider and wider.

She was appalled!

Elanna, let's try this again, just to be sure. What you're telling me is: 'You and Sanjay. . . ?'

I could tell she was close to losing it completely. She looks heavenward and cries out:

Oh my *God!* Hey bhagavana!

Well, okay, at that moment, I was feeling pretty repentant . . . about a lot of things. But, somehow, I still couldn't stop myself from trying to justify my actions.

Rakhi, listen, please try to understand. It was a very complicated time. And I really wasn't myself. Plus, it was long ago. Almost like in another lifetime, or something.

Did it happen, or didn't it?

Well, as I said before, it did – 'kind of' happen. Look, I already told you, I was sorry.

Haran ha! I– I can't believe it. You and Sanjay? Ew-w-w! BARF! YUCK, YUCK, YUCK! You and Sanjay? That haramazada, I'm gonna kill him. And you? I'll straighten you out once and for all. How dare you. . . !

She kept on railing, on and on.

I stayed quiet. All of this was becoming more than just a little humiliating, but after a while, her self-righteous pique of eighteen-year-old prom-queen hysteria began to get to me. It starts to feel a little old, you know, and I mean, who among us needs that? Let me tell you, what I really wanted to say to her was this:

"Oh yes, meri jahn piyari, it is true, I had Sanjay. And so what? That's just how it is, here in this world, my dearest, it's all one great, big, ugly trailer park. Oh, and by the way, take my word for it, little girl, he's lousy."

Yeah, that's what I wanted to say.

But I didn't.

I showed some restraint.

In any case, it wouldn't have mattered, because Rakhi wasn't listening to me, anymore.

Once again, she's faraway.

Rakhi dances ecstatically on the other plane. She's naked. She sways. She throbs. The dance is sensual, seductive. It's the sleaziest, sexiest movie-scene dance you ever saw. Her taut eighteen-year-old body struts and glows, her arms and legs undulate. But Smith isn't interested. With a bored look, he buttons up his shirt and knots his tie. He retrieves his coat-jacket and tosses it over his shoulder before he finally deigns to look back at Rakhi with a dismissive sneer. Rakhi stops and stares, and strikes an indignant pose. Hands on hips, feet shoulder-width apart, as she calls out after him heading over the top of the hill in the meadow.

"Yoo-hoo. . . . Oh, yoo hoo! Mr. Smith?

Mr. Smith, over *here*."

Back in the cave, Smith looks us over. He's sweating profusely and breathing hard, as he attempts to pull himself out of the sexually-satiated daze that Rakhi has left him in on the other plane.

Rakhi's expression now breaks out into full pout.

"Ooooh, Mr. Smith, you don't believe all those things that bad lady said about me, do you? I don't have a clue what she's talking about. I'm not this Joanna Fredrick Jones person, or whatever her name is. My name is Rakhi and I'm just a simple nach-dance-girl. Please, please, Mr. Smith, I didn't do anything wrong."

She blinks at him. Rapidly. Like some mindless ninny.

Smith wipes the sweat away from his lip. When he speaks, his voice is ragged and deep.

"Sorry, meri chocolate flavored chuppa. Sadly, I think the good times are behind us. It's gotten rather, boring. But one thing is definitely true, my Sheila, you're not Elanna Forsythe George. You see, I've met her and she'd never beg for her life like some conniving, cowardly, two-bit Bollywood munchlette. Your type sickens me, all you fanny-jiggling, attention-starved wannabe's who'd do anything to make it."

His fingers snap.

"Get the bags," he growls.

The thick goonda beside him mumbles.

"Uh, but Smith, Rita said to keep her safe."

"Rita's not here, is she? Now go do as I tell you. Bring 'em out!"

As Smith untied Rakhi, the three goondas carried four sacks to the middle of the cave. Smith laughed and whispered in our ear with cruel delight. "So, it looks like the dance competition is back on, my little red-hot cinnamon tart. But, I thought we would give you a bit more of a challenge to spice up the pot."

The men turn the bags upside down. Two cobras dropped out from each bag onto the floor. Angered by the rough treatment, the eight snakes coil. They hiss and lunge at the three men, who've already backed up out of their way.

Smith laughs. "So you wanted to be in the movies, din'j'a? Let's make a movie, now. We'll call it 'Dances with Snakes'. Isn't that original?"

Smith shoves her hard towards the snakes.

Rakhi stumbles forward.

She rubs her wrists as she bites her lip.

Don't provoke him, Rakhi. Just focus on the dancing and let me take care of the snakes.

No, no, no. You're going to have to dance, too. You need to do exactly as I do.

What? No, not me, Rakhi, I can't dance. (I mean, okay, perhaps I could sway a little. But there was no way I could ever move like her. Oh, maybe I could shimmy enough to hypnotize a *single* snake? In a pinch, if I had to, but that was it.)

Rakhi, however, wasn't interested in my excuses.

I'm sorry, it's the only way. Here's what it comes down to: you have to dance just like me, or we're all going to die. You, me, Johnny, and Sanjay, too.

For a long moment, I said nothing. I was feeling baffled, and rather incredulous, in fact, about the whole damn thing.

Rakhi, you're not only a genius, you're an unborn devi-child. How could I ever dance like you?

She's exasperated.

GAWD. Don't worry so much. All you have to do is let go of your jiddi atma, all your silly doubts, and your seemingly unending supply of negative reinforcements, and DANCE!

It's that easy.

Just

LET

GO

and BE for once. Okay?

Okay Rakhi, I'll do my best.

Great. And don't worry. Just follow me.

Before I could protest further, she's walking with cautious reverence to the place where all the cobras gather, coil and slither on the floor. Rakhi stands and looks at each snake, carefully, then meets the gaze of the largest one. Her eyes smile. She's calm. Fearless. She folds her palms in front of her heart. Closes her eyes.

Waiting, sensing, listening. . . .

In my mind, I could hear the largest cobra hissing an inquiry.

"Who are you?"

"I am a servant of Lord Shiva. Before I was in this form, I knew you."

"Everyone who comes here says they are a servant of Shiva. But they lie."

The other cobras hissed their displeasure. "*S-s-s-strike her!*"

"You are wise, oh Naga Ma. We humans are complicated creatures, as are the Nagas. You know that to kill an innocent is pappi. Be careful, you don't want to garner bad karma."

The snake's tongue flicks the air.

"Yet, there are two of you. This other one, she is a servant of Maha Kaali."

"Yes. She fights the evil asuri that people carry in their hearts and minds, and she's destroyed some of those who have neglected the wisdom and compassion of the Nagas. These people standing behind me, they are the ones who kept you in the sack and tossed you on the floor. They want you to destroy me and this other one."

All the snakes hissed loudly. "They use fear to blind us-s-s. We would have struck without discrimination so that the Laws of Karma would weigh against us-s-s. . . ."

Rakhi closes her eyes. Deep down, I can hear the call of the punji. Her body begins to sway. A slow, flowing rhythm courses through her limbs. Rakhi opens her eyes and steps toward the cobras. They rise tall from their coils, curious as they watch. Hypnotized by her smooth, round movements, their serpentine bodies begin to sway too.

Elanna, do you feel it? Let your body go. You can do this.

Okay, I'll do my best. . . . I'm with you.

I'm tryin' to copy Rakhi,
As she. . . .

Twists her limbs. Strikes a pose. Sends her voice up to the ceiling. (And beyond.) Lifts our cry up into the sky.

> *"Dhoom-a daka laka laka Dhoom Dhoom*
> *SHA-BOO-O—O-M!"*

In the upper reaches of our cave, it echoes:

> *SHA-BOO-o-o-M*
> *sha-booo-o-o-m*
> *boo-o-o-m*
> *boom. . . .*
> *boom ... boom*

A fierce, funky bhangra beat now permeates Rakhi's voice. She's ecstatic. Smith and the three goondas look up, mouths a'gapin,' astonished by Rakhi's compelling rhythms. Our vibe echoes on, higher and higher into the darkness above us.

And, then, we cry it up again.

> *"Dhoom-a daka laka laka Dhoom Dhoom*
> *SHA-BOO-O—O-M!"*

And again, it echoes:

> *SHA-BOO-o-o-M*
> *sha-booo-o-o-m*
> *boo-o-o-m*
> *oom. . . . .*
> *boom ... boom*

Now, Rakhi rattles off a scat. It's a staggering line of rapid fire raga-skaa-bhangra-hop improv, spiced with complicated polyrhythms:

"*Dhoom a daka laka laka sha-ba-da she-da a-daka sha-boom kaboom dhoom DHOOM!- a daka laka laka laka daka laka daka laka daka laka laka laka....a laka daka laka dkadad alaka daka!*"

And the beat goes on. Then, at an opportune moment, Rakhi kicks it. Her song begins, and it goes like this:

> *Coyni Meri Jaise Vaise.*
> *Jaise Vaise*
> *Jaise Vaise*
> *Jaise Vaise*
> *Coyni Meri Jaise Vaise.*
> *Jaise Vaise*
> *Jaise Vaise*
> *Jaise Vaise*
> ----------
> *There's No One Like Me*
> *Like Me*
> *Like Me*
> *Like Me*
> *There's No One Like Me*
> *Like Me*
> *Like Me*
> *Like Me*

Rakhi smiles, delighted by the echoes her voice makes. She puts her fists on her hips. She talks it up some more:

> *Oh pho Oh pho Oh pho Oh pho*
> *Ye garabara kiya ha? Oh well. Chalo*
> *Mein kahsvati ti*
> ------
> *Oh my (Oh my Oh my Oh my)*
> *What is this mess? Oh well*
> *What I was saying was–*

Soon, a bass guitar begins to *Boombra-Boombra*. Just as a snare drum goes 'hoppety-skippetty-poppety-slap-BAM!' I run. With Rakhi. Past the snakes. Onto the altar before the 20 metre high Bhujangen. We shake it all over, 60's style.

The rhythm's contagious.

Then, after a few more bars of beats, Rakhi starts singin' the verse:

> *Arreh*
> *Meri jaise koi nahee hai*
> *Koi vasi chal nahee hai*
> *Meri devdut ke saman*
> *aur kamottejak dolana*
> *Dhoom Dhoom Dhoom*
> *. . . . A-daka laka laka*
> ------
> *Hey Hey Hey*
> *Hey there's no one like me*
> *Who moves like this?*
> *My angelic appearance*
> *and sexy, rockin' dance moves.*

Somewhere, a dhol pounds. We flip off the altar. Cartwheel past the snakes. Stopping directly in front of Smith and his men. The music halts. Everything goes tacit. Then, Rakhi launches solo into a brand, new raga-hip-hop-bhangra rap:

> *What? A face like mine?*
> *A body like this body?*
> *Choro na*
> *I'm an original*
> *Kamala hai!*
> *Get off it*

The inevitable bass rushes back in, resuming its pounding.

Dooru-*dooru-dooru da doobie das*

As a 60's-slapback'd guitar joins up:

Wakka tikka wakka Slpnnag-ang-ang-ang-an-ng

Rakhi spins and stops. I follow. Trip a bit. Recover the stance. We eye the men. Seduction. Yeah. "Tease 'em with words."

> *Yeah, yeah, yeah, YEAH, YEAH, so*
> *Can you walk this way?*
> *Can you TALK this way?*
> *Ha Ha-ha-ha Drrrrrrrrr AH*
> *Ha ha Ha ha*

Rakhi and I stomp across the room. Sashay to the left and to the right.

> *Da-da Da-da Da-da Da-da*

(The eternal guitar punctuates)

> *Oiy meri jaise koi nahee hai*
> *Es dhunia me aur es jurava me*
> *Drrrrrrrrrrr-AH! Soonia?*
> *Dhoom-a daka laka laka*
> *Dhoom-a daka laka laka*
> *Dhoom-a daka laka laka*
> *DHOOM DHOOM SHABOOOM*
> *But c'mon, that's just TrrrrASH talk*
> *Kaun ha meri sat?*
> *Haan, ve haan*
> *Oh there's no one like me*
> *In this or any universe*
> *You hear me?*
> *Who's with me?*
> *Yeah. Right on.*

More and more, I feel my arms, my hands, body, legs and feet come alive. Every fiber of my being wants to move. The music is calling me, and I submerge to the urge to groove. My hips slide from side to side. My arms swirl and flutter. My feet stomp, tap and stutter.

> *Chan Channa Chan Chan!*
> *Chan Channa Chan Chan!*

We're in sync. Rakhi and I turn to our captors. She smiles. A giddy come-hither smile. Beautiful hands. Lithe limbs. Voluptuous hips and breasts. A long, slim waist somewhere in-between.

One goonda gaped.

Another smiled.

The thick one next to Smith leers openly at our liquid-undulating body(s).

Robert's eyes grow more and more evil.

Somewhere, mallets are plunkity-plunking on the strings of a santoor.

A dhol punctuates the end of the stanza.

DHOOMa-dhooma DAT-**DHOOM!**

"*Oh-ohhhhhhhhhhhh,*" Rakhi sings out.

The tempo picks up.

Then, it exploded.

> *Thump-da-thump Dada dada dada Thump-da-thump*
> *A TA-TA Tinga linga linga linga heyyyyyy*
> *ARIPA Pah pah pah pah*

The rhythms lift me. Hands clap. I'm crouching. Leaping. Walk like an Egyptian. 'Hoola-hoo-boo-boppin' across the floor. I change light bulbs. Beckon my lover. Shoo away bad boys. I run from my thundering heart, stop to gaze into my true love's face.

"Not bad, Elanna, not too bad. Watch this."

Rakhi one-steps, two-steps, three-step–hops up next to the thick goonda by Smith. She looks at him with saucy, smiling eyes. She hip-checks him, giggles and scurries away in a flurry. He almost tumbles into Smith. Rakhi looks back at him over her dancing shoulders, winks and blows him a kiss.

The thick goonda blinks.

Dhumk-da-da dhumk dhumk.

"Hmmm," says Rakhi, puckering her lips up at him. With her hands she plays her midriff like a drum, as she mouths the sounds.

"Thunka thunka-dee thunk thunka-dee Thunka thunka-dee thunka-dee Thunk"

Staggeringly, the thick goonda begins to move towards her. Arms reaching. Hypnotized. Smith grabs him, yanks him back, and snarls in his face.

Rakhi throws her head back, and laughs. She dances away and comes to stand with the still swaying snakes, grooving to the sound of the eternal jam. Her arms windmill as she spins around the group of cobras. Leap! Whirl! Hop! The snakes follow our lead, wiggle and dance across the room. All three goonda's are entranced by our graceful movements.

But Smith's not giving up.

Rakhi jumps out in front of him. Kicks up her heels, spinning, hopping, Jatti-style. . . .

Drrrrrrrrrrrrrrr ah ha, ah ha
ArrriPAH! ArrriPAH! ArrriPAH! ArrriPAH
Chakae-chakae CHAKALO

HAAN HUH!
Coyni Meri Jaise Vaise
Jaise Vaise
Jaise Vaise
Jaise Vaise
Coyni Meri Jaise Vaise

Jaise Vaise
Jaise Vaise
Jaise Vaise
Coyni Meri Jaise Vaise
Jaise Vaise
Jaise Vaise
Jaise Vaise

She stops a little way from our captors, puts her palms together in front of her heart, and stands perfectly still. She closes her eyes. I feel her enter a trance, breathing deeply. We stand there quietly together, listening for the quietude amid the sounds all around us. We become One.

In my mind, I could hear the Mother Cobra hissing:

> *"As sisters you grew together.*
> *But as brides you live in separate homes.*
> *And though you will long for one another*
> *You must now dance alone."*

Now, Elanna, dance exactly as I do.
Um, okay, gotcha.
Rakhi steps out. So do I.
She spins like a top.
I follow.

She taps, heel and toe. I'm a peacock. I'm a snake. A river flowing into a lake. Rakhi, me, and the cobras dance. One heart, one mind, one spirit. Krishna and his Gopis. Khol-lined eyes flit side to side. Hands clap. Bodies invite. 'Come hither, come hither!'

Fa Fa-fum Fa
Fa-fum Fa
Fa-fum Fa
Fa-fum FA FA

On the ethereal plane, Rakhi and I join hands. We spin 'round and 'round. I see her. She laughs. Her hair sails behind her. Her eyes grow big. *She sees me.* We throw our heads back, and laugh.

We spin faster. We spin. Faster. On and on and on and on and on.
Until we stop.
Out of breath.
Still holding hands.
Rakhi stares at me, amazed.
She's flushed and breathing hard.
She gives me a nice big smile.
"Good to see 'ya. Pahali varrh."
She was right. It was the first time.

Then, I spotted Robert Smith, staring at us in horror and dismay over Rakhi's shoulder. His eyes widen in disbelief. A fury's coming over him.

Wider and wider, with deepening ire, furious-er and furious-er, Robert stares. He's fuming.

"S-S-S-S-T-O-P this! Stop this now. I've had quite enough . . . of this."
He glares at me.
"Oh no, Elanna Forsythe George. Not *you* again. You just don't know when to stop, do ya? Well, you won't get out of *this* alive. Shoot 'em all."
"RUN," Rakhi cries as she pushes me to cover.
We dart across the room to hide in the space between the altar and the giant cobra. The first shot rings out. The bullet misses us by inches, ricochets off the walls; its echoes reverberate all over the cavern.
Ptwang Tawang–awang–awang

More bullets follow.

Pitchoo Pitchoo Pitchoo pwawa-a-a-ang PEEEoooooo
Pitchoo Pitchoo Pitchoo

Crouching down behind the stone altar, I could feel my heart pounding in my ears. Being in my own body again felt—quite odd. Can you imagine trying to get used to that in the middle of a gunfight?

"Are you all right?" Rakhi yells at me.

"Yeah," I heard my own voice say.

Smith's screaming. "GET 'EM, GET 'EM BOTH."

The goondas move toward us. However, the sound of their footsteps is followed by a loud hissing. We peek over the slab to see the cobras on the floor, slithering toward Smith and his men.

"What? Well, shoot them too. Shoot the damn snakes!" Smith growls.

Then, from somewhere high up above, a disembodied voice shouted out.

"HOLD IT SMITH, POLICE."

What?

Who was that?

Somehow that voice seemed . . . familiar.

"W-w-what-s-s-s this?" Smith hisses. Robert and his men look around, trying to discover where the voice was coming from. I spotted Johnny and Sanjay in the far corner of the cave, still struggling to untie themselves.

The familiar voice rumbles down through the cave once again.

"GIVE UP SMITH. THERE'S NO WAY OUT."

Smith's look of surprise turns to spite.

"Listen, we've got hostages down here. So, if you don't give us a way out, a lot of blood will be on your hands."

Just then, one of the cobras lunged at the leg of one of Smith's men. The goonda yelped and fell to his knees, clutching at the wound. Another snake sprung forth and sank his fangs into the man's neck. The man fell to the ground, his body twitching in spasms.

That was it. Smith lost it.

". . . Shoot ALL the damn snakes!

". . . Keep an eye on the cave entrance!

" . . . Don't let any prisoners escape!"

The chaos escalated, as Robert and the remaining men began firing at the snakes. Above the din I could hear the mysterious man calling out, yet again:

"FIRE AT WILL, MEN."

Coming in from all directions at once, I watch as bullets float by. The explosions, echoes, and ricochets that follow, aren't far behind.

> *Pitchoo-pitchoo-pitchoo*
> *Pff-pff-pff-pff BLam Pitchoo-eeeet*
> *Ratta tatta tatta tatta Ptwaaaaaang Pweeeeoo*
> *Ratta tatta tatta tatta*
> *Ratta tatta tatta tatta*
> *Ratta tatta tatta tatta*

The cave walls reverberated with sounds.
   Snakes hiss.
   Men shout.
   Guns fire.
   Bullets bouncing.

His-s-s-s-s. . . . Aaaaaah GAWD DamN . . . Pitchoo-Pitchoo-ptwang Pitchoo pwawooosh-ooosh-ooosh. . . . . "STOP 'em" *. . . Pitchoo-ptwang Hisssss Pitweeeee Ratta tatta tatta tatta Ptwaaaaaang Awwwww . . . .* "GIVE UP NOW, SMITH" . . . "GET UP THERE, YOU. . . ."

Puchwang-wang-wang-wang-wang-wang-wang-wang-wang-wang. . . .

I watched, as bullets ricocheted off the walls and floor. One hits a statue in the wall, rebounds and catches one of Smith's remaining two goondas in the middle of his back. The man hits the ground, hard, and stays there. Not moving. The Mother Cobra lunges at him to make sure he's finished. Robert Smith sneaks out from behind another statue. He takes aim at me. I duck down. His incoming bullet hits the sacrificial altar.

PWANG-WANG-wang-wang-wang-WANG

Two more shots ping off the giant Bhujangen behind us, missing Rakhi by only inches.

"We're sitting ducks!" I shout.

Then I saw it. A gun three feet away from the altar. The goonda who went down must have thrown it when he got hit. I lunge for it, just as a bullet whizzes by. I look up in time to see the thick goonda heading for the altar towards Rakhi. I roll over and take aim above her head.

"Rakhi, get down!"

BLAM!

Blood erupts all over the thick goonda's face. For a moment he's standing there, looking like a big, giant, red poppy, then he topples over, falling backwards to the ground.

I look over at Rakhi. She's staring. Horrified. Her eyes are round as saucers.

She's pointing at something behind me.

"Look out!"

I spun around swiftly, and swallowed hard.

Robert Smith was standing there, only a couple of feet away with his revolver raised, cocked, and aimed, ready to fire.

"Drop your weapon. And get up."

I had no choice.

He had me.

Dead to rights.

Point-blank.

I knew I was about to take one right between the eyes.

They say that you'll never hear the one that gets you; but at that range, I was quite sure I'd have the special privilege of seeing it coming. *It's too late to do anything*, I told myself. My eyes widened a little, as I tried to accept the fact I was staring certain death right in the face. My whole life flashed before my eyes. My mom and dad, Captain Stewart; Beeji, 'Ricky-Rick-Rakesh,' Simryn, Rajesh Sharma. . . .

I kept wondering where I might end up next.

Then

BLAM!

I heard a shot.
But, curiously, I saw no bullet coming.
What?
Why not?
I just stood there, waiting.
And waiting.
Until it seemed like I'd been waiting forever.
My mouth was dry as dust.
I swallowed.
Huh?
What just happened?
Then, it occurred to me, I was still standing there.
What?
Could I be . . . still alive?

When my vision came back into focus, I realized Robert Smith was staring right past me, now. Into nowhere. He blinked. His eyes were full of despair and dismay; I could see blood oozing from a wound in the center of his chest. His face registered confusion as his mouth fell open, while his revolver swung in a graceful semi-circle around his index finger, before it slipped off and dropped to the ground. His knees buckled. He tumbled straight down on top of his unfired weapon.

His face hit the ground, hard.

SPLUT!

There was nothing I could do but stare, as Robert's life exited his body. On its way to the recycling center of the universe. Or, who knows? In any case, Smith was gone. His remains lay there at my feet. Utterly still.

Neither a good-guy nor a badmash, now. All labels removed. Nothing left now but an empty jar, ready to be crushed, meshed, mashed and melded; heated, melted, formed, re-formed, filled and re-filled; repackaged and redistributed. Or whatever.

I sighed.

As I looked up from Smith's already-cooling body, my eyes fell upon a tall, handsome man dressed entirely in black, standing only six feet away. The man had a steady grip on the lethal, state-of-the-art police revolver that he was holding in both hands. A silent, thin puff of smoke curled up from its barrel.

Who?

I gaped.

I blinked.

I couldn't believe my eyes.

I blinked several more times to see if it was true.

I was taken aback.

I was speechless.

Finally, I could hear my own voice, barely audibly, saying:

"Ricky?

"Rick?

"R-R-Rakesh?"

I closed my eyes and shook my head, as vigorously as I could, to clear away the crazy cobwebs.

NYPD Lt. Rakesh Chandra slowly lowers the Luger-P108A to his side.

His revolver's still smoking.

He stares at me.

Our eyes meet.

Our gazes lock.

I kept wondering how long I was going to keep holding my breath.

So, I let it out.

I shook my head, again. I held back my heart, which was about to burst wide open. I quelled the sounds of the swelling violins from the opening strains of the soaring, romantic pavane that was playing somewhere in the deep, background-music of my mind.

Yeah. I was trying to keep a *firm* grip on reality.

Later on that day, I stood outside the cave with Ricky while our agents were finishing rounding up Rita's remaining goondas from the surrounding jungle. Rita, herself, had already been captured. She was standing, not far away wearing handcuffs, under guard by a specifically-assigned team of Nomad non-sensitives. The second-in-command of the rescue operation, a tall, young blonde Aussie Nomad officer, emerged from the cave to stand right in front of her.

He stared at her, looking her straight in her eyes.

Rita glared back at him with a now-impotent gaze.

"Officer, I demand to know your name, number, rank, and your supervisor's name. Mark my words, as soon as we get back to Mumbai, I'm going to have you fired."

"I'm sorry, ma'am. We're not local police. This is an international matter. The Australian, Indian and U.S. governments have authorized this special investigation to find and arrest those linked to the murders of three people on American soil: Simryn Gill, Mona Prajapati and Jai Krishna, a pizza delivery driver from Buffalo."

Rita tilted her haughty chin at the young agent. "I've never even heard of any of these people. What does the Australian government have to do with this?"

The Aussie's lip curled up a tad.

"Your friend, Robert Smith, was responsible for the sudden and mysterious death of his mother a few years back. Large amounts of acrylimide were discovered in her tissue during a new autopsy. and that made our case similar to these other seemingly-unrelated deaths in India and America."

Rita blanched. ". . . what does any of this have to do with *me*?"

"Mrs. Chawla, we have received documented information and evidence from a former high-up member of an underground organization in Mumbai. He's provided video evidence against yourself and Robert Smith. The evidence also seems to point to your involvement in the suspicious deaths of Rajesh Sharma, and in the sexual assaults and murders of some individuals now known to be his offspring."

"Rajesh Sharma? Hah! Everyone knows he had a heart attack. The man died from his own excesses."

The Aussie said nothing. His gaze remained fixed on Rita.

Finally, she hissed. "Who perpetrates these lie-s-s-s? Bring them to me now!"

"They'll all come, Mrs. Chawla, in good time." He nodded to the Nomad team. "Keep her here until arrangements can be made for her transport."

We watched as the operatives lead Rita away. The officer came over and stood with us. "We had quite the task finding you, Ms. George. If it weren't for Lieutenant Chandra, we wouldn't have made it in time."

I glanced over at Ricky.

Our gazes locked again.

The Aussie agent continued. "Sanjay Menge, the man we found tied up inside, has agreed to turn state-evidence against the Bollyood cartel. Our organization will have to put some powerful and clever people in charge of guarding both him and Mrs. Chawla. Especially Mrs. Chawla."

I nodded, solemnly. Then, I remembered something. "But . . . there were two men tied up in that cave. What happened to the other one?"

"The other? We found only one man, Ms. George."

Dammit! Somehow, Johnny Akkarah must have managed to slip away during the chaos. I looked around, wondering for a moment if I could pick up his vibe and follow. But I knew immediately, I wouldn't be able to; he'd be long gone.

The Aussie agent turned to Ricky. "Thank you, Lt. Chandra, I think we can take things from here. We'll call you if we need any more help."

Ricky smiled. "Thanks for hanging in there with me."

The Aussie nodded and turned his attention back to the tasks at hand.

Just then, I saw Rakhi walking toward us, still wearing the now dusty and torn sapphire-blue dress she'd put on for Karishma's birthday party two days ago. She'd tied her long black hair back in a chignon, so she could help attend to the casualties. She caught Ricky's eye. "Lt. Chandra, what's going to happen to Sanjay?"

"Sanjay? He's agreed to turn evidence against the cartel. And, after that, he'll have to live under special Nomad protection, in a psychic deep-freeze, so to speak, for a long time. Most probably for the rest of his life."

Rakhi's eyes glisten. She blinks.

"Oh, I see."

"Will you be okay, Rakhi?" I asked her.

"Oh, yeah. Sure. I'll be fine."

"If you ever need anything. . . ."

"Haan. Don't worry, I'll call ya."

Rakhi began to walk away. But then, she turned back to look at me for one last time.

I bit my lip.

"Goodbye, Rakhi."

"Yeah. Namaste."

Ricky and I watched as she wandered back over to help with the half-crazed cobras and wounded goondas.

"Who's she?" Ricky asked.

I smiled. A big, sad smile.

"She's Rakhi."

"Where'd she come from?"

I swallowed.

"I . . . I'm not sure, Rick, but it doesn't matter anymore."

I spun around to him and searched his face.

"Listen, Lieutenant Chandra, I'll do the questioning around here, and what I want to know is: what the hell are you doing here? How did you ever manage to burst in here, right on cue like Mighty Mouse and save me just in the nick of time? How'd you find me? How'd you ever pull it off?"

He peered at me with those gorgeous brown eyes of his. Then, he smiled a big, sad, yet happy smile. I could feel myself blush. I lowered my eyes. He took my chin in his hand and raised my face up gently. I lifted my eyes to meet his. Once again, our gazes locked.

He frowned.

"Know this, oh Chiti Devi, I have my ways."

He closed his eyes and his mouth descended towards mine.

After that, I'm not sure. When our lips met, I must have swooned or something.

Because everything went black.

Epilogue

Rita Chawla and other members of the cartel, were in the news for months. Thanks to Sanjay's testimony, Rita was implicated in the murders of Simryn and her six siblings. As the weeks went on, other witnesses came to the forefront. The cartel and its activities came out in the open. A few brave actors, actresses and directors brought forward broken contracts, complaints of misdirected royalties, and charges of blackmail, for the purpose of extracting big concessions from the superstars. After that, no matter how many chits Rita Chawla pulled, none of them could save her.

However, one thing was clear. Underneath the new sense of freedom and the fresh air of true confessions, the cartel would still be there, hanging out in hidden Bollywood backstreets, biding its time, waiting and lurking. Rita Chawla, and all the people she was connected to, were only the tip of the iceberg. As for Johnny Akkarah, I never found out what happened to him. He disappeared. After the incident in the cave, he never surfaced again, at least not in any Nomad lore or reports that I ever came across.

Ricky and I? We were married that same evening in a quaint, Vegas-style wedding chapel in Mumbai. The ceremony was presided over by an Elvis-impersonating, Syrian Christian priest. We spent the next two months honeymooning in a sailboat north of Mumbai off the shores of Goa. We stopped at secluded spots along the bird-filled banks of the rivers, poking around centuries-old cathedrals and temples. One day we found a deep cave behind a great waterfall. We came back to it many times to make love to the waters rushing out over the entrance of the cave. At night, we returned to our boat and slept as it rocked, anchored in the swelling waves of the Arabian Sea.

After that, we returned to New York, and resumed our careers as paramystical crime busters.

And, that's where the story ends, you hope?
 Happily-ever-after, like we'd all wish for?
 Well, it did, for a time.
 But 'to love is to lose,' as they say.
 And 'all love-stories must come to an end.'
 Both sayings are true.

The end for Ricky and I came painfully soon. Three months after we came back together from India, I got the call. Ricky had taken a bullet in the line of duty. The microseconds I stood there holding that phone seemed liked centuries.

Beeji, Captain Stewart, and I rushed to the hospital. I sat in the ICU all through that night, holding his hand, trying my best to use my abilities and keep him here, wanting more than anything for him just to open his eyes and look at me. But he still didn't make it through the night. I solved his murder. But that's a story for another day. For now, it's sufficient for you to know it was bittersweet in the end.

At the funeral, I sat like a zombie in the front row with Beeji and Ricky's sisters. As friends and colleagues got up and spoke about him, his work, the sense of honor he brought to the police force, I watched Rick lying there, looking peaceful and handsome as ever in his uniform, but without breath.

I couldn't believe it.

I kept expecting him to sit right back up.

But he didn't.

Afterwards, Beeji and I grieved for many weeks while the South Asian community in New York kept us fed, and did their best to provide us with comfort. Things got better only slowly, and it was many months before I resumed my normal activities. Then, one sunny, lazy summer day, it must have been at least a year after the shooting incident, Beeji gave me a long, knowing look with her tired, dancing, age-old eyes.

She put it to me bluntly.

"Time for you to go, Baetee."

My mouth hung open, as I looked at her.

I hated it.

I couldn't stand the idea!

But she was firm, and I knew she was right. There'd be no solace for me anymore in New York. Not even amongst the blue, red clay, and moss-colored walls of my beloved apartment.

So, within a few days, all the needed arrangements had been made to liquidate my New York affairs, and I found myself sitting in Captain Stewart's office, tying up a few Nomad loose ends and chatting amicably with my best old friend.

He gave me one last, long look.

"Where are you planning to go, Elanna?"

I met his eyes from across his desk. "I don't know, John. I only know this. There'll be a great big field of buttercups waiting for me."

Rolling the Credits

Cast
Heroine(s)
Elanna Forsythe George

Rakhi Chand

Client
Simryn Gill

The Victim
Rajesh Sharma

Simryn's Family
Karishma Chawla

Suraj Amir

Suresh Sharma

Robert Smith

Sarama Verghese

Roopa

Muna

Munjinder Kaur

Makhan Singh

Romantic Interest
Lt. Ricky Chandra, NYPD

Supporting Appearances
Abendabun

Amandeep Khan

Turin

Ami Upadhyay

Pumi Upadhyay

Rama Upadhyay

Chand Upadhyay

Channo, the Village Sweetheart

Kristina Ivanovic

Fatima

Gary Dhami

Gurdave Kaur

Harshad Verma

Homer Smith

Jeetain

Johnny Akkarah

Laila Durga

Miss Pinky and her girls

Minoj Patel

Mona Prajapati

Nandita "Beeji" Chandra

Ominotago

Pool boy in Buffalo

Raj Balrou

Ram

Rita Chawla

Sanjay Menge

South Asian Niagara Falls lab assistant

Martin Johnson

Marla Johnson

KWOL Camera man, Rajnesh

KWOL Hostess Indu ji

KWOL Reporter Ramala Premnath

'Anil Negendra'

Gary 'Chamcha' Dhami

Carribean-born doctor

Lila Prasad

Rashbir Dulku

Misc Law-Enforcers:

RCMP Constable Rodney Phair

Niagara Falls Police Trent and Jones

Patrol Officer Jones

(BPD) Buffalo Police Department:

Captain Jones

Homicide Response Unit leader

Jackson

Fulkner

Dylan

Robertson

Nichols

Drenth

Lt. Simms

Newsome

Officer George Rudy

Det. Sergeant Frank Martin

FBI:

Agent Zeke Smith

Anonymous agent-in-black

NYPD:

Captain John Stewart

Geraldo

Fitzpatrick

SWAT team-leader

Gods, Entities and Goddesses, Creatures & Things:

Bicky

Cobra at Buffalo International Airport

Dorango - multi-voiced bird

Goddess Kali Ma

Makhan Singh

Sentient Cobras in Cave

The 'Bhujangen'

The She Wolf

Musicians & Singers

Jagroop & Korina Mangel

Meghana Prasad

Cameos & Walk Ons:

Asif Salam a.k.a. 'Vinod Kumar'

Baby Simryn Gill

Clerk in the Ye Old One Stop Sex Shoppe

Sikh man in Buffalo convenience store

Blond samurai-waitress

Bobby Nihal

Buffalo Police Department Receptionist

Crazy Lady on the Street
Phony overcharging psychic
Elaine, BNIA car rentals clerk
Evening waitress at Mom & Pop Motel & Diner
Emergency doctor & nurse in Buffalo
Four Bollywood starlets
Anonymous Indian delivery driver in Buffalo
Irate woman at Bollywood Film Festival
John, the gas station attendant in Buffalo
Mani, Front Desk Clerk at Bollywood Planet Hotel
Young /older Manu (Munjinder Kaur)
Prem
Mr Anand
Niagara Falls Hotel Clerk
Niagara Falls 911 operator
Philip the doorman
Ranjit Singh
Roopa, Simryn's mother
Security guard at New York Hotel
The-man-in-the-suit-and-tie
Waitress at Seven Flowers Teahouse
Hostess at Roshnan Asima
Young Makhan Singh
Waiter at Giorgione's
Young Rajesh Sharma

Songs

Music from 'Meri Dil Ka Tara:'
'The Sun Calls Me'
'Without you'
'Say You'll be mine'
'Meri Dil Ka Tara Utarna'
At the 'Bollywood on Broadway Ballroom & Theatre Facility:'
'Chup Chap kiyoo haa?'
'Mera Munder Ke Samalan Walla'
'Healing Song' by Ominitago

Goodbye to New York:
'Mud Sleepy River Blues'
Bara Banta Casino Songs:
'Dhoor Dhoor dhiyan Ha Mere Mitra' by Korina Mengale and Jagroop
'Not the Usual Blue' by Christina Ivanovic Seredova
Sanjay and Rakhi duets:
'Kiya ho giya?'
'Makhan Jasa dil'
At Roshan Asima:
'Kiss, Kiss, Kiss' by Meghana Prasad
Finale
'Coyni Meri Jaise Vaise' by Rakhi Chand

Locations

Bara Banta , 'The Big Deal'
Beeji's house
Bollywood On Broadway Ballroom and Theater Facility
Bollywood Planet Hotel
BPD Police Precinct
Buffalo Airport
Buffalo Hotel
Buffalo Hotel sauna and pool
Bungalow at the edge of the jungle
Chatrapati Shivaji International Airport in Mumbai
Dhoni Maach Restaurant
Elanna's New York Apartment
Gas station in Buffalo
Giorgione's Pizza
Henry's Cafe in Soho
Harshad and Laila's Mumbai apartment
Hospital Room In New York
Johnny Akarrah's Bungalow
Mom & Pop Motel
Nataraja Dance Academy
JFK Airport in New York
Niagara Falls Hotel
NYPD 23rd Precinct

Parkade next to the NYPD 23rd Precinct
Rakhi's apartment
Restaurant in Niagara Falls
Roshan Asima
Sanjay's Beach house
Seven Flowers Teahouse
Shansui Restaurant
Suite 1509 of the Bollywood Planet Hotel
The Dhoni Maach restaurant
The Ethereal Plane
Transcendental nightclub
Typical Truck Stop Diner next to Mom & Pop Motel
Unnamed underground temple outside Mumbai
Forensic lab in Buffalo
Unnamed hot dusty pathway in India
Unnamed opium den
Unnamed dusty street in Western at high noon
Ye Olde One Stop Sex Shoppe

efgpublishing

Notes

First Epigraph:

MacKendrick Karmen, *Divine Enticement: Theological Seductions*. New York: Fordham University Press, 2013.

Second Epigraph:

Neil Young, "Cinnamon Girl." Everybody Knows This Is Nowhere. Lp. Reprise. 1970.

Chapter 4:

Page 102 cites a lyrical line from the the Bollywood movie, *Laila Majnu*. Sundhendu Roy. director. (1976). Laila Majnu [Motion picture]. India: Famous Video

Chapter 5:

Ch. 5 title cites the traditional *Atha Tantroktam Devi Suktam*.

Miscellaneous:

Except as noted above, all other lyrics written by N.K. Johel, with the exception of *Not the Usual Blue* (Ch. 1) by N. K. Johel, D. Michael Gerow, and Elin Plumb.

Elanna Forsythe George is the intellectual property of efg publishing and is open to authors wishing to tell their own cultural or subcultural story. efg publishing will consider all submissions, based soley on the quality of voice and storytelling.

'Dhanyabad, Shookria, Mereban'

Thank you to all the people who supported me throughout this project. No man or woman is an island. I would first like to acknowledge the following, hard working people who assisted me in editing and developing the many characters and stories in Bollywood Storm. I am greatly indebted to you:

D. M. Gerow, S. N. Buckley, H. Dent, V. Bedard, T. Lisle, M. DeRosier, Elin Plumb, contributor to the song 'Not the Usual Blue'. B. Kompani, who heard the entire first novel-in-progress read on Skype, and in listening, helped us hear the language and set the tone.

Editors: Alyssa Linn Palmer, R. Feenie.

Proofreader: J.C. Chan.

My readers from first draft to final edits:
D. McDonagh, J. Belanger, S.D. Wilson, D. H. Gerow, S. Sangha, M. Walker, R.A. White, S. Hassey Laughlin, S. Sandhu, K. Birak, T. Plesner, K. Marsden,

J. Rabu, P. Wilson, C. Kirkland, J & N Dharampal, M. Amar, L. Gerow.

Family, friends and acquaintances
J. Johel, S. Wilcox, C. Johel, M. Behm, R. Doman, Dr. L. Falls, B. Hallas, P. Chatha, K. Woolverton, G. Cheema, T. Bergey, F. Khamseh, A. Safari, J. Riego de Dios, M. Pradhan, L. Mudgar, B. Kompani, C. Giles Lawson, J. Greenberg Beutner, J Massey Tripp, P. Shrotriya Khan, F. Campos Metha, R. Scmidt, R. VanAssche Bueter, S. Craik Wadden, M. Joh, D. Fletcher, M. de Marchena, J. Lloyd, J. Josephsen, R. Hein, Elvis Pizza in Surrey, and finally, Saphire, Dx, Kelly, Hans & all the poets on BT.

The Bus 640 Crew:
M. D'Mello, C. Diotte, S. Radcliffe, J. Collins, K. Gordon, B. Freeman Nestman J. Christensen and C. Rivers who all asked me about the book, laughed with me, and encouraged me during the NaNoWriMo first draft as we commuted to and from work each day.

The Legendary Fireside Cafe Spoken Word Wednesday Night Attendees: R. Speed, A. Keech, D. Loverock, P. Smith, R. James, K. Sloan, D. Stanley Daoust.

My parents, siblings and inlaws, many, many friends and relatives, all of whom I cannot possibly thank here.

In Remembrance of my mother, Kashmir, and my nani ji, Nacchatar Kaur whose storytelling and folklore from India inspired me. And Santa Singh Johel, my grandfather, whom I never met, but whose life journey has always facinated me.

God.

About the Author

N.K. Johel is a third generation Sikh-Canadian. Her grandfather (who was born in the 1860's or so) emigrated to North America in the first decade of the twentieth century. Yet, due to many complex, historical happenings during the mid-twentieth century, she didn't even begin learning English until she started primary school.

She gravitated to the fine arts during her school years in Lake Cowichan. As a young adult, she moved to Nanaimo to study theatre at Vancouver Island Univerity, and then to Vancouver to study painting and fine arts at Emily Carr Institute of Art and Design. Her interest in literature developed informally. She credits Toni Morrison's *Jazz* and Michael Ondaatje's *Running In The Family* as the works that rekindled her interest in writing.

Notes on Typefaces

Body text is set in Janson, the mis-named typeface designed by Nicholas Kis, a Hungarian living in Amsterdam, circa 1685; it is a typeface of excellent readabillity.

Title headings are set in Frutiger, the self-named typeface by the famed Swiss designer Adrian Frutiger, originally intended for use on the signs at Charles de Gaulle Airport, Paris, France.

Subtitles, chapter headings & irruptions within the text are set in *Adagio Sans*, a typeface with true italics and many weights, developed in 2014 by the Polish foundry, Borutta Group.

Chapter opening characters are set in the Calluna typeface, released in 2009 by the Dutch designer Jos Buivenga.

EFG
PUB